Songbyrd

This book is a work of fiction. Names, characters, places, and incidents either are products of the author's imagination or are used fictitiously. Any resemblance to actual events or locales or persons, living or dead, is entirely coincidental and not intended by the author.

First Paperback Edition: June 2016

For information on subsidiary rights, please contact the publisher at rights@jollyfishpress.com. For more information about the book, please visit our website at www.jollyfishpress.com, or write us at:
Jolly Fish Press, PO Box 1773, Provo, UT 84603-1773.

Printed in the United States of America

THIS TITLE IS ALSO AVAILABLE AS AN EBOOK.

ISBN 978-1-63163-074-3

10 9 8 7 6 5 4 3 2 1

For each of my beloved characters, on and off the page, who have taught me much along the way. This journey belongs to all of us.

Songbyrd

a novel

ANNA SILVER

JOLLY
FISH
PRESS
Provo, Utah

I

One.

Day one. One more new school loomed before me. One more minute for me to try to pull myself together. One more breath . . . and then another.

Two.

Two bright-red doors screamed at me from beyond the sanctuary of my mother's car. Two keys clacked sharply against one another as they swung from the ignition. Two hands shook uncontrollably in my lap.

Three.

Three heartbeats before I could exhale. Three days since my last attack.

Four.

"Innocence."

Her voice was always soft at first, easy to ignore. *Four* . . .

"Innocence?"

Four more numbers to go before I could reasonably expect to stand up without feeling like I might black out.

"Innocence!"

Five.

Five hundred different reasons why I didn't want to be here . . . again.

"What?" I opened my eyes, expecting to see the world swim out of focus before me, only to find that the swells were within, not without.

"Can you handle the paperwork on your own?" my mom asked, curling her dark auburn hair behind one ear. "I've got so much to unpack still." She was trying for cheery, but it came off more apprehensive, like a kid sticking a toe in the surf for the first time, unsure whether the tide of my stormy mood would carry her away with it.

I hated it when she cut me off before six. Counting was one of the only things that kept me sane when the panic started to swallow me. It gave me a focus. A *different* focus. Something besides my jackhammer heart and the taste of metal in my mouth. Eight was my goal. Anything less than that was not enough to hold me together. Anything more overwhelmed me.

Especially nine. *Nine* for the age I was when I realized we weren't like other families. Nine for the number of dads I'd had in the last sixteen years. And every one of them sucked more than the last.

The latest model, Phil, was over fifty, balding with a comb-over to rival Donald Trump, and had a permanent case of halitosis. I still couldn't understand what my mother was doing with him. Oh right, his *money.* It was easy to forget Phil was rich since he sent us to live in his wigwam in the middle of Nowhere, Texas.

"Let's see . . ." I began, slinging the strap of my bag over one shoulder. Eight would have to come later. I couldn't last another second in the car with her. "Mother's name: *Dalliance.* Mother's occupation: *gypsy*? Father's name: *Phil.* Father's occupation—what does Phil do again?"

My mother narrowed her sea-green eyes at me. "He owns several car lots in Austin and San Antonio. You know that."

"Right. Car salesman. How perfect." I ignored her glare and pretended to fish for my ChapStick. My hands, at least, had slowed to a manageable tremble. My heart was another story. "What else? Age: *sixteen.* Siblings: *none.* Residence: *Hell.*"

Mom crossed her arms over her chest and sighed. "Maybe with a little less bitterness once you get inside?"

"Sure." I gave her a facetious smile. "I'm saving all my bitterness for you."

"Look, I know you miss the coast. So do I. But this is a fresh start for us," she said.

"With Phil," I amended.

"Yes, with Phil. We need this."

I needed another move and another dad about as much as I needed a lobotomy. "Why do *we* need this? I mean, I know you've told me, but it just keeps slipping my mind."

"Don't do that." She turned away from me and stared out the windshield. For a second, she looked almost genuine, her eyes full of regret and memories. Then it passed. She shook it off with a small shudder and plastered a fake smile over the sadness. "Frank was . . . well, he was getting too serious. It's for the best. Really."

Somehow, she always made it about her and her stupid boyfriends. "Couldn't you just break up with him like a normal person? We didn't have to move."

"Yes, we did. And you'd better start getting used to it because we're going to be here for a while."

She'd been making that promise for as long as I could remember. So far, the longest that "a while" turned out to be was three years. The shortest was five months. "What makes you think this one will take?" I asked.

"Phil's a good man," she said quietly.

They were all good men once, until they met my mother. I grabbed the door handle to leave, but her hand was on my arm before I could escape.

"Name?"

This was the part I hated most. My name. Not only because it was the last in a long-standing Byrd family tradition of weird names, but because she always, *always* made me put her new boyfriend's last name as my own. I took a breath. "Innocence Byrd."

Her clutch on me grew fiercely tight. "Not Byrd—Strong."

I rolled my eyes and clenched my jaw, willing my nerves to settle. "Whatever." I was out of the car and inside the heavy glass of the double doors before she could stop me, before I would have to start counting all over again. I didn't even look back when I heard her Mercedes pull away.

All schools smell the same. A mixture of graphite, warm bread, and disinfectant. Stonetop High was no different. Once I passed through those front doors, I left the scent of cedar needles simmering in the sun behind me. The office was smaller than at my last school, but at least Stonetop had enough of a population to warrant its own high school, unlike some of the other blips in the Texas Hill Country. Several surrounding towns bussed their kids here.

"Can I help you?"

I turned to see a plump woman with rhinestone-encrusted reading glasses Windexing the white Formica counter. She peered at me over her pink rims.

"Uh, yes. I'm new. I need to register."

"I wasn't aware we'd had any new arrivals in Stonetop," she said, giving me a suspicious once-over. She turned to pull some papers from a file drawer in the desk behind her. Handing them to me, she added, "I make it a point to stay abreast of town business. You from somewhere nearby?"

That was another thing all schools had in common. Office ladies were notorious gossips. "No. We just got in last night," I told her.

Her pink lipsticked mouth twitched. "Mmhmm." She handed me a pen with a big, fake daisy taped to the top of it. "Well, fill these out. I'll need your records, of course. Is your momma parking the car?"

"No ma'am. She left." I scrawled my name across the top of the first sheet, taking up almost all the little letter boxes under *first name.*

A pudgy hand slammed down over the sheet before I could write more, the office lady's lacquered nails gleaming the color of flamingo feathers under the fluorescent lights. "She left?"

My heart did a double flop and sunk to the pit of my stomach where it threatened to start palpitating all over again. *And it begins.* The questioning glances. The need for excuses. My mom didn't exactly provide me with a traditional upbringing. Sending your kid in to register for school alone was typically considered remissive parenting. "We just got in so late. She had a lot to unpack."

"But I'll need documents—shot records, proof of residency, stuff like that."

I reached into my bag and pulled out the manila folder my mom had given me that morning, commanding my hands to steady themselves. "I've got it all right here."

The office lady snatched my folder and tucked her chin so as to get a good look at me down her bulbous nose. "Well, I suppose we can get you fixed up for today. But she's going to have to come in before the week is out and sign these forms."

I nodded. "Okay, no problem. I'll tell her."

"I'm Clair Robichaud, by the way," she said before moving to the copy machine. "But everyone calls me Miss Clair."

I nodded again and returned to my form. There it was, staring me in the face. *Last name.* I set the point of the pen to the first little box and started to write a capital *S* for Strong, as in, *Phil Strong*. The last time I did this, it had been Carver, for Frank Carver. Before that, Kakos, for Yura Kakos. He owned a string of Greek restaurants in southern California, so at least we ate well for those fourteen months. In between Yura and Frank was the one we weren't allowed to talk about anymore.

I swallowed against the feel of his name in my throat, against the wellspring of fear that rose every time he edged his way into my memory. Being the daughter of Dalliance Byrd was tiresome, but being her man was deadly.

Screw it, I thought. I was only two years away from being eighteen, getting out on my own and living the life I wanted to live, in one place. It was time to start practicing being myself. I scratched out the *S* I'd started and wrote *Byrd.*

Under *Mother's name* I wrote *Dallia Strong.* She didn't like for people to know her full name. I supposed the irony of the connotations was too much for her liking. Aside from me and my Aunt Summon, no one called her Dalliance anymore.

If she wanted to sacrifice her identity for Phil's, so be it. I was tired of playing by her rules. I left *Father's name* blank.

"Morning, Miss Clair," a masculine voice sounded behind me, making me start. "You're looking rather festive today. I didn't think the Juniper Festival was for another four months."

Miss Clair waddled from the copy machine to the counter and leaned on her elbows, her cheeks going the same color as her nails. "Jace Barnes, you could charm the honey from a nest of bees."

I flipped over another page and continued scribbling, glimpsing his tall, lean form out of the corner of my eye.

"Mrs. Stark sent these for you," he said, passing a handful of papers across the counter.

I could feel the heat of him next to me, and I bristled against it. *Breathe, Innocence.* His long fingers drummed the counter to my right, and the army green of his cuff, fraying slightly at the hem, seemed more vivid than anything else in the room, even Miss Clair's nails. It was suddenly very hard to concentrate. *Breathe.* I could do this. I could hold myself together long enough to get out of this office where the air wasn't thick with boy and Miss Clair couldn't spring any more sudden movements on me.

Boys always did this to me. They made me extremely nervous,

conscious of everything about them in a pronounced way—what cologne they preferred, what they had for dinner the night before, if they did their homework that morning in pencil or ink, if they spent a lot of time in the sun the past summer. Details others would never pick up on or even care about would overwhelm my system to the exclusion of all else. To say they were distracting was an understatement. And inevitably someone would catch me staring, or a comment would slip out that gave me away, and I quickly became the freak who made them uncomfortable, who knew more than she should. When I was nine, my mom's fiancé Roger paid for me to attend a fancy all-girls school on the East Coast. It was ten months of blissful relief. I would trade my right arm for that kind of break again. But it had only grown worse over the years. And after Salinas, after *him,* it was nearly unbearable. Now, every guy was a reason to be on high alert. None of them were safe.

One.

I focused on the memory of *relief,* a feeling I hadn't known in years, and forced myself to finish off the last of the forms. I held the stack out for Miss Clair, trying very hard not to look to my right. "Here. All done."

Two.

I could feel him watching me.

The office lady's smile faltered as she took the papers from my hand. "Well, isn't this perfect timing? Jace, maybe you can show our new student around before you return to class?"

Three. Oh, no. Say no. Please, say no.

"Sure." His voice was medium deep, with a touch of gravel underneath.

Four.

I sucked in a breath and steadied myself, pasting a tentative smile into place. I knew before I even turned that his eyes would be blue.

Five.

My eyes followed his jacket sleeve up to the bronze skin, pausing at a little mole left of his jaw, and continuing across the sloping angles of his face. He had dark-blond hair that almost met his shoulders in back, falling in the kind of wavy layers that I'd gotten used to seeing on surfers and skateboarders when we lived with Yura. His lips were thin and twisted in a half smile. His eyes—cerulean-edged with aqua centers.

Six.

Everything started to release inside me. He was a lot better looking than I'd anticipated. But it wasn't his face that was so irresistible. It was something else. Some inner, nameless light that shone through his slight slouch and his sideways smile. Miss Clair could sense it, too.

Seven.

She handed him a sheet of paper. "Here's her schedule. Give her the lay of the campus so she doesn't get lost."

He turned to her. "Sure thing." His aura was bright and casual, full of easy charm.

Miss Clair gave me a taut smile. "Welcome to Stonetop, Innocence Byrd."

Eight.

2

"*Innocence Byrd.* That's quite a name. Your parents hippies or something?"

I nervously licked my lips and smiled tightly. When it came to my name, I'd already heard it all. "Yeah, my mom is pretty bohemian." Understatement of the year.

Jace stopped in front of a set of three pairs of solid doors. "This is the cafeteria," he said, his eyes skirting mine like twin birds. "There's another entrance from the library hall behind us."

"Okay." I looked away, bashful.

He glanced at my schedule. "You have the same lunch as me. Look." He moved just behind me and held the schedule out, pointing with his free hand. I pretended to care, but I couldn't get past the feel of his breath against my cheek. I stared at his mismatched shoestrings.

We started walking again.

"Where did you move exactly? Not the old Farmer house?"

I shook my head, tendrils of strawberry blond flashing in my peripheral. "No. Um, we're in a lodge of sorts. It's my mom's boyfriend's place. There's a bunch of land. I think it's on a ranch road. The 180-something? I don't know. It was dark when we pulled in."

Jace nodded. "Oh yeah, 186. Huh. There're a few places back there. You're not at the Humboldts', are you?"

I shook my head again. "His name's Strong. Phil Strong." Jace pointed out the B-hall computer lab on our way toward my math class.

"Oh yeah, the Strongs. I know them," Jace said, grinning, before we both realized what he'd implied.

Them. Great. Not a *he.* A *them.* The air grew thinner around me. It wasn't the first time my mother had come between a man and his family. After Roger's wife had tried to use her as a witness in an ugly custody battle, I figured Mom had learned her lesson. But she'd grown increasingly desperate in the last few years after . . . well, after we'd learned just how far she could push a man. She had been careful with Yura and Frank. She must be slipping.

"Hey, I didn't mean anything. I mean, I'm sure your mom's great and all. Mr. Strong's personal life is his own business. I haven't even seen his wife or kids up here in years." Jace was backpedaling so fast he was practically doing somersaults.

My shoulders dropped, and I hugged my notebook and papers even tighter to my chest. "Don't worry about it." *I'm used to it.*

"No, really," he said, stopping in front of me. "I'm sorry. My mouth has a mind of its own sometimes. It's a small town."

I smiled to reassure him, but I was desperate to change the subject. "So, you're into comics?" I asked lightly.

His face brightened. "Yeah. How'd you know?"

How did *I know?* My brain raced through the details I'd collected since meeting him in the office a few moments ago: handsome, casual, favorite jacket, mismatched shoestrings, charming personality, a junior like me because he shared my lunch period. Nothing about comics. My throat constricted. It must be there somewhere, buried in the flood of details drowning my brain, but I couldn't pinpoint where. "Uh, just a guess really," I managed to squeak out.

"Is it that obvious?" He laughed.

My muscles began unknotting. "No. I'm good at reading people. Well, boys." *Oh crap, did I just say that?*

Jace's eyes locked on mine, teasing. "Read a lot of boys, do ya, Innocence?"

I felt the flush creep its way over my face to my hairline. "No. I just meant boys are more open is all. Girls are better at hiding things."

He laughed again and bumped me with his elbow. "With a name like that, what could you possibly have to hide?"

If he only knew. "Anyway, what's your favorite comic?"

"Right now I'm really into *Saga* and *X-Men*. You?"

"I've seen a couple issues of *Saga*, but I'm not really a comic book reader." I curled my hair behind an ear, a habit I'd picked up from my mother, and kept my green eyes cast down. "I prefer novels."

"Ah, the literary type," he remarked. "I can see that. Let me guess, bodice-rippers and highlanders?"

A laugh escaped me. "Uh, no. Fantasy, a little sci-fi, but mostly just whatever captures my attention." Really, it was whatever paperback I could pick up in a roadside gas station or find in my new school library. Traveling light meant I couldn't drag them with me, but books had become the friends I was never able to make. Stephen King's *Under the Dome* from a truck stop in New Mexico. A tattered copy of *A Confederacy of Dunces* taken from the motel lobby outside San Bernardino. The first two books in the *Eragon* series at my school library in Corpus.

"I can work with that. I'll make you a comic lover in no time. There's a good shop just this side of Austin. Maybe I could take you sometime?" Jace stopped again, leaning into me.

The sudden intensity in his eyes coupled with the nearness of him sent my nervous system into overload. My heart thudded in my chest and everything took on a vibrancy it normally lacked. The muddy green of his jacket, the stark white t-shirt underneath, the azure horizon of his gaze, the sun-colored strands in his hair. I could smell the traces of his soap lingering on the skin of his neck with the clarity of detergent. I squeezed my eyes shut and opened them. If I had to start counting again, it would be the third time that morning. I would be setting a record even for myself.

I looked up from the numbers in my brain to the number on the door and pulled my schedule from his fingers. "This is my class," I said, stepping back. "Thanks for showing me around." I ducked into the classroom before he could press me further.

I trudged up the caliche drive, my fair skin baked pink in the afternoon sun. The memory of the spray-spattered wind of the coast was shriveling in my mind under the Texas heat. The Texas Hill Country, I learned over the course of my first day at Stonetop High, was a decade deep in unforgiving drought. I could feel my very soul wither with the lack of moisture. A stiff breeze kicked up a cloud of chalky dust to drive the point home.

God, I missed Corpus Christi.

Hitching my bag higher up on my shoulder, I glimpsed our new limestone house gleaming a hundred yards up the walk. The only thing worse than the obnoxiously long bus ride from Stonetop High to Phil's lodge was the equally obnoxiously long driveway I had to walk once the bus let me off. Phil had used the property for deer hunting, so the mile-high game fence and chained gate meant the bus couldn't get any closer than the ranch road that bordered this side of the property.

The door was unlocked, thankfully. I crumpled behind it in the heavenly blast of air conditioning, locking the door behind me. "You really shouldn't leave this unlocked," I called, wondering if my mother would even hear me. It didn't matter that we were so far off the beaten path that there was nothing to fear out here but scorpions and rocks. You could never be too careful, especially when it came to Mom and her boyfriends. I'd learned that the hard way.

She came into the den, a dishrag in one hand. "I knew you'd be home soon. So how was it?" Her brilliant smile did little to brighten my outlook.

"Torture," I said, throwing my bag into a corner and following her into the kitchen. "It's, like, a zillion degrees out there."

She rolled her eyes. "Innocence, don't be dramatic. We've been in Texas for more than a year now. You're used to the heat."

I pulled a soda can from the fridge and pressed it to my forehead. At least she'd gotten around to the grocery store. "No, we've been in Corpus. At Frank's beach house. I'm telling you, this Hill Country place is a whole other breed of Texas."

"But it's not as humid," she said.

"Exactly," I lamented, popping the top. "It's like the Sahara out there."

"Phil's coming up on the weekend," she told me, throwing a handful of utensils into an empty drawer. "He's got a surprise for you that will make it all better."

I doubted that. "Speaking of, how come you didn't tell me Phil was married?"

She busied herself unpacking the near-empty box. We lived like nomads. We moved so often, and left so fast, we didn't take much with us. Some clothes, a few personal items, a box or two of kitchenware and DVDs. This whole unpacking charade was part of the routine though. Part of her inexplicable need to pretend to lay down roots, to pretend to occupy a place.

I kicked the box away from her. "I'm serious. I thought you said no more husbands?"

She sat back on her heels and looked up at me. "Don't be angry, Innocence. It was a simple mistake."

"No, it wasn't! There's nothing simple about a wife and kids, Dalliance!"

Her eyes turned hard as glass. "They'll never know we're here. He had one foot out the door anyway."

I couldn't believe she was justifying it. "Careful, Mom. Your desperation is showing."

She rose slowly to her feet, her five-foot-nine frame besting mine by only a couple of inches. "I will not allow you to speak to me that way."

"Someone needs to speak to you this way! What kind of woman can't be on her own for more than a few weeks at a time? Huh? What kind of mother drags her kid from one doomed relationship to the next, hiding out in vacation properties and bachelor pads, in and out of strange men's homes? I could call CPS on you. Do you realize that?"

Her hands shot out and seized me by the shoulders. "You wouldn't. Innocence, please. Try to understand," she pleaded.

I shook her off me. "What's there to understand? That you're a serial girlfriend? Some kind of codependent nut who drives men crazy? None of them can handle you. You know that! You're going to ruin Phil like all the rest. And he has a wife, Mom, and children. Isn't it enough that you're destroying my life? Do you have to ruin their lives, too?"

"No," she said, wiping at the sharply slanting angles of her cheekbones. "No, that's not going to happen this time."

My mother had the sort of face that graced magazine covers. She could have made a killing as a model if she'd wanted to, but she had an aversion to publicity of any kind. But that wasn't what drew men to her like flies to rotting sugarcane. It was something deeper. Her perpetual brokenness called to a primal masculine need they couldn't fill any other way. She was a drug, an intoxication they couldn't get anywhere else.

I sighed, feeling the fight flood out of me. She was so delusional there was no point. "Of course it is," I said. "And then we'll hit the road again. Like vagabonds. Or worse, fugitives."

Something in her gaze sharpened at that last word. "Don't say that," she said, moving to retrieve the box I'd kicked earlier.

"Why? What are you running from, anyway?" I picked anxiously at the top of my can.

There were times like this in the past where the truth stretched between us, holding her just out of my reach. And it seemed that with one word she could bridge that gap forever, if she only chose to. But she never did.

She looked at me over one shoulder, holding me in her gaze. Maybe this time she'd finally let the truth win out. Maybe this time she'd finally tell me what we were really leaving behind besides a string of brokenhearted men.

She tucked her hair behind one ear and turned back to the box, and I knew the possibility of the moment had passed. "I love you, Innocence. I'm not running away from something. I'm running toward it."

I wanted to hate her. I really did. She wasn't normal. She wasn't what other mothers were, or even other women. She probably wasn't sane. Sometimes, I wasn't even sure she was human. I wanted to hate her for what she was, and more, I wanted to hate her for what she wasn't. But somehow, I couldn't.

"I love you, too."

3

One large suitcase and one small box—that was all I'd brought with me from Frank's beach house in Corpus. The suitcase lay open on the bed, *my* bed, though it didn't look or feel anything like mine. The dark plaid coverlet resembled something from a JC Penney catalog, all hunter green, navy, and maroon. I ripped it off the mattress and wadded it in a corner between the rough cedar dresser and the taupe-painted wall. A row of stitched mallards lined the edges of the sheet underneath. I wondered who used to sleep here. A son? A daughter? They probably loved navy and maroon.

I sighed and sat on the edge of the bed, pulling over my single box of personal items. I could already see the lavender fringe smiling at me from the top where I'd folded and stuffed my favorite blanket. I dragged it out, letting the thick knit unroll over my lap, and buried my face in the fuzzy softness of it, breathing deep. It still smelled of sea salt. My heart broke for the third time that day.

It wasn't that I cared all that much about Frank. He was okay. They were all okay. It wasn't even that his beach house was all that nice, or that Corpus was anything special. But we'd never strayed too far from the coastline, not if we could help it. And I guess with all the moves and all the changes, the one thing that stayed constant in my life, besides my mom—who was a constant mess—was the sea. If I'd had a home at all, it wasn't in any building or city or town. It was the ocean. That was my home.

Behind the lingering scents of Corpus life, I could smell the fainter, sweeter aroma of my Aunt Summon, who'd made the blanket for me as a birthday present when I was four. She always smelled like oranges and jasmine and deep, rich earth. I adored her. The one good thing about this move was that we would be closer to her. Unlike my mom, Aunt Summon had anchored herself to a compound south of Austin, a real off-the-grid kind of lifestyle that was all about free love and living off the land. I'd been there once or twice, but we never stayed long.

I threw the blanket over my bed and already the room felt better. Feeling merciful, I decided the ducks could stay. I didn't have any other sheets anyhow. I took out a couple of bottles of perfume and a small jewelry box, placing them on the dresser. I threw a paisley silk scarf that had been my mom's over the lampshade. The soft light washed the taupe walls in rose, and I felt like I could breathe a little easier. I set my laptop on the nightstand and plugged it in to charge. I had one small silver frame with a picture of my mom and me standing in front of Pfeiffer Beach in Big Sur. You could just make out the frayed edge where I'd had to tear *his* face out of it. The endless blue behind us made me think of Jace's eyes.

I didn't crush easy. Boys were just too uncomfortable to be around, too full of signals and stimulus for me to enjoy them. I couldn't imagine what it must be like to actually *want* to spend time with one—until now. Jace's presence threw me into a tailspin like most guys, maybe worse, and I couldn't stop thinking about him. But unlike the discomfort I felt around other boys, I was hungry to know more about this one. He seemed so genuine compared to most of the guys, or girls for that matter, that I'd known. And after skirting the coastline of this country from one end to another, I'd seen a lot. I had to remind myself that I'd only been in his presence a few minutes, and my judgment might be influenced by that easy smile and sexy slouch.

The soft knock at my door sent my daydreams fluttering like butterflies. I opened it, and my mom handed me a phone.

"What's this?" I asked, turning the sleek touch-screen phone over in my hand.

"New phones. I took a little trip into Austin today to get us set up." She passed me a slip of paper. "That's your new number."

We'd ditched our old ones outside of a gas station in Beeville. She never wanted them to be able to reach her when we left. Not after what happened with the one before Yura.

"Smart," I said. "Thanks."

She smiled tightly. "I know this is hard on you, Innocence. I really do."

That was it. No apology. No promise to change. Still, acknowledgment was something.

"Yeah," I replied. I wasn't about to tell her it was okay because it wasn't.

She opened her mouth to say something then shut it again. We stood there silently for a moment. "Well, your Aunt Summon is already in there. And I saved my new number in there, too. And Phil's."

Like I would call Phil. Oh well, let her dream. "Okay, Mom. Thanks."

She nodded and turned to walk away, then stopped. "I'm right down the hall if you need me tonight. I mean, if you have one of the dreams."

I nodded and closed my door. I didn't want to think about the dreams. Or the panic attacks. Or the fact that any loud noise left me unhinged. I didn't want to remember life before the smell of burnt coffee made it impossible to breathe. When I was so naïve I could actually sleep eight hours straight knowing the front door was unlocked. Maybe the lack of moisture here would shrivel that part of my brain. I lay down on my bed and pulled up Aunt Summon's number. I'd hit *call* before I even realized it.

"Yeah?" the voice on the other end asked after one ring.

"Aunt Summon?" I don't know why I said it like a question; I knew it was her.

"Hey, Songbird! New number?" My Aunt Summon always sounded like she was living in the middle of a party. Not because of background noise or anything, but her voice was full of life and possibility. Somehow, she hadn't gotten my mom's gene for wistful sadness.

"Yeah. Mom tossed the old phones after we called you."

"Probably better," she said. "So you all settled in? How do you like the new place?"

I blew out my breath in frustration. "It sucks."

Aunt Summon laughed. "Come on, Bird. It can't be that bad."

"It is."

"Worse than Frank's shag carpet?"

Now I laughed. "Yes."

"Worse than Yura's cigar smoke?"

"Definitely. That kinda grew on me."

"Gross, Bird. Don't say such things."

I laughed again. And then, despite how well I'd held them in all day, the tears came anyway.

"Oh, Songbird," I heard her coo over the phone. "I'm so sorry."

At least somebody was sorry for this joke of a childhood I was getting. "I hate it here."

"I know."

"It's so dry. There's nothing to do. This house is full of dead animals and gunslinger decor. What does she see in him anyway?" My voice cracked.

"A place to land, honey. He's just a place to land."

"One minute, we're stopping to trade in our car, and the next, she's moving in with the owner of the car lot. How does that happen?"

"It's just your mother's way, Bird. It's all she knows. I know it's hard, but you have to find a way to forgive her. She just wants to take good care of you."

"This is not taking good care of me! Why can't she get a job like everybody else?"

Aunt Summon sighed long and heavy. "I wish I could say."

She said it with an ambiguous note. Like it wasn't that she didn't know; it was that she *did,* and she really wished she could tell me, but she couldn't. I wanted to ask, but I wasn't sure if I was just reading too much into it.

The truth was my Aunt Summon didn't work like a normal person either. But at least with her it was some kind of lifestyle choice, thumbing her nose at society's restrictions and all that. And she did work. She worked her ass off on her land. She had a real green thumb and a rocking body because of it. She was only two years older than my mom, and like her, she'd been graced with exceptional bone structure and buckets of charisma. She also had my mom's abhorrence for the limelight.

"Are you gonna be okay?" she asked after a moment.

I sniffed. "Yeah. I'll be fine. I always am, right?"

"That's my girl," she said, the smile audible in her voice. "How was your new school?"

"Same as all the rest—lame. I met a cute guy in the office though."

"Really? Cute enough for you to tolerate him for more than ten seconds?"

"Maybe," I admitted.

"Well, that *is* pretty cute. I need to see this guy."

"He's kind of spectacular. He's so attractive it almost hurts to look at him, but it's like he doesn't know or doesn't care. He's into comics, and he's really *nice.* He even asked me out, I think." Talking about Jace made me smile through my tears. He was the one bright spot in this very dismal turn of events.

"Already? Go, Bird. You've got your momma's magnetism."

"I didn't say yes. Not yet."

Aunt Summon took a breath. "Well, nothing wrong with taking

your time. But I have to tell you, that's kind of hard for Byrd women. We, uh, we have a habit of rushing into things."

I rolled my eyes even though she couldn't see. "Speak for yourself. I'm nothing like that."

"You might be more cautious by nature than the rest of us, but you're young yet. Just . . . take it easy. This is a strange time in your life. Not because of the move and everything, but because of your age. Things are gonna start to happen that you might not always understand or know how to control."

I clicked my tongue. "Sum, are you trying to talk to me about sex?"

"Hell no!" she gasped, but I was fairly certain that was exactly what she was up to.

I chuckled. "No offense, but I'm pretty sure you are not the beacon of purity the school would advocate for this talk. We have a counselor for that."

Aunt Summon exhaled long and slow. "Don't waste your time on counselors, kid. Trust me. They will never understand the complexity of a Byrd woman."

I could just make out the white disc of the moon rising between the black branches outside our window. Stale cigarette smoke and bleach burned my nostrils. In the background, the television spoke in useless whispers, its blue blur a small reminder that there was life outside this room.

I blinked until the hem of the pillowcase came into focus. Behind me, I could hear the muffled noises of his kisses, the creak of her ties rubbing against the knobby posts of the bed. He wanted to possess her, just like the rest of them. Only, he was succeeding.

She screamed and the sound of his palm against her face cracked through my memory. His cursing was followed by a tirade of tears and apologies until he dissolved into a completely illogical rant that I couldn't make sense of anymore. The only sound that mattered was the sound of her soft cries and my own breathing. We were still alive. There was still hope.

The mattress groaned as he pushed off of it. The water faucet rushed on. He was in the bathroom. I rolled over and met her eyes on the bed across from mine. The absolute terror in them swelled until it filled me like the sound of the running water. Until I broke, and my own scream came gushing out like a geyser of misery.

I sat up panting, Aunt Summon's lavender blanket clutched in my white-knuckled hands. *"Mom!"* I screamed with such force that the picture of us at Big Sur toppled over.

She bolted through my door before the breath had fully left my lungs. "Innocence, sweetie, it's me. I'm here. It's Mommy." Her fingers brushed over my face and hair, tangling in the soft curls at my shoulder. "I'm here. I won't let you go."

I buried my face in her neck and tried to breathe her in. Her smell was more familiar than my own face, a road map of sea breezes and nightshade blossoms. I sobbed against her until the tension left my body, flowing out of me like a retreating tide.

"Shh, there, there," she said over and over, alternately patting and rubbing my back. "It's all over. All over. He'll never hurt us again. No one will. I won't let them."

Finally, I laid back against the pillow once more, the little mallards there a small comfort. I was on Phil's sheets in Phil's house, not the stiff motel bed of that haunted room.

"It's getting worse," I said quietly, rolling over and letting her smooth the hair back from my damp face.

"I know," she said. Her voice was low and sad.

"Will it ever go away?" I whispered.

"Of course it will, sweetheart. You just need time. We're going to get lots of time here."

Her voice was soft like ruffles in the dark. I wanted to believe her. I needed to believe her. "Stay with me."

"Always," she whispered into my ear as she lowered herself next to me on the pillow. The solid warmth of her buffered me against the dreams and memories, against the terror. "I'll never leave you, Innocence. I'll never let them separate us."

She meant *him,* not them. He tried to take her away from me. They all did really, but none had ever gone that far. Not like him. In the end, she was just too strong, too sharp. He broke himself against her like a wave splitting against the rocks.

4

The only thing worse than the first day at a new school is the second. I'd gotten next to no sleep and had only a handful of clothes to choose from. Then I had to trudge up the dusty drive to the bus stop, only to have my black skinny jeans covered in a fine layer of caliche residue. This place was going to cost us a fortune in laundry detergent.

The buses dropped us off behind Stonetop High, which completely disoriented me, and I was late to my first class. My locker wouldn't open no matter how hard I tried, so I had to lug all my new textbooks with me the entire day, and then the strap broke on my schoolbag after lunch. I was slumped over in the hallway scrambling to collect my papers as kids tromped by leaving dusty tread all over them. But it was the shove to my ass which sent me sprawling on my face that really pushed me over the edge.

I clambered up and got to my feet, spinning around to find three guys in letter jackets cackling behind me. *Seniors.*

"Cute scarf," one mocked and then proceeded to dissolve into laughter again.

I looked down and saw that my favorite sky-blue scarf had come unwound and was hanging inordinately low on one side. There was a giant dirty footprint across it that read *Adidas.*

I pulled it off and let it slide to the floor. Mostly, I managed to avoid each school's squad of assholes. Somehow, this time, I hadn't.

Heat flooded my body from the ground up in embarrassment, shame, anger. The air was thin and my heart was racing, but I was somewhere beyond the fear, somewhere I couldn't count my way back from. My face burned with humiliation and something much deeper, an incalculable rage that I had only ever felt once before in a cheap motel room in California with my mother tied to the bed next to mine.

Without warning, without thinking, I flew at the guy in the middle. Guttural fury enveloped me in its grip, and my fingers found his face, digging in like talons as I shoved hard. His head whipped back, but his flesh caught under my nails, leaving deep bloody trenches on both cheeks.

"Jesus!" one guy cried looking from his buddy to me.

The guy I'd attacked had eyes wide with shock, round as brown saucers.

"Are you fucking nuts?" the other guy yelled.

I took a step back, my own shock sinking in. But the middle guy, whose face I'd just shredded, turned and slapped the one who'd yelled at me across his head.

"Don't be such a dick," he said, one hand to his face. He looked at me, repentant. "We're sorry."

My eyes flooded over with tears I couldn't stop. The bell rang shrill all around us, shredding my nerves along with my sanity. I snatched at my broken bag and ran down the hall, leaving half my papers and three perplexed jocks behind me.

In the bathroom, I splashed cold water over my face until the tears stopped. I used a pencil and the running water to clean the blood out from under my nails. I forced myself to take deep breaths until my cheeks went from fire-engine red to petal pink. I counted to eight and then counted again . . . three more times. When my hands stopped visibly shaking and the threat of vomiting passed, I knew I had myself together enough to face a crowd. I slipped late into class.

My algebra teacher looked up at me as I slid apologetically into my desk.

"Miss Byrd, how nice of you to join us," Mr. Sikes said.

There were a few giggles, but mostly everyone ignored me as I fumbled to get out my book and find the page they were on. When I finally reached it, the door to our class opened and Jace walked in, a pink slip in his hand. He handed it to Mr. Sikes, and his Mediterranean blue eyes found mine instantly.

"Well, Miss Byrd. It seems no sooner than you've found us, you're being called away." Mr. Sikes waved the pink slip in my direction. Everyone *ooohed.*

I let the air spill out of me and slid my book back into my broken bag. Rising, I moved to the front of the class and took the paper. Jace held the door open for me, a sympathetic smile on his face. My heart raced as I passed him to get out of the class.

In the hallway, he said, "It's not serious, don't worry. Just a counselor's note."

I bit my lip.

"Rough day?" he asked, bending his head to try to make eye contact.

I looked at him. "Beyond rough. I hate new schools."

Jace shrugged. "I wouldn't know. I've never been outside Stonetop."

"Well, trust me," I said. "Moving sucks."

"You move a lot?" he asked, something more than simple curiosity in his voice.

"More than most."

"But you think you'll be here a while?" His faded denim shirt was rolled to the elbows and left open over the dark-colored indie band t-shirt he wore underneath.

"I dunno," I said with a shrug.

"This way," he directed, guiding me down another hall. "I was hoping I'd have plenty of time to convince you to come to Austin with me. To check out the comics, I mean."

I didn't say anything. What could I say? I never knew when the day would come. The day when I got home and my mom would be shoving a suitcase and a couple of boxes frantically into the trunk of the car, my Aunt Summon already on the phone, and telling me to grab a soda and get in, it's time to fly. Hell, it could happen tomorrow for all I knew.

Once when I was about nine, I'd tried to work out a pattern to her flight behavior, thinking if I could just find some rhyme or reason, I could take peace in the predictability of it. But there was no method to her madness, and I realized that it was the men—not her—who determined when we would leave. When it came to them, we were both blind. Neither of us could ever tell how long they'd hold up against the desire, how long they'd last before they wanted her too much.

Jace stopped in front of a wood-grained door. "Don't worry," he said, scratching at his thumb. "Mrs. Kleberg is really nice. I'm her aide. She'll go easy on you."

He opened it and we stepped into a bright office with a tiny waiting room, complete with love seat and iron end tables. Pamphlets on everything from safe sex to bullying were fanned across the wooden coffee table in front.

"Hold on," Jace said, knocking at another door. A woman with dark curly hair popped her head out.

"She here?" the woman asked.

Jace nodded and stepped aside so she could see me.

"Hey there, Innocence," she said with a cheerful tone. "I love your name. Come on in."

"Thanks," I said quietly. Her office smelled syrupy sweet from an apple-scented candle burning in the corner. I sat in front of her desk in a padded green chair. My scarf was coiled on top of her desk calendar.

"So," Mrs. Kleberg started. "I'm sure Jace told you about me. I don't bite, I promise. You can call me Wanda. All the kids here do."

I swallowed and looked at her mutely.

"Typically, an altercation like the one you were in earlier would result in serious disciplinary action, but I know you weren't responsible. Kurt admitted to the bullying, and we have a strict no-tolerance policy for bullies here at Stonetop."

Her smile was chalky white and friendly. She wore very little makeup, and her soft blue eyes were warm and inviting. Perfect counselor features. She couldn't have been out of her thirties.

I nodded.

"Mostly, I just want to check in and be sure you're all right. Being a new student is traumatic enough without something like this happening. Would you like to tell me a little about what transpired between you and Kurt?"

Oh boy, how to proceed. I took a breath and said, "He kicked me. I don't know why I snapped like that. I mean, it's been a rotten day. And he was a real dick, but—sorry. He was a *jerk*. So were his friends. I just didn't sleep much last night because I keep having these dreams, and then this happened. It kind of threw me into a fit of sorts." I was word vomiting, and I couldn't stop myself.

Mrs. Kleberg jotted some notes on a piece of paper while I talked, her dark curly-haired head bobbing as she nodded. "Mmhmm."

"Why are you doing that?" I stopped and asked. "What are you writing down?"

Mrs. Kleberg looked at me. "No worries, dear. I'm just keeping notes of our talk for your record. The district is very serious about how we report and handle incidents of bullying."

"Oh. Okay." I relaxed again into my seat. "So, am I in any trouble?"

Mrs. Kleberg sat her pen down. "I'm not gonna lie. Fighting back physically like you did is really frowned upon. But under the circumstances, what with your being brand new here and Kurt's firsthand admission of guilt, I think we can let this go. That said, it is on record.

Another mess up like this could result in major consequences for you. Do you understand that?"

I nodded.

"I've known Kurt and his family a long time, Innocence. I have to say, I was really surprised by what I saw today. The nurse called me down after he came into the clinic. Kurt is—well, he's very confident. Sometimes too confident. If you catch my meaning. And it's not the first time he's been suspected of crossing the line with another student. But I have never, ever seen him so distraught and contrite over his own behavior. Between you and me, your little retaliation may have been one of the best things to happen to him. I don't think anyone else has ever had the guts to stand up to Kurt Meier."

I wasn't sure what to make of this. Was she telling me what I did was good or bad? I recalled the startled brown eyes in the hallway and how quickly he'd turned on his own friend to suddenly defend me. It was odd.

Mrs. Kleberg picked her pen back up and asked, "Tell me about these dreams. You said you keep having them?"

My head snapped up, and I eyed the counselor warily. Why would she ask me that? But then, I'd been the one to bring it up. *Stupid.* "It's nothing. It's just these recurring nightmares. Night terrors? They're not uncommon. I feel panicked, and then I can't go back to sleep."

"Do you ever have these feelings of panic while you're awake?" she asked.

I wasn't sure how much to tell her, but I didn't want to lie. After all, she was giving me a pass for literally attacking another kid. "Sometimes," I admitted. Only my mom and Aunt Summon knew that.

"When?" she asked.

"I don't know. Whenever something happens that reminds me of—" I caught myself just before I said *him.*

"Of?" she questioned.

"Of the dreams," I lied.

"Like what? Give me some examples."

I shrugged. "The smell of burnt coffee, television chatter, scratchy sheets. Stuff like that."

Mrs. Kleberg gave me a funny look and kept writing. "Pretty specific. What else? Any other symptoms?"

Symptoms? How did we get to symptoms? Symptoms of what? "I don't know." I shifted uneasily in my seat. "I have trouble concentrating sometimes. In class and on homework and stuff. I feel anxious a lot." Basically my life had become a series of fight-or-flight moments strung together. *Like right now.*

Mrs. Kleberg nodded knowingly. "Uh-huh. And do you have many friends, Innocence? I know you just moved here, but back home? Did you have any trouble forming or maintaining friendships there?"

Why was she asking me all this? Of course I had no friends. I rarely stayed anywhere long enough to make them. Did she have any idea how long it takes to insert yourself into a circle of girls? And there was no way I could make friends with a boy. They sent my nerves skyrocketing. "Not really, not a lot of friends. But I don't try that hard. I'm kind of an introvert."

"Even introverts need friends." Mrs. Kleberg tapped her pen against her lips. "Hmmm. Have you told anyone else about this? Your parents maybe? A doctor?"

I shook my head. "My mom knows about the dreams. I haven't seen a doctor in years. Why? What's wrong with me?"

Mrs. Kleberg smiled warmly. "Don't be alarmed, Innocence. There's nothing *wrong* with you."

That was typical counselor speech if I ever heard it.

"What you're describing sounds an awful lot like PTSD though."

"What's PTSD?" I squeezed my bag to my chest. I was in high school. I didn't like anything with the letters S, T, and D in it. Fortunately,

I was also a virgin. So I was pretty sure Wanda was barking up the wrong tree.

Mrs. Kleberg folded her hands over her desk. "Post Traumatic Stress Disorder. It's a condition that sometimes follows a traumatic event. The dreams, the irritation, the panic. These are all classic PTSD symptoms."

"Oh," I said, not sure where she was headed with this.

"Can you think of something that might have triggered the disorder for you? A trauma you might have experienced a few weeks or months before these symptoms started?"

I shook my head. "Not really."

"It can be anything from a car accident to emotional abuse. Nothing rings a bell?" Her blue eyes were full with concern.

Or men who hold you and your mother hostage for days in a crappy motel outside of Salinas? Does that count, Wanda? "No."

Mrs. Kleberg sighed. "Look, Innocence, I know you're new here and it's going to take time for you to trust me, but I want you to know that I'm going to stay on top of this. I'm going to keep an eye on you and see how your symptoms are progressing. If things don't improve, I'll need to call your mother and recommend you to a therapist with the skills to help you."

One call from Wanda and we'd be a hundred miles up I-35 before Jace could say *comic book.* I couldn't let that happen. "You don't have to do that. My mom is looking for a sleep center in the Austin area. I'm sure we'll figure it out." It was a lie, but it was going to take more than *I'm fine* to convince Mrs. Kleberg to stop nosing around in my mental health.

Mrs. Kleberg pursed her lips. "I'm not sure a sleep center is going to cut it, but maybe it's a start. I'll check in with you in a few weeks, okay?"

"Sure," I said, standing. "Am I excused?"

Mrs. Kleberg handed me my scarf. "Try to hold on to your accessories, Innocence. And stay out of Kurt's way for a while, just in case he returns to his old self."

I crammed the scarf into my crippled bag then reached for the door.

"And Innocence," Mrs. Kleberg said just as I pulled the door open. "Stonetop is glad to have you and your mother join our little community."

We'd see about that.

5

I couldn't put today behind me fast enough. The only thing redeeming about it was the nap I got in sixth period. When the final bell rang, I practically sprinted for the door. The sweltering bus ride and powder-cloud driveway of Phil's lodge sounded wonderful after the day I'd had.

I was about three feet down the hall when I noticed the stares. Not just one or two people, but dozens of kids were eyeballing me as I passed, their expressions wary and curious. I didn't know what to make of it, but then I felt his hand on my shoulder.

I turned, expecting—hoping, even—to see Jace's radiant face behind me, but instead, Kurt Meier was there. My claw marks were still an angry red on his cheeks, glossed over with antibacterial cream.

He reached for my broken bag. "Let me carry that for you."

I paused. "Uhh, that's okay."

His face fell a little. "No, really. It's the least I can do."

Uncertain, I slackened my death grip as he pulled the bag from my arms. It was insanely heavy. A part of me was grateful.

"Where are you parked?" he asked as we started down the hall, pairs of ogling eyes watching our trek.

"No, I—I ride the bus," I told him, embarrassed.

"Come on, I have a truck. I'll give you a lift." His broad shoulders and muscled arms were apparent even under the thick sleeves of his varsity jacket. It was way too hot for a jacket of any kind in my opinion. What was with the boys in Stonetop?

"I don't know. The bus is fine. I don't mind," I replied, starting to reach for my bag, my mind already racing through the numbers that stilled me in times like these.

He held the bag away from me. "Forget it. I'm giving you a ride."

I didn't know what to think. First, he'd made me eat tile, now he was carrying my bag and offering to drive me home from school *after* I'd practically rearranged his face with my fingernails. Mrs. Kleberg had warned me to stay away from him, but under the circumstances, I wasn't sure what to do.

"Okay," I said reluctantly.

I followed him into the student parking lot. A couple of people stopped us along the way to talk to him, and I felt like his pet two-headed goat with the way they looked at me. I was beginning to understand my mom and Aunt Summon's hatred for unsolicited attention. No one spoke to me, but I got a lot of lingering looks. No one dared to ask Kurt about his face. I wondered if everyone already knew, or if his imposing physique and the hard expression in his eyes when they saw me kept them quiet. I decided to find out.

We stopped at a red pickup truck and Kurt opened the passenger door for me, setting my book bag on the floor mat. I climbed up and let him close the door, praying I wasn't making some kind of huge mistake. When I was little, I'd watched the movie *Carrie* on TV with my mom, where these kids invite an awkward girl to prom only to make her the butt of their joke. It was cruel, and she used her fire power to burn everyone to a crisp. I, unfortunately, had no fire power. If Kurt intended to humiliate me in some way, there wouldn't be much I could do about it. But he seemed peculiarly sincere, and a large part of me doubted he was that gifted of an actor. I hoped that part was right.

Kurt got in and started the truck. "Where we headed?" he asked.

"Um, it's off Ranch Road 186. I can show you as we get closer."

Kurt nodded and began to back out, his arm stretched across the back of the seat, uncomfortably close to my shoulder. Jace was standing next to an old blue beater. His eyes caught mine through the windshield as we made our way through the lot. I looked down and tried to lean away from Kurt's arm, feeling suddenly ashamed.

"I'm really sorry," I said when we got on the road. "About your face."

Kurt shrugged. Even with the scratches, he was a handsome guy. High cheekbones and a strong nose, thick eyebrows over his brown eyes, a glowing tan and cropped dark hair. He had a rugged, athletic prowess that set him apart. "Don't be. I deserved it."

"Everyone keeps saying that," I said with a sigh. "But I still feel rotten. I don't usually freak out like that."

Kurt smiled at me, and it was open and almost kind, though not as infectious as Jace's smile. "Everyone should mind their own business. I am sorry about today. We shouldn't have done it, ganged up on you like that."

"Why did you do it?" I asked. I was genuinely curious. What made a guy like Kurt—popular, handsome, accomplished—want to pick on a girl no one knew?

He shrugged again. "If I told you the truth, you wouldn't believe me."

"Try me," I said.

His dark eyes found mine and lingered there. My nervous system kicked into overdrive, and the saddle leather smell of his bench seat filled my nose. The whir of the air conditioning grew uncomfortably loud, and I was suddenly very aware that his palms were sweating. He was *nervous.* I was making Kurt Meier nervous.

"You were there," he said with a devilish grin. "And you had a cute ass."

"So you felt the need to put your foot up it?" He was right; I didn't believe it.

"I don't know," he said sighing. "It was an impulse. Stupid, I know. And then you turned around . . ."

"So?"

He looked at me, his dark brows drawing close over his equally dark eyes. "So everything changed when I saw your face."

I blinked and turned away, feeling very self-conscious under his gaze. I looked at the translucent reflection of myself in the passenger window. I lacked my mother's ruddy skin tone. She looked almost golden in the right light, and I was always pale. Where her deep auburn locks were near maroon in some places, my gentle curls were strawberry with blond streaks. But I had her moody green eyes and proud cheeks, even if my chin was daintier than hers and my nose more upturned. I had enough of Mom and Summon's DNA to know I was attractive, but I was hardly the showstoppers they were.

I looked back at Kurt who was still watching me in between checking the road. "Why?"

He shook his head. "I don't know. I just—I mean you're beautiful, but more than that, I *felt* something. I felt your feelings, I guess? I felt sorry. But not like pity. Call it a revelation. I saw what a douche I was in your eyes."

"I never said you were a douche," I told him.

"You didn't have to."

That was true. "So now what? Does everyone know? About today, I mean."

"Probably. I didn't say anything, but Riley and Josh blabbed I'm sure. And it's kind of written all over my face," he said with a laugh.

"I just hate that everyone knows it was me," I said quietly. Physically attacking the most popular guy in the twelfth grade like some kind of crazed she-cat wasn't exactly the best way to establish yourself at a new school.

"Don't worry about it," he said, patting my leg. "I'm not going to let anyone mess with you over it."

The feel of his hand sent spikes of adrenaline through me, and I shifted uneasily.

"It's up here on the right," I said, pointing. He pulled the truck into the bit of drive that stretched between the street and the gate.

"Isn't this the Strongs' place?" he asked.

"Yeah," I admitted, hoping he wasn't camp buddies with Phil's kids or anything.

"Huh." He looked at me. "Your mom must be hot."

I blinked, not knowing what to say. I wasn't sure if Kurt was great at math, but he certainly put two and two together pretty quickly. At least he wasn't judging us for it.

"She is, actually." I started to open the door. "Thanks for the ride."

"Sure. Can I call you sometime?"

My stomach tightened. Two guys in one week? I just wasn't ready for this. "I don't think so," I said, climbing out of the truck and closing the door behind me.

I fiddled hastily with the gate and didn't even bother to close it before running up the drive toward the house. From the window in my room, I watched his red truck pull away.

"Whose truck was that today?"

Her voice was low and grave behind me, and I froze between the open doors of the refrigerator where I'd been rooting out something to eat. "No one. Just this guy from school."

I plucked up a soda can and an apple and closed the doors. Turning, I took a bite.

"Innocence, I don't want you running around town with boys you just met," she said, folding her arms. The deep violet chenille of her three-quarter sleeves looked soft despite the hardened poise of her stance.

"I wasn't running around anywhere. He just gave me a ride home from school."

She didn't budge.

I set my soda on the counter and opened it. "Besides, you're one to talk," I said darkly.

Her eyes narrowed. "I'm a grown woman. You're still very young."

Exasperated, I threw my hands up. "Mom, it was just a ride from school. It's not a date or anything. I didn't even give him my phone number."

"So this isn't the boy you told Aunt Summon about? The one who asked you out?" She took a step toward me.

I sighed. *Damn you, Sum.* I had a way of forgetting that the only other person as close to my Aunt Summon as me was my mother. "No!"

She advanced on me, her gaze probing. "Are you telling me the truth?"

"Why are you being so paranoid? He's just this asshole from school who was kind of rude to me today and felt bad for it, so he gave me a ride home. It's not a big deal." I gulped my soda and hopped up to sit on the counter.

"What do you mean *rude* to you? Did he hurt you?" Suddenly, she switched from interrogator mode to nurse mode, checking me over for scrapes and bruises.

I pulled away. "No. It was more the other way around."

She stopped. "You hurt him?"

I nodded and pursed my lips. "A bit."

"And then he offered to drive you home?"

"That's what I said." I really didn't want to relive today's incident with Kurt, and I had to tread carefully. I didn't want her catching wind of my appointment with Mrs. Kleberg.

She exhaled and began braiding her long hair over one shoulder. "You shouldn't accept rides from strangers."

"He wasn't a stranger. And I hate the bus. You know that."

She eyed me and looked away. "I'll have to talk to Phil about this."

I huffed. “Yes, let’s see what Phil has to say.” Hopping off the counter, I started to leave but she caught my arm, twirling me back around.

“I’m serious, Innocence. No boys.”

“You know, I’m going to have to date some time, Mom. They don’t really stock chastity belts nowadays.”

“I just think you’re still too young. And I know Phil wouldn’t approve.”

That literally sent me into a fit of laughter so ironic, I could barely catch my breath. “Phil is in no position to weigh in on the morals of teen sexuality. In fact, he’s in no position to weigh in on morality of any kind. At least Frank had the decency to pretend I wasn’t there most of the time.”

My mom looked stung, but she knew it was true. While she and Phil pretended he was my insta-father, Frank only ever cared about her. I could have waded into the ocean and drowned for all he would have noticed. I liked it better that way. I didn’t need Phil taking his parental guilt out on me.

“I’m not talking about morality. You’re not like other girls, Innocence. Dating . . . it’s going to be different for you.”

“Spare me the *you’re special* speech, Mom.” I rolled my eyes.

“I just mean that women in the Byrd family have a certain history. That’s all.” She opened her mouth to continue but I cut her off.

“I will be nothing like you.” The vitriol in my tone changed the energy between us from typical angst to something deep, twisted, and deadly serious.

Her eyes narrowed again and she straightened. Tension rode up her spine, leaving her rigid and ready to pounce. I waited for the defensive strike, but it never came.

Instead, her shoulders slumped and her eyes watered. A weariness fell over her like a sunset, and she said simply, “I’m counting on it.”

Then she walked away.

6

Phil stood beside the silver coupe beaming at me like a kid who'd just used the potty for the first time. The only thing brighter than his smile was the flawless paint job, glinting in the midmorning sun. Or maybe the polished flesh of the bald spot peeping through the combed-over crown of his head. He'd removed his tan cowboy hat in my mom's presence to hold it over his bulging gut instead.

I looked from him to my mother in disbelief. She, too, was smiling, but hers had a calculated edge.

"You have to be kidding me," I stammered, nearing the tiny car. I was barely out of my pajamas, fully prepared to sleep my first Stonetop Saturday away when Mom insisted I come outside. We'd only been here a week, and Mom had convinced Phil to give me a new car. That was fast work, even for her.

"I told you I'd talk to Phil about it," she replied, walking over and patting his arm like he'd been a good dog.

Was all this really in response to my ride home with Kurt? One little ride from a boy and they were giving me a car? I should have started acting out years ago. What would I get if she knew I'd registered under my own name? I stared at her, wondering why she would go to these lengths. What was this really all about?

She just grinned innocently. "I told you I wanted you to be happy here, darling. So does Phil."

Phil, who at this point hadn't managed to wipe the goofy smile from his face long enough to speak for himself, suddenly recovered his faculty of speech. "That's right, Innocence. Stonetop is your home now. Your mother and I want you to accept it."

I rested my elbows on the rounded roof of the sporty Mini and gave Phil a glossy smile. What he wanted was for me to shut up so that my mother would stay put in this cedar and limestone cage he'd given us.

"Wasn't there something else?" My mother said under her breath, nudging Phil with an elbow.

"Oh! That's right." He scrambled to pull his wallet from his slacks. Taking out several credit cards, he held them out to me over the roof of the car. "The keys are inside," he said.

I took the plastic from him and shuffled through them rapidly. AmEx, Visa, MasterCard. They were all here, a full house. All in Phil's name. "What's this for?" I asked him as I pocketed the credit cards.

He looked at my mom, who urged him on with an encouraging nod. "We thought you'd enjoy a day of shopping. On me, of course. Your mom told me you didn't get to bring much with you."

I ran my tongue over my teeth thoughtfully. Roughly translated, Phil was paying me to get out of the way for the day, so he could be alone with my mother. I wanted to throw it all back in his face, but then I thought of the hellish week I'd had. To top it off, I was going to have to wear last Monday's outfit again this Monday if I didn't get some new things. In light of all that, I couldn't bring myself to pass up Phil's offer. I hated myself for it, though. It brought me one step closer to being just like her.

"Honey, what do you say to Phil for his generosity?" The syrup in her voice made me sick.

I sighed and shot my mother a look of disgust. "Thanks, Phil," I said flatly. Smirking, I added, "I'll be sure to pick something up in town for you, too, Phil. Don't worry."

He broke away from my mom's radiance long enough to contort his face in confusion. "For me?"

I plastered on a dazzling, fat-cheeked smile. "Sure. You know, a little something to take home to the wife and kids, so they don't ask where you've been all day."

Phil's jowls went limp and his eyes bulged. Beside him, my mother was crimson with anger. Before either of them could respond, I dove into the driver's side, slammed the door, and started down the drive.

Maybe I was for sale, but at least I set the price.

I was on the road before I'd even had time to consider where I was going. I turned onto the street that led to our town square and parked in front of the old drugstore across from the courthouse. Phil had left the Mini with a nearly full tank. I cut off the ignition, turned off my phone, and went inside. I figured I could buy a road map or get the clerk to give me some directions.

The interior of the drugstore was small and musty but bright thanks to the large glass windows in front. I snatched a bag of lollipops off a shelf and made my way to a circular display of maps and sunglasses near the door. I popped a grape lollipop in my mouth for breakfast, plucked a Texas Highways map from the display, and tried on sunglasses. The sun was blinding here, but it only made me miss the sight of it glinting off the waves of the many beaches I'd known and lived near.

"I think that pair definitely suits you," a familiar voice said.

I turned to find Jace grinning behind me as I pulled the black plastic shades from my face. "Oh, hey. Want a sucker?" I asked, holding up the bag and feeling completely ridiculous. I hadn't seen him the rest of the week at school. I was beginning to think he'd changed his mind about me.

Jace took a green-apple one and eyed the map in my hand. "Going somewhere?"

"I, uh, I'm supposed to go shopping," I said, my smile faltering as the morning's events came back to me. "I don't really know where I'm going."

Jace tugged the map gently out of my hand and put it back on the rack. "Let me take you," he said.

I froze. A whole day in Jace's company would surely send me into a total breakdown. I was already fighting the inevitable trampoline heart his presence caused in me. How would I ever stay centered long enough to try on clothes? "You don't really seem like the mall type," I told him.

"Neither do you," he said. "But we gotta get the essentials somewhere. So can I tag along?"

I thought about my mother, about how much she would freak when she found out—taking Jace in the car meant to keep me from spending time with any boy.

"Sure," I said before I could change my mind. "I could use the company."

"Great," Jace beamed. "Let me just drop this off."

He passed an empty prescription bottle across the counter to the pharmacist and jogged back over to where I was paying for my candy and sunglasses.

"You sick?" I asked him.

"What? Oh, no. It's for my mom." He looked down. "She's been on meds for the last three years. Antidepressants."

"Oh," I said, embarrassed at my prying. "If it makes you feel any better, they don't make a pill for whatever's wrong with my mom."

Jace laughed and caught my eye. My heart sped up about three times as fast. "Thanks. It does," he said.

7

My car felt about two times smaller with Jace's good looks taking up all the available oxygen in it. I tried to focus on his directions and not the fact that I could hear his heart beating under the steady thrum of the bass on the radio or that I was aware of the exact distance between our legs in the cramped interior.

I switched lanes, and my fingers fumbled on the gear shaft. I took a deep, shuddering breath. *One, two, three. Easy, Inn.*

"Are you okay, Innocence?" he asked.

"Yeah, it's just been a shaky morning." I couldn't tell him that the sound of his breathing was louder to me than the engine of a car, or that I could smell the fabric softener in his t-shirt over the new-car scent of my seat.

He placed a hand over mine on the gear shaft. "You wanna talk about it?"

I shook my head, the heat in his palm searing against my hand. Then I looked at him. "Phil's not my stepdad, okay?"

Jace's expression was open and understanding. "Okay. I get it."

"No, you don't. And that's all right. I just—I don't want you to think certain things about me because of how my mother is." I didn't know why I was blurting all this out. It was just—this boy, this stupid boy, all beautiful blue eyes and big open heart.

Jace laced his fingers through my own, pulling my hand into his lap. "Innocence, my mom's been clinically depressed for the last five years, and my dad drinks too much. We're not our parents. I would never pass judgment on you, or your mom for that matter. I don't know you well enough, but I want to. If you'll let me."

Could I let someone in? And not just anyone, but a boy—one that yanked a thousand tethers on my senses without even trying?

I swallowed and concentrated on the feel of his pulse against the skin of my wrist. "I'll try," I said, giving his hand a little squeeze before pulling away. And I meant it. It was the best I could offer.

He guided me to a mall in west Austin, but even surrounded by fluorescent lights, food court smells, countless people, and an endless array of merchandise, I zeroed in on Jace again and again like a homing device. It was as though my system went on autopilot: destination *Jace*.

"You haven't bought much," he said just outside of the third clothing store we'd visited that day. He glanced at me. My ears caught his pulse throbbing beneath the surface of his neck, my nose—each individual pheromone he was letting off. I *knew* he wanted me. But I was frozen in that knowledge and completely unsure what to do. So I put all my energy into resisting. The more I resisted, the more he wanted to touch me. And the more he wanted, the harder it was for me to resist him.

I looked into my single, meager shopping bag and shrugged. "I got a pair of flats and two t-shirts. What are you talking about?"

Jace laughed. "For a girl with a handful of credit cards and free reign, that's pretty sad. Shopping isn't really your sport, is it?"

"I'm usually better at this," I admitted. "I'm off my game."

"Is it me?" Jace asked.

I stared at him, pretending he couldn't feel the threads of attraction weaving between us when I knew he could. *Of course it's you.* "No, of course not. I wouldn't have even found the mall without you."

"Okay," he said, taking a sip from the iced coffee I bought him. "The next store we go in, we're each picking out three things for you, and you have to buy them. No matter what."

"Fine." I sighed. "We'll try your way."

We ended up trying his way for the next seven stores, including a shoe store and the bookstore, where I introduced him to Peter S. Beagle and he introduced me to Brian K. Vaughan. In a matter of a couple of hours, I had several loaded shopping bags.

Eventually we ended up at a table outside the Chinese restaurant in the food court. Jace's plate was nearly empty. I had a plate of sweet and sour chicken that was going cold. It was hard to eat when you could smell someone's tea-tree scented shampoo with every bite.

"So I take it Phil isn't your mom's first conquest," Jace said casually.

I shook my head. "He's just the latest of many."

"How many is *many?*"

"A lot." I counted back under my breath. "Nine, I think. I don't know, I can't remember past a certain point. There may have been one or two more when I was really little."

Jace's brows rose in surprise. "Wow. She must be a real romantic, your mom."

"No. It's not like that for her. She doesn't *love* them."

"Oh, come on. Surely she's been in love with a few of them at least."

I stared at him, realizing for the first time how absolutely untrue that was. "No, none of them. Not one." I wasn't sure how I knew that, I just did. It's not like she ever said it to me, but it was understood. I knew my mother. And I knew I had never seen her in love.

"What about your dad?"

I shrugged. "Never knew him. I doubt she really cared for him either, given her track record." I knew practically nothing about him. Even Summon never brought him up.

Jace slurped his soda and eyed me. "So what do you think it's about, then?"

"Survival." The word slipped out before I had time to register it, but I knew it was the unabashed truth. These men, every single one of them, for my mother, were sheer survival. Hers . . . and mine.

Jace wiped his fingers with a napkin and wadded it up. "Sounds a little predatory."

He was right. It was. And yet, hadn't I accepted a ride from Kurt? Wasn't I accepting Jace's help now? I didn't think she *hunted* men, she just used the resources available to her. Like my Aunt Summon had told me, *it's all she knows.*

"Maybe," I replied. "But it's not like she's vicious or anything. Sometimes, I feel like she's on the run. Like there's something she's not telling me. And all these guys and all the moves, they're just her way of putting as much distance between us and . . ."

Jace leaned toward me. *"And?"*

I sighed. "I wish I knew."

"So . . . a couple of your teachers stopped by Mrs. Kleberg's office. I'm not supposed to listen, but I overheard your name. They were concerned about you sleeping through class."

"Great," I muttered. "I guess Mrs. Kleberg's even more worried now."

"You could say that. She's pretty serious about you getting some kind of help. I—um, worry about you, too."

"I'm really fine."

He didn't seem convinced. "Look, Innocence. I don't know what's up between you and Wanda, but basically everyone in the school knows you peeled the grin off Kurt Meier's face with your fingernails. And while nobody's really faulting you for that too much, because let's face it, he *is* a dick, it's pretty volatile. I know you have some issues with your mom, and I know everything here is new for you—"

"Jace, what are you getting at?"

He took a breath. "I think maybe you should listen to her and talk to your mom about seeing someone. It could help. When my mom's depression was at its worst, Wanda helped me see that the best way I could help her was to focus on helping myself. It's normal to want to fix everything for the people we love, but sometimes we end up broken in the process."

"It's not that easy," I told him, crossing my arms. I liked the feeling of his trust, and I liked Jace and knowing everything about him, but I didn't need another person putting pressure on my mom and me. He didn't understand. When the pressure got to be too much, my mom would blow Stonetop altogether and start over again. I didn't want that. As much as I missed the coast, I wanted to settle for a while. I'd given my real name. Aunt Summon was nearby. And I had Jace. It wasn't much, but it was a start. And it was more than I could say for anywhere else we'd lived.

"Sure it is."

"You don't know my mom, Jace. You don't understand."

"Then help me understand," he said. "I like you. I had a lot of fun with you today. Being around you—it feels right, like that's where I'm supposed to be. I don't want that to get messed up."

"I like you, too," I told him. "But I just met you. I know you're trying to help, but you don't get it, and I can't explain it to you in a ten-second window in the mall food court."

"Then let's go somewhere," he said. "Somewhere you can talk about it."

I fidgeted with the handles of one of my shopping bags. Part of me screamed to say goodbye and go home. It was unreasonable to trust this boy I barely knew. I'd never told anyone about Salinas. I couldn't afford to. The dreams, the anxiety, the constant fear—they made sure I remembered that.

But just as I could sense his attraction to me as a tangible thing, I could also sense his caring. The sentiment in his voice, the slope of his shoulders, the warmth in every smile. His sincerity was like a blanket

I could wrap up in. To say he didn't care would be like insisting I was dry while standing in the rain. This was a new experience for me. Jace had no hidden agendas. I liked the feel of being someone's focus for a change.

I squinted against the fluorescent lighting and let him reach across the table for my hand.

"Come on, Innocence," he said. "I don't bite."

I pursed my lips but nodded slowly. It wouldn't matter where I was. In my mind, I was always stuck in Salinas. "I have trouble sleeping."

Jace raised one eyebrow.

"I have nightmares," I told him. "Recurring nightmares."

"What of?" He was being casual to keep me calm, but he was tense underneath. The scent of his adrenaline sent little spikes through our conversation.

"A motel room," I said. "Near Salinas."

"That sounds awfully specific, Innocence," he said carefully.

I nodded. Was I really going to do this? Was I going to tell someone the darkest secret my mother and I ever shared? "That's because it's not just a dream. It's a memory."

"What happened in that motel room?"

One, two, three.

I swallowed against the bile searing my throat and blinked back the beginning swell of tears. *I killed a man.* "I—I don't like to talk about him."

My heart kicked into high gear, awakening a tremble that crept down my arms into my hands. *Four, five, six.*

Jace gave my hand a little squeeze. *"Him?"*

My gut turned to jelly. *Seven.*

I looked at him; his blue-green eyes were the sea I missed so much. I could do this; I could face what happened in Salinas with Jace by my side.

"What did *he* do to you?" Jace looked at me with a mixture of fear and rage.

What more did I have to lose? The panic was there. The fear was overwhelming. I had come undone years ago already. There was no putting the pieces back together. This game I played of holding it all in was just that—a game. Why keep playing? *Eight.*

"He held us. Tied us up. Kept us hidden in that room." The tears slipped over my cheeks unbidden. It wasn't even what he did to us that truly haunted me. It was what *we* did to him.

"For how long?" Jace's brows were deeply furrowed.

"Two days . . . maybe three." I dashed the tears from my cheeks.

"Christ, Innocence. Have you told anyone about this?"

I shook my head. "No. And you can't either."

"But you got away—the police? They helped you, right? They know?" He gripped my hand tightly now in his.

"We got away," was all I said.

"Did you know this guy?" Jace was trying to piece together what little tidbits I'd given him, but he was missing the most important part of the puzzle—and he would never, *never* know it. No one would.

"He was one of my mother's boyfriends. We were leaving. He tracked us. Followed us. Found us." I exhaled. "I don't know—I don't know what he would've done if . . ." I couldn't finish that sentence.

"But he didn't," Jace said. "He didn't hurt you, did he? I mean, he didn't rape you or anything?"

I shook my head. "No. He knocked my mom around some. Scared the crap out of us. He was crazy, Jace. I'd never seen him like that. Anyone like that. He was completely insane when he got to us."

"Anyone who would hold two women hostage is clearly unstable."

"No. You don't understand. He was totally fine before . . . her."

"Your mom?" Jace asked.

"She has this effect on them. I can't explain it. It's like she's their drug. And if they have too much, it breaks their minds. But we always leave before it can get that bad. She—she knows when to back out."

Jace didn't believe me, I could tell. He thought it was the trauma talking, that I was paranoid.

"I'm not making this up," I told him. "I've lived my whole life this way, *her* way. I know what she's like. It's not . . ."

"Normal?" he supplied.

Human. "Right."

Jace sighed. "Innocence, I know what it's like to have a crazy mom. It sounds like yours could use some serious help herself, but right now, we need to focus on you. Making sure you're safe. Making sure you have what you need to be okay. These dreams sound serious. Nobody comes through something like you did unscathed. You need real help."

I pulled my hand back and folded my arms over my chest. "You think I'm the unstable one?"

"No, that's not what I'm saying." Jace ran his fingers through his hair. "I'm saying there are doctors who are trained to help people overcome major trauma in their lives. And what you went through, that counts as major trauma. It's not going to just go away. It's going to take work."

"No doctors," I said with finality.

"Why not?" He looked mystified.

"We don't need people in our life," I told him. "It'll only make things worse . . . with her. If you truly like me, if you want me to stay here, then no doctors."

Jace blew out his breath. "Fine. What about Wanda? Would you talk to her at least?"

"Mrs. Kleberg? I don't know."

"If I let her know what you've been through, how scared you are, I'm sure she'll give you time—"

I threw a hand up. "No, Jace. Promise me. You cannot tell her, okay? No one. You can't tell anybody what I told you."

"All right. But only if you promise to talk to her. It doesn't have to be about Salinas, not yet. But at least talk to her about your mom and all the moving and stuff. She's really helpful. When they were trying to straighten out my mom's meds and things were pretty bad at home, she was the one person I could talk to about it. She's not like most teachers or administrators. She truly cares, you know?"

Yes, I did know. And I also instinctively knew that however much Mrs. Kleberg "cared," her meddling would only cause more problems for us. But I couldn't explain that to Jace. "Yeah. I'll think about it," I lied.

Jace's serious expression broke into a shining smile. "Good."

"And Jace?"

His eyes met mine with a tender attentiveness that turned my stomach to mush. "Yeah?"

"Thanks for being my friend." He didn't know it, but the truth was, Jace was the first real friend I'd ever had. My only friend.

He beamed. "If you'll let me, Innocence, I'm hoping to be much more than just your friend."

I blushed a deeper red than Kurt Meier's pickup truck.

"Well, you've gotten a hell of a lot of shopping done thanks to me. Want to see a movie or something?" Jace stood and began grabbing at bag handles.

I wanted to open him up and live inside him, like a shell. I wanted the safety and comfort of him around my shoulders to buffer the rest of my life. But more than any of that, I wanted to kiss him until neither of us could breathe.

None of those things were an option.

"I do," I said, pushing my fantasies of him to the place where all my needs and desires went to die. "But my mom is expecting me and it's already late. I should get home."

The gate was open when I pulled up a little after nine o'clock at night. I rolled down the drive slowly after closing the gate, feeling oddly vulnerable. "It doesn't have to mean anything, Innocence," I told myself, but adrenaline spiked my blood like vodka. My fingertips tingled and heat washed over me. I hated unlocked doors.

I used to leave doors unlocked all the time. Call it childish naïveté, but I always felt safe with my mom nearby, like she was impenetrable. That's how *he* got to us outside Salinas. I'd gone out for a Coke from the machine and left the door unlocked behind me. He'd been watching from a rented car across the parking lot. When I came back, she was already tied up.

I shook the terrible memory from me with a shiver and parked a few feet inside the gate. I left my bags where they were and stalked toward the house, every nerve on high alert. A raggedy old pickup sat empty in the drive. The dents along one side catching the moonlight like cupped hands. Phil wouldn't be caught dead in a green beater like that.

I tensed and took light, deliberate steps onto the front porch. The front door wasn't fully closed. A little nudge and it swung inward on oiled hinges, making no sound. I stepped into the entry, noticing a thousand details at once: the light on in the kitchen, the disheveled throw on the sofa, the ugly leather sandals sitting at the base of the stairs, and the clink of glass against glass.

"Dalliance, you need another glass, so stop whining," the all-too-familiar voice floated to me from the kitchen. "I just tried her cell again and it's still dead."

Aunt Summon. I exhaled in relief. I'd been dreading facing my mom after this morning, or even worse, my mom *and* Phil. This would go much smoother with Aunt Summon to pave the way.

There was a sniffle, and then my mom's voice cracked through the kitchen. "I just don't understand why. What teenager runs away the day they get a new car? I thought it would make her happy." She sounded shattered with worry, and a pang of guilt swept through me. I had shut my phone off because I didn't want to argue. I never meant for them to think I'd run away. I started toward the kitchen to let them know I was home.

"Dall, I've been telling you for years, Innocence is not that shallow. She's not a normal teenager, and you know that."

I switched paths, moving instead to the bottom step of the staircase, and sat down in the dark where I wouldn't be seen.

"You don't know that she's anything else, either. Given the chance, Innocence could live a perfectly human life. That's what I'm trying to give her," my mother snapped back. "She's not like we were. Not entirely."

Human . . . Not normal. Human. I'd known since Salinas, maybe sooner, maybe since I was born, that there was something very different about her, about *us.* But this went deeper than I wanted to dig.

A long, frustrated sigh escaped Aunt Summon. "You're kidding yourself, sister, if you think she's going to grow up to be anything other than what she is . . . what *we* are. It's in her blood, Dall! And you're denying her the truth of her existence."

"It's not the only thing in her blood," my mother hissed. "She can fight it."

"I'm telling you, she's getting older. It's coming out, and in the end she's going to hate you for trying to keep it from her. You should just tell her and get it over with."

Tell me what? My mind spun like a bouquet of pinwheels. I knew my mother was keeping something from me. I'd felt that for a long time, maybe forever. And here was Aunt Summon confirming it. But the question was *what* . . . and why?

A sob caught in my mother's throat. "I can't! Don't you see? She's safer this way. She trusts me, even if she doesn't like this life. Once she knows, she could act on it. She'll leave a trail. What if they come for her like they did him? What if the police put something together? Anything could happen. She's too young—she'll make mistakes."

"We all do in the beginning." There was more clinking as I assumed my Aunt Summon was refilling her own wine glass. "Some of us are still making them."

My mom huffed.

"It's gonna happen anyway," Aunt Summon said. "She won't be able to resist her instincts. Not forever. Only she won't know what she's doing. That's a recipe for disaster if I ever heard one."

"If the worst happened—if she turns out like me, or even Florid, she would know nothing of it. What harm could she do? If she has no control over it? She hasn't been taught, like we were. It'll be useless to her. She can live a different life. And she'll be safe that way."

High-pitched laughter filled the air. "Ah, Dalliance. You really are in your own world, aren't you? She'll never be safe because she's one of us, especially if she hasn't been taught *what* she is and trained how to control it, how to use it. Do you think caging a bird makes it any less capable of flight? Or takes away its desire to taste the sky? There's such a thing as blood memory, Dall. You should tell her, and you should train her so she can protect herself. Just think what happened to Aleister the last time you tried to deny what we were. And if anyone realizes that she's his daughter, they won't care whether she knows about us or not—not if they intend to finish what they started."

"They can't know that," my mother whispered. "No one can."

I strained my hearing to its limit to hear her. The fragility and terror in her voice frightened me. They were talking about my dad. More than I'd ever heard of him before. Getting down on my hands and knees, I crawled toward the kitchen so as not to miss a single word.

"One look at her and anyone would know," Aunt Summon said. "She's a Byrd woman all right, but she's got Aleister written all over her, even without the accent."

I was so intent on hearing them, I completely missed the hall tree to my right, another of Phil's antlered contraptions. I hit it with my knee, and it made a small scraping sound across the wood paneling.

Sounds of clinking tile followed as both women put down their wine glasses. Fortunately, I'd at least made it to my feet by the time they raced into the hall.

"Hey," I said brightly. "I got a ton of stuff at the mall. Maybe you could help me with all the bags?" I tried my best to wipe my face of any incriminating spy expressions.

My mother gasped and threw her arms around me. "Oh god, Innocence, I was so worried! I thought something had happened to you. Why weren't you answering your phone?"

I hit the side of my head and said, "Total derp moment. I ran out so fast, I didn't notice my phone wasn't charged. I'll have to pick up one of those car chargers. The mall was so loud anyway, I probably wouldn't have heard it."

My mom stepped back, looked me over, then bear-hugged me all over again.

"Geez, Mom. Hug much?"

She laughed, tears shining in her eyes. "I'm just so relieved. You have no idea."

"You and Phil were the ones who told me to go shopping," I reminded her. "Hey, Aunt Summon! Are you staying the night?"

Aunt Summon gave me a queer look, then said, "No. Now that you're home safe, I think my sister can manage on her own. I got a lot to do at the farm first thing in the morning. Gotta get up bright and early, Songbird." She rubbed her knuckles across the top of my head.

"Right," I said. "Commune life calls. I get it."

"Listen, why don't you and your mom come out next weekend and stay with us? You're so close now. Surely Phil can spare you for one weekend?" Summon looked at my mom expectantly, whose mouth promptly fell open.

"Mom, please!" I begged. I could use the chance to wrestle some more info from my Aunt Summon concerning what I'd overheard tonight.

My mom dropped her hands to her sides in surrender. "Okay, but just one weekend."

"Yes!" I jumped and clapped my hands like a little kid.

Summon laughed. "Come on, Bird. Walk me to my truck."

I followed her out to the drive and held her door open as she climbed into the cab of her fossil of a vehicle. "You know, Aunt Summon, Mom could probably get Phil to give you a new truck."

She grinned. "No thanks, Bird. I like mine just fine. Got it all rigged up to drive on nothing but old restaurant grease and goodwill."

I shook my head. "You are so weird."

"It runs in the family," she retorted. "So watch out."

I laughed, but her face dropped suddenly, and she leaned toward me. "I mean it, Songbird. Be careful, okay? There are things at play that you don't fully understand. I can't talk much now. *Later*. This weekend, all right?" She looked to where my mom stood in the open doorway watching us.

I swallowed and nodded, not certain if I should tell her what I heard.

Summon waved at my mom and closed her door, giving me a peck through the open window. "When you and your mom come out, I want you to do the driving, okay?"

I narrowed my eyes, confused. "Sure, Sum. Whatever you say."

She rolled up the window, and I stared at her, watching the intensity of her blue-green eyes, *Byrd* eyes. Then I ran down the driveway to open the gate and move my car for her. I'd half hoped she'd stop at the gate and tell me what all this was about, but I was still inside my car when she passed. Whatever Aunt Summon had to say, it would have to wait until the weekend for me to find out. And then, only if we could get away from my mother long enough. *To hell with that.*

Upstairs, I called good-night to my mom after getting the last of my bags inside and shut my bedroom door, flicking off the ceiling light to make it convincing. I flopped on the bed and drew my purple blanket up over my head as my laptop flared to life beneath it, illuminating the space around me like a woven blue cave.

"Aleister" was obviously the name of my dad, and his accent must mean he was foreign. Unfortunately, I had no such nomenclature for the mysterious *they* my mom and aunt kept referring to. And *they* were somehow connected to my dad—not in a good way from what I could gather. I didn't know if that's what Summon wanted to talk to me about next weekend or not, but whatever the case, I wanted to be ready. I needed to learn whatever I could on my own because those two were obviously hiding something, and I clearly couldn't count on them to fill me in. And on the off chance Summon's little rendezvous played out, maybe I could have some questions prepared for her.

I pulled up Google and typed in various spellings until I found the most likely one. It was all I had to start with. Maybe if I could learn more about my dad and whatever happened to him, I could also learn more about the mysterious *they,* and in turn, more about *us.* A flood of search results greeted me.

Most of them were about an Aleister Crowley, some crazy occult guy in a goofy hat. He died in 1947, so he was clearly—and gratefully—not the sperm donor I was looking for. I had to sift through about six pages of him before other, less famous, Aleisters began to pop up. One from an indie band. Another from the cast of a popular TV show. Both too young to be my dad. Eventually I hit on two articles. The first was from the scientific journal *Genetica Applied,* dated two years before I was born. I clicked on the link. The headline read, *Controversial Leading Geneticist Aleister Helling to Found CAGE, the Central Authority on Genetic Experimentation, in the U.S. Next Year.*

Only the first few sentences of the article were visible.

> *Britain's leading geneticist, Aleister Helling, finds favor in the U.S. for his pet project, CAGE. Helling's previous research on gene therapy is sure to provide the foundation for his new program, but the scientist*

> *is uncharacteristically silent on the subject of CAGE, venturing only to say that his funders have complete confidence in him and his tight circle of associates.*

The rest was plastered over with a message about needing a paid subscription to access the material. I still had Phil's credit cards and considered paying the fee, but if he showed my mom his statement for any reason, she'd know something was up. Besides, after perusing the *Genetica Applied* website a little more, it was obvious most of what they published was written in a level of geek jargon too far over my head for me to grasp. I doubted the article could tell me much more.

The second article was a tiny snippet from the *New York Times.* It was dated seven months prior to my birth. The headline read, *Promising UK Geneticist Victim of Murder Mystery*. I could read all of this one, though there wasn't much.

> *After countless delays in the upstart of his U.S.-headquartered research lab, CAGE, famed British geneticist Aleister Helling was found dead in his East Coast apartment from multiple stab wounds. Baffling forensic evidence suggests the wounds were self-inflicted, though detectives negate the possibility.*
>
> *"There's just no way a man could stab himself twenty-seven times with that much force," said leading investigator James Todd. "Nor do we have any evidence that indicates Helling wanted to end his life."*
>
> *Despite first appearances to the contrary, authorities insist on calling it a homicide, though they're no closer to uncovering who was behind the brutal attack.*

I didn't need to know any fancy words to understand this one. It was plain enough. *This* Aleister, Aleister Helling, might be my real dad. He had the name, he had the accent, and he fit Aunt Summon's mysterious "remember what happened to Aleister" spiel. Which meant I now knew his last name, I knew what he did for a living, and I knew that he'd been killed. Though I still wasn't clear on why. And I wasn't the only one. More searching didn't turn up any new leads or suspects in my father's murder. His case had gone cold.

Which left an even bigger question. Were my father's killers the mysterious *they* my mom and Aunt Summon kept referring to? And if so, why would they be interested in me or my mother?

8

The acrid smell of charred coffee roused me from dozing. Whatever we'd brewed that morning was black tar against the bottom of the pot he'd forgotten to unplug. Next to me, his incoherent ramblings droned steadily on. I opened my eyes, letting my lids flutter against the dim light, feeling my lashes move against the rough pillowcase. My wrists were bound together and zip-tied to the bed frame. The plastic chafed against my irritated skin.

He sat on the edge of her bed, stroking her face in his madness until she began to whisper. You don't want to do this. *Then he would slap her until the tears rolled from her eyes and wet his fingertips. This was followed by more babbling.* Love, love . . . mine . . . *Intermittent sobs choking in his throat. I'd been witnessing it for hours. What frightened me most was seeing her powerless.*

What frightened me more than that was whatever would come when this mad routine ended.

The scream tore out of me before I was even fully awake. And then she was there, tucking herself into the bed next to me, running her fingers lightly over my bare arm like feathers. "Quiet, my dove. I'm here."

I rolled into her and squeezed my eyes hard until the tears stopped wringing out from between my lids. Until exhaustion drained me of my fears and promised to carry me away into oblivion. "Why?" I choked out against her chest.

"Because he was sick," she whispered.

Lovesick. Heartsick. Head sick. Was there any difference? He was all three in the end. "No," I corrected. "Why does loving you ruin them?"

There was a deep sigh that I could feel reverberating beneath her sternum, then a pause in the darkness. "Because it is my curse. But it doesn't have to be yours. Never yours."

What she didn't see was that it already was. Being her daughter, living through it with her, made her curse my own.

I drifted back to sleep in her arms, and at dawn, she was gone.

School was a blur of chatty girls and open-book boys, of demanding teachers and frivolous lectures. I fell asleep in almost every one of my morning classes. I escaped to my car during lunch for a nap. I sat in my fourth period feeling an invisible tug that compelled me to leave the room and follow it, like a string pulling on my focus. At first, ignoring the urge heightened its intensity, but eventually it relegated itself to the back of my mind. It followed me into the next period and the next, always shifting its direction. And the only thing it didn't distract me from was Jace. That's when I realized it *was* Jace. I'd become strangely aware of Jace's presence at all times. He wasn't in any of my classes, and I didn't see him at lunch since I skipped, but I could *feel* him wherever he was in the school, like a tether of energy extended between us, tying him to me.

It made me feel oddly strong. It made me feel powerful. Like I was drawing something from him that buoyed me in a raging sea.

"Innocence," Mr. Sikes practically shouted, waking me from my reverie.

I sat up and blinked.

"Your quiz? You going to pass it up or cuddle it for the rest of class?"

I looked down at the blank sheet of paper under my folded arms. I'd totally spaced out. I hadn't answered a single question. The other kids sniggered at Mr. Sikes's sarcasm.

He was my only male teacher and a real hard-ass. I wanted to crawl under my desk. Obediently, I passed the paper to the girl in front of me, who shot me a sympathetic glance before handing it forward.

Mr. Sikes took it from the boy at the front of our row. He looked from the paper to me and shook his head. "After class," was all he said.

When the bell rang, I was slow to gather my things. I let the room empty out of all other students before I rose and approached his desk.

Without looking up at me, Mr. Sikes said, "I don't give do-overs."

"Okay." I shifted from one foot to the other. I was wearing a cute pair of green flats Jace had picked out for me. They pinched my toes.

"Not for anyone," he added, shuffling through the stack of quizzes until he came to mine. "Give me one good reason why I should make you an exception."

He looked up at me, the thick hair of his eyebrows like furry brown caterpillars perched over his glasses.

Because my mother and I were effectively kidnapped, and now I have horrible nightmares from the trauma? But I couldn't tell him that. "Because I need one," I said instead.

Mr. Sikes blinked behind his thick frames and pulled them off. He pinched the bridge of his nose and sighed. "That shouldn't be good enough," he said, then handed me my blank quiz paper. "But it is. I want it first thing in the morning, you understand?"

I nodded and slid the paper into my bag, turning for the door.

"And Innocence," he called.

I turned back, meeting his eyes. They were an unsettling brown to me all of a sudden, ringed like the inside of a tree trunk.

"Can we keep this between us?"

Was he asking me for permission? It felt like it, but I told myself it was only a trick of phrasing. "Sure," I replied.

He nodded. "If you need anything else . . ." I heard him finish as I passed through the door. Even at the end of the hall, I could still smell his cologne.

"Ride?"

I glanced up into the expectant grin of Kurt Meier, who was suddenly at my side in the hall after the final bell rang. "No thanks. I have a car now."

He trotted ahead of me and turned around. "You sure? What about something to eat? Are you hungry?"

"Not really," I admitted, feeling Jace moving nearer where his hall would soon intersect our own. I was pretty sure other girls in school were not energetically stalking their crushes like I was. And after last night's big reveal, I couldn't help but wonder if this had something to do with whatever was up with my family. Maybe we were some kind of new, useless breed of psychic.

Kurt was clipping people left and right with his massive shoulders, obviously not caring. His face was healing. The scratches were nearly gone.

"Maybe give me your number then? If you get hungry later . . ."

I wanted to see Jace, but I didn't want to bump into him with Kurt in my path. I reached out and grabbed his arm, pulling him back the direction we'd come and down another hall. We stopped outside an empty classroom. "I don't think giving you my number is a good idea," I told him.

His melancholy was practically tactile, but he quickly recovered. "Anything you need, Innocence. Anything at all," he said emphatically.

It was the second time someone had made me that offer today. I frowned. "I *need* someone to give me the answers to this algebra quiz. And I *need* to get some sleep. And I *need* a break from boys tonight."

Kurt waggled his fingers at me in a *gimme* gesture. "I took Algebra

II last year. Got an 87 average. Give me your paper, and I'll take care of it for you."

"What? No. I didn't mean—I was just being rhetorical."

Kurt looked at me very seriously, which seemed atypical for a guy like him. "Innocence, you need to rest. You're not going to get that worrying over some stupid quiz. Give it to me and I'll do it. Then you can have everything you need. I'll give it back to you in the morning."

I'd never let someone else do my work for me before. And with a little rest and effort I could score much higher than Kurt's B+. But I was exhausted and he seemed so sincere. Under the circumstances, I'd be lucky to get a C on the quiz. It was too tempting. I handed him my paper.

"Now go home and get some sleep, okay? I'll find you before first period tomorrow."

I nodded mutely. Maybe Mrs. Kleberg was wrong about Kurt. Maybe he was a better guy than any of us gave him credit for.

A scrawny underclassman in glasses and an Avengers t-shirt passed by and stared at us. "See something that concerns you, faggot?" he bellowed at the poor kid, who looked away and hurried his pace.

Maybe not.

"Really?" I rolled my eyes and started to walk away.

Kurt grabbed my arm. "What?" He looked pained.

"You were so rude to that kid for no reason," I said. Did he seriously not get how offensive he could be?

"That upsets you?" he asked.

I wanted to scream at him, but I swallowed my rage. "Yes, Kurt. That upsets me."

"Oh." His mouth went round, and his eyes were transfixed with this apparent revelation. "Should I go after him?"

"No—just leave it. You'll probably only terrify him more." I sighed. "Thanks for taking my paper. It's just this once, okay?"

He beamed. "Whatever you say."

I started to pull away from him, and he asked, "Innocence? Maybe we keep this between us?"

The déjà vu sent chills racing up and down my spine. Were he and Mr. Sikes drinking the same Kool-Aid? And why did it seem there was suddenly much more meaning to those words than they were used to carrying? "Yeah, sure," I agreed and walked away.

9

I dropped my new book bag next to the same green chair I'd sat in before and tucked my hands under my thighs to keep from fidgeting. Mrs. Kleberg watched me with an open, relaxed expression that I figured was intended to encourage me to spill my guts. Someone should tell her it wasn't working.

"Well, Innocence, I'm so glad you came to see me today." Her smile wasn't fake or hostile, but I still felt like prey in a dark corner.

I'd tried to put Jace off all week. I made excuses to Wanda not to stay after school and whined that I was too behind in my classes already to meet with her during the day. Meanwhile, I'd picked up my quiz from Kurt—92—and traded him three sheets of algebra homework that I could have easily done myself. I didn't know why I was giving in to his need to help me. Maybe it just felt good to be the one taken care of for a change. I relented and agreed to sacrifice a solid half hour to Wanda Kleberg's desire to help. I wouldn't miss Ms. Shelby's incessant droning about prohibition during U.S. history anyway. Now, here I was, staring into her kind, you-can-trust-me counselor face.

I gave Wanda a tight smile and kept mum. I didn't share her sentiments, but I was trusting Jace that this wouldn't go too far. I could put Wanda off my trail by giving her just a little, while I held the really heavy stuff back. Stuff like kidnapping, manslaughter, and whatever it was my mom and Aunt Summon had been discussing in the kitchen that night.

She rose to close her door and reseated herself comfortably. "I know you don't want to be here," she said matter-of-factly.

My eyebrows rose.

"Jace didn't really have to say it, but it was implied that he'd put considerable effort into this."

"It's nothing personal, Mrs. Kleberg. I'm sure you're really very nice and good at your job. I just—I like to keep private things . . . *private.* You know?"

"I get it," she said, lifting her hands in an *I surrender* gesture. "Believe me, I do. It's not my intention to pry. But I have certain concerns, and I told you, I am going to keep an eye on you. It's my job to make sure my students are okay. All of them. You're here now, so you're one of my students. You matter to me."

"Thanks," I said, though I wasn't sure I meant it.

"Have you talked to your mom about our visit the other day?" Her elbows rested on the solid oak desk, right next to the picture of her and her husband skiing and the blown-glass candy dish.

"No," I admitted.

"Any particular reason?"

I met her bright eyes and told her, "I don't think she'd like it very much."

Mrs. Kleberg leaned back in her chair. "But you weren't in trouble. Not really."

"I know," I said as I exhaled. "My mom doesn't really like it when we call attention to ourselves. She's, uh, kind of reclusive." It wasn't exactly true, but it was close.

Wanda steepled her fingers in front of her chest. "I see. And you were afraid she'd be angry with you for getting my attention?"

"Yes." I rocked side to side on my hands and pressed my lips together, not knowing what else to say.

"Do you get much attention at home, Innocence?"

I blinked. I knew where this was going. That I was acting out. That I didn't get enough parental attention, what with no father and a mother who was always moving from one man to the next. But it wasn't like that. My mother wasn't one of those pathetic, low-self-esteem cases who drank too much and let men beat on her. I didn't know what she was exactly, but she was different. "Enough," I replied.

Wanda jotted something on a tablet and looked up at me. "Have you thought any more about the dreams? About what may be causing them?"

I stared at the picture of her and her husband. A blanket of white rose up behind them. Their faces were pink-cheeked and cheery, shining in the sun reflecting off the snow. They looked happy. Simple and happy. How could two people like that know anything about my mother and me? How could their perfectly simple, American-pie lives even begin to comprehend what we had been through? What we were? I couldn't even grasp it.

"It's just all the moving," I said. "It takes a while for me to adjust."

Wanda stared at me, her face totally unreadable, and then she jotted something else down. "You're certain about that?"

No. "Yes, of course."

She sighed. "Jace said you've moved a lot."

What else did Jace say? "Yeah. It's kind of crazy really. But I'm used to it."

"I find that hard to believe," she said, plucking a jelly bean from the candy dish on her desk. "I want you to come back next week and talk with me again. I'm going to give you a pass—you pick the time. Just pick a different class period so you don't fall behind in any one subject."

I took the pink paper she was holding out to me and frowned. *Great. More personal time.*

"If I don't see you by Friday, I'll come looking for you. I don't want to call your mother . . . but I will."

"Can I go?" I asked, gathering my bag in my arms.

"Innocence, try to lighten up a little, okay? I'm not the enemy. I think we can learn a lot from each other."

I looked back at her then, seated with one leg tucked beneath her behind that big wooden desk. Her loafers sat empty on the floor. Her coral toenail polish, happy vacation photos, and marble Texas star paperweight were replete with all the pure, altruistic goodness a life like hers could muster. A life that would never be like mine. I was the daughter of Dalliance Byrd. I had roamed with her. I had suffered with her. I had killed with her.

What could a woman who eats jelly beans possibly have to teach me?

IO

I'd failed Aunt Summon. We were up bright and early Saturday morning to make the drive out to her place for the weekend, but I'd been plagued by another nightmare and was too sleepy to argue when my mom pulled the keys from my hand.

"Innocence, don't be ridiculous. You can hardly keep your eyes open," she'd said as she unlocked the passenger door and ushered me in. "Lie back and get a little sleep on the way."

This is exactly what I did—for the entire two-hour drive south.

I awoke to my mom's gentle shaking, her hand alternately patting and squeezing my knee. "We're nearly there, sweetheart."

I rubbed my eyes and pushed myself forward, letting blood and energy make the slow climb back up to my brain. Despite her hesitation when Summon invited us, my mom seemed positively enthusiastic now. Her face glowed. She had her hair down and loose around her shoulders, pushed back with a pair of expensive Louis Vuitton sunglasses.

"Gift from Phil?" I asked, noting her flashy new shades.

"What? Oh! These? Yes," she said with a happy grin. "You like?"

I shrugged. They were nice, but I'd long since stopped being impressed by the expensive gifts her men lavished on her. Especially when I knew how much of it would get left behind at the next breakup.

She frowned a little, and I almost felt guilty for dampening the radiance of her smile. *Almost.*

"Please, Innocence. Let's not fight this weekend, okay? I just want to enjoy this while we can. It's so seldom that I actually get to *see* my sister." Her full bottom lip puckered in a little pout, and I sighed.

"They're nice," I caved.

She quickly ripped them from her head and handed them out to me. "You want 'em?"

Of course, I was pretty used to this, too. It wasn't unlike her to ply me with whatever gifts she'd been bestowed in order to ease the latest transition. "No," I waved them off. "What would you tell Phil?"

She tossed them in my lap anyway. "Whatever I want. He'll just buy me another pair."

That was probably true. I picked them up and slipped them on despite my moral misgivings. They sat high and wide on the bridge of my sculpted nose, their little rhinestone *V*'s twinkling at my temples. They would do. For now.

My mom turned sharply to the right before twin steel posts that framed an equally menacing wide steel gate, the bars set so closely together you could scarcely make out the slivers of light between them. The gate was already open, and a dark-haired man with a grisly five o' clock shadow waved to us from beside it. A call box waited on the left, but my mom passed it and pulled through.

"Who was that?" I asked, looking over my shoulder as he grew smaller behind us. I watched him swing the gate shut, chain it, and lock it several times.

My mom's thick lashes flitted as she cut her eyes at me. "No one. Just another of your aunt's *helpers*."

"Did she make him stand out there just to let us in?" I turned back around in my seat and watched the scruffy blur of foliage beneath the towering trees as it passed on both sides of our vehicle.

"It's not a bad deal for them. They get to stay here for free after all."

Something about the way my mom said *them* made my skin crawl. Like they weren't people. Like they were broken-in animals. Rodeo horses or circus elephants.

The forested scenery continued as we moved slowly down the red dirt road, past sweet gum trees covered in spiky balls and fat-limbed oaks with canopies like giant umbrellas and blue-green cedars. It had been so long since I'd been here, I barely remembered the place. I didn't remember the gate, or this long road through dense, uncleared land.

"Has it always been this overgrown?" I asked, looking out my window uncertainly. "I don't remember this."

"Summon values her privacy," my mom said. "Always has."

I looked at her and crossed my arms. Despite the blazing Texas heat, I suddenly felt chill.

At last, our car broke into a fountain of sunlight as we passed from the trees into the open acres at the heart of my aunt's place. Here were the fertile patches of garden I remembered, spread like a checkerboard across the land. Several men were out and about, gloved hands full of garden tools, tan faces set with easy smiles. A black-and-white dog trotted behind one guy on a small red tractor, its giant wheels crawling slowly down the road. He waved at us as we passed.

"Wow. Aunt Sum sure has her fair share of tasty morsels around here, doesn't she?" Tractor guy's hulking biceps and rugged good looks had not been lost on me.

My mom sniggered, something I rarely heard her do. "Summon has a type, that's for sure."

The big wooden house loomed ahead of us, the cedar siding a deep red-brown that made everything within a hundred yards smell fresh. It felt good to be here. Right, even. My mom seemed lighter than normal. The heavy veils that always shrouded her misty green eyes seemed to part. I took a long breath and let it out, tasting sunshine and possibility on the air.

We parked and opened the doors, getting out to stretch our legs as Aunt Summon trotted down the front steps to greet us.

"'Bout time!" she shouted, her golden-red hair pulled into a high, bouncy ponytail, little wisps dancing free around her face like flames.

Her eyes fell on me where I stood leaning on the open passenger door. I saw her smile waver for a split second before she regained it. I wanted to explain about the dream and being too sleepy to drive, but I didn't think I should bring it up in front of my mom. Summon hugged me fiercely, just the same.

"Well, come inside," she said. "I made vanilla-orange scones, and there's fresh whipped cream on the table."

My mouth watered as I moved up the porch with her arm around my shoulder. My mom was laughing out loud on the other side of us at something Summon had just said. The fragrance of fresh-baked bread and cedar warming in the sun filled the air around me. My lungs breathed deep and long. My muscles felt loose as cooked spaghetti noodles. My heart rate was the last thing on my mind.

I could get used to this, I thought.

"Help yourself, Songbird!" Summon shouted from the kitchen where she was already putting on a pot of fresh beans and ham hocks for lunch.

I drizzled some sweet cream on my scone, took a bite, and let the flavors melt in my mouth. My mom was standing at a large plate-glass window in back of the house, looking over the view. Whether she was enjoying the land or the men, I couldn't say.

Summon moved into the room after a few minutes, a steamy mug of coffee in one hand. "See something you like, Sis?" she asked with a smirk. "Or someone?"

I almost choked on my scone.

My mother turned back to face us and came to sit at the table where Summon had laid out her breakfast buffet: scones and cream, a carafe of coffee, sliced melon, hard-boiled eggs, and a platter of greasy, fried bacon. "It's beautiful, Summon," she said with a sigh. And just like that, the abysmal sorrow that always plagued her was back. It skirted across the windows of her eyes like spirits in a vacant house.

Summon patted her shoulder soothingly, and I had the distinct sense that I was looking in on something that transcended this mere moment, that I was catching a glimpse of some long-buried secret between them. "What's mine is yours, sister."

My mom reached her hand up to cover Summon's, a sad smile toying at the corners of her perfect lips. "Ditto," she replied with a hint of sarcasm. It was almost like a joke between them, but no one was laughing.

I cleared my throat. "It's been so long since I was last here. I feel like I've forgotten everything."

"Good! Then I have an excuse to give you the tour again." Aunt Summon's cheeks were a weathered pink from wind and sun and her perpetually cheery disposition. "Finish your breakfast, then I'll take you around. Introduce you to the new guy—Alvaro. He's from São Paulo. That's in Brazil." She said this last bit with a purr and a wiggle of her hips.

"I think you can spare her the introductions," my mother said, her eyes narrowed on Summon.

"Such a sourpuss," Summon said, exasperated. She gave me a wink when Mom wasn't looking.

I wouldn't mind basking in the masculine glow of all Aunt Summon's eye candy for a day or two, but truth be told, my mind kept returning to Jace. What was he doing right now? Did he have his shirt on or off while doing it? The tether of energy that seemed to hold him to me when we were both at school was pulled too thin to be felt at home, least of all here. I missed the constant presence of it. Of him. I hoped I could make it until Sunday—we'd planned to have a lunch date at his house after I got back. It wasn't the comic book store, not yet, but it was a start.

I swallowed the last of my scone and grabbed a couple slices of bacon. "Okay. All set!"

Aunt Summon clapped her hands and wrapped an arm around my waist. "Come on, Bird! Let's go see the sights while your momma gets settled."

Summon used a Kawasaki Mule to get around her property quickly. It was like a golf cart on steroids.

"Isn't this cheating?" I asked her as we passed yet another shirtless male on his way toward the broad, aluminum barn.

She waved at him and slowed to a stop so he could catch up, ignoring my question. "Hey, Sam! This is my niece, Innocence. The one I've been on and on about?"

He held out a hand to me. "Oh yeah! Hi there. I'm Samuel."

I shook his hand lightly and tried not to blush. Sam—Samuel, *whatever,* had an unbelievable six-pack and a winning smile. His hazel eyes and long, mocha-colored hair went a little too nicely with his bronze skin and strong jaw.

"You heading over to look at Janie?" Summon asked him, all business now. "She's our new heifer, got a loose tooth and won't eat right," she said to me.

"Yes ma'am," Samuel said, giving her a nod. "We'll get something down her. Don't worry."

Summon smiled languidly. "I know you will, Sam. You're so good with them."

He smiled back at her.

"I'll be by later," she said to him, and I didn't miss the suggestion riding just under her words. "Maybe."

He waved us off as the Mule picked up speed again, and Aunt Summon turned just before the barn to take me out to where they kept the bee boxes.

"He a close friend of yours?" I teased.

Summon gave me a dazzling smile. "Bird, they're *all* close friends of mine."

I wasn't sure I wanted to know what she was implying. I let her steer the Mule in silence until we were well past the barn and the gardens, where one of the far pastures met the wooded perimeter. She slowed and stopped under the far-flung shade of a hundred-year-old live oak. The drone of bees could already be heard from the stacks of white and pale blue boxes on the edge of the pasture.

We got out and walked over to a wooden picnic table sitting empty under the oak. "What do you think?" Summon asked me. "Pretty close to heaven, isn't it?"

To me, after years of being dragged from one town to the next, one man to the next, in my mother's shadow, this *was* heaven. I told her so.

She nodded approvingly. "This kind of living, it's in our blood, Songbird."

I snorted. "Are you sure you and my mom are related? Did it skip over her? Cause this kind of life is definitely not in her blood."

Summon turned her green eyes on me speculatively. Like mine and my mother's, they were a teal color, but Summon's were clear and bright where my mother's were deep and restless. "She tried it once, you know," she said now. "Your mother. More than once, really. Tried living here with me."

"You're kidding." I could not picture that.

Summon nodded. "Oh, yeah. She wanted this, Bird. Bad."

"So what happened?" I asked. Instead of filling in gaps, Aunt Summon was only showing me how much more of the puzzle I had to work out.

Aunt Summon perched on the edge of the table and slipped off her sandals to let her toes curl in the soft spring grass. "Didn't work out," she said quietly. "But not for lack of trying."

I sat next to her and leaned in. "What do you mean *didn't work out?* What's to work out?"

Summon looked out over the sedate pasture, across the haphazard stacks of hives. Her eyes went somewhere far away, like my mother's often did. When they came back, they were full of tears. "Chalk it up to sibling rivalry, I guess."

I didn't know what to make of that. My mom and Aunt Sum had the usual sister relationship with usual sister squabbles, but they were inseparably close with an unspoken respect for one another. Rivalry was just not something I ever saw between them. And if they both wanted it so badly, where did the rivalry come in?

"I don't understand," I said simply.

"I know you don't, sweetie," she said, brushing my hair back from my face. "You know, Grandma Byrd and her two sisters shared a place just like this one? Theirs was back east. Your mom and I grew up there. It was a gem." She shifted her weight and looked around. "We sold it after Grandma Byrd passed. Her sisters were already gone. Your momma and I thought it was best to move on."

I'd been hearing about Grandma Byrd and her gaggle of sisters since I was little. My mother and Summon both adored their mom. Like me, they'd grown up without a father in their life.

"I thought Grandma Byrd had three sisters," I corrected her. "You said she lived with only two."

Summon whipped around to face me, her eyes suddenly sharp. Catching herself, I watched her force the muscles in her face to relax and smooth out. "Yeah, well, it didn't work out with the last one—Florid. She couldn't get along with everyone else."

Florid, huh? Now we were getting somewhere. "Kinda like you and mom?"

My Aunt Summon sighed then, and that sigh was full of so many unspoken words, so many regrets and sorrows I would never know, that it hung in the air between us like rotten fruit. "Exactly."

"If all the other Byrd sisters lived happily ever after on this magical farm back east, then what was Florid's problem?"

Summon eyed me. "It takes a special sense of community to live together on a place like this. A common cause. It requires certain . . . *sacrifices.* Florid was never really the sacrificial kind. She wanted things. She had ambitions."

I raised an eyebrow. "And that's bad?"

"No, not in and of itself. But the way we go about getting those things can be. The things we're willing to do, the people we're willing to hurt. She needed to be in control. She was a manipulator and worse."

"How much worse?"

"Much." Her one-word answer didn't say a lot, but her look spoke volumes.

I swallowed. "Did she ever get caught? Get arrested for anything?" Maybe I could look into my family's criminal history online when I got home.

"No. She was too clever for that. She was a bad seed, Bird, but she wasn't stupid."

"And no one ever told on her? Her sisters didn't call the police or report her or anything?"

Summon stood. "Of course not."

The way she said it, almost like she was offended by the idea, made me feel like I had stumbled into the deep end of the pool without my floaties. "W-why not?"

Summon's green eyes were hard as glass. "She may have been evil, but she was still a Byrd."

II

It seemed my family was compelled to protect the skeletons in their closets. Gathered into the Mule, our ride back to the house was silent until I finally found the courage to bring up the driving thing. "Sorry I didn't drive here like you asked."

She cut her eyes at me and looked away. "No worries, honey. Maybe next time. Hopefully, since you guys are so close now, you can stay more often—for short visits at least."

I nodded. I would like that. "Why did you want me to? Drive, that is."

Summon shrugged, but there was something mechanical in it, something forced. "Just thought it would be good practice. And . . ." Her voice fell away.

"And what?"

"Well, I'd like for you to know the way. The way here. In case—I don't know, in case you ever needed me or something." She patted my knee and forced a tight smile.

"Oh," I said. Then, trying for a little more courage, I added, "Does this have something to do with my dad?"

Summon's foot slammed on the brake of the Mule, and I hit the back of the black pleather bench seat. The Mule skidded to a fast halt, and Summon gasped.

"Jeez, Aunt Sum! Are you trying to kill us?" I couldn't help it; my heart was thudding in my chest with a frantic rhythm. My breathing grew thin and fast, and it was all I could do to squeeze out the first few numbers of my calming countdown.

She took a deep gulp of air and apologized. "Sorry, Bird. I wasn't expecting that."

I got to eight, huffed, and looked at my feet. "It's not like I don't know I have a father," I told her. "I took biology."

"No, I know. You're right. But, you never ask about him. I figured you thought he was dead or something, like your mom and I thought about our dad when we were little. Mother—Grandma Byrd, she never talked about him. We figured it was the grief."

"Did he? Die?"

Summon's eyes were quizzical. "Who?"

I huffed again, exasperated. "I don't know. Your dad. Mine. *Both.*" Maybe if I played dumb, she'd spill a few more beans than the Internet did.

"Oh." She smoothed her ponytail, though it did no good. Her fly-aways framed her face like frazzled petals. "Yes."

My eyes bulged, and she quickly recovered herself. "I mean, our dad. Your mom's and mine. He did die. Anyway. And your dad . . ."

"What about my dad?"

"You really need to talk to your mom about this, Songbird. It's not my place—"

"Sum, just tell me." I already knew anyway, and my mom was even less likely to tell me anything than Summon. Deep down, my aunt knew that.

"He passed years ago," she said at last. "Before you were born. Your mom doesn't like to talk about it. It wasn't an easy time for her."

I nodded, squinting in the sun as my pulse resumed a normal rhythm. "I guessed as much. I won't tell her you said anything."

Summon patted my knee. "You're a smart kid. Smarter than your mom gives you credit for."

I teetered on the brink of telling her what I'd overheard and what I'd read online. I needed her to give me more first.

"Anyway," she continued before I could get up the gumption to oust myself, "Why would you driving here have anything to do with that, with your dad?"

"I don't know," I said. "That's why I asked you." I began to tug nervously at a piece of hair by my ear.

Summon slid a finger under my chin and pulled until I met her eyes. "Bird, what's going on?"

"Why don't you tell me," I snapped. "Because Mom's never going to do it." I'd never spoken to my Aunt Summon that way before.

"What are you talking about?" she said, incredulous.

I couldn't believe she was going to play stupid with me. I'd come here to see her and have fun, but I'd also come here for answers. I thought, after everything I heard her say the other night about how unfair it was for my mom to keep secrets from me, that she would spill the second I asked her. She'd said we'd talk this weekend. I thought she would be honest with me. Now, I felt wrong. I felt *wronged.* If my own mother, and even Aunt Summon, wouldn't be straight with me, who would? The Internet had already rendered the little it had to offer on the subject. Tears pricked my eyes like sand in the wind. Embarrassed, I buried my face in my hands.

Aunt Summon's strong arms wrapped around me supportively. "There, now. Bird, what has gotten into you? What's this all about?"

"I don't know. You said we'd talk, and there's this woman at school who keeps bugging me, and—"

"What woman?" Summon asked. She pulled back from me until I would look at her. "Songbird, what woman?"

I sniffed. "The counselor."

Summon narrowed her verdant eyes. "Why would the counselor be bugging you?"

I sighed. "I—I kind of got in this fight. Well, not a real fight. I just scratched this guy and—"

"Whoa, whoa, whoa. Slow down. You're fighting at school?"

"No. I mean, it only happened once." I turned my pathetic, tear-stained eyes up at her.

"Your mom knows about this counselor woman?" She bit her bottom lip.

I shook my head slowly from side to side.

"Probably better," she said. "How did you end up fighting with a guy anyway?"

"He was picking on me. I don't know. I got so mad. I kind of lost it and clawed his face. I hadn't slept the night before because of the nightmares."

"And now the counselor thinks you're some troubled teen?" She said this as if she already knew the answer.

"Basically," I told her. "She's real nice though."

"Aren't they all?" Summon said. "Listen, Bird. You keep a tight lip around this woman, understand? The less you tell her, the better. And do not, under any circumstances, tell your mother about this. I just got you guys this close, and I am not about to lose you already."

I nodded and took a deep breath.

"We'll talk more, Bird. Okay? But right now if I don't get you back to the house, your momma's liable to get testy."

There would be another chance—lots more, before the weekend was through. Next time, I promised myself, I would be direct. I wouldn't wait for what Aunt Summon volunteered. She obviously wasn't going to give much away on her own. Next time, I would tell her what I heard, what I knew, and demand she fill in the blanks. *Next time.* Right now,

I'd had as many confessions as I could handle. "So, you don't think I'm bad or anything? For losing my cool like that?"

"Songbird," Aunt Summon said, her normal, easygoing self shining through again, "there isn't a bad bone in your body. He was probably asking for it. And probably . . ." She took a long, hard look at me. "He's real sorry now. Isn't he?"

I grinned. "He keeps doing me all these favors and asking for my number. It's kind of weird actually. How did you know?"

"Call it a hunch," she said with a laugh, a laugh that indicated there was a lot more to it than a hunch. "When you're a Byrd woman, sugar, things like that are just part of growing up."

My mom was pacing the floor when we got back. She'd changed from the sundress she wore up to a pair of loose linen slacks and a sleeveless knit top. Her feet were bare, but it looked as though she were about to wear a hole through the pine floors.

"You look antsy," I commented as we came through the door.

She paused and took a deep breath, both hands on her hips. "What took you guys so long? I was about to come out looking for you!"

"Chill," I said. "I was getting the full tour, remember? It's not like anything's gonna happen when we're surrounded by all those trees and fencing. This place is a fortress."

Mom didn't say anything. She glared at Aunt Summon, who looked apologetic. "I took her out to see the bee boxes. That's all. It was a little drive. And the Mule is slow."

"You should have come out anyway," I told her. "It's a gorgeous day, and it's really nice out there." I smiled, but apparently I wasn't getting the transmission about what a screwup this was because my mom only frowned.

Aunt Summon was silent behind me.

"Go upstairs, Innocence," my mom said. "I need to talk to your aunt. Alone."

I looked from her to Summon, who gave me a small nod, a queer look growing on her face. "What the hell is going on?" I asked, facing off against their wall of red hair and secrets. "You're both acting weird."

My mom's eyes fell on me hard. "I said *go upstairs.*"

I started to turn for the staircase but stopped and faced both of them. "I'm getting real tired of this," I said, my voice smooth like steel. "There's something going on. Something you two aren't telling me. If you think I haven't noticed, then you're both blind."

My mother's face was as rigid as a marble statue and twice as beautiful, even in her anger. But there was something more behind it—fear.

Before I could turn back for the stairs, the bathroom door swung open and a woman stepped out into the tension. Seemingly oblivious to it, she looked from my mother to Summon to me, and a wide grin broke across her face. "You must be Innocence!"

I froze, unsure how to respond. She looked like a younger, grungier version of Summon. Her hair was a brash red, with tips that were bleached from brass to white. She had a nose ring and hoops that went all the way up her ears, and she was dressed all in black with ripped jeans, clunky boots, and an oversized dyed military jacket covered in old patches. Dramatic black wings lined her eyes and her lips were the color of polished garnets, but her skin was as pale as moonlight. A tattooed silhouette of a black raven marked her left hand between her finger and thumb.

Happy as she was to see me, the same could not be said of my mother. "Innocence, upstairs! Now! Tempest, if you take one more step toward my daughter, I'll end you myself."

The woman's smile dropped and her eyes rolled. She couldn't be more than thirty.

"Dall, don't you think you're overreacting a bit?" Summon asked.

Wrong question. My mother narrowed her eyes.

Summon turned to me. "Innocence, please. We'll save the introductions for later."

I crossed my arms over my chest. I was really, *really* tired of the cover-up. And now here was my aunt's wicked doppelganger standing in the living room before me, and they were still trying to hide things.

"I'm not gonna wait forever," I said placidly. "If you don't start explaining soon, I'll go find my own answers." No use mentioning I already had, and Google was next to useless on the subject.

My mother said nothing. Aunt Summon looked away guiltily. And Tempest, whoever she was, shot me an appraising smile. I ascended the stairs until they were all out of view. Then I sat down just around the top corner and listened for the fallout.

"Well, that was cute, Dall. Now she really suspects something," my Aunt Summon began in a low, exasperated tone.

"This is your fault," my mother replied. "When did *she* get here? Why didn't you tell me?"

"Because I knew you'd react just like this!" Summon shouted back.

"With good reason," my mother told her. "One of us has to have some sense in this family. And keep your voice down."

"Hi pot, remember me? I'm kettle!" Aunt Summon didn't seem to be grasping the concept of "lowered voices."

"Does she live here now?" Mom questioned her.

"No! She just needed a place to crash for a bit. That's all."

"Uhhh, do I get to be a part of this conversation *about me* at all?" I finally heard Tempest interject.

I crawled carefully down the staircase until I could just peek around the corner and make them out. My mom and Summon were facing off in the living room while Tempest had plopped herself on the sofa with a bored expression.

"No," they both answered in unison.

Tempest pulled a pair of dark sunglasses out of her pocket and slipped them on. "Kill me now," she droned.

"Gladly," my mother snapped.

"Dall!" Summon sounded really angry, angrier than I'd ever heard her. "Whatever your misgivings, Tempest is family. Remember the meaning of that? Byrds stick together."

My mother turned her back on them both. "Not all of them," she said sourly.

Summon sighed and rubbed a hand across her forehead. "I thought I told you to stay in the bunkhouse."

Tempest shrugged. "Sorry, the toilet was clogged. I had to go, and all of your boy toys were out working the fields. I came in to use the bathroom. So sue me."

My aunt looked skeptical. "Whatever. Do you think you could just give us a moment? Alone?"

"Wanna send me upstairs without my dinner, too?" Tempest replied coolly.

My mother shot Summon a darkening glance.

"Outside would be better," Summon said. "For now."

"Fine," she conceded. "I'll go take a smoke break. But I'm taking this with me," she said, snatching a Marie Claire fashion magazine off the coffee table. "Just so I don't die of boredom out here in the sticks." She made sure to slam the door behind her.

My mother spun on my aunt. "How dare you—"

"Look, Dall, before you lay into me, just hear me out. She's only staying temporarily. She just—she needs to get on her feet is all. You, of all people, should understand what that's like."

My mother shook her head slowly from side to side. "You can't possibly believe that line of crap, can you?"

My aunt looked deflated. "What would you have me do, huh? She turned up on my doorstep. You want me to just turn her away? She's got no one, Dall! What if that were Innocence out there? Is that how you'd want someone to treat your daughter?"

"No, but—"

"But what?"

"She's not my daughter, or yours. She's *hers!* It's not the same thing."

"Isn't it?" my aunt asked, sitting back on her sofa.

"What the hell is that supposed to mean?" My mother's long, dark red hair swung as she spun to stare down at Summon.

"Dall, you're no saint. None of us are. Would you have someone condemn Innocence for your crimes because she's your daughter? Because that's what you're asking me to do to Florid's."

I rocked on my heels at that. So Tempest was Florid's daughter. The notorious Florid Byrd, committer of countless unknown crimes and shatterer of family trees. I never even knew Florid had a daughter, that there was anyone in this family anymore besides the three of us.

"I'm not, I haven't—"

"You know what I mean," Summon said more gently. "It's just a figure of speech."

"You should have told me," my mother said quietly. "I would have waited until she was gone to bring Innocence here."

"There wasn't time," Summon told her. "You were already on your way when she showed up."

"This whole trip was a bad idea," my mother said, sitting next to Summon. "And you know I don't want her out there, not for long, not around your *brood.* It's too risky."

"I thought you said she was different, huh? That she was normal. Human."

My mom sighed. "I said she had a chance at a normal life. That's different."

"Relax, Dalliance," my aunt responded, her voice softening. "Nothing would have happened. She was with me the whole time, and we only saw a couple of the guys. Even if she's like you, she's young. I'm the stronger one. My frequency will win out. It overpowers hers."

Frequency . . . I'd never heard the word the way my aunt used it, but it reverberated inside me like the name of an old friend. *My frequency . . . overpowers hers.* Whatever it was, she wasn't just stating that she had it; she was implying I did, too.

"I'm sorry," my mom relented. "It just feels so awful not to be able to go out there with my own daughter. What's she going to think if I sit in the house all day while you get to tool around and be the fun one? I guess I'm just a little envious and a little paranoid. It's still hard, being back here. It's hard thinking that Tempest can be here with you and I can't."

"I know it is, honey," Summon said. "You can come out for spells. I mean, only Alvaro is new. I think I have the others pretty well under control. A little time outdoors is not going to wreak too much havoc."

"No," my mom said with a sigh. "I won't chance it. You don't deserve that. I won't be responsible for doing to you what Florid did to our mother. If Tempest wants to take her chances with you, that's her business. But I won't do that to you."

"Tempest is no threat," Summon said. "She has none of your or Florid's power. But suit yourself. Just remember, Dall. However much you're alike, you and Florid are two different women. You're not her clone, Dalliance. And neither is Tempest. You're not destined to turn out like her—bitter, alone, miserable."

"No," my mother said. "I'm worse."

There was a pause, and then my aunt said, "So. What are you gonna do? About Bird, I mean. She's up there now. She knows more than she's telling. I think it's time, Dall."

"I can't," my mom said in a whisper. "I just can't, Summon. I can't take that from her, the security of believing she's like everybody else."

There was low chuckle. "You really think she believes that, honey?"

"I don't know. I hope so. It's the best I can give her."

"Even after Salinas?"

"Especially after Salinas," my mom replied.

"You and I both know what happened in that motel room, sister. I know you want to believe it was only you, but it wasn't. You were too weak. He was too far gone. She helped you, and you know it."

"No," my mother gasped, her dark auburn hair pooling like blood around her face. "I refuse to believe that. I—I could never forgive myself."

"Yes you could. And you will. Because it's who we are. And it was self-defense. Innocence is one of us, like it or not. Aleister or no Aleister, she's a Byrd, through and through."

There was an audible sob from my mother. It killed me to see her like that, much as I hated some things about her. We never spoke about what happened in Salinas, not directly, but it was always there between us. A shadowy persistence that taunted us, guilt made manifest.

"She did it to save you, Dalliance. And I'm willing to bet she knows that, and she wouldn't take it back." My aunt's voice was gentle but firm.

I watched her wrap her arms around my mother as she had me earlier that day, watched my mom melt into her embrace, needing that support. And I knew, beyond a shadow of any doubt, because my aunt had dared to put words to what we'd only allowed ourselves to think, that we were both killers.

Silent tears coursed down my cheeks, hot and wet and honest as the day was long. A man was dead because of her. Because of me. And my Aunt Summon was right. I wasn't sorry. I was guilty, but not sorry. I'd do it again. As surely as I was my mother's daughter, I would destroy him—anyone—to save her.

"You see," my mother's muffled voice came floating up to me. "I am worse. If what you say about Tempest is true, then Florid only destroyed herself. I condemned my daughter."

12

My tongue bucked against the cotton gag, protesting. The corners of my lips stung. It was the scream, the one I released when she looked at me from across the room, so lost and helpless, that made him gag me. I couldn't scream anymore. I couldn't even cry anymore. Everything—my hope, my fear—everything inside me was dried up.

He sat between us on the floor, his back to the chipped veneer of the nightstand. Elbows on knees, head in hands, soft ramblings pouring between his spread fingers. Mine . . . mine . . . mine . . .

How many hours had passed like this?

Ray, *I heard her say now. She'd been silent for so long, the terror her only gag. But something was brewing as he dissolved on the floor between us into a puddle of madness. Desperation. We were at the end of our line. The pistol at his feet said as much.*

Ray, *she whispered softly, turning so her body angled toward him, so her voice reached his ears. Her eyes became intensely focused, sharp as needles, pupils receding to pinpoints, then mere slivers of black.* There's only one way now, Ray. *Her voice was determined but tender as a caress.*

His head shook, sweat wetting the hair around his face. He wouldn't look at her. He knew.

Listen to me, *she said gently, so gently.* You know I'm right.

I watched, unable to speak, unable to help. Frozen on my godforsaken bed. But I wanted to. Something in me rising, stirring like a phoenix in the ashes of my soul, knew she needed me. Knew that bound and gagged, I still wasn't helpless.

It has to be, *she said simply.* You.

He shook his head violently then, crying out to keep her voice from reaching him. He stood, holding the gun above her, her pupils quivering with fear. Beneath the gag, I gasped. I could feel the string she held him on snap like an invisible cord.

The end was upon us, my worst fears about to be realized.

I kicked out and caught the back of his right thigh with my foot. Not enough to hurt him or even make him stumble. Just enough so he would turn, out of reaction, and look at me. It was the window I needed, and the only one I would get.

I couldn't speak, like she could, with his gag tied across my mouth. But I didn't need words. Not for this. Once his eyes met mine, they caught like a sheet on a barbed fence and tangled there. He was hung. He couldn't look away. I dug into him with everything I could muster, every ounce of strength I had left. The force rose in me unbidden, yet familiar, something that had been there all along. And I felt his will bend before me, soft and pliable as a lump of wet clay. Felt it give and finally break. He was mine.

Behind him, she lay flaccid as he cut at her ties, first one wrist, then another. She watched, motionless, as his trembling hands raised the pistol to his mouth. This is the only way, Ray, *she said calmly, her eyes fixated on him, on me, on what I was doing to him.*

I held firm, even in those final seconds. My focus never wavered. Every detail of him infused me, absorbed into me, so clear. The scabs encrusting his knuckles, the missing button on the collar of his shirt, the smell of sweat and coffee and steel in the room. His eyes never left mine.

Until the shot rang out, and his body hit the floor.

"Ray!" His name was a hiss on my lips, one I hadn't spoken in over a year. It slithered out of me like steam before I could bite it back. The sobs racked my shoulders in the dark as the soft, familiar hands found them, soothing.

"There now, Songbird," she said. Summon this time, not my mother. "Another dream?"

I'd forgotten in the horrors of my sleep that we were at her house for the night. I nodded and pressed my face against her neck. "It was . . . it was Ray. It was Salinas all over again," I choked out.

Summon pulled back from me. She wiped at my cheeks to dry them, and the soft glow of the night-light in my room glinted off the whites of her eyes. "No, honey. That's over and done now," she whispered. "He can never come for you again."

Didn't she understand? Didn't any of them understand? "He comes for me every night," I told her. "He always will."

"What's all this?" she asked, studying my face in the dark. "What are you saying, Bird?"

I swallowed my fear, but like a lump of dry bread stuck in my throat, it went down painfully slow. "I know what I did, and so does he. He's haunting me. He'll never let me forget."

Summon's eyes widened and her jaw tensed. Her face was white in the halo of her fiery hair falling loose across her shoulders. "Why don't we sit out on the porch," she said suddenly. "Take in the night air. I don't want to disturb your momma."

I let her take my hand as I followed her silently down the dark staircase, her white gown fluttering around her calves like a ghost in the unlit space. She looked back at me once, her face tight and imploring. I moved wordlessly behind her, understanding. Not a word until we were outside, beyond my mother's hearing.

The night was damp and alive with sound. Cicadas so loud I couldn't hear my own thoughts for several seconds. Summon slid the front door closed behind us, careful not to let the latch click audibly, and gestured to the porch swing. I sat down, taking in the feel of the slick, painted planks against the back of my legs, adjusting the quilted throw pillows—one at the small of my back, one in my lap.

Summon sat next to me, her eyes intently on mine, and the swing shook beneath us. "What did you do in Salinas, Bird?" she said quietly.

She knew the answer to that as well as I, had basically said so to my mother that very afternoon, but she was drawing me out. She wanted *me* to say it. Could I?

My fingers toyed with the corner of the pillow I was holding. "I killed Ray." My eyes met hers.

"Ray took his own life," she said, her voice barely more than a whisper. "He shot himself."

I shook my head slowly from one side to the other.

She swallowed. "Songbird," she said carefully. "Whatever it is you think happened in Salinas, what matters is that *Ray shot himself.* Do you understand me?"

I understood her, but I didn't want to play this game any longer. I didn't *think* anything. "I know what happened, and so did Ray. So does my mother and . . . so do you."

Summon looked away, her eyes searching the stars for some kind of guidance she wasn't getting. She looked back to me. "I do," she said at last.

I let out a breath I didn't realize I was holding. Was this it? Were we being real with one another now? Finally?

"But I want you to remember that it wasn't your finger on the trigger. Is that clear? In the eyes of the police, of everyone else, Ray took his own life."

"And in our eyes?" I asked, pressing her for more.

She sighed. "In our eyes you did what you had to do to protect yourself and your mother."

Now it was my turn to sigh.

"And I'm damned proud of you for it, too," she added, her natural spunk taking over.

I nodded, a single tear sliding down the swell of my cheek to my chin. I watched it drop onto the pillow in my lap, a dark bloom of wet on the light fabric. Now that we'd said it, now that it was out there, could this be the last tear I cried for Ray? Could I kiss the panic attacks, the racing heart, the jumpiness and queasiness goodbye? Somehow, I didn't think so.

We were quiet for a while, letting the truth settle between us like dust, letting the night sing songs of comfort to our frazzled nerves. Where to go from here? Something was out we could never take back. Something I'd been carrying inside myself for so long. Something my mother didn't want between us.

Finally, I took a breath and asked, "What's a *frequency?*"

Summon's eyes shot to mine, her demeanor dancing back from the calm she'd just about found. "You heard."

She wasn't asking, so I didn't answer.

She nodded curtly. "What else have you heard?" she asked me, probing my face with her eyes for clues.

"Enough," I said.

Summon settled back against her side of the swing. "Oh, Bird. Is this where the father question came from?"

I nodded.

"I should have known," she said. "*She* should have known. Where do I even begin?" she asked herself.

I shrugged. "You can start by telling me what a frequency is."

Summon clasped her hands in her lap. "You already know the answer to that, I'm afraid. You used yours in Salinas . . . on Ray."

That. The stirring, the building, the invisible force that pushed against him until he crumbled before it, malleable, succumbing to my will, my needs, over his own. That was a frequency. *My* frequency.

"That's a strong example, of course," she said now. "But it was what the situation warranted at the time. Impressive, I must say. You take after your mother a lot."

Those were not words I ever wanted to hear. As much as a piece of me marveled at the power of it, *my* power, I had no desire to go through life like my mother, to use people like she did.

"I shouldn't be talking to you about this, you know," Summon said, filling in the silence I let linger between us on the swing. "This is your mother's place, to have this conversation, to—to tell you about us. She would kill me—"

"I won't say anything," I cut her off.

Summon nodded, pressing her lips together.

"She's never going to tell me anyway," I said pointedly. "But, I think I've known for a long time in my own way that she was different. *We* were different."

"I want to say more," Summon whispered. "I've wanted to tell you for so long, Songbird. But I have to respect your mother's wishes. She's just not ready to face the truth about you."

"Aunt Summon," I said, my voice high with the query playing on my lips. "Please, tell me. What are we? I need to know."

Before she could even open her mouth to respond, a shadow emerged from around the corner of the house bringing a low, sinister chuckle with it. "Go ahead, Sum, tell her. Tell her everything."

Tempest climbed the steps to the porch, the cherry of her cigarette glowing a venomous orange like her hair against the night. She had her military jacket on over a long white cotton nightgown. Her lips were curled into a teasing smile.

My aunt practically hissed. "Tempest, what the hell are you doing out here in the dead of night?"

Tempest grinned. "Can't a girl have a smoke?"

Summon eyed her. "How much did you hear?"

Her cousin glanced away, took a drag of her cigarette, and shrugged.

"Enough. But don't worry, I'm good at keeping secrets." She pretended to lock her lips. "Mum's the word. Anyway, don't let me interrupt. You were just about to tell my sweet cousin here all about our Byrd family history, right?"

Summon pursed her lips. "You are more trouble than you're worth."

"So Mother always told me," Tempest concurred.

My aunt winced at that. "You shouldn't hold on to bad memories," she told her.

Tempest turned her eyes on me, a deep, pitiless brown, not the green of my mom and aunt. She looked as if she had another smart remark on the tip of her tongue, but she bit it back. Instead, she said, "I think Innocence should know just how twisted our family tree grows. It's not fair that there's a Byrd who knows even less about being a Byrd than I do."

"That's not our decision to make," Aunt Summon told her. "But for once, I agree with you."

"What Dall doesn't know won't hurt her," Tempest suggested. "I'm sure the kid can keep a secret as well as any of us. She is a Byrd after all." Smoke curled out from between her lips.

I didn't know why she was arguing for me when she barely knew me, but I hoped she won. She may look the most unstable, but she was making more sense than anyone else. I wondered how much of her rock-and-roll appearance was an act.

My aunt eyed her. "Tempest, I've already said my piece on this. And it doesn't concern you."

Tempest stiffened. "That's right. I forgot my branch of the family tree was forfeit when my mother went AWOL." Her voice was hard and clipped like rusty nails.

"I didn't mean it like that," Summon began, but a deeper, more gravelly voice cut through the night air.

"Everything all right?"

Sam stood on the porch stairs in an open button-down and flannel pajama bottoms, his hair tied back behind his neck. He leaned against the corner post and looked at me, his face a mask of concern. At first, I thought he was talking to my aunt, but the intensity of his gaze zeroed in on me in a way that made me practically squirm in my seat. A charge was building between us, not unlike my own energetic tether to Jace.

Embarrassed, I wiped away any remaining tear streaks and cleared my throat, suddenly aware of my own vulnerability, compelled to erase it.

"Sam," Summon said, jumping up. "Everything's fine, really. We were just talking. You can go back to your own cabin."

Tempest backed up a step and flicked the butt of her cigarette away.

Sam didn't budge. He just kept staring at me. The hair on the back of my neck began to rise.

"Why doesn't she tell me that?" he asked after an uncomfortably long moment.

Summon looked over her shoulder at me. "Crap," she muttered. "Come on, Songbird, we gotta get you back inside."

Tempest looked from Sam to my aunt to me. "Summon, what's going on here?"

"No time to explain." Summon held her hand out to me. "Come on, Bird. Inside."

I rose to take her hand, and as I did, I noticed several more shadowy figures marching steadily across the dark lawn toward the porch. Aunt Summon's helpers—more like a reverse harem. Like Sam, they were drawn by something. It took a moment before I realized it was me.

Tempest saw them, too. She moved toward us to follow us inside.

"No," Sam snapped suddenly, throwing out an arm to break Summon's grasp on me. His eyes were narrowed at her. Something was very *off*. I could taste Sam's aggression like salt in the air, and it ran across my skin like static electricity.

Summon looked shocked. Her eyes found mine, and I could sense her fear building.

I gazed at Sam and let my muscles spread beneath my skin, loose and lean. I opened all my senses to him, picking out his smells and flavors, his essence from the dozens of others in the night, coming from the men that were nearing the house. My eyes slammed into Sam, fierce and unyielding. "Go to bed, Sam," I said simply.

He caved, nodded, and turned to leave. Summon pulled me toward the house, relief and anxiety warring on her beautiful face. We turned to see my mother framed in the doorway just as a wave of four guys neared the first step.

"What's going on here?" my mom snapped, her anger crackling around me in the dark. Her eyes danced between the three of us on the porch—me, Summon, Tempest.

Summon's face fell. "She had a nightmare, Dall. We came out to talk it off, but . . ."

My mother's eyes took in the guys crowding at the base of the porch stairs. She looked from me to my aunt with understanding and anger floating across her expression. "We never should have come here," she said, pulling us both into the house and slamming the door.

The sun was just beginning to rise over the interstate, and a gray light diffused everything in its path, softening the hard lines of my mother's face as she sat next to me in the driver's seat. I fiddled with the expensive sunglasses in my lap, the ones she'd given me on the ride up. The silence filling the car was deafening.

"Thanks," I said. "For these." I gave the sunglasses a little wiggle.

She didn't even look at me.

I sighed. "Are we gonna talk about what happened back there?"

My mother pinched the bridge of her nose. She flitted her eyes at me, then held them on the road ahead. "Innocence, there are things you are too young to understand just yet. Your Aunt Summon's lifestyle is . . .

unique. There's no point in explaining it to you right now. It's something you'll have to come to terms with when you're older."

Was she serious? Did she really expect me to buy this? "*Unique*? Is that the best you can come up with?" I scoffed.

Her lips pursed.

"Christ, Mom! Your lifestyle is unique. My lifestyle is unique. Hell, *Grandma Byrd's* lifestyle was unique. All the Byrd women are 'unique.'" I emphasized her choice of words with air quotes. "Tempest certainly is. Think you could be a little more specific?"

She ran her fingers through her hair and snatched the sunglasses from my lap, sliding them over her cool, green eyes. It was nowhere near bright enough for shades.

"Cute," I mumbled. "Real cute. While we're at it, how come there are no Byrd men? Huh? How come we have an entire family history made up of only women?"

"Of course there are men," she said with a huff. "Don't be ridiculous."

Now I was ridiculous? "Funny, no one ever talks about them. I don't even know a thing about my own father. You realize you've never mentioned him to me? Not even once? I don't even know his name!" This last bit was a lie. I knew now, thanks to my superior eavesdropping skills and Google, but no thanks to her.

She thought she was hidden behind those dense lashes, but I could still see her eyes go wide when I mentioned my father, even in profile. "Your father . . ." she began pathetically, searching for something she could say that would shut me up. "Well, I'm not really sure who he was. It's a little embarrassing to admit, but the truth is, there were several men in my life at that time, and I was never certain which one was your dad."

This, I knew for a fact, was a load of crap. First of all, I overheard her myself referring to Aleister as my dad with my aunt. Second, my mom was no Aunt Summon. She didn't do more than one guy at a time. She could barely handle one, let alone a hoard—or what had she called it? A *brood.* I knew this about her. I'd watched her at it my entire life. "Bullshit," I said frankly.

"Innocence!" she scolded, shock in her voice, on her face, rippling between us in the car.

"Utter bullshit," I repeated, in case she didn't catch it the first time.

"You do not talk to me that way," she spat. "Do you understand?"

"Well at least I'm talking," I yelled back, my voice wobbling with the flood of emotion behind it. "Which is more than you ever do! At least I'm not pretending all these things aren't true, that whatever that was at Aunt Summon's didn't happen, that Salinas didn't happen, that frequencies aren't real!"

Her mouth dropped open, and it was several long seconds before she composed herself enough to respond. When she did, I knew I had made a terrible mistake in saying that last part. "I have no idea what you think you are talking about, but I'm not going to tolerate another word."

I crossed my arms and sulked silently the rest of the way home.

When we pulled into the familiar drive of Phil's property, she carefully and stoically extracted herself from the car while I threw open my door, clambered out, slammed it shut, and began stomping toward the front door.

"Innocence," she called firmly from behind me.

I turned and glared at her.

"I want your phone."

"What?" My *phone?* The phone was important. That was how we stayed connected. That was how she reached me at school in the middle of a Wednesday when she'd suddenly determined it was time to move on. Or called to ask what I needed from the mall when she shopped for new stuff after we'd settled somewhere else. The phone was crucial. She knew that. What if there was another Salinas? Another Ray? What if I wasn't there to help her? What if she wasn't there to help me?

Her face shifted, almost softened, then went rigid again. "You heard me. Give me your phone."

I dug into my bag until my fingers clamped around the cool metal of my latest phone. I hadn't even had this one long enough to buy it any accessories. I held it out to her, my bottom lip protruding against my will.

She took it, cool and distant. "If you're responsible, I'll replace it for you . . . eventually. But for now, I think it's best if you take a little break from Aunt Summon."

I was perfectly responsible. Always had been. I had to be, living with her. What she meant was if I stayed quiet, kept my mouth shut, and stopped asking difficult questions. And now, I'd lost my only connection to the one person who I could count on to tell me something, *any*thing, about my father . . . about myself.

13

I couldn't call Jace now that my phone was confiscated, but I was determined not to skip out on our plans together. After everything that had happened, I *needed* Jace. He steadied my nerves like the glass of red wine my mom was pouring downstairs. I could bide my time and sneak out once she fell asleep. Hopefully, Jace wouldn't mind if I showed up early.

It took a few hours, but as I'd predicted, my mom curled up on her bed and sacked out a little before noon. Our impromptu departure before dawn had left her tired and crabby, and she was expecting Phil that afternoon. I didn't even bother unpacking my overnight bag. I left it in the middle of my bed and took a quick shower, slipping into a clean cotton dress from my closet. Glancing at my bag before I tiptoed downstairs, I decided it could wait until tonight. First, Jace. Then, maybe, I could unpack all the residual emotions left over from our trip along with my bag. I still wasn't sure how I'd sort it all. I might have processed Aunt Summon's Byrd family backstory as a hereditary flair for dramatization, but then Tempest appeared, confirmation in the flesh. Her "secret cousin" routine unnerved me, and I was really unclear on where she fit among the skeletons now marching out of the closet.

I easily made my way out the front door to my car. Sliding it into neutral, I backed it quietly a few feet down the drive toward the gate, pushing on the hood. I wanted a little more distance between me and Sleeping Beauty when I started the engine. I just needed a few hours. If she was up when I got back, I'd tell her I went out to get something to eat.

His directions were tucked in my glove box, but I didn't need the house number. When I turned on his street, I could literally smell which house was his. There was something so comforting about Jace's scent: the undertones of laundry detergent were homey, and there was a clean, papery scent that made me think of curling up in his arms with my favorite book. Deeper than that was a hunger for him. There were times it took everything I had not to crush my face and hands against his skin and drink him in.

His house was ideal on the outside. Brown brick, two stories, pretty new. A cut-glass front door winged by potted geraniums. Green, clipped lawn sliced in two by a meandering sidewalk. Dormered windows. The driveway was empty, but I parked at the curb and walked up to the low brick stairs in front of the door. I was worried that they might not be back from church yet, but the doorbell brought a short, slender blond woman, her bobbed hair and brilliant teeth striking against her tanned skin.

"Well," she greeted me brightly, "you must be Innocence."

I smiled as she ushered me inside. "I know I'm early."

"No problem. Jace is right upstairs."

I looked up to see him leaning against the railing, his blue plaid shirt already unbuttoned and his loose-fit jeans tattered only at the hem. I grinned to think that this was his version of dressing up.

"Hey, you," he called. "Couldn't wait, huh?" He cut his laughing eyes to his mother. "What can I say, Mom? She can't live without me."

My face turned several shades of crimson.

"Oh, don't mind him," his mother said. "He's always such a tease." She gave me a nudge toward the stairs. "Go on up. I'll call you both when it's time to eat."

It was hard to imagine this woman as crazy or depressed. She seemed to exude easy confidence, like her son. Nothing about her appeared out of place. Then again, no one would look at my mother and think *predator.*

I passed an open study on the way to the stairs and saw a man with thinning hair and glasses propped on a love seat, a drink in one hand and the paper in the other. He didn't smile or say hello or even turn to look at me. The chill surrounding him reached me in the hall.

I rounded the top banister, into a game room that overlooked the entrance below and stood there shyly. "Sorry, I'm too early. There was this thing with my mom, and I wasn't sure I'd get to come if I didn't leave then."

Jace's eyebrows went up. "Sounds intense." He reached for me, pulling me close. "I'm glad you're here," he said into my ear, his breath teasing the soft curls by my face.

My knees started to buckle, but I managed to stay on my feet. God, I'd missed him. What was this hold he had over me? I broke away to sit on the sofa.

He sat next to me. "You could have called. I would have fixed myself up or something." How did he always stay so happy? Everything about this boy made my heart glad.

"My mom took my phone." I scrunched my mouth up to one side.

"Sucks," he said. "She going to give it back?"

I shrugged. "Who can say? She says she'll get me a new one later if . . ." I couldn't exactly get into the details of the exchange.

Jace's fingers toyed with mine. "Yeah?"

"I don't know. Something about being responsible. Whatever. It was stupid really. Just a dumb fight we had on the way home. She's mad. She'll cool down and get over it." I hoped.

"I take it the trip didn't go so well then?" He ran his fingers lightly up my arm, and goose bumps broke out across my skin.

"It was fine," I lied. "My mom's just tired and cranky."

"I hope so." He sighed. "I can't imagine not being able to reach you."

Neither could I.

Jace leaned in so that his sun-colored waves brushed against my own pinkish tresses. "Maybe after we eat, you and I could go somewhere . . . alone."

I let my breath out slowly. *Easy, Innocence.* He was intoxicating this close. It made it hard to think, much less speak, clearly. "Okay."

"You have no idea how much I missed you," he said softly, his lips only inches from mine. My own parted slightly, heady for the kiss I was sure was only seconds away.

"Jace, could you come and set the table please?" his mom called up, breaking our connection.

I turned my head away and smiled bashfully.

Jace leaned back and sighed, a laugh playing on his lips. "I'll be right back," he said, eyes sparkling. "Do. Not. Move."

"Yes, sir," I agreed, watching him skip down the stairs.

I could hear the clink of dishes sounding downstairs as I stood to stretch. I looked around the casual room, feeling wrapped up in Jace. The chambray-upholstered sofa, the family portraits on the wall—hell, even the ping-pong table let off a feeling of *Jace.* Jace's hair, Jace's eyes, Jace's sideways smile, it was all part of this room.

I followed the strongest vibrations of him to a short hall with two doors. One was open to reveal what must be his bathroom. There was an empty bottle of his tea-tree scented shampoo on the floor next to a still-damp towel. The other door was open just a crack. I gave it a push and peeked inside. A messy bedroom opened before me. Jace's unmade bed, dark navy sheets with a black plaid comforter. His open closet where a pile of t-shirts littered the floor. A dark wood dresser topped with his iPod dock and school books. Across the room, between two windows, his desk and laptop.

Slowly, I picked my way through the discarded shoes and comic books. The air in here was so thick with him it was like a cloud of Jace all around me. A delicious, intoxicating cloud. Without thinking I moved through it, breathing him in. On the other side of his bed, I sat down in the black computer chair and ran my fingers across the keys of his laptop, imagining his own fingers there before I arrived, feeling the heat from them still. The computer sparked to life, coming vividly out of sleep mode, and my breath caught in my throat.

The headline glared back at me in bold, black type: *Salinas Shooting, Monterey Man Found Dead in Motel Room.*

Beneath that, smaller print read: *Homicide yet to be ruled out.*

My eyes darted across the opening lines.

> *Esteemed Monterey resident Ray Caldera, 49, was found shot through the head two days ago in a motel in nearby Salinas, Calif. While police suspect suicide, the brutal scene is still being investigated for signs of homicide.*
>
> *"Wear to the bedposts and disheveled blankets indicate a possible struggle," says Detective Jerald Briggs of the Salinas Police Department. As of yet, no suicide note has been found.*

My heart thudded a frantic rhythm in my chest as my eyes skipped down the page.

> *Caldera served as a civil trial judge in Monterey County's Superior Court for the last five years. He was the youngest judge on record in Monterey's history. He is survived by estranged ex-wife, Rachel Caldera, and four-year-old son, Mason.*

My heart seized within me. *Son?* Ray had a son? I had no idea. He never said, never spoke of him. There were no pictures, no phone calls from his ex-wife. Nothing to indicate he'd had a family . . . before us. Warm tracks down my cheeks caused me to look away from the screen finally. I reached up to feel the wet trace of tears. I didn't even know I was crying.

Ray wasn't exactly the paragon of father figures. He partied hard, gambled often, and struck me as the type who'd never met a woman he didn't like. Of course, once my mom was on the scene, a lot changed. She became his new drug of choice, and I don't think he ever stopped using long enough to notice another woman after her. I wasn't surprised his ex-wife and son wanted nothing to do with him, but it didn't change the fact that I had taken a boy's father away. Because of me, reconciliation would never be possible.

> *"The testimony of any witnesses will be crucial in the ongoing investigation," Briggs says. Anyone with information that might pertain to the crime scene is encouraged to come forward and speak with police.*
>
> *"Any details or leads are welcome. Informants are assured that their identities will be kept confidential. We just want information." Detective Briggs and other officers assigned to the case can be reached through the Salinas Police Department.*

My mind was spinning circles inside my skull. *Ongoing investigation.* My mom said that as far as the authorities were concerned, we left Ray and our ties to him back in Salinas. She made me think we were safe, untouchable. I wondered now if she'd seen this and kept it from me. Or had she deluded herself, too? If anyone saw us arriving or leaving that motel, if anyone talked to the police about my mom's relationship with Ray, we could end up on the wrong side of this Detective Briggs real quick. The only thing worse than learning Ray had a son was learning that we weren't in the clear, not even here in Stonetop, Texas.

One, two, three . . . I couldn't count fast enough to erase what I'd read.

"Innocence?"

I practically leapt out of my skin. Usually, I could feel Jace coming from across Stonetop High, but I was so engrossed in my own thoughts, in the frantic counting that might bring me an inch closer to sanity, that I'd never picked up on him drawing near in the same house. I stood and stared at him, pain, embarrassment, and anger all fighting to consume me.

He took in my tear-streaked face and the glowing headline on his screen behind me. His face flushed. "I can explain," he said.

"I don't think you can," I managed.

He slid his hands in his pockets. "I'm just worried about you. That's all. I wanted to see—"

"If I was lying?" I finished for him, anger rising and winning out behind my words.

"No, of course not."

I didn't know what felt worse. That he knew the facts—He knew Ray's name. He knew about the gunshot, the apparent suicide. Or that he knew the implications. He also knew about the suspected homicide. The "wear to the bedposts and disheveled blankets." And he knew about Mason, Ray's son. Something that was news even to me. This secret, private torment of mine was laid open for him to examine. Did he not believe me? Or was this some kind of thrill, having all the ugly details? Was I a puzzle to solve? "You were researching me."

Maybe if I just held onto the anger, the other feelings—the worse ones, like shame and guilt—would fade away.

"It's not like that," he said quietly.

"Really?" I glared at him. "Because that's how it feels." I couldn't stand there with that screen behind me any longer. I had to get away—from Ray and his family, from his memory, from my runaway pulse, from the guilt and the fear, and from Jace. I bolted for the door, pushing past him when Jace tried to stop me.

"Innocence, please! Just give me a chance to explain." He was behind me on the stairs. "I only wanted to understand you better. I thought if I knew more about what you went through, I could be more of a support to you."

From the corner of my eye, I could see his mother craning around the door to the kitchen, trying to get a glimpse of what was happening. I ripped the front door open and ran to my car, hopping in before he could stop me. I needed to go somewhere I could breathe again. He stood on the lawn as I pulled away, but I made it a point not to look back.

The sound of my mother's soft snores informed me that I hadn't been missed. Stepping lightly on the stairs, I returned to my room and closed the door behind me, its tiny click the only sound I made. I cradled my face in my hands, leaning against the inside of my door, and let the frustration and shame leak out of me. It was stupid to leave like that, but what choice did I have? How could I face Jace again?

How could I stand Stonetop without him?

Everything about this weekend, everything I'd been looking forward to, had gone horribly, terribly wrong.

I stepped to my bed and swept an arm across it, sending the overnight bag I'd left there crashing into the dresser and spilling across my floor. I was all set to throw myself across the ugly plaid comforter and cry myself to sleep when I noticed the corner of something peeking out of my toppled bag. I sniffed and kneeled beside it, dragging the item in question out with my fingertips. The worn blue cover of an old book slid easily into my lap.

I hadn't packed any books.

I turned it over to read the title; dulled gold-leaf lettering spelled out *Young's Concordance of Mythical Beasts.* Weird. Did it get in my bag by mistake? I didn't remember being around any collections of old books recently. And it hadn't been in there when I packed for the trip; I knew that. It had to have come from Aunt Summon's. But how?

I flipped open the top cover and found Aunt Summon's fast, sprawling script rolling across the inside.

Dear Songbird,
Grandma Byrd gave me this on my thirteenth birthday. You're a little behind schedule, but I think it's high time it got to you. I hope you enjoy reading every page as much as I did. You'd be surprised what you can learn. / Be careful with it and keep it safe. It's an heirloom of sorts.

All my love,
Summon

I fingered the slash mark she'd made by mistake and smiled to myself. Aunt Summon was always sloppier than my mom. She could afford to be.

I flipped to the last page. There had to be well over two hundred pages. I wasn't so sure I was going to enjoy every page as much as Aunt Summon thought I would. I had enough reading to do for school. I didn't really have time for a dry rhetoric on classical mythology published in . . . I checked the copyright. *1865?* Summon wasn't kidding. This book was old.

Gingerly, I turned back a sheet to reveal the title page. Running from the top left-hand corner down were the carefully etched signatures of the book's many owners. At the bottom, I recognized my aunt's loose, slanted handwriting, a little less steady than it was today. *Summon Byrd.* Above that, my grandmother's name in black scrolled letters. *Harmonious Byrd.* Above that, in tiny, dark cursive: *Melodious Byrd.* Was Melodious my great-grandmother or her sister? Above her name, long, looping script spelled *Temptation Byrd.* And above Temptation, the very first signature read *Serenade Byrd.*

I ran my fingers over the indentations of each signature, marveling. Five generations of Byrd women. Did any of them ever marry? Ever take another name? I'd always thought being Innocence Byrd was such a short stick, but I wondered how these women felt. What was it like to be Temptation Byrd, or Melodious? There was nothing innocent about my life. Was theirs truly anything tempting or melodic?

I smiled. However much I disdained certain things about my mother, about myself, it still felt good to hold this book in my hands. To feel a connection to these women who'd held it before me. I was glad it had found me.

I grabbed a black ballpoint pen from my bag and pulled the cap off with my teeth. Carefully, just below Aunt Summon and leaving plenty of room for the next several generations, I added my name to the list: *Innocence Byrd.*

I flipped to the beginning and began to read. *Young's Concordance of Mythical Beasts* was about as exciting as it sounded. True to its name, it listed in alphabetical order every fantastical creature from legend and mythology known in the eighteenth century. Lengthy descriptions for each beast, given by Young himself, were followed by references to and even some excerpts from folk tales, classical myths, and archaeological finds. All in the nauseatingly formal speech that characterized the Victorian era. It was truly soporific.

I was only a few pages into the *A*'s when I decided Aunt Summon was evidently off her rocker. Somewhere between *Afrit* and *Angels* I was supposed to find the answers to all my burning questions? Was she serious? Was this her way of trying to turn me off her trail, give me just enough to make me think she was helping without really giving me anything at all?

I slammed the book shut and set it aside. About all I was getting from *Young's Concordance* was a vocabulary boost and a migraine. She probably hoped giving me an heirloom would make me feel connected to my heritage, and somehow that would ease my sense of being utterly lost in the sea of *WTF* moments that were becoming my life. Why she wanted me to read every daunting page was a mystery I couldn't solve without a couple of aspirin and a good night's sleep. Unfortunately, thanks to my mom's control issues, I couldn't call her and just ask. But

Mom couldn't hold out forever. The phones were important. Phil would get clingy, she would get antsy, and I would get cellular once more. Then I would ring Aunt Summon, ask her about the book, and hopefully get the CliffNotes version to *Young's Concordance of Mythical Beasts.*

14

My mother and I spent the next three weeks avoiding one another as much as possible. Awkward silences were broken only by necessary questions and strained one-word replies. There seemed to be no way to come together after the debacle at Aunt Summon's, which I still didn't fully understand. So instead, we steered clear of each other. In her attempts to avoid me and my knowing stares and unspoken questions, my mother began spending most nights in the city with Phil. It hurt me, angered me, and left me alone and scared, but I had been forbidden to speak about the one thing I really needed to talk about. My pride would not allow me to talk to her about anything else, least of all how much I hated her being gone.

While home had become an exercise in avoidance maneuvers, school was not much better. I could still feel Jace wherever he was within the walls of Stonetop High, and I dodged him like the plague. I ached to see his winning grin and dancing eyes, but frankly, I couldn't stand to face him after our confrontation. It was embarrassing to have run out like that, no matter how necessary. And it was discomfiting to know that the truth about Salinas was no longer just *my* dirty little secret—well, mine, my mother's, and Aunt Summon's. Now this boy, this outsider, knew too. Or knew enough, at least. Enough to make my skin crawl every time I remembered that subhead: *Homicide yet to be ruled out.* How could he look at me and see anything other than a freak, a killer? How could he not be suspicious?

The only person I had any regular contact with anymore was Kurt. He met me in the halls, offering little favors, begging for my number. It did no good to tell him my phone had been taken from me. He just kept asking.

I needed Aunt Summon's sage advice to deal with Kurt. I needed it on a lot of things. I could've emailed, but I wasn't sure this was the kind of thing I wanted documented in cyber history for my mom or anyone else to find. I didn't trust my computer's recycle bin. I'd read that everything you ever did on your PC was more or less still stored there for the truly tech-savvy to find. No, it was best to wait until I could talk face to face or at least by phone.

Another lonely weekend loomed ahead of me. Fridays, everyone else's favorite day of the week, had become the worst for me. Mom often stayed in the city. I had a car, but with no phone and no friends, there was nowhere for me to go. I picked at a hangnail from behind my desk and sighed to myself. In front of me, Mr. Sikes was droning on about the importance of standardized testing. His eyes met mine more than once, but he didn't call me out for lack of attention. In fact, he'd become considerably more lenient toward me since our little exchange about my quiz, which was odd, considering his tough-as-nails reputation.

Out of nowhere, the flat of his hand slammed hard against the top of another student's desk two rows over. I nearly leapt out of my skin along with every other kid in class. But I doubt every other kid felt their mouth go dry and their stomach turn over. I doubt every other kid had only a few numbers between them and complete meltdown. When his hand hit that desk, the gun went off in my mind all over again.

"Eliza Miller, any reason why you don't find my lecture important enough to look at me when I am speaking?"

The poor girl stuttered incoherently, rattled as she was. She was unable to take her gaze off Mr. Sikes's fuzzy knuckles, which were still sprawled across her desktop.

"I suggest you keep your eyes on me for the next twelve minutes," he said. "Class isn't over yet."

Everyone was focused now, but I couldn't seem to slow my sprinting heart rate. Adrenaline coursed through me, making Mr. Sikes's voice sound very far away. My preoccupation with everything that had occurred a few weeks ago was making me less aware of my surroundings, and this had caught me by surprise. I had already counted to *six* and was feeling no better for it. The lights overhead were blinding, and I could smell the moldy carpet of that motel room wafting back to me.

I raised a hand and waited for Mr. Sikes to notice.

"Yes, Innocence?"

"Um, can I be excused?" I blurted. I needed to get out of this room. The sudden start felt too much like being caught by Jace that day in his room and being caught by Ray in another. Hot tears were already stinging the corners of my eyes.

He didn't even ask for a reason. Mr. Sikes simply nodded once and carried on speaking. I gathered my things quickly and stumbled from the room just in time for the first rebellious tears to splash against the hall tiles.

My heart still raced ahead of me as I wandered down the hallway trying desperately to stifle the flood. In a few moments, I had the tears under control, but they had been replaced by racking hiccups, each one a little spasm of fear. I rounded a corner and leaned against the wall of lockers, holding my breath in hopes that it would suffocate the hiccups. I began my count again.

One . . . two . . .

With my forehead pressed against the cool metal and my eyes squeezed tight, I didn't notice if there was anyone else in the hall.

"Innocence?" Her voice was small behind me, small and kind.

I spun around, blowing out the breath I'd been holding like a popped balloon. "Wa—Mrs. Kleberg!"

I'd quieted my tears, but their traces still glistened against my cheeks, and my eyes and nose were undoubtedly rimmed in pink. It took Wanda about half a second to notice.

"What's going on, hon? Bad day?"

I tried to shake off her concern. "Oh, no. Just these damned hiccups. Mr. Sikes frightened the class. I guess that's what brought them on."

She gave me an odd, appraising look. "Why don't you come to my office for a few minutes? Pull yourself together."

"I couldn't. I, uh, I have another class soon and—"

"No, I insist. Come on. Jace will be glad to see you."

Seeing she would not take no for an answer, I reluctantly followed her down the hall toward her office. Inside the brightly lit waiting area, Jace was seated comfortably on the love seat reading a Ray Bradbury novel, his ratty All Stars propped up on the coffee table full of brochures.

His eyes rose slowly until they met mine. He quickly lowered the book and sat up, concern all over his face. I looked away, stung by the sight of him. I didn't want any more of anyone's concern. I just wanted to be left alone.

"Have a seat, Innocence. I have a couple calls to make, and then we'll chat," Wanda said pleasantly before slipping into her office and closing the door.

I lowered myself into a chair across from Jace and stared awkwardly at my knees.

"Please look at me," he said quietly.

I huffed and flicked my eyes up to his.

"I can't stop thinking about you. About what happened. I've been so worried—"

"Don't be," I said briskly before he could finish. "I'm fine."

"Clearly," he said with biting sarcasm.

As if in response, I hiccuped violently, my own body validating his observation. *Dammit,* I cursed myself. "Look, Jace, I don't know what you think this is between us, but I'm not your concern. The last thing I want is your sympathy."

"Ouch," he said, leaning back.

I hadn't meant it to come out sounding so mean. What I'd meant was that I wanted him to like me for me, not because I was some problem to fix. It made me feel like my mother to think I was attracting him simply on the merits of my broken, sordid history rather than for who I really was.

"I didn't mean—I don't—ugh, I don't know what I mean." I ran my fingers through my loose hair, frustrated.

Jace's expression was gentle, patient, daring me to make my meaning clear, to undo the hurtful words I'd just spoken. It almost frustrated me more. Before I could say anything else, Mrs. Kleberg opened her door and beckoned me inside. He shot me a sympathetic glance as I entered, but I only looked away.

I took the same familiar seat I had before and leveled my gaze on the nosy counselor opposite me. What was I going to tell her this time?

"So," she began, her fingers steepling, "tell me what had you so upset in the hallway."

"I told you already. Mr. Sikes got angry. He slammed his hand on a girl's desk. It just, it made me jump is all. Then I had a hard time calming down."

"Why were you in the hall?" she asked.

"I asked to be excused."

"Going anywhere particular?" Her flat blue eyes raked over me.

I shrugged. "No. Just trying to cool off."

She folded her arms over one another on her desk. "What about the tears? I know you were crying, Innocence."

The one bright spot in the last three weeks of near isolation for me was that Wanda Kleberg had been out of my hair. What with my good grades, thanks to Kurt's devotion, and Jace not fretting over me day in and out, she had backed off considerably. How had I managed to run into her, of all people, when I did—of all times?

I pursed my lips and said, "If you must know, my mom and I have been fighting. Things are a little tense these days. So I'm on edge."

Her eyebrows went up. "Anything I can help with?"

"Not particularly."

"Trouble at home is my specialty, remember?" Her attempt at humor was well meaning, but it had no real effect on me.

"It's not a big thing. My mom took my cell phone because I yelled at her. I'm getting it back soon."

Wanda didn't look convinced. "Why on edge then? I mean, if it's no big deal."

She had me there. I frowned but didn't respond.

"You know, Innocence, being easily startled is a symptom of PTSD. Have you given any more thought to the treatment we talked about?"

"Lots," I lied.

"And?"

"I'm just trying to figure out the right way to talk to my mom about it." These days, I would be doing good to figure out how to talk to my mom at all.

A thin smile played on Mrs. Kleberg's pale lips. "Well, maybe I can help with that."

"I don't—" I started, when I heard a feminine voice just outside the door, a voice I knew only too well, even if I hadn't heard as much of it lately. I stared at the closed door, my jaw slack, terror oozing its way up my spine.

"You see," Mrs. Kleberg was saying, but her voice sounded a hundred miles away, "I decided to give your mom a call."

So that's what she was doing in the hall. She'd been coming to get me for this very meeting. I looked back at her, and before I could stop them, the words had tumbled out. "What have you done?"

Her expression tightened, defensive and confused, but before she could respond, the door swung open, and there in the frame and the glare of the fluorescent lighting stood my mother. Her silk maxi dress was a deep forest green, making her eyes spark like tumbled gemstones. Her hair was pulled neatly over one shoulder, spilling down her chest in mahogany and maroon waves. But behind the perfection of her appearance and effortless beauty, a barely restrained tension brewed, emanating off her like heat on asphalt. She would have my head for this before we got home. She had never been called to school for me before. It was at the top of the *Don't* list.

"Mrs. Byrd," Wanda said, rising, and I nearly choked on my own tongue. Now I had done it. Now she would know I'd registered under my real name instead of Phil's.

Next to me, my mother's face waxed pale, but she recovered herself with a pretty smile and an outstretched hand. "Please," she said casually. "Call me Dallia."

My mother sat in the chair beside me, and I watched Jace's face disappear behind the slowly closing door. I was trapped.

Mrs. Kleberg looked us both over, taking in my poorly concealed anxiety and my mother's cool demeanor, before she launched headlong into our visits and her suspicions that my nightmares might be part of a larger disorder known as PTSD. She even told my mom about the run-in with Kurt.

I wanted to crawl under my chair and hide, but all I could do was sit unmoving and refuse to meet my mother's eyes as she listened calmly—too calmly—to all of Wanda's concerns.

When Mrs. Kleberg was finally done, my mother stood and smiled placidly at her. "I can assure you, Wanda, that Innocence's father and I will take all of this into consideration. We'll look into finding her a reputable therapist in the area. Really, I just can't thank you enough for caring about her as much as we do."

Wanda was all self-righteous smiles. "I'm so glad to hear that, Mrs. Byrd. Innocence had me quite convinced that you would not take this so well."

Only *I* noticed how my mother flinched to hear her true name. Only *I* noticed the veins straining under the skin in her hand as she reached for the doorknob. Only *I* noticed that her voice was unusually high. Wanda was oblivious to all these signs.

"Well, Innocence has always been a trifle high strung," my mother said as she pulled the door to. "A bit of a Nervous Nellie."

The counselor's smile slipped at that, but she completely missed the steely glare my mother gave me as she looked back over her shoulder. "Come on, baby," she said, her voice sweet as honey and twice as thick. "Let's get you home for some rest."

As we made our way through the waiting room, Wanda crammed some pamphlets on PTSD into my mother's hand with a final goodbye and a promise to call on me again sometime next week.

Stupid woman, I thought, glancing back to take in every detail of Jace's face as I looked on it for the last time. *I won't be here next week.*

My mother flung the pamphlets into the nearest trash can as we sped down the hall.

"I think this is a record, even for us," she shot as we pulled into Phil's long drive.

"What do you mean?" I asked, even though I already knew.

She parked the car and got out. I did too. Looking at me over the roof of it she said, "I mean go upstairs and pack your stuff as quickly as you can. You know the drill."

"But why?" I pleaded, planting my feet. "She's just a stupid counselor. She's just doing her job. Can't we pretend that you got me the help? I mean, Phil's doing fine, isn't he? You said—you said he was strong."

My mother was already at the door, her back to me. She turned and leveled her cool, deep-sea gaze on me with the weight of an anvil. "Maybe we could have, Innocence, if you hadn't given her your real name."

So it was my fault? That's what she was telling me? I was so desperate to stay, to stick somewhere, *anywhere,* and now we were leaving because of me. In my hopeless attempt not to be like her, I was becoming my mother. I couldn't let that happen.

"So what?" I took a step in her direction. "It's just a name. What difference does that make? Nobody knows we were there in that room! The police don't know. They're not looking for *us.* They might have a few useless witnesses, but they don't have our names. No one knows about Ray but you, me, and Summon!" *And Jace,* my heart thudded, but I bit that back.

"Shut up!" She rushed at me, slapping me across my face. "I never want to hear you say that name again. Do you understand me?"

I bit my bottom lip until the warm metallic trace of blood slipped over my tongue. But I could not keep the tears from falling.

Instantly contrite, her hands wiped frantically at my cheeks. "Oh, Innocence! I'm so sorry. Please, please, let's just go. It's not just that, honey, it's not just Salinas. I—I can't tell you. Not yet. You just have to trust me. But you can never, *never* use your real name."

I stepped back from her, my own eyes falling hard and cold on her like hail. "Why should I pretend to be somebody I'm not? I'm not Phil's daughter! I'm yours. I'm Aleister's!"

The shock stuck her to her spot like an arrow in its mark. Her mouth fell open. Her hands dropped to her side. Her face contorted into some never-seen-before expression that made her suddenly look her age. Her wild hair danced on the rare breeze. "Where—where did you hear that name?"

Her voice was quiet now, fearful, whispering.

I sniffed. "You. Talking to Summon. I overheard."

Her hands flew to her mouth, stifling a cry. And the hard shine of her beautiful eyes became soft with fresh tears. "No," she gasped between her fingers. "No."

My posture slackened. I'd only seen this side of her once before, terrified and vulnerable. And that didn't end well. "Mom, it's okay." I attempted to calm her. "I didn't hear that much really."

But her head kept wagging side to side. She snatched at my wrist, her eyes darting around us, checking the trees. The confidence that defined her was lost. "Come on, we have to get you safe inside. I have to go."

I pulled away and she spun on me. "You didn't tell anyone else, did you? You didn't give his name?" She was recovering some of her composure, but fear had her in its firm grip and it wasn't letting go anytime soon.

"No," I assured her. "No one. Why—"

Her hand was over my mouth before I could finish. "No. No more. We can't speak of this. Not here. Not now. Go upstairs and gather your things. I—I have to go to Phil's, but I'll be back soon. We'll leave before nightfall."

She'd never gone to see one of them before we left. But then again, we'd always left *because* of them. This time, we were leaving because of me. Because I'd committed some unpardonable sin, some unspeakable crime. Something far worse than Salinas. Something to do with who—*what*—we really were.

But what could be worse than killing a man?

She was scaring me.

"Why? Why do you need to see Phil? Let's just go, like always. Okay? You were right. We should go."

"I need money," she said plainly. "I have to get as much out of him as I can before we leave."

"We'll pick up another one on the way like we always do, Mom. We'll find someone with money. It'll be fine. Like always." Her panic was clawing its way up my arms and seizing in my chest, a fist around my heart.

Her head shook. "No, Innocence. That's not enough. Not this time. We—we need to go far. And I don't think we should look for another man for a while. It'll just be you and me for a bit. Somewhere far."

"I don't understand," I pleaded with her as she marched back to the car, determined. "I don't want us to go."

I didn't know why I was suddenly so afraid when only moments before I'd been willing to risk it all. Something in the way she trembled and tried to look brave for me. Doubt riddled my determination, and a gnawing sensation of loss, of some utter devastation lurking around the corner, began to fill my insides.

She looked up at me with the car door open and put a quieting hand to my cheek. "I know you don't. I guess you're due some answers, aren't you? We'll talk on the drive. Okay? We'll trade cars and then we'll talk. But right now I have to go and see Phil, so we can be safe. I have to get us as much money as I can for the road. It won't take long; he's very pliable. I just need an hour or two. I'll be back by the time you're done packing. Lock the door."

I nodded, even though everything inside me screamed to not let her leave.

"Take this," she said, pulling my phone from her pocket and handing it to me. "You still have the cord?"

I nodded, palming the cool metal.

She smiled wanly, lashes wet and glistening. Then, she suddenly threw her arms around me, holding me so close my breath came in shallow gasps. "I love you," she whispered into my ear. "Always remember that."

I pulled back, nodding. "Of course, but—"

The crunch of gravel cut me off. We both turned to see the patrol car rolling up the drive. Next to me, my mother was still as stone and twice as pale. It stopped just short of us and the driver's side door opened, but the lights never stopped spinning, the engine never stopped purring. Fear stuffed my insides like cotton.

"Dalliance Byrd?" the officer asked as he approached, his hand resting on his gun holster. Another man emerged from the passenger side dressed in a dark suit. He took a few steps but stopped near the hood.

My mother swallowed and forced her eyes to meet the officer's. "Yes."

"I'm Officer Reyes and this is Special Agent Monroe."

My mother took a breath, her glance cutting to me then away.

"May we come inside?" Officer Reyes asked.

"We were just about to leave," my mother said coolly. "Can this wait?"

"I'm afraid not," the officer replied. Behind him, Special Agent Monroe was silent, too placid to be believed. "We'd like to ask you some questions."

My mother's gaze dropped. She took a long breath and turned to me, her eyes full of words she couldn't say. She wrapped her arms around me in a quick hug. "Pack up," she whispered so they couldn't hear. My reply stuck in my throat.

Finally, she looked back to Officer Reyes. "Not here."

He nodded once. "We could go down to the station."

In response she stepped toward them. Special Agent Monroe held the door for her.

"Mom!" I regained power over my voice just in time to watch her slip into the car.

Officer Reyes seemed to be noticing me for the first time. "We should only be a few hours," he said. "Is there someone you can call? To stay with you?"

I swallowed and clutched my phone. *A few hours?* That was a lot more than "some" questions. I nodded at him. "My aunt. She lives nearby."

"Good," he said. "Give her a ring. We'll be in touch."

He turned and I blurted after him, "Is everything okay? Is my mom in some kind of trouble?"

Officer Reyes looked back at me and pursed his lips but didn't reply. He got into the car without another word.

The patrol car turned and drove away from the house. My mom never even looked back.

Why? My unspoken question seemed to follow her retreating face down the drive until she was swallowed in a cloud of dust.

Wrapping both arms around myself, I watched until I could no longer see the blue and red glint of their spinning lights, realizing only after she was long out of my sight that I'd forgotten to say goodbye.

15

I fidgeted on my bed anxiously. I hated waiting. Chalk it up to years of always taking flight, being on the move. I glanced around the room again, triple checking in case I'd missed anything. I'd packed Summon's blanket, my pictures, my scarves, my laptop, a few basic toiletries—toothbrush, etc.—and as many clothes as I could cram into my bag, rolling them up into tight little cylinders. With the extra time, I'd grabbed a paper grocery bag downstairs and threw some more clothes and shoes into that for good measure. I hated to leave a stitch behind. Not because they were any nicer than the clothes I could buy once we found a new place, but because Jace had picked most of them out and they reminded me of him.

Thinking of Jace made my heart squeeze with longing and pain.

I had my car and the keys, but was there really time? I couldn't chance not being here when she returned. She'd been so frightened before the patrol car pulled up, I didn't want to give her reason to think anything bad had happened. I had my phone back, but somehow I couldn't bring myself to call him. What would I say anyway? Goodbye? *Sorry I showed up out of nowhere, led you on for a few weeks, and acted like a complete ass before getting ready to take off again.* There was no way I could look Jace in the face now, no matter how badly I wanted to.

I also hadn't called Aunt Summon like Officer Reyes told me to. At least not right away. When I did finally call, her voice mail picked up. I left her a quick message. I didn't want to freak her out, so I willed my voice to be steady and told her to call me as soon as she could. I didn't mention the cop or the detective. I also didn't want to freak myself out any more than I already was. Saying it would make it too real. I'd tell her when she called. Or better yet, I'd let my mom tell her. They'd have to release her sooner or later, and once they did, we would hit the road. This time, I wouldn't whine or beg or even flinch. This time, I was ready to be in the driver's seat.

I rolled over and peered at the clock. Seven fifteen. She should be here by now. Maybe the police weren't turning out to be as *pliable* as she thought. But that seemed unthinkable. My mom had been doing this for years—manipulating men, getting in and out of tough spots. This was her game. She knew how to read 'em. Surely Officer Reyes and Special Agent Monroe were as soft as every other man underneath their badges and uniforms, as easily led, as desperate to please. There probably wasn't a man on this earth who was a real match for her.

Except . . . maybe . . .

It's not the only thing in her blood, my mom had said to Summon that first night I heard them talking about me. Whatever we were, whatever was responsible for the frequencies, it was genetic—inherited. But apparently I had inherited something else, too. Presumably from my dad. Something I could use to balance out—no, *fight* was how she put it—my instincts from her side of the family. Did that mean that my father, this Aleister guy, was the only match for my mother's power? Was he the only one who was truly strong enough to withstand her influence? If that were true, she never would have left him if he hadn't died. Isn't that what she wanted, a man who could be near her, take care of her, without folding like a house of cards under her pressure? I could have known a normal childhood in one place with two parents *if* . . .

My blood turned cold in my veins. When I'd said my father's name, she'd been afraid. More afraid than I'd ever seen her, even in Salinas.

It wasn't Aleister who frightened her; it was his killers. When it came to whoever murdered my father, it seemed my mother was the one yielding. Or should I say running? Because the truth was, we'd been running long before Salinas, before Ray. It wasn't the cops who scared my mom. Or not only the cops. It was someone else. Someone who, for whatever reason, wanted my father dead. Someone who might want us dead, too.

I tucked this away with the million other questions I intended to ask once we were safely on the road. I checked the time again. Nearly eight o'clock. Surely she'd be here any minute. I continued to stare at the clock as all sixty seconds of the next minute ticked painfully away.

Right.

I flipped open my bag and dug inside. Aunt Summon's book was a hard angle against my fingers, and I pulled it out for a second look. She'd wanted me to read it, though after my first dry attempt, I still had no clue why. With little else to occupy my mind, it was the perfect distraction.

It only took a few pages before my eyes were drooping, but I paused on a paragraph in the chapter on harpies.

> *The renowned immortal steeds of Achilles were the conjugal offspring of the harpy, Podarge, and her lover, Zephyros, the West Wind.*
>
> *Harpies were originally depicted in art as beautiful women with wings and referred to as lovely-haired. Later they were repeatedly depicted as harrowing half-bird women. It is unclear whether this was a matter of mere confusion with the more terrifying sirens, or if the species had undergone some significant transmutation, though many scientists and mythologists of the day would refute this notion. There is also some question as to whether harpies and sirens were, in fact, one and the same.*

I hated to break it to him, but the scientists and mythologists of today would refute a lot more than Young's notion that harpies transmuted. Apparently, Young had forgotten the operable word in his title: *mythological*. Which was in clear contrast to his use of the word *species*.

Even so . . .

My fingers brushed the hand-inked illustrations. There was something about the creatures' weaponized beauty. I flipped in the book to find *sirens* and found a woodcut image of a woman on a rocky ledge overlooking a ship on the water. Bare chested with feathered hair and scaled legs, she held a lyre in her hands. The faces of the men in the ship were angled toward her, but she seemed to be looking past them, through them, to an endless horizon. Her face was an expressionless mask, but I could read the serenity and sadness warring between her eyes.

I stared at her for a long time, tracing every detail, each string on her lyre, each wave of her hair. I could feel the spray of the ocean as it would have been against her skin, a kiss. The only kiss she could truly treasure. The only kiss she could trust. The only genuine kiss she would ever know. I looked at the men's faces in the ship, blank as slates as they stared at her. It was the most depressing image I'd ever seen. My tears plopped wet and new on the page.

Not for the men, whose craft was sailing straight for the wall of stone that held her above them, unreachable, where it would splinter into a thousand pieces. Their suffering would end quickly. But for the woman, the *siren,* whose misery would endure a thousand ships. She would never feel the soft touch of a man's arms around her. She would know only the love of the coarse rock, the fleeting wind, and the vast sea.

I knew what she was looking for out on those waves.

She was waiting for a man who would never come. A man strong enough to resist her charms and avoid the death trap below her.

But she could never know a man such as that. Because a man who could resist her would simply sail away.

If such a man existed at all.

My breath caught. This wasn't distracting me at all. In fact, I found something familiar in their sharp faces, something that reminded me of my mother and Aunt Summon and how completely alone I was right now. I snapped the book shut again and glanced at the clock. Five till nine. What was keeping her? Were they taking blood samples or something? Did they go to the neighboring station in Austin? A nagging concern was making itself known in the pit of my stomach, and with every tick of the clock, it was blossoming into festering doubt.

I pulled Aunt Summon's sweet-smelling blanket out of my bag and across my weary shoulders. Rolling over, I tucked her book to my chest. I was so tired after the day we'd had and I wanted to be awake for the car ride so my mom and I could finally talk. Surely, if I let my eyes drop closed, if I drifted into sleep, she would be here in no time and we could finally leave Stonetop and all my uncertainties behind.

My throat was raw with screaming. I sat up, wrapping both hands around my neck, coughing on the terror that had filled me. The dream again, the nightmare. Only this time, something was very, very different.

Something was wrong.

There was the same musty motel room. The same scratchy sheets. The same push as my frequency drowned out the fear building inside me. The same gunshot.

There was the same thud as a lifeless body hit the floor.

But when I'd looked down, it wasn't Ray's body lying like an empty shell between the beds. It was my mother's.

I blinked and rubbed my hands briskly over my face. Something else was off, too. Not just the dream. My throat burned. I'd screamed myself awake. There were no footsteps in the hall. No softly spoken words. No comforting hands smoothing my hair.

Sunlight streaked the blinds in bright stripes. I looked around. My bag was at the foot of the bed. Aunt Summon's blanket was tangled around my shoulders. *Young's Concordance* had left an indent against my breastbone. The clock read 7:17. Hadn't I fallen asleep after eight?

Something tapped at the recesses of my brain. 7:17. Not p.m.—*a.m.* It was morning. I'd fallen asleep waiting for my mother to come back from the station, expecting to leave last night. The nightmare had woken me, and unlike every other time, she hadn't come to wipe my tears and soothe my nerves. She wasn't here. She'd never come back at all.

I rolled off the bed and fumbled for my toothbrush in my bag. In the bathroom, I pelted my face with cool water. I didn't understand. Where was she? Why hadn't she returned? She said she'd give me the answers I was due. She said we were leaving. Last night.

If something held her up, if the cops were proving more resistant than expected, why didn't she call? Even if they'd arrested her—which they hadn't—she was allowed a phone call. I grabbed my cell and found her among my meager *contacts*, pressing her number and waiting for it to ring. An automatic voice mail message sounded instead. It wasn't even her voice. Either her phone was dead, or she'd turned it off.

Or they'd taken it from her.

I tried to stay busy, looking up various U.S. maps and dreaming up new destinations for us. Anything to keep my mind occupied. Anything to keep me from checking the clock. Anything to keep the fear at bay.

I nibbled on some blueberries and had a cup of Greek yogurt, but my stomach was hopping like it was full of crickets. Finally, I crawled back on top of my bed. I fell asleep to the ever-growing instinct that maybe my mother wasn't coming at all.

The sound of knocking pulled me from the void of slumber. The clock read 3:03. I bolted from the bed and flew down the stairs, still rubbing my eyes. *Finally. She was back. We'd leave. She'd explain everything.*

As my hand gripped the slick brass knob, it didn't dawn on me that she would have a key to let herself in. That thought didn't settle over me until the door was already open wide, and my mind registered enough of the silhouette looming before me to know that it was not my mother.

I squinted against the light, my heart turning over in my chest like a car engine. My pupils couldn't recede fast enough to take in the warm, brown eyes brimming with concern. I only knew that I'd made a terrible miscalculation. I drew in a sharp breath.

"Innocence? You all right?" His voice broke through my panic, and I exhaled shakily, suddenly happier than I ever expected to see Kurt Meier.

I threw my arms around his neck, surprising both of us.

Slowly, he pried me off of him. "Whoa there. What's up?"

Sheepish, I backed away, letting him step inside. A sob caught in my throat, escaping as a pathetic whimper.

"Something wrong?" he asked, peering at me.

I shook my head, but he didn't look convinced. "Why are you here?" I asked.

He shrugged his massive shoulders. "You weren't at school yesterday. I thought I'd come by and check on you. See if you needed anything."

I wasn't sure what to say to that. "Thanks?"

Kurt ignored my tone and looked around curiously. His eyes landed on one of Phil's taxidermy treasures, a buck over the fireplace mantle in the living room. "Sweet! A twelve pointer!" He moved into the living room to study it more closely.

Come on in, I thought, closing the door behind him.

"You know how hard it is to get one of these things?" he said, turning to me with wide eyes.

I shrugged. I had no clue. Nor did I care. "Kurt, my mom's gonna be back any minute. It was sweet of you to come by, but you should probably go."

He narrowed his eyes at me, not in a mean way, but in a thoughtful one. "You don't feel right," he determined.

"What?" My jaw slackened.

"You're afraid. I can feel it. What's wrong?" His voice deepened and his muscles coiled beneath the weight of his jacket.

I began to pick up on little things. The subtle highlights in his hair. The salty taste of his perspiration in the air. "Why do you say that?"

"I dunno," he replied. "I can just tell. Like I said before. I *feel* things about you. I feel your feelings."

"Then why don't you feel how much I want you to leave?" I didn't mean to be rude, but my nerves were strained to the limit, and I didn't want to explain myself to Kurt of all people.

He peered at me again, and then he grinned, his chiseled cheeks dimpling slightly. "Because you don't. You're glad I'm here. You're alone."

I swallowed. Was he right? I searched myself. Behind the panic and the urgency, there it was. The relief. And deeper than that, the absolute understanding that what Kurt said was true. I was alone.

I sank to the sofa, folding my hands absently in my lap, staring blankly out the window. She wasn't coming. The strange way Officer Reyes had pursed his lips when I asked if she was in trouble. The hug before she left—so tight it almost hurt. Like it would be the last hug she ever got. Was she preparing herself then? Was she telling me goodbye? Or had something gone horribly wrong? The tears rolled effortlessly to my chin. Did she try too hard to press them? Did they crack under that strain and turn on her?

"I have to make a phone call," I told Kurt, bolting from the room. "Be right back," I shouted as I pulled my phone out and found Aunt Summon's number again. I danced from one foot to the next in the kitchen as it rang. *Pick up,* I practically screamed in my mind.

"Summon's harem hotline," a mocking tone said. At least it was a real voice this time. Summon would know what to do. She could help me.

"Aunt Sum? It's Bird," I blurted. It was a wonder she got connection at all with all those trees around.

"Well, hello Innocence." The voice turned chipper. I could hear the smile through the line. But it wasn't my Aunt Summon's voice at all.

"H-hello? Who is this?"

"Have you forgotten about me already? I'm hurt. But it wouldn't be the first time. We Byrds have very selective memories."

"Tempest?"

"Bingo." I could almost picture her dark cherry-red lips forming the 'o' at the end. "What can I do you for?"

"Uhh. Is—is Aunt Summon there?"

"Somewhere. She's out in the fields oiling down her hired hands or something. Who knows really? This place is huge."

"Yeah. So, no chance you can get her for me?"

There was a low laugh. "Can you hold for, like, three hours?"

"Right. Well, can you just tell her I called? And tell her to call me as soon as she gets in. It's . . . important."

"Is everything all right?" Tempest asked, her voice laced with something akin to concern or curiosity—I couldn't tell which.

"No." My voice cracked. "But she'll know what to do. Just have her call me."

"Sure, Innocence." She dropped the sarcasm entirely. "If you need anything, just call back. I know I'm not Summon, but I am family. I can help."

"Sure. Okay. Thanks." I pushed *end* and took a breath to steady myself. I was so grateful for the sympathy that it threatened to crater me all over again. Even if it was from someone I barely knew.

"Innocence?" Kurt was beside me in a heartbeat. "What's going on? What can I do?" He must have heard the panic in my tone from the living room and come to my rescue.

I blinked mutely at him, irritated. What was he doing here? Why was he always shadowing me like this? How did he know things about me? Things I barely knew myself?

His hands fluttered over me nervously, birds with nowhere to land. "Are you hurt? Shit. How can I help you?"

My stomach growled between us, answering for me.

He jumped. "Food! You're hungry. Let me take you to dinner."

I looked up at him absently. Everything was going to be fine. It might take Aunt Summon a little time to get my message, but she would call back. She would figure out how to help my mom. And I did need to eat, after all. Maybe this would take my mind off of things until she called. I needed to feel normal, to keep the panic at bay. I nodded at Kurt in spite of my anxiety. "Okay. Just dinner."

Kurt reached down and took my hands in his. "You like Mexican?"

I followed him to the door. "Sure." I slid into my flip-flops and wiped the remaining tears from my face with the hem of my oversized t-shirt. We would laugh about this later, my mom, Aunt Summon, and I. We would talk about the time her phone died, and the patrol car got that flat seven blocks from the station, and I thought something terrible had happened, and in the end, everything had all worked out. And we would laugh and laugh. And I would remember this dinner with Kurt and how scared I'd been and how silly it all was.

Once outside, I locked the door behind us.

"I'll drive," he said, giving me a funny look and guiding me to his truck with a hand at the small of my back. I sat next to him with all the presence and expression of a stone as we rolled down 186, turning my cell over and over in my hands. Everything felt so surreal, like I was trapped in a Dali painting, a world of melting clocks and long-legged beasts on parade.

Maybe she just decided I was too much of a risk. That she was safer without me. Maybe they released her hours ago and she bailed on me and Phil. But that didn't fit with the incredibly protective woman I'd known. That wasn't my mother. She didn't make decisions just for herself. She made them for *us.* Maybe I hated some of those decisions. Maybe I didn't always understand. Maybe she used the men she met. But she never *used* me. She loved me. And she made her choices based on that.

I needed time to think, to examine the situation more closely. If the police found something on us from Salinas, something on my mother, and tracked our real names, they would have arrested her, wouldn't they? We'd be splashed all over the news by six o'clock. At best, I'd be shuffled off to God knows where. At worst, my mom and I would be sharing a cell and fighting over orange jumpsuits. We had to get on the road. As soon as we could, we had to get her out of there and hit the bricks. We could disappear. Maybe cross the border. New names, new hair color, new man, new home, new lives. Like witness protection, only less official. We were experts at that by now.

"Kurt, stay with me?" I asked with as much confidence as I could muster.

His eyebrows went up.

"I think it would be best if I didn't go back to the house alone. I can explain later."

Kurt looked at me like he wasn't sure whether to believe me or not.

I did the only thing I could. I summoned a little of the force I'd used that night on Sam. "Kurt, please. I really need you to do this."

Need appeared to be the magic word with Kurt. He gave me a brisk nod and turned back to the road. Like it or not, I'd climbed right into my mom's old role. At least Kurt was easier on the eyes than Phil. Looking out the window, I watched the barbed-wire fencing and scrubby landscape fly by, feeling a little safer with Kurt's big red truck between me and the rest of the world.

16

Kurt hovered conspicuously in the doorframe, his signature jacket thrown over one shoulder. He looked edgy and unsure.

"Come in." I sniffed, balling the tissue I'd grabbed in my fist and forcing a smile. "I just need a minute."

Seeing my mom's car sitting empty in Phil's driveway when we returned from dinner seemed to send home the message that this was all really happening. My mom was gone, maybe in trouble. I was alone. There it was.

I'd broken down all over again before I could even make it back inside, but I'd been careful to keep my face angled away so Kurt wouldn't see the tears. What was it about a girl crying that made even the most macho men practically quake with awkwardness?

The worst part was not knowing. I had no clue what was happening to her at that station. I couldn't erase the image of her falling apart when I'd said my father's name. She looked so completely freaked. Or the sight of her head hanging down as she climbed into the back seat of Officer Reyes's car.

No, the worst part was not being able to tell anyone. I had no one I could trust except Summon, but she hadn't returned my call yet. I was afraid to call the station and ask what was going on. I didn't want the police anymore involved in our lives than they already were. I realized now that whatever my mom believed was threatening us all those years on the road was very real. We never really left Salinas behind. It was always there, trying to catch up, waiting for the opportunity to come between us for good. And if she'd been right about that, then she was right about other things, about whatever—whoever—we'd been running from before we ever met Ray.

All the years of being *Innocence fill-in-the-blank* had been for a reason. She'd spent a lifetime trying to protect me from them, and now it might all be blown because I'd used my real name *one* time.

Kurt's eyes wandered over me nervously. "You still want me to stay?"

He should be on his way home by now. I knew that. But I'd used—what?—my *frequency* to stop him. Just a little nudge to enlist his help and hold off the inevitable departure and ensuing loneliness. His will pressed against mine, his need to do the right thing. He wanted to call someone, a doctor, his mom, the authorities. He wanted to keep me safe the way that he'd been taught how. But I'd been taught a different way. No one was safe except another Byrd. We had no authorities.

"You didn't touch your dinner."

"Umm," I stalled. I needed to pull it together if I was going to keep him on my side of this fucked-up equation. I needed him to believe that I was all right . . . mostly. I needed him to keep his mouth shut when he wasn't by my side. I also needed to him continue helping me until I figured out what I was going to do. At least until Aunt Summon got here. "Yeah, I, uh, wasn't feeling the Mexican food. Maybe we could just order a pizza?"

"Reno's delivers," he offered. He hung his jacket on the hall tree. "I already skipped practice so . . ."

"Great," I said with a forced smile. "You can stay."

He shrugged. "Yeah, I guess."

"Why don't you call?" I suggested smoothly. "I'm just going to clean up a bit."

He pulled out his smartphone while I ducked into the bathroom to wash my face. *Hold it together, Innocence,* I told myself as I looked at my reflection in the mirror. I could fall apart once Kurt was gone, but right now, I needed him to be here. I needed him to be strong.

I was sounding like my mother already.

"They're on their way in thirty," he said as I emerged from the half bath. A triumphant grin sat squarely on his face.

"Good. What do I owe you?" I asked, pretending to search my pockets, but inwardly I was letting that force eke out ever so slightly.

"Nah, I got it," he said easily.

Excellent.

"Besides, I beat the shit out of that delivery kid, Derek, last year. He usually just gives them to me."

Not excellent.

I smiled thinly at Kurt, feeling the fear snake around me in loose coils. This wasn't a dog or a cat I was training. This was a person I was manipulating. A guy. A big one. How long could I keep this up? How far could I push him? Something inside me wanted to know, but I felt like the circus tamer in the cage with the tigers. What happens if I lose my hold? If my frequency slips? Even for a second? What happens if Kurt figures out what I'm up to? I'd probably read or heard about a dozen tiger attacks in my lifetime. Didn't those guys always end up mauled at some point?

It hit me with the force of a tsunami. What I was doing, what my mother and Summon did, wasn't just morally and ethically questionable. It was dangerous.

The doorbell exploded through the crowd of thoughts overrunning my mind. I jumped up from the sofa to get it.

"Pizza's here," Kurt called.

"I'll get it," I told him.

"Let me. If it's Derek—"

All the more reason for me to get it alone. I put a hand on his shoulder to keep him seated. "I've got this."

"Suit yourself," Kurt said with a bit of a pout, but he handed me two twenties to cover it. "Just don't overtip that little freak or he'll get a big head."

I was pretty sure Kurt had made certain poor Derek wouldn't know what too much confidence felt like for the rest of his natural life. "Whatever," I told him and scrambled for the door.

But when I opened it, I didn't see a scrawny kid with thick glasses and cystic acne standing there. Instead, I was looking into the stern face of Officer Reyes. My mouth fell open.

"Innocence, right?"

I nodded. "Yeah."

"Your aunt around? The one you called?"

Behind me, Kurt's voice boomed. "I know you're out there, Derek!"

I rolled my eyes and stepped out on the porch with Officer Reyes, closing the door behind me. "Sorry," I said, looking up into the policeman's clean-shaven face. "That's my friend. He's a little high strung."

Officer Reyes raised his brows but didn't say anything.

"My aunt is out picking up a pizza for dinner. Is everything okay with my mom? Is she here? Can I talk to her?" My arms were crossed tightly in front of my chest as I craned to look past the officer to his car.

"I'm afraid not," he said frankly.

"What do you mean?"

Officer Reyes frowned and looked at his feet. "Your mom is being taken into police custody for now. This really isn't something I should discuss alone with a minor. I need to speak with your aunt as soon as she returns, and she can relay any information she sees fit to you."

"C-custody? You mean, like jail?"

He sighed. "Innocence, please have your aunt call the station tomorrow. She can ask for me directly." He turned to go.

"Wait!" I clutched at his arm. "You have to tell me something. This is my mom we're talking about."

Officer Reyes turned his dark eyes onto the hand I still had wrapped tightly around his sleeve. A strange look crossed his face. "Your mom is safe. I've already said enough. Have your aunt give me a call."

I released my grip and watched him walk back to his car. He paused at the door and looked at me for a long moment as if he were considering something, then he ducked inside and was gone. I didn't even have a chance to go back inside before the red Camry with the glowing *Reno's* sign pulled up.

"Kurt, pizza," I called in a flat voice, passing him the twenties as he came to the door.

Kurt was three slices deep, even after a full plate of enchiladas earlier, when my cell finally buzzed. Say what you will about him, the boy could eat. I was still picking at my pepperoni. "I'm gonna take this in the kitchen," I said, darting out of the room as I pressed *answer*. "Hello? Aunt Summon? You there?"

I'd called her as soon as Officer Reyes left but only got her voice mail. I left a short message telling her to buzz me ASAP and tried hard not to cry into the phone.

Tempest's voice filled the space between us instead of my aunt's jovial tone. "Hey, kid. I just wanted to check on you. There's a border collie giving birth tonight by the barn. Your aunt is pretty tied up. Everything okay? You sounded upset earlier, and your message sounded urgent."

The veneer of calm I'd tacked so artfully into place for the last half hour around Kurt split wide open, and my tears rushed to the surface. "She's gone," I tried to keep my voice down so Kurt wouldn't overhear again.

"Who?" Tempest's tone was controlled, but I detected a note of increasing alarm. "Who's gone?"

"My mom! She was going to go see Phil—we needed money, and

she said we had to go really far this time—but then a patrol car showed up and there was this cop and a 'Special Agent Monroe' and they said they only had a few questions, but she wouldn't let them in. They took her to the station. They took her and . . . she never came back. Reyes was just here, and I really need to talk to Aunt Summon, and—"

"Innocence, take a breath," Tempest commanded. "I can't follow you. A bloodhound couldn't follow you when you talk that fast. Now slow down and tell me everything."

So I did. I told her all about Wanda calling Mom and our fight outside. I told her how Mom looked more scared than I'd ever seen her because I registered under my real name. I told her about Officer Reyes, and Kurt, and how Summon needed to call the police station.

"You did right," she said. "The less contact you have with the cops, the better. We need to keep this between us. In the family, so to speak. I'll tell your aunt."

The word "we" took a load off my shoulders. I wasn't in this alone. My mom wasn't either. I had Summon and Tempest. I had family. "I'm so scared," I told her. "What if something terrible happens to her and it's all my fault?"

She sighed. "Innocence, whatever's happened, it's not your fault."

"But why isn't she back yet? She should be able to use her, you know, her frequency to get out of there. Why would they take her into custody?"

The line went silent. Then after a minute, Tempest said, "I've been given a gag order on that subject when it comes to you. Sorry, kid. It's a condition of my stay. As for the rest, I don't know why they haven't released her yet, but we need to keep our heads. I'm going to go talk to your aunt, and we'll get to the bottom of this, okay? But you have to stay calm for me. We can't have anyone else catching wind and coming in on it. This is . . . *delicate*."

"Okay. When do you think she'll get here?" I asked, sniffling.

"Get there?"

"To pick me up," I finished. "I'll have to stay with you guys until we figure this out."

There was a long pause in which my unease grew before she responded. "I know this is going to sound harsh, but you can't stay here."

"What?" My voice cracked all over again.

"The authorities have your mom. There's obviously an ongoing investigation. If you bolt, they'll come sniffing after you here. We can't have that."

"We don't have to tell them where I'm going. I'll just leave."

Tempest groaned. "You're not thinking clearly. You've had a shock. If your aunt takes you without alerting anyone, the school will report your absences. And we're back to square one with the whole investigation thing, only this way she'll look even guiltier. That won't help your mom's case any."

"Case?" My mom had a case? She didn't *have* a case. She *was* the case.

"But she's so off-grid. They'll never find her place. Will they?" I was desperate. She couldn't just leave me here to face this alone.

"Look, kid, even if that were true, don't you remember the last time you were here?" she sighed. "If you stay here, it'll wreak havoc with the guys. Without saying too much, I don't think your aunt can control them. Not around you. It's not safe."

"Oh." I didn't know what to say to that. "Will she come stay with me then?"

"If she can get away," she said. "Maybe."

"Maybe?"

"Listen, Innocence, there's a lot you don't understand. Your aunt can't just leave this place. She's what's holding it all together."

"But I told the police I would call her." She and Tempest wouldn't just leave me alone here, would they? "That she would call them."

"You did, and she will," Tempest replied. "Look, maybe I can come.

For a little while, at least. I'll talk to Summon and we'll work this out. You have to stay brave, okay? This is no time to lose your cool."

That wasn't much comfort. Tempest was my cousin, but I'd only just met her. Still, it was better than being alone. And if Aunt Summon trusted her, so could I. "I guess . . ." My voice trailed off.

"Give me a little time. I'll talk to your aunt and tie up some things here. Call me if you need to. I'll text you my direct number."

"All right. What do I do in the meantime?"

"Act normal. Go to school. Then go home. And let me know if you hear anything more from the police. When I get there, we'll figure it out together."

I agreed and tried to hide my disappointment.

"In the meantime, do your best to keep a lid on that Byrd mojo of yours. We don't really know what you're capable of yet. Until your mom and aunt decide to fill you in, I can't say more. But you're not ready for that level of responsibility."

"Okay. I'll try." I decided not to mention that I was already using it on Kurt. Maybe when Tempest got here I could weasel some information out of her. At least she wasn't pretending none of it existed. Right now, I didn't care so much about what we were and what it all meant though. I just wanted to help my mom. "Tempest?"

"Yeah?"

"Do you think she'll be all right?"

"She's a Byrd, isn't she?"

"Yeah." I wasn't really sure what all that meant yet, but it was a loaded question.

There was a long pause. "Innocence, your mom is a force. She knows how to take care of herself. She's been doing it for years."

"Right."

There was the sound of a lighter catching and a long deep breath as Tempest lit one of her cigarettes on the other end of the line. "Try not to worry too much, kid. There isn't a person on this planet who can get close enough to hurt her."

I wanted to believe that, but we both knew it wasn't true. Someone already had. And he would have hurt her worse if I wasn't there. *Ray.*

My alarm sounded its angry buzz, and I slammed a hand against it to shut it up.

Welcome to Season One of the Innocence Byrd Show. *In this episode, Innocence returns to school and tries to appear completely normal while secretly worrying her mother has been imprisoned for first-degree murder.*

I trudged to the bathroom for a shower, stopping momentarily in the door of my mother's room. Kurt carried her bags back up for me last night, but I didn't have the steel to unpack her things. Not yet. A piece of me still wanted to believe she would be back at any moment, and when that happened, we needed to be ready to leave fast.

I didn't want to go to school today. All I wanted was to think over those days in Salinas with a fine-tooth comb, searching for anything that we might have overlooked that the police could have found as a clue. But I also didn't want to send up any more red flags, especially with Mrs. Kleberg. I needed to do what Tempest told me and make it look like all was well on the home front while she and Summon pieced this puzzle together and figured out what to do.

Before I left, I decided to arm myself. I still wasn't entirely sure how frequency worked, but I did know it was the only weapon I had. Dark leggings and a teal wrap dress with a colorful Chinese fan print seemed perfect. I patted concealer heavily over the purple pits beneath my eyes. I even blew my hair dry, pulling it into a curtain of loose, shining strawberry waves. For the final touch, I used lip gloss.

When I got to the school, the halls swarmed as usual—kids, teachers, admin. I felt like a sore thumb, like the truth of my situation was evident on my face, but no one seemed to notice. I slipped easily down the halls unchecked, moving from one class to the next as though nothing had changed. Only Mr. Sikes seemed to register the difference.

"Everything all right, Innocence?" he asked when I tried to slink out of his room after the bell.

I dropped my shoulders and attempted to look casual. "Sure. Why?"

He stared at me and for a moment, the look was oddly similar to Kurt's when he'd been standing in my living room. A look that said he was reading between my lines. If it weren't for Eliza Miller clearing her throat when she handed him her paper and he didn't take it, we might have stayed locked like that for another several minutes.

Mr. Sikes reddened and thanked her in a monotone, relegating the paper to the top of a stack on his desk. He glanced back up at me, careful this time not to look too long or stare too hard. "No reason," he said amicably.

I pursed my lips and turned, feeling as though I'd been caught in a suggestive position with my math teacher. It was creepy—like *now-I-need-a-shower* creepy. But Mr. Sikes wouldn't let me go that easy. He stopped me at the door, pushing a twenty-dollar bill into my hand.

"Wha—?" I couldn't even get the full word out.

"Just take it," he demanded urgently. "I'll bring more tomorrow."

Panicked and unsure what to do, I stuffed the bill in my bag and hurried out of the room. I didn't need Eliza or anyone else witnessing that transaction.

Flustered by my run-in with Mr. Sikes, I slammed headlong into someone taller than me a few feet down the crowded hall. I backed up a step, apologizing, and let my eyes focus on the screen-printed tee in front of me, green with a white unicycle stamped in the middle. My nostrils flared and took in the aromas of tea tree oil and wet clay. I knew this smell, organic shampoo and art class, second period. I knew this chest—chiseled beneath the casual clothes.

I looked up into Jace's aqua gaze, and a sigh slipped out before I could stop it.

The corners of his mouth rose slightly. "Glad to see me?"

Jace. I hadn't thought about Jace. How could I have forgotten? I'd get to see him again. Or would I? Could I chance being around Jace and keeping my mom's custody a secret? Could I hold Kurt on a string and keep fawning over Jace, too? It didn't seem likely.

"Yes." I didn't know why I said it, but there it was. I was immeasurably glad to see him. I wanted to spill my guts to him, cry on his shoulder, beg his forgiveness and advice. But I couldn't do any of those things if I was going to keep my mom's situation a secret.

He grinned and reached up to pull on a strand of my hair. "You look . . . pretty. You look really pretty today," he said.

I bit my lower lip and tried, really hard, not to smile up at him. But it was impossible. He'd said the magic word—*pretty.*

"Come to lunch with me?" he asked then.

I froze. "What?"

"I'm going to grab a bite off campus. Come with me, please."

"I don't know," I said. "I'm already in trouble. I shouldn't skip."

Jace beamed at me. "I'm in good with all the office ladies. Trust me. I'll make sure you don't get counted out."

I remembered Miss Clair dissolving into a girlish puddle before his charms the first day I came here. And Mrs. Kleberg certainly thought he hung the moon. Probably he had every one of them wrapped around his little finger. I still shouldn't go, but I needed this. I needed an hour with him, an hour to feel happy.

I looked up at him, hitching my bag higher on my shoulder. "Just lunch," I agreed.

His smile widened, and he laced his fingers through mine. I knew then, if he asked for a day, a week, a *year,* I wouldn't be able to refuse.

The café was small and nearly empty. Our tiny table was tucked back in a shadowy corner not far from the bathrooms. I didn't want to sit too near the front windows. I didn't want to feel exposed.

"We should do this more often," Jace said, his brilliant smile lighting our little space like a flashbulb.

"I would like that," I admitted. It was true. I would. Whether or not it was smart was a different thing altogether. With so much worry gnawing at my nerves, for my mom, for myself, I wasn't sure how present I could be for these little dates. It felt wrong to enjoy myself with Jace when so much was at stake right now.

He laughed. "Awesome. How 'bout tomorrow?"

Say no. Say no. Say no. "Sure."

And just like that, this stolen moment felt like one of the most important things in my world. I was supposed to be gone. Stonetop should have been miles behind me by now. Jace should have been someone I already referred to in the past tense. Yet, here I was, splitting a club sandwich, being given a second chance. I might not ever get this again. Maybe tonight they would come for me like my mom. Or maybe they would finally come to turn me over as a ward of the state. I had this moment only, for all I knew, and selfish as it may sound, I intended to bask in it.

I reached brazenly across the table and curled my fingers around his. "I'm sorry," I said. "For the other day. I overreacted. I know you just want to help."

Jace gave my hand a squeeze. "You were right to be angry. I get it. It was an invasion of your privacy."

I nodded and took a sip of my soda. "It's just that sometimes I feel like . . ."

He stared at me expectantly.

"Like that's the only thing you see in me. Something to fix."

Jace leaned forward, his face a dozen shades of serious. "I don't want to *fix* you, Innocence. You're perfect to me as you are. That would be like saying the Mona Lisa could use a few adjustments. I just want to see you happy. I thought if I could put myself there in that room with you, if I could get a handle on what you experienced, I could understand your resistance to outside help, and I could be closer to you somehow. That's all."

The breath slid out of my lungs, and my gut fluttered with a tide of emotions that came too fast to name. "You make me happy." *Or as happy as I can be under the circumstances.*

As soon as I said it, I practically kicked myself under the table. What a lovesick thing to say. I felt like an ass, but Jace didn't seem to mind. And it was true. Only Jace could help me reach for some kind of silver lining in the black cloud that was my life.

"Good," he replied, giving me a sexy, one-sided smile. "Then we can solve your problem and mine at the same time."

"What's your problem?" I'd had enough of my own for the moment, and getting into my issues right now was dangerous territory. Two cute grins from Jace, and I'd be spilling the "jailbird mamma" beans. His do-gooder heart wouldn't be able to keep him from calling Counselor Wanda.

"My *problem,*" he said with inflection as he laid a tip on the table and we stood to leave, "is that I can't get enough of you, Innocence Byrd."

The ride back to school was short and filled with the textured intonations of Jace's new favorite band. He said the name, but I couldn't remember it. I couldn't remember anything except his last words to me in the café.

When he said he couldn't get enough of me, did he mean like a crush? Like the way I never got tired of the sound of his voice and the warm feel of his presence? The way you never tire of your favorite blanket or favorite book? I hoped so. But something darker was seeded within me with those words. He could mean like a drug. An addiction you ride for all it's worth until it destroys you. Like all the men my mother had left in her wake, desperate for stronger doses of her. Hungry for a high that would only mean their end.

I couldn't let myself think that. Not about Jace. I couldn't picture him that way, broken and addled and cloying. I wouldn't let myself do that to him. I would never, *never* use my frequency on Jace. I swore it to myself right there in the passenger seat of his car.

I thought of Ray and swallowed hard. I prayed that was the difference, but I wasn't completely convinced. Mr. Sikes cramming a twenty in my hand flitted across my memory and I shuddered. I hadn't used my frequency then. Not intentionally. But he'd reacted as if I had.

Jace's hand found mine across the seat, and he beamed at me as he pulled into a parking spot. "Back as I promised," he told me, killing the engine. "Long before the coach could ever become a pumpkin."

His Disney reference was cute, but it cut to the quick of my fear. I wasn't worried about Jace's glamour fading. He was so pure. Pure comic books, and soft t-shirts, and classic novels, and indie bands. He was purely himself. Purely wonderful.

I was another story, a darker tale.

I let him take my hand outside the school doors and pull me close. I let his lips graze my cheek quickly before letting go and walking inside. But I couldn't meet his eyes.

I was no Cinderella.

When my glamour faded, Jace would see me for what I truly was.

A monster.

17

I was at Kurt's truck when he finally made his way into the student parking lot after the final bell, shoulder bumping and high fiving a dozen different guys in the process. I'd slept a tad better last night, and I managed to get to school without incident. Still, I couldn't shake the sense that it would be safer not to go home alone. Surely Tempest would be here in a day or two. Until then, I needed to get my sense of security somewhere else.

Kurt saw me leaning against the cab and thrust his chin at me in greeting, a hundred-watt smile lighting up his face. A tiny brunette in a frayed denim mini stepped into his path before he could reach the truck, stopping him midstride.

I watched his eyes fall to hers and his smile drop. I saw him fiddle nervously with the strap of his backpack. He nodded a few times and his lips moved as he answered her. Her posture stiffened, her arms folded tight in front of her. He glanced at me, said something else, and she turned to aim her dark, furious eyes at me.

I knew her. Laney Reyes. Very cute, very popular junior. Student council member, track star, president of the Spanish Club, among other things. I hadn't been at Stonetop High long enough to get her full resume. But at last her name clicked. *Reyes.* The officer on my front porch last night must be her dad.

It didn't occur to me that Kurt might have a girlfriend, but it made sense as I watched her stalk away, her stick-straight hair gleaming like burnished ebony in the sunlight bouncing off the cars. She looked pissed, and a wave of regret sank over me. Would their relationship survive Hurricane Innocence?

In my mind, I argued that I needed Kurt more. Laney was going home to loving parents and a normal teen life. I was going home to another man's house, an absent mother who may or may not be facing life without parole, and the realization that I was designed differently than the average girl. But apparently, whatever I was, it did not come without a conscience. And I hated myself a little more for hurting someone in the process of trying to take care of myself.

"Wanna hang?" Kurt asked brightly as he threw his pack into the bed of the truck.

"Don't you have practice?" I asked. I'd learned yesterday that in addition to football, Kurt played baseball and had been on the swim team until last year.

He shrugged. "Not really."

That wasn't the same as a *no* and I knew it, but I would take it. I *really* didn't want to go home alone.

"Follow me then?" I asked, nodding toward my car a few spaces over.

"Your place again?" His eyebrows arched.

"Sure." I pretended it was his suggestion.

He started toward the driver's side.

I nodded and walked toward my car, feeling a little lower with every step.

When we pulled up in front of the house, a black Mustang was parked in front. It had white racing stripes painted across the top and had been wrecked on one side. Tempest was sprawled across the hood, her red hair fanned out like spilt paint around her dark glasses and dark lips. The radio was blaring Joan Jett from inside the still-open door. She flicked her cigarette away as we pulled up and hopped down to greet us.

"God, I thought you'd never get here," she complained, snatching her keys from inside the car and closing the door. "It's hotter than the face of the sun out here. You could have left the door open for me."

Kurt's eyes took in the earrings, the black jeans, and the ripped tee.

"Tempest, this is Kurt. Kurt, this, uh, is my cousin, Tempest."

"Pleasure," she said flatly.

"I didn't know you were coming," I told her.

"I said I'd be here, didn't I?"

"That was two days ago."

She shrugged. "I told you, I had to take care of a couple of things first."

"Where's Aunt Summon?" I asked as I led them to the front door and unlocked it.

"Back at the ranch. Where else?" Tempest grinned.

Inside, Tempest flopped onto the sofa. Kurt looked uneasily from me to her. She pulled her sunglasses down her nose and beamed at him. "Would you be a dear and bring me something cold to drink? I am positively drowning in perspiration over here."

Kurt gave me a questioning glance.

"Go ahead," I told him. "I'll take one, too."

He rolled his eyes and marched off to the kitchen while I slipped into the living room.

"So, did Summon call the station and talk to Reyes?" I asked Tempest.

"Yeah, course."

"And?"

"And she's taking care of it."

I dropped my backpack on the floor. "What do you mean 'taking care of it'? Taking care of it *how?* I need to know what's going on with my mom and why they're holding her."

Tempest tossed her sunglasses onto the coffee table and sat up.

"Look, kid, your mom's in deep. I'm not gonna lie. And this Reyes is . . . immune to her charms, if you know what I mean. Summon can handle it, but it's gonna take time. She's not like your mom. Her influence is more subtle."

"What does any of that mean?" I snapped.

Tempest's eyes grew cold. "Keep your voice down," she insisted. "You don't want brawn-over-brains in there to hear."

I sank into an armchair and put my head in my hands.

"Don't worry," she said in a gentler tone. "I can stay for a while. I've got my own issues to resolve, things I might have to leave to take care of now and again, but otherwise I'm here for you. Okay? Summon sent me. She wants you to know that she's working on getting your mom out. And once that happens, you guys are home free. You just have to be patient."

I nodded. "Is she going to call me?"

Tempest glanced away, her eyes roaming over the wind-twisted trees out the window. "If she can. They're probably watching your phone. She wants to lay low. Handle as much of this from afar as possible. But as soon as it's safe, she'll buzz you."

If whatever my mom had gotten into was enough to keep Aunt Summon at bay in my hour of need, then it was way worse than I feared. We were so screwed.

"In the meantime, you've got me."

Something about the black-clad apparition stretched across Phil's sofa didn't exactly evoke the comfort and confidence I was hoping for. But Tempest was my cousin, she was one of us—whatever we were. And I had to trust her. I had no choice.

Kurt came in and set two cold soda cans on the coffee table.

Tempest popped the top and took a sip, then grinned and pulled a leather-bound flask from her back pocket, tipping a little of its contents into her can.

Kurt eyed her. "What's that?"

"Just a little something to soften my edges," she said.

"No drugs," I demanded. "We're already in enough trouble, Tempest."

"Relax, kid." She sat back, crossing her legs. "It's just bourbon."

Kurt grinned and held out his can. "Can I have some?"

Tempest passed him her flask and looked at me. "I like this one. He can stay."

I'd like to say Tempest's presence was a comfort, but it was more like a rock in my shoe, grating and constant. She watched me when she thought I wasn't paying attention, ate anything good we had in the house, and smoked inside even when I asked her not to. But she was family, and that seemed more important than her poor roommate qualities. I may not have liked the rock in my shoe, but it reminded me I had a foot.

Then, three days later, I pulled up to find her loading a gray duffel bag into her trunk.

I hopped out of my car almost before I could even get it into park. Running up to her, I placed a hand on the open door of her wrecked Mustang. "Hey, what's going on?"

She slammed her trunk closed and gave me a loose grin. "Nothing. Just a little business trip."

"You're leaving?" My voice came out much higher than I intended. "Shrill" would be the appropriate word to describe it.

She laughed. "Relax, kid. It's only for a few days. Two, if I'm as good as I think I am."

I had no idea what she was talking about. "But . . . what about my mom? Is Aunt Summon going to come while you're away?"

Tempest tied her dyed military jacket around her waist and lit a cigarette. "We've been over this, Innocence. Your aunt is doing all she can *from her place.*"

I narrowed my eyes. "So you keep saying. I just can't believe she wouldn't even call me—"

Tempest shook her head. "You are such a pain." She reached into a partially zipped backpack she had slung over one shoulder and pulled out an envelope. "I wasn't going to show you this because she asked me not to, but since you're basically calling me a liar, I don't see that I have any choice." She waved it before my face before letting me snatch it from her.

It was stamped and addressed to Aunt Summon's place and ripped open across the top. The return address was to an attorney's office in Austin. I pulled the one-page letter out and read over it quickly. It simply confirmed their receipt of some paperwork Summon had sent them and promised they'd be in touch soon. It described my mother's case as "precarious" and "grave." I folded it up and passed it back, depressed.

"Happy now?" Tempest shoved the envelope back in her bag. "Maybe next time you'll believe me. We are trying to protect you, Innocence. Anyway, I'll be back soon. You'll barely even know I'm gone."

I couldn't believe I was about to be on my own again so soon. My lungs began to feel tight and my heart sped up. The sun grew unbearably bright. I would be a ball of anxiety without her, without someone. I searched my mind for something to keep her with me, to hold her here. Anything was better than being alone. Even if it meant listening to Tempest's favorite metal bands and eating the burnt toast she served every morning. She was company of a sort. "But I'm a minor! I can't be alone. What if the police turn up and they want to talk to you? I told them I called my aunt to come stay with me. They'll take me away if they find out otherwise."

Tempest took a long drag on her cigarette, chuckling around her filter at my panic. "All you'd have to do is tell them I ran an errand. Haven't you ever lied before? But they won't turn up. So you have nothing to worry about."

Something about her tone in that last statement, so sure of herself, made my spine tingle. "How do you know?"

She cut her eyes at me, and they were such a deep, brooding brown they almost looked dyed like her jacket. "I just know. Now move, I've got a job to do."

I took a step back but eyed her as she started past me. "What kind of job?"

Tempest stopped midstride and looked down at me. She tucked a stray hair behind my ear. "The kind I can't talk about, Innocence. But if you're good, if you show me you can keep it together while I'm gone, while your mom is away, then maybe one of these days I'll take you with me. Maybe even give you a cut." There was something like tenderness in her touch, like a mother would touch a daughter, but it didn't feel quite right.

"A cut of what?"

She laughed at that. "You're too much, you know that? *A cut of what.* Of the money, fledgling! Duh. A girl's got to earn a living. Even if she is a member of this family. I don't have all those hotties your aunt has to keep me warm at night. I make my own way. Someday, you will, too."

She climbed into the car and closed the door, still shaking her head at the joke I hadn't realized I'd made.

"I like this," Kurt said, his big grin blinding me.

"What?" I asked absently, my pencil poised over an algebra problem. I was stomach down on Phil's sofa while Kurt worked at the coffee table. We were into our second week of afternoons like this. Kurt at my place doing homework was becoming part of the routine. As was Kurt skipping practice and Kurt ditching Laney.

Tempest was gone . . . again. Whatever it was she needed to "take care of," it usually kept her away for two to four days. Then she would show up out of nowhere, usually with something new in tow—a gift for me, a new car, a new leather jacket. She was also never short of cash.

I didn't ask her any more about her little adventures. And she didn't offer much up, except to say she was tracking down Mom's exes. So far, no one was a threat to Mom's case, though there were still a couple of the real early birds she had yet to track down. Roger, Yura—they'd all moved on in one way or another, rebuilding from the wreckage of their lives after Storm Dalliance passed through. In a way, I was glad to hear it, though it didn't do much to ease my fears about where Mom actually was or what might happen to her.

Aunt Summon did finally text me but didn't say much more than to hang in there and listen to Tempest's advice. I texted her back and told her I would, but that I missed her and really wanted to see her in person. I asked her to call whenever she got a chance. I was beginning to forget the sound of her voice.

Every time I asked Tempest for details about my mom's case, she would give me the same spiel about not being allowed to tell me too much. For someone so tough and rebellious, she sure seemed to be following the rules my aunt laid out for her to a T. I said as much to her one afternoon while Kurt was in the bathroom.

"I have a lot to make up for," she told me. "My mom wasn't exactly the family favorite. I'm not going to win any favors by blowing off your aunt's orders."

"Just tell me how serious it is."

Tempest hesitated. "You tell me. How far would your mom drag her own name down in order to protect you?"

My stomach dropped. Anything. My mom would do anything to protect me, just as I would, *had,* for her.

In the meantime, I kept Kurt on his leash to make myself feel better, especially since I never knew if Tempest would actually be around. This new part of my schedule wasn't one I was overly fond of but very grateful for. Every day that he followed me home, I could breathe easier walking in the front door. He always stayed until dark and locked up behind himself as he left.

"Earth to Innocence. Hello?" Kurt's voice cut through my thoughts. "I said I like doing our homework together. I like it better than just doing yours for you."

My eyes met his, and I looked away. I could see it there, deep at the core of his pupils, that growing hunger. Soon, this wouldn't be enough. He'd want to stay later, come over on weekends, spend the night. He'd want all of me, more of me than there was to give, and when he couldn't get it, he'd go to pieces. I knew how this worked. I just needed to hold him together long enough to get a plan formulated. I promised myself that when Aunt Summon finally called, I'd talk to her about staying at her place. Maybe if I stayed inside and didn't leave the house, we could manage it.

"Good," I said quietly. "That's good, Kurt."

He bent back over his textbook.

My mind wandered to the one new part of my schedule that I *was* fond of—lunches with Jace. We went to our same café, sat at our same table, every weekday now. I told him I was still grounded, so he didn't try to push for anything after school, which was good. I needed to keep these two halves of my life separate. Jace in the afternoons; Kurt in the evenings. I couldn't bring myself to *use* Jace, but I couldn't make it on my own without using someone. Kurt was a convenient target, and the callous truth of that brought my self-loathing to a fever pitch. But it wasn't enough to keep me from doing it. I was my mother's daughter now, in most every respect, like it or not.

Tempest told me not to use my frequency, but what she didn't know didn't hurt her. And I didn't need much with Kurt. Kurt was strong, protective, and easy to dominate. Just a little nudge here and there, and he stayed in line. He didn't ask too many questions, did anything I asked of him, and had plenty of money and connections. I wouldn't risk what I was doing to Kurt on Jace. And Jace would never understand my predicament unless I used my frequency. He'd be full of questions and concerns, and for reasons I couldn't quite explain, I didn't want him bumping into Tempest just yet. He and Wanda would be on the phone to the authorities in a matter of seconds, getting an earful about my mom's situation. And there was no way Mrs. Kleberg would find Tempest to be a suitable guardian. I just couldn't trust him with this.

I sighed and threw my pencil down. "I can't concentrate," I muttered.

Kurt smirked. "I have that effect on girls."

In spite of myself, I actually laughed. Underneath his Texas-ass-kicker exterior, Kurt had a decent core. I liked to think I was helping bring that out in him. Thanks to my . . . *intervention,* he'd stopped himself from sweeping the gravel with Derek the pizza guy's face last week. It was progress of sorts.

"You're such a goon," I told him.

"Thank you?"

I rolled my eyes. "Come on, I need groceries. Let's go to S-Foods."

I'd managed over the weekend thanks to Phil's credit cards, which my mom had conveniently forgotten to collect from me after my day with Jace at the mall, and some cash Tempest had given me. But I didn't want to use them more than I had to. I didn't know how much time I had before Phil stormed down here and demanded them back. Demanded everything back—the cards, the cars, the house. The fact that he hadn't yet made me wonder if she'd managed to call him or something from the station. Maybe that's part of what Summon was "working on." I figured if another couple of weeks went by without hearing from him, I could assume so. Even then, it would only be a matter of time before he woke up and took care of the dead weight squatting on his property. Summon better have figured something out for us before then.

"I'll drive," Kurt agreed, stretching.

I tried not to notice his six pack when the hem of his shirt rode up. Kurt was hot. And he wasn't stupid, even if he acted like it sometimes. If his heart was as big as his pecs, I might be interested. But he would never be Jace, whose heart *and* pecs were perfectly proportioned.

"Shouldn't your mom be doing this?" Kurt asked as we scooted out the front door.

"I told you," I said, locking it behind us. "She's working that new job for Mr. Strong in San Antonio. Late hours."

S-Foods was the only real grocery store in Stonetop. Knowing that, they took considerable liberties with their pricing.

"Innocence?" Kurt's voice snapped me from my price comparisons.

My hand was frozen on a box of cereal. I shook off the grief that was creeping up my chest and lowered the box into our cart. "Just reading the label," I assured him when Kurt's brown eyes searched mine.

We moved on. I grabbed a dozen cans of soup and several different kinds of granola bars. I wasn't one for cooking. My mom never really taught me. She didn't know much herself, and we were always moving too often to keep up with the supply of utensils and appliances needed for decent meals. Not like Aunt Summon, who could whip up a bowl of melt-in-your-mouth comfort in two heartbeats.

"You should come to our house for dinner," Kurt suggested, eyeing the contents of the cart. "My mom cooks most nights."

I looked at him wondering how many family meals he'd missed recently on account of me. What must his parents be thinking? I couldn't face that firing squad. I couldn't look his mother in the eye knowing what I was doing to her son. "I, uh, am kind of shy around people I don't know."

"Come over and then you'll know them," he said as though I were missing something painfully obvious.

"No." I looked at Kurt, angled myself so I would be facing him head-on. "In fact, I think you should go to practice tomorrow."

Kurt's eyes clouded over. "You don't want me to come over tomorrow?"

"That's not what I said. I just don't want you to get in any trouble."

Kurt stepped close to me, and I had to look up to see his face. "But . . . you *need* me."

Uh oh. I gulped down the shame and fear that rose like bile in the back of my throat. "You can come by after if you want, but you can't keep missing to spend time with me. I'll be fine for a little while."

He looked like he was going to say something else, to argue again, and I put a hand out, spreading my fingers wide against his broad chest. My frequency hummed through my fingertips as I let it pour into him slowly. "Just check on me after practice. All right? And tonight, once you drop me off, go home for dinner."

A big waft of Kurt rushed over me—a tide of Axe body spray and car leather. The hint of a five o'clock shadow seemed suddenly bold along his jaw, and I realized for the millionth time what incredible shape he was in, every muscle tightly wound beneath the surface of his skin. The more I deliberately used my frequency, the more I seemed to hone in on all the tiny details of Kurt.

He nodded mutely until I took my hand away.

I sighed, glad to have escaped that little emergency. Then his hand shot out and grabbed mine, pulling it to his chest where it had rested only a moment before.

"Kurt? What are you—?" I started, but he stared down at me, his eyes sharp as flint.

"Innocence, when you touch me, I . . ." He couldn't quite find the words to finish.

I tried to pull my hand away, but his fingers were clamped firmly around my wrist. He jerked me to him, so that my entire front was pressed along his body.

Crap. "Kurt, please let go," I whispered. "We're in a store."

"Innocence? Is that you?" someone said from behind me.

Kurt relaxed and I jumped away, turning to see Jace's mom standing behind me. She was pushing a cart that was nearly full, mostly from several large boxes of wine. Apparently, she was self-medicating her depression along with whatever prescriptions she had. She saw me eye her groceries and blushed.

"Hi, Mrs. Barnes," I said with a short, spastic wave. I couldn't imagine what it must have looked like Kurt and I were doing in the middle of the pasta aisle. I'd been after some mac and cheese before his little invite and grope-fest.

"You ran out so suddenly the Sunday before last, I never got to say goodbye." Her eyes shot up from my reddened face to Kurt who was hulking behind me like my personal body guard.

"Sorry, uh, about that," I stammered. "There was a little misunderstanding."

She nodded twice. "Well, I'm glad to hear you two have cleared it all up." Her eyes traveled to Kurt again, questioning. "Jace says he's been seeing a lot of you lately."

Behind me, Kurt stiffened at Jace's name like a wall of muscle. "Yeah, it's been great. Lunch buddies."

Her face slackened, then pulled back into a plastic smile. "I'll—I'll let Jace know you said hello."

"Okay." I grinned with even less sincerity than she did. "Thanks."

She began turning her cart to go back the way she'd come when Kurt boomed out, "Tell Jace I say hello, too, okay? It's Kurt. Kurt Meier." It sounded more like a demand than a friendly request.

She lifted a hand to wave her fingers at us without looking back.

Yay, male posturing, I thought. I rounded on Kurt. "What was that?"

He shrugged. "I didn't know you and Jace Barnes were so close," he said with an accusing glare.

"We're friends, Kurt. Just like you and me. *Friends.*" It wasn't completely true, but I was more focused on making sure Kurt knew where our relationship ended rather than where mine and Jace's picked up.

His lips pressed into a hard line. "Come on, Innocence. Don't give me that. You know this is more."

He had a point, but it wasn't the one he was trying to make. "What ever gave you that impression?"

Even though Kurt had been at my house every afternoon for the last couple of weeks, I'd been careful. I didn't let him get too close. I kept my hands to myself, and I did my best to be sure I didn't cross the *flirting* line. But I'd be lying if I didn't admit that the frequency had formed a connection between us that defied the boundaries of normal friendship and skirted dangerously close to attraction.

"You were all over me a second ago," he pointed out.

"Not by *choice,*" I hissed.

"You put your hands on me first."

Two points: Kurt. My breath escaped in a slow whistle. I was not going to convince him of anything other than what he believed. I knew that. My mom could never have convinced those men, no one could, that they weren't anything more to her than a roof over her head and food in her mouth—a means to an end. Not that she'd ever tried.

The frequency seemed to work by playing up every fantasy these guys had, blinding them to reality. The weird thing was, I didn't think I was Kurt's type without it. I was nothing like Laney Reyes. She was peppy and extroverted. I was sullen and introverted. She was dark haired with doe eyes and packed curves. I was fair haired, my eyes full of secrets, my curves pulled long and lean. Sometimes I felt like the frequency was there before I willed it, making Kurt believe he was seeing something different when he looked at me than I did.

"Whatever," I groaned, grabbing the cart and heading towards the checkout line. "Let's just go."

"Don't worry, Innocence." Kurt glued himself to my side. "I'll pay for these."

18

I skulked down the hallway warily, not sure if I wanted to meet Jace after yesterday's run-in at the store. I could only imagine what his mother must have said to him and what he must think of me now.

"There's my favorite girl," I heard from behind. I spun with a smile only to see Kurt gaining on me.

"Going somewhere?" he asked.

Of course. Mrs. Barnes's slip about our lunch dates yesterday—well, technically *my* slip—had tipped Kurt off to his competition. So here he was, ready to claim whatever time I wasn't already spending with him.

"Bug off, Kurt. We'll talk later, okay?" I cast an anxious glance over one shoulder and bit down on my lip hard.

"I thought we'd talk now . . . over lunch." He looked down at me, resolute.

"Can't," I told him. "I have plans."

Kurt's brow furrowed low over his brown eyes, and his face shifted from hunky underwear model to angry Cro-Magnon. "With him?"

Here we go. "Not that it's any of your business, but yes. With Jace. We—we do lunch. It's a thing."

"What kind of thing? A *date* thing?" He crossed his arms, making his biceps bulge under the short sleeves of his polo.

"A *food* thing. Okay? We're friends. I told you."

Kurt squinted at me. "Then why are you so nervous?"

"Because you're looming over me!" I pointed out.

He took a visible step back and let his arms drop to his sides.

"Everything all right over here?" Another voice piped in. Mr. Sikes had apparently been on his way out, too, when he came across us. He stood possessively near me and cast an authoritative glance up at Kurt.

"Fine," Kurt shrugged. "Innocence was just inviting me to lunch with her *friend*, Jace."

Mr. Sikes raised a brow and studied me through his thick tortoise-shell frames. "That true?"

"Not exactly," I answered. "But we're fine." I let a little willpower ooze into the words. The last thing I needed was the two of them hovering when Jace rounded the corner.

"I'd be happy to escort you myself, Innocence, if Mr. Meier is being a bother."

I scowled at Mr. Sikes. I'd spent two weeks scurrying in and out of his class as quickly as possible so as to avoid another weird confrontation. Yet, here he was, practically on cue, as though he'd never noticed my avoidance tactics. "No, I—"

"Dude!" Kurt exclaimed. "Pretty sure that's illegal."

And gross.

Mr. Sikes shot Kurt a death stare. "So is loitering, young man, in most establishments. I suggest you move along before I report that you're bullying Ms. Byrd for a second time this year. Another infraction would result in suspension, I think."

While I was grateful, I was also concerned. I had dragged Kurt into all this. This time, he wasn't to blame.

"Mr. Sikes, no. It's fine. Kurt was just leaving for the cafeteria." I latched onto Kurt with my eyes, boring deep into his own so he wouldn't argue.

He responded to the link between us, his posture softening as a slow grin found his face. "Yeah, going. See ya, Innocence."

"Later, Kurt!" I called to his retreating bulk. I turned to Mr. Sikes. "See? All better."

But something in the brown swirls of his eyes was deeply unsettled. He moved nearer to me, hands fumbling low near his waistline.

I panicked and tried to move away, but his furry knuckles clutched at me desperately. A wave of relief washed over me as I saw him extract a tired black wallet from his coat pocket. He crushed two crisp hundred-dollar bills into my hand. My nose burned with the smell of money and his aftershave, his finger fuzz grating against my skin like Velcro.

"Take these," he said in a breathy tone I'd never heard him use before. "I know you need them."

"Mr. Sikes, I—" I pressed the wadded money against his stomach. What I needed was for him to cut this out.

He slipped the wallet back into a pocket and held his hands up as though I were pointing a gun at him. "No. No," he repeated as he backed away, launching himself into a jog down the hallway toward the doors outside.

I stood there, dumbfounded, watching him disappear. When a hand slipped over my shoulder, I nearly jumped out of my skin. My mouth was as dry as if I'd been sucking on old bones, but my palms were sweating bullets. "Ku—!" I started to shout, but it was Jace smiling broadly beside me.

"Ready?" he asked, his blue eyes full of promise.

Maybe Mrs. Barnes hadn't said anything.

"Uh, yeah," I said, recovering myself.

Jace's eyes widened at the sight of the crumpled hundreds in my hand. "Okay, okay! I'll let you pay. Just put that away before someone sees it."

I looked down, dazed, and stuffed the money in my bag, trying to play it off. "Right. This one's on me."

Jace's hand slipped easily into mine. "I like a girl who can take care of herself and her man," he joked as we headed for his car.

If he only knew.

Tucked away in what I liked to think of as *our* corner, with Jace teasing my fingers in his, I relaxed a little. The waiter had already taken our order, and I was sipping at my lemon water like it was the last drink I might ever get.

"Slow down, there's more where that came from," Jace said with a good-natured smile.

"How do you stand this climate?" I asked with a laugh, backing off my straw. "It's like the Badlands. I'm still not used to it."

His aquamarine eyes crinkled with his grin. "You've moved around a lot. Surely this isn't the first arid destination you've called home?"

I shook my head in earnest. "No, it is. We kind of had a thing about the coast for a while."

Jace looked puzzled. "Any particular reason?"

I thought about the flirt of salt and sand on the wind, the slick feel of my skin in the ocean spray, and the endless sunlit days. My heart twisted wretchedly. *About a million.* But the truth was, I didn't know why we'd always skirted the edges of the continent.

I looked up at Jace and shrugged. "Not that I know of. Preference, I guess?"

"Kinda strange, isn't it? I mean, if your mom is really how you describe her, it seems like she wouldn't be that . . . selective."

He had a point of sorts, but my mom was a subject I strayed wide and far from around Jace. "Maybe." I didn't know if he was really onto something or simply overanalyzing.

"You should ask her," he said, giving my hand a squeeze.

I tensed instantly but forced myself to ease up with my old, familiar counting routine. "Yeah, I will." *Liar.*

I hated keeping things from Jace, but I didn't really see any alternative. Whatever was growing between us, whatever *this* was, I didn't want to risk it. It was like a gift I'd always asked for but never thought

I'd receive, and I just couldn't stand to let it go now. Being with Jace was like breaking the surface, coming up for air in a world that had dragged me deep into its abyss. One day, probably soon, I would drown in it. Like my mom, like a wrecked ship, I would simply sink, never to be seen again. But for now, Jace was my life preserver, my raft to normal.

"Ehh-hmm." There was an insistent clearing of a throat to my right, pulling me from my thoughts.

I looked up to see Laney Reyes stamping an agitated foot next to me. Her arms were doubled over her pumpkin-colored Texas Longhorns t-shirt, and her black, little eyes were burning holes in my hand, still tucked in Jace's and resting on the table.

"Cozy?" she asked with a snort.

I sucked in air and tried to cast my eyes anywhere but hers.

"Laney, hey," Jace said casually, his own eyes darting between our expressions. Hers, livid. Mine, guilty.

She leaned toward me, making it clear that whatever she'd come to say, it was aimed at me. "What's your deal? Kurt's not enough for you?"

I pulled my hand from Jace's and forced myself to look at her. *You deserve this, Innocence. Take it.*

She glared at me hotly. "I know what you're doing. I know all the time you're spending with him," she practically spat.

Jace turned to me. "Him *who*?" His look was tender and questioning and somehow a hundred times more difficult to bear than hers.

I opened my mouth to answer, but Laney did the honors. "Kurt! *My* Kurt. We're not broken up, you know."

I squirmed in my chair.

"Kurt Meier?" Jace asked, leaning away from the table.

Laney barely spared him a glance. She was driving all her fury into me. "I don't know what you're doing t-to get him to—" Her mouth screwed up as though she couldn't bring herself to say it. "You must be some kind of slut," she finished. "Or worse."

"Hey! Wait a minute—" Jace started, his chivalry kicking in despite the evidence piling up against me.

Laney threw a hand up to silence him.

I searched desperately inside myself for the familiar hum that I'd used lately to get out of tight spots like this, but my frequency had abandoned me. My eyes met Laney's and held, thinking I could somehow stir it, that I could match my will against hers and get her to eat her words or back down at least. Not only was I not having any impact on her, except for making her angrier with my brazen staring, but I couldn't even feel the push of it within me. My willpower wilted before her on the vine.

Meanwhile, that *or worse* she'd tossed at me made it clear she knew something about my mom. No doubt she overhead things when her dad let off steam about work at home.

"Don't you have anything to say for yourself!" she finally screamed.

"It's not what you think," I managed.

Laney huffed. "Right. I've heard that before. But you're the one who thought wrong. He doesn't love you. And when he's done with you, which he will be soon enough, he's going to throw you away like the wasted trash you and your mother are."

Her eyes were bright with what I realized were angry tears, and I felt utterly defeated. I was so guilty. Even if it wasn't what she was thinking, even if nothing *physical* had occurred between Kurt and me, it wasn't because *he* didn't want it. And wasn't that only because of the desire I fed to him?

I looked from Laney to Jace, my cheeks stained with humiliation, but he wouldn't meet my gaze. He just stared at the table blankly.

She dabbed at her eyes and pointed a trembling finger at me. "I will find a way to ruin you."

I didn't doubt it.

She shot a quick look at Jace and her resolve softened a little. "I'm sorry, Jace. I thought you should know." With that, she spun and stormed out of the café.

The air rushed out of me in a shuddering exhale when the door closed behind her. A wall of sensory input flooded into my every cell. I could feel the heat pouring off of Jace, the tension mounting in his chest and lungs. I could hear the muffled *whoosh* of blood in his veins, like pressing a seashell to my ear at the beach.

I reached thoughtlessly for his hand, but Jace pulled instinctively away. Something he'd never done before.

"Innocence, what's going on?"

I fumbled for the right words and landed stupidly on, "With what?"

He looked up at me, his face red and hostile. "With *that!* With you and Kurt. With me? With your mom?"

I had to tackle this hornet's nest one stinger at a time. "I don't know. She's obviously heard some things about my mom and Phil. People . . . people form opinions. It's not the first time."

"And the rest?"

"There's nothing between Kurt Meier and me. She's just . . . paranoid." I fiddled with the strap of my book bag.

"I saw you ride with him that day, which is pretty weird for someone who supposedly isn't involved with him. And everybody knows you attacked him in the hall. And my mom, I mean, she said—but, I didn't believe her . . ."

Jace looked hurt and confused, and I wanted to wrap my arms around him and somehow explain. But I couldn't. Because the truth was stranger than fiction. Because what was really going on between Kurt and me was far worse than he or Laney could imagine.

Jace rose, throwing a twenty on the table. "I'm not hungry anymore."

I bounded up, grabbing at his arm. "Wait, please."

He sighed and turned to me. "What am I to you?"

Everything. How could I tell him that now? With Laney and his mother's accusations fresh between us, it would sound so cheap. My tongue lolled in my mouth.

"Say something!" he demanded, breaking my grip on his wrist with a shake of his arm.

The press of my frequency slammed against the backs of my eyes, thrashing inside me like a restless lion in a cage. It would be so easy. But I couldn't do that, not with Jace. It would be a parody of us. A Xerox. And a copy is never as good as the original.

My eyes welled. "It's not what you think," I whispered.

Jace scowled at me. "Yeah, you said that already," he muttered and left me standing at our table.

19

I fell across my mother's bed and wept uncontrollably. Too dispirited to return to class, I'd made the short walk to the high school parking lot from our café and driven myself home. Now, I buried my face in the rumpled spread and breathed in the last remaining whiffs of her scent, a subtly seductive smell—sweet on the surface but gathering in complexity underneath. To a man, it would have been irresistible. To me, it was simply *home.*

"Why aren't you here?" I asked out loud, but resounding silence was my only answer.

I felt so helpless. While Summon made phone calls and looked people up, what was I doing? Playing house? My mom needed me, like in Salinas, and this time I could do nothing to help her. I didn't even know where to begin. Tempest kept telling me to keep a lid on my frequency, but no one would explain exactly what it was yet. Or how to use it properly. If there was a way that didn't end in people blowing their brains out.

The blinds were closed, and my mom's room was dark. I rolled over onto my back and rubbed at my eyes like a sleepy child. I wanted her here. To hold me and comfort me. I didn't care anymore about how we lived or what we really were. Aunt Summon's infectious grin floated across my mind, and I resolved again to convince her to let me stay at her place. It was Friday. I could pack tonight, leave in the morning, and hunt her down. If I just showed up, she couldn't turn me away. And without Jace, there was nothing to stay for. Tempest was away on one of her mysterious business trips. By the time she got back, I'd already be settled in.

If I didn't find Aunt Summon—well, I had Mr. Sikes's two hundred dollars and a little mileage left on Phil's cards. Maybe I should pack and hit the road myself. Do like my mom. Find a man near a car lot, trade out the Mini, leave him in the dust before he realized what hit him. Could I be that ruthless? I wasn't sure.

Was how I treated Kurt any different? Not really.

I lay there wondering how old my mother had been the first time she took to the highway, moving from man to man the way a kid swings from one monkey bar to the next. I didn't really know. We'd been like that for as long as I could remember, but I imagined she started roaming before I came into the picture. Summon said they tried to live together and failed miserably. Had that been the start of her gypsy ways?

Knocking, bordering on pounding, broke me out of my reverie. At the base of the stairs, I rubbed my head and peered through the beveled glass set in the door. Kurt's handsome face stared at me, cut and angled like a Picasso painting by the decorative window. I opened the door before his fist could meet it again.

"How'd you—" I started to ask, when he brandished the copy of the gate key I'd had made for him last week.

"Ah," I said with a nod. Maybe not my most brilliant idea.

"You weren't at school. I looked for you after." Noticing my puffy eyes and splotchy complexion, he stepped inside without waiting for my invitation.

I closed and locked the door and followed him into the kitchen. "Yeah, well. I wasn't really up for it. Your girlfriend paid me a little visit at lunch."

"I heard." Kurt looked tense. "I took care of it."

My heart stilled in my chest and my extremities chilled. "What do you mean, Kurt? What did you do?"

He shrugged and headed to the fridge for a soda. "I dumped her."

I fell against the counter with a sigh of relief. "You scared me there for a minute."

Kurt gulped down several mouthfuls of generic orange pop. "What'd you think I meant?" he asked, curious.

I didn't want to tell him. There was no way to describe what men became capable of under the frequency's mind-numbing effects. No way to describe the crazed gleam in Ray's eyes as he toyed with the pistol between us in that motel room, ready to off us both to escape his wretchedness.

"Nothing," I said, looking away.

Kurt moved closer to me and set his half-empty can down. "Laney's all right. But she's not you."

I groaned. "Kurt, you know there's nothing serious going on here. You didn't have to break up with Laney for me. I hope you weren't mean to her. I know where's she's coming from." My throat tightened with the strangle of rising guilt.

He leveled his most earnest gaze on me and leaned close, rubbing his hands up and down my arms. "Say what you want, Innocence, but the way I feel about you— *around* you—is very serious."

Little shivers danced up and down my traitorous skin, and I couldn't bring myself to break away from him. For a moment, I felt I could see myself in his eyes, and I was glorious. I swallowed hard, worrying that the addiction to the frequency I'd seen in my mom's boyfriends could work both ways. It felt good to see yourself the way they did. And after how Jace looked at me today, and how low I'd felt, I couldn't resist Kurt's vision of me. I didn't want to feel like I had in the café ever again. I didn't want to see myself as the monster I was becoming.

I cleared my throat. "I don't, I mean, I *like* you, Kurt. You know I do. And I appreciate you very much. But my feelings aren't—"

Kurt leaned down with a wicked smile playing on his lips. His breath was syrupy sweet from the soda. "Innocence? Stop talking."

I froze, knowing what was coming and feeling as helpless against it as I would have been against a speeding train. This wasn't supposed to be his moment. A first kiss was supposed to be romantic and with someone like Jace. But this close, Kurt was beginning to feel less like a need and more like a want.

Kurt's lips brushed mine and his hands tightened around my arms. He whispered little kisses along my jaw, and when his lips found mine again, they parted hungrily, tasting me with careful flicks of his tongue.

My eyes slipped shut, and I let my mouth open against his, exploring. His body pressed into me, the counter digging into my lower back, and I felt as limp as a wet noodle in his grip. Flames sparked low in my belly, warming me in delicious tingles.

I wanted him.

The sudden realization was so startling that my eyes flew open, and I turned my head to the side, alarmed, breaking our connection. I pushed against Kurt's chest until he backed up an inch or two, and I tried to catch my breath.

Kurt chuckled, and the sound was gruff and sexy. "Too soon?"

I looked at him, pressing my fingers to my lips as though I could undo the feel of his own there, and my eyes widened.

"Come on, Innocence," he said. "We've been dancing around this for weeks now."

I slid down the counter until I couldn't feel the heat of him on me anymore. I shook my head. "Not me."

Kurt ran a fist of fingers through his close-cropped hair. "Coulda fooled me."

"I think I need you to leave," I told him. I couldn't do this anymore. I couldn't have Kurt here. Not just because it was getting harder and harder for him to resist me, but because I wasn't sure I could go on resisting *him.*

My heart may have been somewhere else, but my body was very present—my traitorous body. Somehow, my frequency had not only affected him, it affected *me,* rising between us like a tangible monster. I'd felt it, and it had felt good, but also . . . wrong. Inhuman. My kiss was no better than the siren's in Aunt Summon's book.

He could read the desire, and my fear of it. "Okay," he said after a moment's hesitation. "Okay. For now."

I followed him to the door, resisting the urge to clutch at him and beg him to stay. I felt like two people—half Innocence and half something else, something that wanted Kurt but would suck him dry and abandon him without a second thought.

He turned in the doorway and let his fingers trace the trail of kisses he'd left along my jaw earlier. "This isn't over, Innocence."

I nodded and closed the door, leaning against it as I listened to his retreating footsteps crunch down the drive. I was in over my head, and I couldn't ask Tempest for advice without admitting that I'd been using my frequency all along against her and Summon's express orders. For the first time, I considered that maybe their warnings weren't just about protecting me, but protecting everyone else from me.

I tore *Young's Concordance* from my bag, heart pounding. The possibility seemed so obvious, but no one wants to admit they might be a monster. I stared at Aunt Summon's note in the front, comparing her handwriting to mine. My loops weren't as wide, my *o*'s not as open, but I also didn't mimic the tight scrawl of my mom's I'd witnessed over the years, all sharply angled points and pressed letters. God, I missed them both.

I turned to the title page to read over the many names of Byrd women who'd held this book before me. I let my thumb shuffle through the pages, smelling the musty paper in the stirrings of air they created, pretending I could pick up on traces of my ancestresses as I turned back to the image of the siren. My eyes pored over her noble expression and stopped when I noticed a blue slash line peeping at me midway through the text in the caption. It had been drawn over an *n*. I'd missed it before, too transfixed by her grave portrait. But when I flipped back and compared, it was just like the one in Summon's note: blue ink, angled right to left, only smaller. *I hope you enjoy reading every page . . . You'd be surprised what you can learn.* Then, /.

I flipped once more through the yellowed pages, halting on a page near the front. There, midway through the third paragraph, was another blue slash. I checked the page number: 83. The *G*'s. *Gryphon.* Did Aunt Summon want me to notice these pages for some reason? The ink was as fresh as that inside the front cover. Not faded or old. She'd made these marks—I could feel her in them.

I scanned the reading. *Giant bird . . . half eagle, half lion . . . powerful guardians . . . protector from evil . . . mates for life . . .* yada yada. Wow, this Young guy was thorough, even notating the mating habits of his mythological menagerie. While I appreciated the subject, I couldn't understand why Summon would want to point this out to me. I turned to the page before of this one, hoping for something more. And there it was. Another slash. Bold and blue against the tightly packed, miniscule black text.

I flipped between the two pages. *Summon, what are you driving at?*

I flipped ahead again. Nothing.

I turned to page 84. Another slash. Page 85—another. They went on like that for eight pages. Then . . . nothing.

Keeping one finger tucked in *Gryphons,* I flipped ahead some more until more slashes began to appear between the blur of pages. I stopped. Turned back. These started in *Mermaids*, page 137.

I scanned a little. *Beautiful and mysterious . . . associated with unexplained events such as drownings and storms at sea . . . related to mammals of the order Sirenia . . .* and so on. This wasn't adding up.

What did mermaids have to do with gryphons, gulons—a Scandinavian wolverine-like creature that feeds nonstop—and gwyllion, evil Welsh spirits that roam the mountains? Why would she lead me to these pages?

I flipped back through the *Mermaids* markings and noted that one page had two slashes. One in the opening sentence. One near the bottom paragraph. And that's when it dawned on me. Aunt Summon hadn't been attempting to draw my attention to the pages. She'd been trying to draw it to the letters.

Every blue slash was crossing out a typeset letter in Young's ramblings.

I opened to the beginning and flipped until I found a slash, jotting that letter down. I found three more on the next three pages. I looked back over the letters I'd written—*w, e, r, e. Were* or *we're*. It was code.

The first set of slashes was found in the *B*'s. It started in *Baba Yaga*—a Slavic witch—and ended in *Balaur*, an eastern European dragon. It had thirteen letters:

w-e-r-e-d-i-f-f-e-r-e-n-t

I don't know why she even wasted letters on that message. I'd basically figured that much out on my own.

Then . . . nothing.

The pages between slash marks were a break of some kind—like breaks between sentences. I had to determine for myself where one word began and another ended.

The second grouping was the one I found near *Gryphons*. It had twelve letters and was debatable from where I was sitting:

y-o-u-r-e-s-p-e-c-i-a-l

The third grouping was the one that began in *Mermaids*. Only eight letters this time. Eight horrible letters:

n-o-t-h-u-m-a-n

My stomach churned. I was beginning to hate Aunt Summon's message, but I needed to carry on.

The fifth set of letters was under *P.* It started in *Pan*—god and faun—and ended somewhere in *Parandrus*—a shape-shifting stag. Nine letters:

n-o-t-k-i-l-l-e-r

Thanks for the vote of confidence, Summon, but I was pretty sure she was wrong on this one. After all, I was there outside Salinas and she wasn't. Eyewitness to my own fall from grace. I practically had the t-shirt.

I doubted the last two groups held enough letters to clear this all up. But I forged ahead. Seven letters starting under *R* for *Redcaps*—murderous English dwarves. Comforting after my last fun fact. They spelled:

n-o-t-g-i-r-l

The air got thin and I began to tremble.

I wasn't a boy. So far, all she'd told me was what I *wasn't,* but I needed to know what I *was.*

The final group of letters would make that perfectly, alarmingly clear.

The letters began in the *S*'s, under *Sileni*—a special class of satyrs that followed the god Dionysus. They ended beneath the woodcut I'd stared at for so long. The lonely woman on the rocks, the beautiful lyre her call, the men in the ship sailing to their doom.

Five final letters to answer my question once and for all.

I tried so hard to make it say something different. I tried to put the spaces between the letters to make them spell new words, but there was only so much you could do with five letters. And these five letters spelled only one word.

S-i-r-e-n.

Fifty-four letters. That's all it took.

Fifty-four letters to bring the whole world crumbling down around me.

Fifty-four letters that would change me, and my life, forever.

I hated numbers. I was sick to death of them at this point. My heart was pounding, but I refused to resume my familiar count. I was done with numbers.

That was it. These six phrases were somehow supposed to explain everything.

We're different.
You're special.
Not human.
Not killer.
Not girl.
Siren.

According to Aunt Summon, we were sirens. According to Young, we were irresistible, rare, and above all, dangerous. I'd spent the last couple of hours reading and rereading everything Young wrote about sirens. When that didn't suffice, I'd taken to the Internet. A sort of succubus of the sea, sirens were a predatory combination of harpies and mermaids who were known to live along the coastline or on remote islands, scavenging for their survival off the scattered remains of shipwrecks. Shipwrecks *we* caused by summoning the sailors and their vessels to their watery graves with our heavenly music.

I left Summon another useless voice mail. I would lob my questions at Tempest when she got back. I made my way down the stairs for dinner and into the kitchen. Grabbing a cola, a bag of chips, and a carton of strawberries, I trudged back up the stairs again, my mind whirling over Young's and Wikipedia's descriptions. On second thought, maybe I would do my best to fill in the blanks on my own. The less Tempest thought I knew, the more likely I was to get information out of her, and the safer I felt.

Legs folded on the bed, I turned all the information over in my mind as I sucked the flesh from a strawberry. I could think of a few shipwrecks my mother had left in her wake. Or train wrecks. However you chose to label it, what my mother did was wreck the life of the men she summoned to her. In that sense, all the sources were right. But they were also starkly biased. Nothing written from the perspective of the siren. Nothing to explain *why* they did what they did. Nothing but a whole lot of paranoia about evil female archetypes.

The comparisons were easy enough to draw. Our last name was Byrd. My mother and I had traveled the coast moving from one man to the next. We lived by picking off their remains. Because the truth was, from the moment my mother came into contact with a man, he was doomed. And it was his slow descent, his spiral into madness, which fed us . . . for a while. But my mom wasn't evil; she wasn't a killer. Not to mention I had no bird parts the last time I checked—which was about twenty minutes ago. No fish parts either. Maybe I loved the beach, but so did a lot of people. Especially sun-worshipping teenage girls. And I had my own reasons. Reasons that were far easier to explain than being half fish. Also, I didn't have a lyre and I was pretty sure I was tone deaf. I couldn't read a note of music. So much for the *heavenly music.* I may be a Byrd, but I was no songbird, regardless of what Aunt Summon called me.

I ran this loop about two dozen times through my mind, and it kept bringing me back to one question. What did my Aunt Summon mean?

If we weren't Young's literal part-bird-part-fish-part-woman sirens, then what kind of sirens were we?

I knew two things at this point. I knew about frequencies. And I knew about sirens. Twin streams feeding into the same current.

I knew what we were.

20

I was back at the drugstore where I'd run into Jace before we'd gone shopping. Plucking a couple road maps off the stand and grabbing some snacks, I tried not to think about that day while I paid the cashier. Jace had been the only thing keeping me at Stonetop, but I didn't have Jace anymore. Not only because he probably despised me, but because I couldn't risk figuratively drowning him with what I was.

With that string cut loose, however painfully, it was time to say goodbye to Stonetop. I was different. *Not human. Not girl.* I was more. I was a siren. I could save my mom, and hopefully do it before the police who came for her came for me.

I had a small bag of clothes in my mom's Mercedes and a forming, if loosely, plan. I'd left the Mini back at Phil's for a couple of reasons. One, so I wouldn't be spotted by Kurt, Mr. Sikes, Jace, or any other Innocence groupies and be flagged or followed. Two, so that anyone who'd noticed my mom's car since we came to Stonetop would think she was out and about, and therefore still free. If the police weren't ready to release her name to the press, I certainly wasn't either. I figured I would find Aunt Summon's place, and together we would get my mom out . . . today. Summon loved me. She'd left me that message. She would help me once she saw me, once I told her I now knew what we were. She wouldn't have a choice. I would bicycle chain myself to that.

I comforted myself with this conclusion as I started the car and rolled out of town, watching Stonetop recede in my rearview.

Goodbye, Jace.

Everything south of Austin looked the same. Every tree, every road, every town. I pulled over to the dirt shoulder of the ranch road I was wandering idly down and drummed my thumbs against the steering wheel. What. A. Stupid. Plan.

Shifting to park, I snatched up the map open on the passenger seat. I had to be close. I could practically hear Aunt Summon's laughter wafting across the treetops to where I was. Why was this so hard?

I glanced at my phone and considered just calling her and explaining that I was lost, but I knew she would talk me out of coming if I gave her any warning. And that was if I could even reach her. So far, all I'd gotten were a couple of distant text messages. Nope, I would not call. I would find her place myself and make it impossible for her to say no.

According to the map, I'd traveled a little too far west. I decided on a circuitous route to bring me back around directly beneath Austin, hoping I might notice something familiar along the way. If not, I could stop in San Marcos for a restroom break and change tactics from there. The way I saw it, I was willing to cover every single road on that map between Austin and San Antonio. She had to be on one of them.

A flash caught my eye, and a quick glance in the rearview revealed that I was not alone. One of Stonetop's finest was headed up the road in the distance, kicking up a dusty trail behind the patrol car. I swallowed and told myself it wasn't odd that they would be patrolling this desolate strip of asphalt so far from town. Maybe they were just keeping an eye on wealthy ranches in Hill Country.

I turned back to my map and made a failed attempt at folding it back up after marking the road I was on with a blue slash. If I ticked off the ones I'd already checked, I wouldn't end up going in circles. Or at least that was the idea. My hands were shaking too hard. Finally, I crumpled it against the empty seat next to me. I was genetically incapable of map folding.

The cop car was nearing, and as I made ready to pull back onto the road, it started to slow down. Was it waiting for me to pull out? Why wouldn't it just pass me? It wasn't until I saw the vehicle begin to move onto the shoulder that I got scared. They were pulling up behind me.

One . . . two . . . three . . .

I drew in a ragged breath and gripped the steering wheel. My PTSD went into overdrive. Some instinct inside me began kicking and screaming to take over. Were they coming for me now? I couldn't let that happen.

I jerked the wheel hard to the left and hit the pedal. My tires spun for a second against the gravel and dirt before they found purchase and moved onto the road with a lurch. I looked back just as the driver's door of the patrol car was opening. Whoever was inside would get nothing more than a mouthful of sandy Texas loam from me.

But moments later the white-and-blue sedan found its way onto the asphalt ribbon behind me, lights whirling. I floored the gas.

I felt split in two.

Human Innocence was screaming in my head. *Are you insane? Pull over!*

But Siren Innocence insisted the bigger risk was in complying. *You're not one of them, and they'll never understand you. Run!*

Another unmarked road was intersecting up ahead, and I slowed just enough to swing a left onto it without rolling the car. I let out a tense breath as my tires put more and more distance between the road I was on and the sedan, but within minutes it had made the same turn and was behind me again and gaining.

My heart was like a trapped jackrabbit, and my eyes began to water.

I focused on the road ahead and prayed I'd find an opportunity to get away permanently. The patrol car was only a few car lengths behind now. Mom's Mercedes was no match for whatever engine they had. On either side of me, the road opened up into fields, crops of some kind. I hit the pedal hard and poured what strength I had into the car protecting me. I doubted frequencies worked on machines like they did on people, but it was worth a shot. Still, the squad car advanced. It was moving to my left, preparing to come up beside me, probably trying to pass me and cut me off so I'd have to stop. The odometer surged, and I veered left then right, accidentally causing the car to fishtail. Within seconds, the car was next to me, sirens blaring, and I could make out the shadow of a man inside. Pretty soon, he pulled ahead, cut the car sharply to the right, and braked to a horizontal stop in the road. I floored my own brake, tires squealing, and came up only a few feet short of T-boning him.

My heart felt like it was gushing adrenaline. I opened the door and stumbled out, even as the officer shouted at me to stay inside my vehicle. His voice carried down a long tunnel to me, and I gulped the air like I'd just come up from an underwater nap. I didn't feel like a mythological monster. I felt like a human girl who'd just done something really, really stupid.

"Miss Byrd, you are to remain in your vehicle!"

I clutched my side, which had begun to cramp with my frantic breathing. How did he know my name?

Officer Reyes was on me in a heartbeat. I had majorly screwed up. I should have just let him pull me over in the first place. There was only one way out of this, and for once I felt lucky to have access to it.

I took a deep breath and let my eyes catch his. I couldn't risk holding back, so I grinned at him and let the magnetism unfurl within me, twining around us as he stood facing me.

His jaw went slack first, then something behind his eyes did. But there was a resistance inside him that would only let me get so far. Realizing I was harmless, he had me lean against the Mercedes and put my head down. He even brought me a bottled water from his car.

"What are you doing all the way out here?"

"Taking the scenic route?"

He pursed his lips. "Where to?"

I let out a long breath. "I don't know. Anywhere but Stonetop. Your daughter paid me a visit the other day." I needed to change the subject.

His brows scrunched up under his short-cropped hair. "So I've heard. Laney shouldn't have said anything. She doesn't know much, just that your mother is in custody."

"So she knows as much as I do." I crossed my arms.

Officer Reyes scowled. "We've been in frequent contact with your aunt. If it weren't for her intervention, you'd already have been placed under state protection. She hasn't told you anything?"

I shook my head. I didn't want to let Reyes in on the fact that Summon wasn't actually staying with me. I should have kept my mouth shut.

"She's been in touch with us since your mother was taken into custody. We've given her all the information we can, but it's her decision what to share with the rest of the family."

"I know. I respect that. I'm just worried is all." *And clueless.*

Officer Reyes gave me an appraising look. "She's visited the station more than once and given her statement. They even allowed her a short visit with your mother. She didn't tell you any of this?"

My mind went numb. Aunt Summon had been to Stonetop? Multiple times? And she didn't stop to see me? I straightened and tried to seem like none of this was news to me. "I guess she's trying to protect me from whatever's going on with my mom."

"Normally I would understand that, but under the circumstances, I don't think she's doing you any favors to keep so much from you," Reyes said with dark eyes.

I looked into them, afraid of what I might see there. "What do you mean? What circumstances?"

Officer Reyes glanced away. "Innocence, I shouldn't be the one to tell you this, but your mom is in a very grave situation. The sooner you adjust to the idea of . . ."

"Of what?" My eyes narrowed. What was he trying to tell me?

"Of her incarceration," he continued with a sigh. "The sooner you accept that, the better."

"No." I shook my head refusing to let his words seep in.

Reyes placed a hand on my shoulder. "I know this is hard to hear."

"No!" I shouted at him, breaking our contact. "That won't happen. My mom didn't do anything, and I won't let you lock her away."

"It's not me holding the key to her cell. This is a federal case. Special Agent Monroe is with the FBI. We're just cooperating with their investigation at this point. There's nothing you can do about it, I'm afraid. It's in the court's hands."

We would see about that. "What about me? Can I give a statement?" If my mom confessed, so could I. They would never slap me with the kind of sentence she might get. I was young and fragile. My name was *Innocence* for crying out loud.

"You already did, remember?" Officer Reyes didn't look confused, but I must have.

"I did?"

"Sure. Your aunt brought it in."

"Brought it in?" I was no criminal justice major, but I was pretty sure a statement was only admissible if it was given where the police could witness it. Had Summon managed to influence them into accepting a written statement I never gave? I would never incriminate my own mother. Summon must have figured I would let something slip accidentally, something they could use against us.

"A few weeks ago," Officer Reyes insisted. "You can give a second one, but I'm afraid nothing you say now will discount your original statement." When I didn't say anything, he added, "You need to go home for now. Your mom's car is under surveillance, and neither you nor it are allowed to leave the county at this time. It would be best if you stuck close to Stonetop from now on."

I stared at Officer Reyes unblinking.

"Just consider this a verbal warning. For the speeding. And for trying to outrun an officer of the law. We'll let your little jaunt into the countryside remain between us."

"Thanks," I muttered. I started to climb back into my mother's car when something occurred to me. Reyes was being awfully nice to me for someone who believed my mother was guilty of murder. And it seemed like he had a rather soft side for my aunt as well. Of course, Summon and I were innocent in his mind, bystanders to my mother's horrible crime. But still. Something wasn't adding up. "Can I ask you something? What do you think of my mom?"

He blinked and studied me, but didn't respond. "I-I can't—"

I allowed my frequency to bleed into the air between us, just a hint. "Off the record. I'm just curious."

He exhaled. "She was convincing at first."

"At first? What changed?"

He shrugged. "I don't know exactly. Your mom is a beautiful woman. I don't have to tell you that. But once we were able to see past that flawless face, so much more became clear."

Interesting choice of words for a man who was supposed to be "immune to my mother's charms," as Tempest put it. It sounded like she had no problem working her magic in the beginning, but then something got in the way.

"After your aunt called the station, we changed our line of questioning. And that's when your mother finally confessed."

Summon was supposed to be using her frequency on the police, but now I wondered if she was using it to help or hurt my mom. "And what about my aunt?" I asked. "What do you think of her?"

His face flushed, which told me all I needed to know. "She's very cooperative."

I nodded, my whole body going rigid with anger.

As I slid into the car, Officer Reyes closed the door for me and leaned on the window sill. "She may not look it," he said of his own volition. "But your aunt has a good heart. She's a unique woman. Special."

His eyes softened when he spoke about her, and I knew that look all too well. The funny thing was, Summon looked as wholesome as she seemed, all fresh country air and sunshine. And as good as she was at running her brood, none of the guys on her property looked like Reyes did now, like so many of my mom's boyfriends had—bewitched. "What do you mean she may not look it?"

Reyes stared at me. "You know, she has a rough exterior. But that's not who she is underneath."

"Rough as in rugged?"

Reyes shook his head. "As in dark, troubled."

I was pretty sure Officer Reyes was not talking about my Aunt Summon. "Are you referring to her tattoo?" I waited to see if he would swallow the bait.

"The raven on her hand? Yeah, that among other things—the earrings, the goth attire. None of it is who she truly is. It's just a cover, a front. She's been through a lot. She just needs someone to understand her."

And there it was, the magic word. *Need.* I didn't know exactly how or why, but Tempest had been playing the cops and the feds. Did Summon know this was happening? Was this something they cooked up together? Whatever they might be planning, it would have to stay between the Byrds.

I thanked Officer Reyes and backed the car up, turning it around the way I'd come as I sped away, entrenched in my own thoughts. I needed to find out the truth. Most of all, I needed to talk to Summon. Why wouldn't she call the station herself? Why would she send Tempest to do it instead? I thought Tempest was bringing me the answers I could expect to get, but instead, she had only brought more questions.

21

I unlocked the gate with shaky fingers. *Home again, home again.* I was beginning to appreciate Phil's property more. It wasn't Summon's fortress, but it felt a hell of a lot safer than being out in the open, especially after my afternoon car chase reminded me that mythological being or no, I still had limitations.

Of course the feds were in charge. Why else would a "Special Agent" turn up to question my mother? And bugging cars was just one of the many things the FBI was known for. It was silly of me to think I could skip town, track Summon down, orchestrate a heist. Tempest had been right: I had no choice but to stay put.

I bristled with fresh annoyance. Tempest had lied to my face about what she'd been doing. Even if it turned out it was for my mom's good, I wasn't a child, and I deserved to know the truth.

Until I had some definite answers about my mother's case, about Summon and Tempest, I decided I should not only keep my guard up, but reinforce it with bulletproof glass. I took a few deep breaths and trudged back to my car. *New plan, Innocence.*

I would play Tempest's game, keeping the role of the wide-eyed, innocent teenager who desperately needed her and believed everything she said. Right now, Phil was likely still love-addled in San Antonio. I had the place to myself and enough time to launch my own investigation into what really happened to my dad and what was happening to my mom. Somehow, I would figure out how to spring her on my own.

My confidence was shattered when I pulled up and found Tempest sitting cross-legged on the front porch steps, a cigarette butt hanging between her lips. But it wasn't what she was smoking that disturbed me. I got out of the car slowly and walked toward her. She grinned menacingly and drummed her fingers across the cover of *Young's Concordance* in her lap, my decoded message from Summon scrawled on a sheet of paper lying at her feet. She leveled her gaze on me. "So much for family secrets."

I steeled myself. Whatever fierce sort of creature Tempest was, I came from the same stock. "I guess Summon was trying to find a way to tell me all along."

"I guess so." Tempest gripped the book.

"How long have you been back?" What I really wanted to know was how long she'd been in my room while I was gone, but I didn't dare phrase it that way.

"Not long," she said, but her eyes told another story. She flicked her dying cigarette away and leaned forward. Despite myself, I stepped back.

"So what do you want to know?" she said brightly, but her voice sounded thin as paper.

I didn't know if I could trust her answers, but it would be suspicious if I didn't ask her any questions, and frankly, I was starving for as much information as I could get. "Where do I start?"

"You can start with this," she said, holding the book up so I could read the cover. "Legend has it that Young was a friend of the family."

"You mean—"

"He had an affair with a Byrd woman." She flipped open the cover and pointed. "Serenade Byrd herself. They met when she was only fifteen. He was infatuated with her, and in exchange for keeping the mythology act up, she let him in on our family secret. Well, not just our family, but we are part of a very select group."

"So the myths are a good thing? We like them?" I asked her.

She grinned mischievously. "Kid, we love them. Hell, we may have even started them. At any rate, we certainly help them along."

"Why? Doesn't that only draw attention to us?"

Tempest flicked her hair over her shoulder. "What it does is make for an excellent diversion." She flipped though the book to the portrait of the half-bird woman on the cliff and tapped it. "As long as this is what people are looking for, they'll never even believe we exist. We're just made-up creatures, like mermaids or unicorns or vampires. If you even suggested someone might be a siren, you'd have a vein full of Thorazine before you could finish your sentence."

"But that's what we are," I said, pointing at the same picture and trying not to cringe. "Sirens."

"In a way. We're not birds or fish or any of that mythological crap they've been passing down from one generation to the next."

I wrapped my arms around my knees. "Obviously. I can't even sing 'Happy Birthday' in tune."

"Or fly," she added.

"But there are correlations. It's not all make-believe."

"Sure. All lore springs from a kernel of truth. What's music or sound but vibration? It's all just part of the front for our frequencies."

"And what are the frequencies exactly?"

She shrugged. "Who knows and who cares? You're asking all the wrong questions here."

I scowled. "I didn't know there were right ones in a situation like this."

Tempest looked at me a long moment. "Don't ask what a frequency is or why you have one—ask what you can do with it."

Her eyes had taken on a mad gleam, a zeal seething just below the surface. I chalked it up to family pride.

"So this Young guy actually knew the truth about us," I said, changing the subject.

Tempest leaned back. "Of course. He gave a copy of the book to Serenade after it was published. And we've been passing it down ever since."

"Why?" If the book didn't say what we really were, why hold onto it like we did?

Tempest shrugged. "Sentimental reasons, I suppose. Our family is full of ridiculous customs and silly superstitions. Every oldest daughter has received it and written her name in the cover."

Her fingers traced over the different loops of ink. I noticed the raven tattoo on her left hand again, wings outspread, and remembered the goofy look on Reyes's face.

"As I see you've figured out." She slapped the cover shut.

"How many others know about us?"

Tempest dropped the book on the step next to her, suddenly bored. "Not many. And those who find out rarely live to share the news."

Something about the way she said it, as if it were such a casual thing to take a life, made me feel hot and nervous all over, the way you feel when you're worried about being found out in a lie. "Harmonious is my mom's mother, my Grandma Byrd. But Florid was your mother."

Tempest shot her dark eyes at me and gave me a calculating once-over. "That's right. My mother was the baby of that group of sisters. They were always jealous of her."

"Jealous?" That's not exactly how Summon put it. "I heard that she chose a different life than they did, than the kind we usually live, like Aunt Summon."

"She had to." Tempest stood and cut her eyes away from me. "They didn't understand her."

That sounded eerily similar to the tripe I'd heard Reyes give me about her. I swallowed and tried for more. "Why?"

"It's complicated." She looked at me and softened a little. "Our family has always lived a certain way, not because it's the only way, but because it works and they're afraid of anything different. Change isn't something the Byrds welcome. They fear it."

I watched her flip through the *Concordance,* shake her head, and slap it closed. "But that way isn't fair. It forces all the younger sisters to live under the rule of one dominant eldest sister. They have to subject their frequencies to hers, and she gets everything—the men, the land, the children."

"So?"

Tempest glared at me. "So, my mother refused to be subjected to that. She might have been the youngest, but her frequency was the most powerful. And she did what she had to do to prove it."

Goose bumps prickled up my arms. "And what was that?"

"She took what Harmonious treasured the most away from her. And then she struck out on her own and created the life *she* wanted, not the one they tried to force on her."

I couldn't imagine what Florid took that was so precious it was unforgivable, but I found myself sympathizing. Wasn't that my mother's situation after all? And while she and Summon seemed to get along and be in each other's lives, if it had been the other way around and my mom wanted something else, I would have expected a loving sister to support her in that quest. There were always two sides to every story. Florid's might not be as bad as the rest of the family made it look.

"I guess her way made an impression on you." I was commenting on Tempest's rebel look and secretive life on the road, but she seemed offended somehow.

"Yeah, well, I didn't get a choice like she did. Once the Byrds push you out of their nest, there's no going back. I'm guilty by association, and I've made a life for myself the only way I could. They left me no other choice."

I swallowed hard and watched her toss *Young's Concordance* to me before turning for the door, letting it slam behind her. I let her go. Wherever that life had taken her, no one in this family was in a position to judge. We were all Byrds. We were all sirens. And we were all monsters.

Tempest left shortly after, and I didn't stop her. I didn't want her to know that I knew about Officer Reyes until I'd figured out what to do about it. Or at least until I talked to Aunt Summon, but she still wasn't answering her phone—a silence that felt ominous.

I distracted myself with hours of meaningless research. When sirens turned up more of the same—beautiful, seductive women who lured hapless men to their death and sang like Christina Aguilera on steroids—I switched tactics and googled *frequency*. That dragged up a whole lot of scientific mumbo jumbo that did little to explain what *I* was referring to as a frequency.

The sum total of what I got was this: A frequency is a wave.

Of what? Well, that's where it got murky for me. Of movement. Of sound. Of matter. It was like a vibration. Invisible and communicative, everything had one.

And then I came across this quote: *Everything is energy—vibration. Match the frequency of what you want to create that reality.*

As best as I could gather, we were manipulating energy—our own, others', or both—to create the reality someone else wanted. Or, the *illusion* of that reality. Except, at times it seemed more like what I was doing was not convincing Kurt that I was everything he wanted, but convincing him that everything he wanted was me. Which sounded like two different ways of saying the same thing.

Some things were making more sense though. The way I'd never managed to make any real *girl* friends. My excuse had always been that we moved so much, but now I wondered. Maybe it was like Aunt Summon said, because I wasn't a real girl. I was different. Could they tell?

The way I'd always been hyperaware of the boys around me. I didn't know exactly how it tied into frequencies, but I knew it was part of mine. It wasn't just Ray, it wasn't just fear or PTSD, it was my frequency kicking in that made the difference. Sure, Wanda wasn't all wrong. I had been through some serious shit. And that trauma had left its mark on me in the way of panic attacks and bad dreams, but some of what I was interpreting as anxiety could be my heightened senses kicking into gear. It would be up to me to sort out which was which.

Exhausted, I passed out sometime after midnight amid a flurry of papers, my laptop still glowing. For the first time in as long as I could recall, I didn't dream about Ray. Instead, I saw myself perched perilously at the edge of a windy cliff overlooking the sea, the same I'd seen in the siren woodcut. I looked down at the roiling waters and saw the bodies of countless men, some floating unconscious, others scrabbling for purchase against the rock, clawing with bloody fingers, trying to make their way to me. One wore my algebra teacher's face. One, Kurt's face. One, Jace's. Terrified, I turned to run, but as I did, a faceless woman with scalding red hair shoved me so hard I lost my footing and spun out into the open expanse of gray. As I plummeted toward the water, I feared the men I saw there more than the impact—they would tear me to shreds. I put my arms out to brace myself and found a pair of black wings in their place.

I was still staring at my arms in disbelief, shaking off the feathers of my dream, when the knock sounded. Not as insistent as before, but I knew who it was nonetheless, and I knew he wouldn't go away. I may as well answer it.

Grumbling, I stood and looked at the clock. I'd overslept. School started almost three hours ago. No wonder he was here again. I made my way to the front door, not bothering to look as I turned the lock and knob.

"I really shouldn't have given you that—" The words stopped short when I looked up, expecting to find Kurt's dark, penetrating stare and instead saw Jace's intense aqua gaze. "—key," I finished flatly. I'd just seen his face in my dream, clawing toward me. I shivered.

"What key?" he asked, his brows drawing together in a puzzled way.

I looked past him, but his car wasn't in the drive. "How'd you get in here?" I was intensely aware of my poor "sick day" fashion choices. Ripped jeans and a faded black *Rolling Stones* t-shirt I'd dragged with me from Corpus. Barely there makeup. Not my usual colorful self.

For a second, he looked sheepish. "I climbed."

"Climbed?" I echoed, confused. I tried to comb my fingers through my hair inconspicuously.

"The fence. The gate was locked, so . . ." He looked down at the scuffed toes of his Converse.

"Right. Yeah. I, uh, keep it locked for a reason."

He looked hurt for a moment, and his weight shifted back, away from me. "I should probably go."

I suddenly realized how I must have sounded. "No! I mean, you're here. May as well come in."

Jace forced a tight smile, stuffing his hands in his back pockets as I stepped aside to let him in the entry.

I closed and locked the door, taking a deep breath before turning to face him. "So . . . why are you here?"

He shrugged. "Thought we had a date. Remember?"

I glanced through the living room at the television, scanning for the time. Right around noon. "You mean lunch? At the café?"

He nodded. His body language was all wrong: tight, tense, withdrawn. He took a step nearer to me, and I let that small sign feed the ember of hope I'd been carrying around that somehow he'd find a way to forgive me.

I looked down and picked at one thumbnail with another. "I figured, after Friday, that those had been suspended . . . indefinitely."

He shrugged again. "Couldn't stay away."

I assessed those words carefully. Was that frequency talk? Was it more Innocence-you're-my-drug speak, like I'd gotten from Kurt? I'd wanted Jace right here, saying just that, so desperately that for a second I didn't think it mattered. But this was Jace. This was my Mr. Lifeline. I couldn't let him slip into some kind of siren coma under my watch. I had to know it was him and not the trance talking.

"Why?" I said coolly.

His eyes widened slightly, and then he hung his head, running his long fingers through that gloriously tousled mop of blond waves. I had to bite my lower lip to keep from reaching out and grabbing him. The boy looked like he hung with angels.

"I had every reason to be upset, you know," he said, meeting my eyes again, but it lacked the same bite he'd carried when he was angry Friday.

I nodded slowly.

"I just want you to be honest with me, Innocence."

"I was," I told him, but not completely, and we both knew it. How could I be?

He chuckled humorlessly. "Sure. So, you're saying Kurt wasn't here? You and he haven't been seeing each other all this time?"

Crap. "It's not like that," I told him. I was tired of having to defend myself, and I was only sixteen. Was this going to be my whole life? Defending what I did, who I was, to every human that pointed a finger? No. I owed no one an explanation . . . except Jace. He was the only person whose opinion mattered to me outside my own family. Yet, I couldn't give him the explanation he deserved. That would mean telling him what I was. That would mean losing him for certain. "It's not romantic," I added.

Jace rubbed his face with both hands. "So it's platonic? That you're spending all this time with Kurt *I-have-my-Wheaties-with-a-side-of-cheerleader* Meier, and there is nothing physical going on?"

I crossed my arms. "Did you ever think I might be simply tutoring him in some of his subjects? Kurt has to pass with a B-average to keep his place on the team."

"You're a year below him," Jace pointed out.

"We do homework together. That's all." I wasn't backing down. I had no intention of letting my connection to Kurt go any deeper than bodyguard. I'd told Kurt that myself.

Jace blew out a long, uncertain breath.

"What about Laney?" I countered. "What was all that *I thought you should know* stuff?"

Jace folded his arms over his chest. "Laney and I dated for a couple of months last year. It was nothing serious. She's not my type. She's . . ."

"Kurt *I-have-my-Wheaties-with-a-side-of-cheerleader* Meier's type?" I supplied.

Jace cracked a small smile. "Yeah. Yeah, I guess. She's a great girl. Just a little bouncy for me."

"In case you didn't notice, I'm not a cheerleader." Though, that wasn't keeping Kurt from trying to lap me up with his breakfast of champions. But Jace didn't need to know that. I wasn't going to reciprocate with Kurt, and that was all that mattered.

"I noticed," he said grinning.

"So if Laney's not your type, who is?" Maybe he'd say mythological female serial killers, but somehow I doubted it.

"You are." He took a couple steps toward me and I froze. Jace reached his hands up and cupped my face, pulling me to him. His eyes grazed over mine, across my cheeks, down to my lips. He ran a finger along one side of my face, tucking back a stray lock of hair. "These eyes, this face, these lips—that's my type."

I shuddered with need. I didn't care anymore if it was him or the addiction talking. He was so close that he overwhelmed me. All I could see or smell or hear or feel was Jace. His heart beat in my ears like thunder. I was swimming in him, and I never wanted up for air.

Suddenly, his hands were tight around my arms, pushing me away from him. "You're not making this easy," he whispered, a panicked glint in his eye.

I looked up at him from beneath the heavy line of my lashes. "Good."

"I'm not sure I can trust myself around you," he laughed, sliding his hands down until they found mine. "Wasn't I supposed to be pissed at you?"

"I don't know what you're talking about," I said, feigning innocence.

"Uh huh." Jace lifted one hand and kissed my knuckles lightly. "Why don't we find something distracting to do for a while?"

I beamed. Jace was pulling back, restraining himself. This had to be real. Could any guy under the frequency have been able to do that? "Well, they were supposed to run a *Wolverine and the X-Men* marathon on Nickelodeon later today."

Jace beamed. "You know I'm partial to mutants. They're so misunderstood."

I did know, and I was counting on it.

22

It had come a little late, but we ended up having our date at the café after all. Same table and everything. Jace returned after stepping outside to ring his parents and give them his phony excuse about driving his friend Levi home from school sick. He looked at me across our sodas and fries. "Well, that's settled."

I shook my head. "I can't believe they bought that." My mom would never be so gullible. Then again, my mom wasn't around to trick.

Jace shrugged, a grin playing across his lips. "What can I say? I'm just that good."

And yet again, I was happy enough to forget about her absence for a few hours and ride Lifeboat Jace over my veritable ocean of trouble.

"And Levi is okay with being your decoy?" I raised a brow at him. "While you play hooky with me?"

Jace had yet to bring me around any of his friends, and I never wanted to ask. It seemed like everyone at Stonetop High knew him and liked him, but he mostly kept to himself.

"Sure," he said. "I gave him a ring. He'll answer and play it off if they call him."

"And he knows? About me?"

Jace set his drink down and leveled a burning blue gaze on me. "'Course, Innocence. Anyone who knows me knows about you."

I felt the blush spread out from my cheeks like two blooming roses. "You . . . talk about me?"

He laughed a little. "More like I can't shut up about you."

My whole face flushed with the crimson heat of a sauna. I couldn't help the ridiculously obvious smile that crawled across and made itself at home there.

Jace watched me with a satisfied expression. "Don't you tell your friends about me? Where do they think you've been every day at lunch?"

Apparently, Jace hadn't noticed my severe lack of actual friends, or he wouldn't have asked that. "I don't really make friends easy," I answered. I didn't want to come out and say, *you're my only friend.*

Jace flinched, as though it hurt him to think of me being hurt. Then, a giant smile took over and he gave me a sly wink. "Makes me all the more special."

There were no words for how I appreciated that, the way he veered around my painfully obvious deficiencies, trying to make me feel better. "If you say so," I teased.

"Besides, you have all my friends now. Any friend of mine is a friend of theirs." He popped a ketchup-coated fry in his mouth.

I knew what he was trying to do, and it meant a lot. But there was something else in his choice of words that stuck in my throat like a chicken bone. "Can I ask you something?"

Jace swallowed. "Shoot."

I took a breath. After everything that happened today, I needed to say this. I needed to know. Because one Kurt was enough in my life. "Is that what we are? *Friends?*"

Jace sat back and looked at me. "Are you serious?"

I sucked my full bottom lip in and bit it, nodding. "It's just, after all the lunch dates, and the holding hands . . . I mean, I guess I thought . . ." *Ugh.* Why couldn't I just spit this out?

Jace watched me, taking in my awkward gesturing and babbled words. Finally, he said, "Innocence, I have enough friends. I was really hoping you'd be something more."

I dared a glance at him and saw the intensity deepening his eyes. A breath escaped me, flooding the air between us with my relief. "Okay."

"Even though all my *friend* positions are filled, the *girlfriend* slot is wide open at the moment. Think you could handle that job?" His mouth twisted on one side into a wicked cute grin.

I giggled. Full-on schoolgirl giggle. So. Embarrassing. "I can try."

"Try hard," he said, reaching over and giving my hand a squeeze.

Something strangely seductive snaked through me, and I cut my eyes up at him. "I'll give it everything I've got."

Jace let go of my hand to flag the waiter, but his eyes never left mine. "Can we get a check over here, please? *Now.*"

It was nearing seven o'clock. *Wolverine and the X-Men* had laser-eyed, storm-called, and knife-fought their way through a full season of episodes. We were facing the inevitable, and we both knew it. Jace had to leave soon.

Jace cleared his throat and the rumble in his chest vibrated through my shoulder.

"Stay for dinner?" I kept my voice perky. Clingy wasn't good girlfriend material. I was facing another long, tormenting night alone. Ray's face hovered just beyond my consciousness, ready to haunt me again. Only now, it was joined by my mother's. They took turns playing victim in my nightmares, which left me taking turns between skipping heartbeats, breathing too fast, and feeling like the walls were creeping closer.

Jace smiled sweetly and my heart shrunk a size. He was about to tell me why he couldn't. Then his eyebrows pulled together and he looked around, as if really seeing the den for the first time. "Hey, where's your mom?"

I sat up and gave my standard reply. "She works evenings for Phil now, in the city."

The hollow ring of my tone registered with Jace where it hadn't with Kurt. "Innocence," he said carefully, like I was a frightened animal. "What's really going on?"

Something in me crumpled. It just felt so good to really *be* with someone again. When Kurt was here, he wasn't really here. Not of his own free will. He was never completely himself with me, or I with him, because the frequency was always between us, shaping us into people we weren't.

Whatever the reason, I folded under the pressure, and the emotions rushed in, flooding me. I tried to stop it, tried to backpedal, but Jace made me vulnerable in ways no one else did. The tears came fast, swelling, cresting over my lashes, coursing down my cheeks before I could suck them back in.

"Oh, Innocence," he said, wrapping his tan, lean arms around me.

I turned my face into his shoulder until I could staunch the flow and gather myself. Blithering crybaby was a long way from the sexy vixen I thought all sirens were supposed to be. What was it about Jace that made me feel so . . . *human?*

I pulled back and looked up at him, swallowing air. What could I tell him now? He knew something was wrong, but I couldn't tell him the truth.

Jace seemed to see that I was warring with myself. "You have to tell me," he said. It wasn't a demand, but a point of fact. He wasn't going to leave now without knowing what was going on.

I sighed and looked away. "My mom . . ."

Oh god, I couldn't do it. If I told him, he'd be on the phone to Wanda in a heartbeat and I'd be someone's foster kid before year's end.

"What about your mom?" The genuine concern in his eyes was like a weight on my heart.

I hated lying to him like this.

"She's been spending a lot of nights with Phil lately." It gushed out all at once. It wasn't even a half-truth, but the bottom line was the same: she wasn't here and I was alone.

"How many?" He scrutinized me, and I could practically see the social worker cogs turning in his mind.

"Not many," I supplied quickly. "Just, you know, a few a week."

"And you're alone here when she's gone?"

Mostly. Not counting Tempest and Kurt, who didn't count for much these days. I had never let Kurt sleep over while she was gone, even if I was tempted. After our lip tussle in the kitchen, I figured that would be a horrible idea. "Yeah."

"Why didn't you tell me?" he asked, taking my hands in his.

"I didn't want you to worry about me." Perhaps I was being slightly evasive, but it was for his own good and mine.

Jace rubbed at his forehead. "And tonight?"

"Gone," I said. "If she's not home by now, I know she's not coming."

Those words sunk to the pit of my stomach like dead weight, truer than I realized when I spat them out. I knew, if she hadn't returned by now, nearly a month since they took her, then they would never let her go. Summon, Tempest, and I were her only hope, but I didn't know who I could trust anymore. Maybe I was all she had left.

I squeezed my throat around a sob before it could escape.

"Crap," Jace muttered. He looked vexed as he stood and began pacing in front of the sofa.

"What is it?"

"It's just, how am I supposed to leave now? Knowing I'm leaving you here by yourself . . . all night? It feels wrong."

"Oh." Who said chivalry was dead?

Jace stopped and stared at me.

"It's fine, really. I'm getting used to it." I plastered a *see-how-well-adjusted-I-am* smile across my face.

"No, it's not. I just watched you break down in front of me. It's me, Innocence. I know about your nightmares. That means you're here dealing with all that by yourself half the time."

I shrugged.

Jace shook his head. "I can't believe she's doing this to you. What kind of mother leaves her kid alone in the middle of nowhere three to four nights a week?"

The kind who's being held for a murder she didn't commit. The kind who takes the fall for her daughter. I looked down at my hands folded in my lap and hunched my shoulders. I felt small. Insignificant.

"You know Wanda found those pamphlets she gave her in the trash? She has no intentions of getting you any help for your PTSD, does she?"

I frowned in my mother's defense. I couldn't exactly go confessing Salinas to a shrink unless I wanted to end up in a prison cell, too—to say nothing of my mythological heritage. I didn't say this out loud; I wanted Jace to stay, even if it meant he thought less of my mom.

"Come on," Jace said with a sigh, holding his hand out to me.

"Where are we going?" I slipped my fingers into his and stood. "Kitchen," he said, kissing my cheek. "I'll make us dinner while I think of something to tell my parents about tonight."

I rushed through my shower, brushing my teeth with one hand while drying my hair with the other. I settled for damp waves, rubbed apricot lotion across my skin, and threw on my flowery sleep shorts and a loose racerback tank that read *Meow* across the front. Frowning, I wandered downstairs. I hated looking like I maintained the sleepwear selection of a fourth grader. Jace was laid out in front of the television watching a news parody I didn't recognize.

"Do you want me to see if Mom has any of Phil's things here you could borrow?"

His eyes raked over me, and I knew he was totally rethinking this girlfriend thing. First chance I could, I was taking Phil's credit card to Victoria's Secret for some undergarment upgrades.

"Uhhh, no. That's okay. I just need something to brush my teeth with and a place to land. I'm good."

"Okay. Come on up and I'll get you a spare."

I waited outside in the hall while he brushed his teeth, a goofy grin spread across my face. Jace Barnes was in my bathroom right now brushing his teeth to sleep over. Then another thought struck me. How the hell was I supposed to sleep while he was under the same roof?

The door opened and Jace stepped out. His shoes and socks were in one hand. His blue shirt was hung over his other arm, and a thin white undershirt with a V neck was all that separated me from his leanly muscled chest.

"Where do I crash?" he asked.

Right, sleep. "I thought you could take my mom's bed." I pointed to the open door at the end of the hall. "Just leave those in the bathroom. I'm right here if you need anything."

Jace smiled awkwardly. "Sure. You'll be all right? Sleeping, I mean. With the dreams and all?"

I stepped to my doorway and turned around. Jace was hovering behind me anxiously, as though he expected me to start screaming my head off any minute. "Yeah. You know, if you hear anything, just wake me up."

"Can do." He ran both hands through his hair at the same time.

I leaned against my doorframe and looked up at him. His body heat wrapped around me like a hug. "This is really sweet of you, by the way," I told him. "I don't know many people who would care that much."

"Hey, I'm your boyfriend now. It's kind of in the job description—*caring*." His hands slipped into his front pockets, and he gave an easy shrug.

I laughed, feeling the zing of that word—boyfriend—course through me. Was it ludicrous to think I could keep this, *him?* Possibly.

I was probably so deep in denial I was bordering on delusional. But I didn't care. It felt good to forget how scared I really was, to pretend. "Well, anyway, it's sweet."

I rose up on my tiptoes and kissed him lightly on the mouth. He was a delicious mix of sweet mint and salty skin. "Goodnight, Jace."

"Mmmm . . . good night," he said, but neither of us moved, and within a few seconds, my lips were on his again, kissing them slow and sweet. It was different than with Kurt. With Kurt the desire had come as a surprise, a latent reaction, and it didn't run deeper. With Jace a hunger was driving me beyond reason, beyond conscious thought or any feeling other than the need to get as close to him as possible.

I hooked my fingers into the waistline of his jeans and pulled him toward me as I backed into my room, but his hands went up, catching at the doorframe on either side. With effort, he pulled his lips from mine. "Innocence, I can't come in there."

I sighed. "Please. Just for a little while. It'll help me fall asleep."

Jace groaned. "You're killing me, you know that?"

I smiled drowsily at him and gave his jeans another tug. One step in and his right arm fell from the door.

"This is such a bad idea," he said, eyeing me.

Another tug, another step, and his hold on the door broke altogether. Instead, his arms found their way around my waist as I molded my body to his. We toppled onto the bed and Jace caught himself, hovering over me. "You're stunning from this angle," he said with a devilish smirk.

Before I knew what I was doing, my lips were grazing his neck and collarbone.

A groan rumbled in his throat. "Innocence, if you don't stop, I'm not going to be able to hold back."

"So don't hold back," I whispered against his ear, my fingers moving beneath the hem of his shirt. "I want all of you."

Hunger swept him, and he was kissing me with a jolt of untapped passion. My hands were pushing his shirt up, my fingers traced lightly over his ribs, and I felt his body shudder with pleasure against mine.

For a second, there was nothing but Jace. I was losing myself in him. And everything—my mom, sirens, Tempest, all of it—everything but this moment with this boy slipped away. It was the most intoxicating experience of my life. If I could just hold on to him, I could endure the rest of it. Within me the siren was stirring; she wanted this boy more than anything, and she would do whatever it took to have him . . . always.

And then my wrists were being pinned to the mattress, and I couldn't taste Jace anymore. I opened my eyes to see him trembling as he held me, his hands pressing mine to the bed. "Innocence, please . . ."

He sounded out of breath and totally freaked.

I was suddenly mortified. I'd lost complete control in front of him. I pressed my eyes closed and swallowed against the sting of humiliation building inside me. Not to mention, I'd probably been doing it all wrong.

I felt the pressure ease as Jace let go of me and rolled to the side. Then, the caress of one finger down the slope of my nose. "Innocence, open your eyes."

I wanted to shake my head like a stubborn child. I wasn't sure I could look at him again. I must have seemed like some kind of sex-crazed wildcat. I let my eyes flutter open.

He loomed over me, a delicious smile on his face. "Are you okay? I didn't hurt you, did I?"

I shook my head, but I didn't say anything.

"That was . . ." his voice trailed off as he searched for the right word, and I noticed he still sounded huskier than usual.

Horrible. Over the top. Desperate. "Too much?" I tried.

"I was gonna say *incredible.*" He sighed.

"Then why'd you stop?" I asked, completely confused.

"I've never—you make me—uhh, how do I put this? I mean, in a way that doesn't make me sound totally lame."

I scowled. Jace, *lame*?

"I can't think near you," he said at last. "The closer I get, the more my brain shuts down. When you're touching me, it's like no one else exists. When you're *kissing* me? You could be the sun. That's how all-important you seem. I lose all sight of myself."

It sounded just like what I was experiencing. But Jace was brave enough to say it.

"Does any of this make sense?" he asked, uncertainty crossing his face.

"Perfect," I told him. I saw the woman on the cliff once more, and I knew why she held herself out of reach. This was what happened when a siren fell in love. Crushing, all-consuming desire. There were no limits. No controls. No certainty for how it would end.

"Don't get me wrong. It's awesome. And I can't wait to experience every part of you. I mean, *if* you want to and *when* you're ready. But this is so fast; it feels like we're racing off a cliff. I just—I don't want to screw this up."

I raised up on my elbows and kissed him gently, pulling back with effort before I overwhelmed us again. His "cliff" metaphor was more poignant than he'd ever know. "First off, there is no *if*. I'd say I've demonstrated my readiness pretty well already."

Jace swallowed hard.

"But you're right. It's intense. And we should probably give this thing between us some time to stick before we dive in headfirst."

Jace leaned down and kissed the tip of my nose. "You're so cute when you're being rational."

I righted myself on the bed so my head was on the pillow. "Think you can handle a little spooning, Barnes?"

"I'm the champion of spooning," he whispered, and I felt his body shape to mine.

For about five minutes I was perfectly content. And then my fingers began itching to trace circles along the smooth skin of his neck, chest, and shoulders.

"Hey, Jace," I said in a defeated tone.

"Yeah?"

"I'm really trying, but I think you better go to my mom's room."

His breath stirred my hair as he laughed. "Glad I'm not the only one," he said, getting up and retreating to the safety a few walls could provide.

23

My eyes trained on his, unwavering. I felt him fold against me, his own free will giving like wet paper against the force of my frequency.

And then the gun was in his mouth.

And then his finger tensed on the trigger.

And then he dropped from my line of sight.

And then Ray Caldera was dead.

Her fingers worked the pocketknife nimbly, releasing the short blade, and she slid it between my wrists and the black plastic of the zip-tie. But my eyes were trained forward. On the blood spatter on the wall. On the pattern of gore Ray left for me. My work of art.

The only thing stronger than the sickness rising in my throat, which I had to swallow down again and again, was the feeling of satisfaction countering it.

Her arms encircled my head as she untied my gag, and I could smell her saltwater perfume. When I looked down, it wouldn't be her face I saw, staring marble-eyed and lifeless against the floor. That's what mattered.

I sucked in air as the gag left my mouth, working the stiffness from my jaw with shaking fingers. I dared a glance down—just to reassure myself she was alive. He hadn't killed her because I killed him first.

Only, the blood wasn't matting Ray's dark, unkempt hair, but bright blond waves. And it wasn't Ray's crazed, brown eyes that were fixed open. These eyes were aqua blue . . .

I don't know how long I screamed. I was only aware that I was still screaming when Jace finally clamped a hand over my mouth to get me to stop. I bit my tongue until the coppery taste of blood filled my mouth and pressed my quivering fingertips to his face, smoothing them over his cheekbones. Then, I pushed them through his hair until they met at the back of his head.

I had to be sure.

My own face felt hot and sticky from the steady stream of tears. I shook all over like someone with hypothermia. But the night was warm and humid, and the heat of life flushing Jace's skin insisted my vision was not real.

"Y—you're not dead? Not hurt?" I was barely aware of what I was saying as I tried to separate dreaming from waking.

"No, I'm fine. Innocence, please, I'm fine." He used the sheet to wipe some of the wetness from my cheeks.

It only made me cry harder. "I killed you. I saw it. You were dead."

Jace's eyes scrunched, and it was then that I realized he'd turned my lamp on. "It was just a dream. A nightmare." His words were softly spoken, like little caresses against my soul.

I nodded, but I still wasn't sure I believed it. "I was supposed to kill *him*. It's always him. But it was you and—"

"Who?" Jace asked, rubbing my arms briskly to stop me from trembling.

"Ray." I crumpled my hands against my eyes. "I killed Ray. He's dead because of me."

Jace's hands slowed on my arms and eventually stopped. He pried mine away from my eyes and looked at me. "It was just a dream, you understand? It's not real. You couldn't hurt anybody."

But even in the dim light of my bedside lamp, I saw the doubt flicker behind his blue eyes.

I nodded, beginning to gain some control, some awareness. Realizing I'd said too much. Jace tucked himself in beside me, pulling me against his warm, steadily beating chest.

"You poor thing," he kept saying, over and over, as he kissed the top of my head. Until I finally fell back asleep in his arms.

Carefully, I lifted Jace's arm off of me and slid from the bed. I wanted a chance to brush my teeth and hair before he woke. Through the cracks between the blinds, I could see the pumpkin-orange light that indicated dawn was in process outside. We had about an hour before we needed to leave for school.

I pulled a handful of things from my closet and figured I'd sort through them and dress in the bathroom. I cleaned up as quickly as I could and applied a little eyeliner, mascara, and concealer to hide the lavender circles accenting the moody green of my eyes. I vaguely remembered my dream. I remembered screaming and biting my tongue. And I remembered, much as I hated to, telling Jace I had killed Ray.

I could only hope he thought it was more dream gibberish.

Digging through the fast grab of clothes I'd made in the dark, I settled on jeans and a thin boat-neck top and threw them on. I ran downstairs and started a pot of coffee. I inhaled a ripe banana, washing it down with a mouthful of orange juice, and I gave myself a quick once-over in the downstairs mirror before climbing the stairs again to wake Jace up.

Only, when I got to my bedroom door, Jace was no longer in the bed. I stepped inside and saw him standing by my dresser, where my laptop sat open with a blank screen. His back was angled toward me, but his blue shirt was back on and he looked like he'd taken advantage of my time downstairs to brush up for the day, too.

"You're up," I said with a smile.

When he turned at my voice, there was no smile on his face.

Then I noticed what he was holding. In one hand was *Young's*

Concordance and in the other was the paper where I'd worked out Aunt Summon's message. "Innocence?" he said slowly. "What's this?"

I sidled left and he shifted right, like we were circling each other.

"That's private," I told him.

"It was out," he replied.

Touché. Note to self: don't leave Aunt Sum's coded messages lying about when nosy boyfriend sleeps over.

My eyes fixed on the words on the page:

We're different.

You're special.

Not human.

Not killer.

Not girl.

Siren.

God, what must he be thinking? And after last night's murder confession, the word *killer* stood out like exhibit A in a prosecution's case against me. Even if it did say *not* in front of it.

"Jace, I can explain." *Stall. Stall. Stall.*

"I hope so." He scratched at his neck. "I wish you'd finally start explaining something around here to me."

"It's . . . complex."

"I don't care if it's rocket science. I'm tired of you hiding things. Every time I feel like you open up to me about something, it seems there's just another secret to take its place. This, *us*—it's not going to work if I can't trust you."

My breath hitched in my throat. Surely he wasn't breaking up with me already? "You can trust me," I told him, but did I even believe that?

He held the paper up in front of me and the word *Siren* seemed to be screaming from the page. "Can I?"

I gulped. My mind raced over a dozen different ways to begin. But which one was the most likely to keep him from bolting out the door?

The sudden *bam bam bam bam bam!* at the door saved me from having to make a choice yet.

Yes! Kurt to the rescue. "I have to get that," I said, spinning for the stairs before he had a chance to respond.

I was about halfway down when I realized how completely awful this was. Kurt. Here. After Jace spent the night. I'd need a fire hose to keep him from flattening my new boyfriend. If Jace even was my boyfriend anymore.

I ripped the door open before he could start pounding again, but it wasn't Kurt who was beating Phil's door off its hinges. It was worse. Way worse. It was Phil himself.

"Dalliance?" he said weakly, leaning against the wall for support.

He looked terrible. His face was pasty white, like it had been caked in baby powder. And the skin hung loose from the frame of his bones. He'd lost weight. A lot of weight. Gone was the beer gut he'd sported the last time I'd seen him. His comb-over was missing too. In its place, wispy strands of thin, frizzy hair stuck out in all directions, and the gooseflesh of his head sat unprotected. No cowboy hat. No snazzy car salesman duds. He wore—what was he wearing? Was that a night-gown? It looked like one of those hospital gowns that ties in the back. At least he'd managed to drag some velour sweatpants on underneath. And socks.

"Phil?" I stared at him dumbly, not knowing how to react.

His face twisted. "Where is she, you little brat? What have you done with her? Where are you keeping her?" His voice was shrill and fevered.

I reeled from the sudden burst of venom in his words and decided to play dumb. "She—you—she's not with *you?*"

Phil took an unsteady step inside, falling against the wall after he did. My arms shot out to catch him, but he flinched back from my touch. "Keep away from me!"

"Okay, okay," I told him, lifting my hands to show him they were back.

"Dall!" he called pathetically, looking past me toward the kitchen. The sound died in a series of dry coughs.

"Phil, you look like hell. Come sit down." I backed up so he could scoot past me into the den.

He hesitated, peering at me as though he wasn't sure he could trust me, but finally he nodded, his weakness getting the better of him. He pushed himself off the wall and started toward the couch.

I turned to see Jace glaring at me. A few steps in, Phil was going down again. Jace and I raced to his side to help him up. Getting him to the couch, we centered him on the cushions before he flapped me away with his bony arms. It was then that I noticed the hospital bracelet still clamped around his right wrist.

"Phil, are you supposed to be in the hospital?" I was beginning to panic inside. Once he realized Mom wasn't here, where did that leave me? And what would Jace do when he realized she wasn't with Phil, that I'd lied? *Again.*

"They can't help me," he moaned.

Jace cut his eyes at me. "I think I better go call someone."

"No!" Phil shouted, the force in his voice alarming us both. "No one can help me."

"Mr. Strong," Jace said calmly. "You look really sick. I think we better get an ambulance here to take you back."

"There's no going back," he drawled, his eyes whirling around the room before settling on me. "I need her. Do you hear me? I *need* her. Why are you keeping her from me?"

"I'm not," I told him. It was out before I could stop it. Something about the whine and timbre of his broken voice got to me.

"Then where is she?" he begged, his red-rimmed eyes flooding with tears like a child who's lost his favorite toy.

Jace stared down at me, and I knew the jig was up. "In jail," I told them both, my shoulders sagging as the truth flowed out of me.

Phil began coughing again and clutched at his chest, sparing me the tirade of questions I knew Jace was preparing to lob my way.

"Phil, what were you in the hospital for?" I asked him, evading Jace's eyes. Had Dalliance withdrawals done this?

"Heart attack . . ." he muttered. "Surgery."

Christ. No wonder he hadn't come looking for her yet. And then another spine-tingling thought seized me. Could she have done this to him on purpose? Did she use her frequency to stop his heart and buy me time? Was that possible if she were so far away from him? No. I couldn't believe that of her. I wouldn't. I didn't even really think it could be done. But I had only just tasted my frequency. What happened if I pushed it to its limits?

"Shit," Jace said. He sat beside me on the coffee table. "Innocence, we've got to get him help."

"No!" the shout came again. "I'm beyond help. I told you."

I looked at Jace and his eyes dug into mine like an extra conscience. "What can we do?" I mouthed.

He shrugged, but he was looking at me like I should come up with something. I turned to Phil, and my heart wrenched in my chest. He looked like he was dying. And whatever, however it happened, *we* did this to him—my mother and I. To make matters worse, Jace was here, witnessing it all. Seeing just what we were capable of. How could I tell him about my frequency now?

Jace was staring expectantly. Maybe I could use my frequency for good, like when I stopped Kurt from kicking Derek's ass . . . *again.* It was the only thing I knew to do.

"Phil, look at me," I said, squaring my shoulders. The command in my voice was obvious, and he let his eyes rest on mine. He was so weary; I could read it in his gaze. Had he driven himself all this way from the hospital in San Antonio?

"I *need* you to calm down." Phil's hands dropped into his lap obediently.

"What are you doing?" Jace asked.

"Something," I told Jace, before turning back to what little of Phil my mom had left behind.

Phil was weak in every way, but in order to get him to comply, I had to overpower his addiction to my mother. I had to override *her* frequency, which still had some kind of hold on him. The pulse reached out to him and he resisted at first, but his need was too strong. Within minutes, I could feel his addiction transferring to me like a deft tug on an invisible fishing line. It meant I had a new problem on my hands, a *new* Kurt. But at least we could get him some help, and I could buy myself more time. "Here's what we're going to do."

Jace and Phil both stared at me, but Jace's eyes were shifty and alert, where Phil's were transfixed. Jace was afraid. I could taste his adrenaline in the air.

I ignored Jace and honed in on Phil, praying this didn't rub off on him somehow, that he didn't get some kind of contact high from being near me while I used my frequency on someone else, like Mr. Sikes did that day in the hallway with Kurt. "Jace is going to go call an ambulance, and you're going back to the hospital. I'm going to stay here and wait for my mother. Okay? For as long as that takes. And you won't mind, because you want me to be happy, right? You want me to have what I need."

Phil nodded slowly. "As long as it takes," he repeated. "If that's what you need."

I could feel Jace's eyes boring holes into the side of my face, but I ignored them. Instead, I whispered to him from the side of my mouth, "Go get him a glass of water. Once he's calm, we can figure out who to call."

I felt him stand next to me and take a few steps out of the room.

I reached out and put my hand over Phil's. "You're going to get better," I told him, imprinting this on him as my will.

His hand gripped mine. "Of course. You need me."

I swallowed, but there was no going back now. The truth was, every time I used my frequency, it was like flexing a cramped muscle. It felt wonderful. "That's right. I do need you. I need you to be well. And I need you to go back to work. And I need you to let me live here. Okay?"

"When can I see you again?" he breathed.

"When you're better. You can bring me some money next month, and we'll go from there. But around other people, I'm your stepdaughter. And we're not going to tell anyone else my mom is in jail. Except your attorney, who you're going to call for me in the morning. Can you remember that?"

Phil's fingers crushed mine together until it hurt. "Anything for you."

I winced and pulled my hand away just as Jace rounded the corner into the room, a tall glass in one hand.

"Here's the water," he said, but he saw me as I was leaning back, and his eyes fell on my right hand, cradled in my lap.

Bright pink finger marks could be seen across my still-pale skin where the blood flow had been squeezed off.

Phil's fingers.

24

I needed a minute to catch my breath and untangle my thoughts. The only reason I wasn't in full-blown panic mode was because Jace was there. Or was it me? I'd had to push past my panic so many times in the past few weeks, maybe I was getting better at it. But my minute would have to wait.

The door began hammering immediately after Jace's call. He looked at me over the phone in his hand. "Expecting someone?"

No. I went to the door, knowing the only person I'd really care to see—Aunt Summon—wouldn't bother to knock. "Mr. Sikes?" My algebra teacher was standing on the porch with his shirtfront untucked and a large diagonal tear in the thigh of his khaki slacks. He was bent over and out of breath.

"That's a—whew—tall fence," he said between breaths, squinting his eyes behind his glasses.

"Is there some reason you're at my house instead of my school?" I crossed my arms. This was just getting to be too much.

He straightened and peered behind me. "Well, you've been absent. I didn't know if you were okay."

I shook my head. *Unbelievable.*

I felt, more than saw, Jace walk up behind me. "Hey . . . Mr. Sikes?"

Glancing over my shoulder, I saw that my on-again/off-again/on-again boyfriend was as confused as I was.

"Is this something you do for all your students who miss two days of class?" I asked him.

My algebra teacher pulled his shocked expression from Jace back to me. He seemed perplexed. "Well, now that you ask, *no*. But—"

"Did it ever occur to you that hopping a game fence to get onto gated property might be considered trespassing?" I asked tightly. Jace squeezed my shoulder as if to say *be nice*.

"B—but you're a student," he stammered. "We—"

And there it was. The proof that somehow my algebra teacher had been siren-ized by my frequency on the sly. "There is no *we*, Mr. Sikes."

His eyes were round and blinking like an owl's behind his glasses. "You can't mean that, Innocence. After everything . . ."

I felt Jace's hand tighten on my shoulder. There's no telling what tawdry images Mr. Sikes's words were conjuring in his mind. "I do. And what I really need right now is for you to leave."

I hoped the magic word—*need*—would be enough.

"Is it him?" he responded with a sneer in Jace's direction.

No such luck.

"Who, me?" Jace questioned from over my shoulder.

"Has this Adonis seduced you with his youth and vigor?" Mr. Sikes punctuated each word with heavy consonants, practically spitting at Jace as he talked.

Whatever had lured my algebra teacher into my orbit, it wasn't enough to push him out of it. I needed to deliberately use my will to get him to back down, but I had an audience and my mom's ex in the living room. I didn't know if using my frequency on Mr. Sikes would affect Phil, and Phil was so fragile already.

"Please just go!" I whined, careful that nothing else slipped out with the words as I covered my face with my hands.

"Hey! You heard her! Go!" I heard the third voice approaching from behind my teacher, and I knew it all too well.

This. Was. Not. Happening.

"Kurt? Kurt Meier?" Mr. Sikes sounded completely befuddled.

I peered through my fingers to see Kurt running up the drive, brandishing the key I'd given him over his head where it sparkled in the sunlight.

"Let myself in," he said as he stepped onto the porch.

"You gave him a key?" Jace asked behind me, his hand slipping from my shoulder.

I spun to face him. "I can explain."

His brows arched high, but before I could get the words out, Kurt interjected.

"Hey, what's Barnes doing here?"

This was my fault. Every bit of it. I'd made this mess with my inherited mojo. Using my frequency might feel good, but it also made it harder to rein it back. Once it was out, it was out, and my panic this morning must have sent a wave of it big enough to reach the school. Now I had to clean it up the old-fashioned way. "Kurt, please leave."

He shoved his way in front of Mr. Sikes. "Nuh-uh. No how. Where have you been? I backed off like you asked. I gave you space. But I didn't do it so you could skip class with Jace Barnes!"

His finger was pointed dangerously close to my face, and I leaned back as he jabbed it at me while he talked.

"Watch it, Kurt," Jace said in a low voice behind me.

I put an arm out as if to hold him back. "Listen. Everyone's going to calm down. All right? This is just all a big misunderstanding."

Kurt puffed his chest out and inched toward the threshold. "The only misunderstanding is Barnes thinking he can get with my girl."

"*Your* girl?" Jace howled, pressing against me as he rose to Kurt's challenge. "Innocence is my girlfriend, asshat. Why don't you go back to your cheerleader sandwich?"

"I beg your pardon!" Mr. Sikes erupted, shouldering himself a step ahead of Kurt. "I'm the one who's been taking care of her!"

At this point, all three of them were pressing in so close around me I could barely draw a breath. If I didn't do something fast, I was going to get pounded by six different fists at once when they all started swinging. But they weren't exactly listening to reason at the moment. "Kurt, you're a good friend, but Jace is—"

I never got the rest out.

Kurt gave Mr. Sikes a hard shove, sending him to the ground between us, while he reached for Jace. Mr. Sikes crumpled against my legs, causing my knees to buckle. I fell left against the door but managed to stay upright. Just in time to miss Jace's swing, which connected with a hard crack against Kurt's square jaw.

Unfortunately, it wasn't enough to level Kurt to the boards of the porch. He stumbled back but retaliated quickly, intending to send Jace flying backward but clipping my chin in the process. It interrupted his momentum and helped Jace stay on his feet but also caused me to cry out in pain.

"Look what you did, you dick!" Kurt yelled, as though it was Jace's fault somehow.

"Me?" Jace shouted back. "You hit her!"

"Enough!" another fierce voice cried as a loud crack split the air like a gunshot. No, not like a gunshot, I realized suddenly. It *was* a gunshot. I couldn't see through the tangle of limbs, but I didn't need to. I would know that voice anywhere, even if it had been a few weeks since I heard it last.

"Everyone take five steps back, now!"

Instantly I felt the pressure of bodies ease around me as Kurt and Jace disengaged, and poor Mr. Sikes scrambled to his feet. They all wore terrified expressions.

Kurt and my algebra teacher parted like the sea, and I could make out her fiery halo of blowing red waves and the tight pull of her beautiful features. Aunt Summon was marching up the drive in a pair of old cowboy boots and a printed sundress, with a hunting rifle aimed at the sky. And she looked pissed.

At nearly six feet tall with her leanly muscled limbs all exposed, hair to rival a Celtic queen the likes of Boudicca, and enough attitude to give a rattlesnake a run for its money, she was a daunting figure. And brandishing the rifle didn't hurt.

Clomping onto the porch, she pushed her way past Kurt and Mr. Sikes and grabbed me by the arm, pulling me close. "I suggest you two find somewhere else to be. *Fast.*"

Mr. Sikes straightened his glasses and glared at her. "Innocence, do you know this woman?"

"Do you know that it's legal to shoot trespassers in the state of Texas?" Summon shot back.

"It's okay," I assured him. "She's my aunt."

Summon lowered the rifle and poked it into his belly. "That's right. So back off, Tubby."

Mr. Sikes scowled but began stepping backward from the rifle until he was off the porch, at which point he turned and ran down the drive toward the gate.

Kurt smirked.

Summon swung the rifle in Kurt's direction and his hands flew up. "You, too, Jock Itch. Scram."

His brows lowered menacingly, but he began backing off as well.

"Wait," I called before he got too far. "I need the key."

Kurt looked from me to Summon, who held the rifle firmly trained on him. "Just drop it," she snapped.

He reached in a pocket and fished it out, letting it clatter to the ground as he continued backing up. Summon didn't budge until we heard the rumble of his truck starting and watched it vanish up the road.

Then, with an unexpected force, she spun on us both and shoved the rifle at Jace.

"Whoa!" he hollered, jumping back a foot.

Summon's eyes narrowed. "Hit the pavement, kid. I'm taking care of Innocence now."

I placed a hand on top of the gun barrel and pushed it down gently. "No, Aunt Summon. Not Jace. He's cool. He's with me."

She cut her eyes at me carefully. "When you say *with* . . ."

"Sum, please don't shoot my boyfriend," I clarified.

That seemed to satiate her. That and Jace's petrified expression. She set the rifle down, leaning it against the doorframe, and caught me up in a swift hug. "Boy, am I glad to see you, Songbird!"

25

"I can't believe you're starting your own brood, you sly little devil!" Summon clapped me on the shoulder cheerily after setting me down. Pushing past me, she eyed Jace on her way to the sofa, throwing me a *not bad* wink over her shoulder. But she came up short when she found Phil stretched out looking pathetic.

Summon blinked at me. "Innocence, what's going on here?"

"Why don't you tell me?" I stormed. "I didn't know you were coming. Where have you been all this time? Why did you send Tempest, and why is Tempest pretending to be you to the police? What are you doing to help Mom?" I had about a million more questions loaded, aimed, cocked, and ready to fire, but Summon interrupted me.

"Whoa, whoa, whoa! One thing at a time. What's all this you're saying?" Summon's face contorted with perplexity.

Phil moaned from the sofa.

Jace crossed his arms. "Yeah. I'd like to hear this, too."

My stomach dropped somewhere deep and sour where the light couldn't reach it, like the Mariana Trench. I focused on Summon. "You mean you don't know?"

She drew a deep breath. "Know what? All I know is that I haven't been able to get a hold of my sister for the last several weeks. At first, I thought she was just really pissed at me about Tempest. But then I got scared, thought you both might have hit the road again without telling me. That's why I came. I was checking to see if you were still here."

"But . . . you texted me. Didn't you get my voice mails?" My mind was flooded with so many sick possibilities at once, I couldn't keep up.

"Bird, what voice mails? All I got from you were a few texts about hating school and missing me."

Something was not adding up here. "I-I called. I left voice mails. I thought . . . I mean, Tempest said—"

Summon held up a hand to stop me. "What does Tempest have to do with this?"

Jace watched us both silently, his own face registering what I was just beginning to piece together.

"You didn't know she was staying here?"

Summon laughed. "Honey, your mother would sooner flay that girl than let her stay under the same roof."

The force of the realization pinned me to the floor. She didn't know. Summon really didn't know anything. This whole time.

Summon's eyes seemed to read something of what was happening in my brain. Her expression cratered and guilt flash crossed it. "Oh, Songbird. What's happened?"

I sunk into the armchair. "I'm so sorry, Sum. I thought you knew. It's Mom. They've taken her."

My aunt's eyes went wide as silver dollars. "Bird, where is my sister?"

It took the better part of an hour and another glass of wine to fill Summon in on everything she'd missed. Jace quietly listened in while I spilled the details, everything from Mom's arrest, to Tempest's "business trips," to decoding her message, to Phil showing up here after his heart attack. I finished with the brawl she'd just witnessed on the front porch, the results of my frequency gone wrong.

Summon pinched the bridge of her nose, sighed hard, and then cut her eyes at me. "Bird, I owe you an apology. A big one. When I couldn't reach Dall, when I thought—well, let's just say I am the world's worst aunt. If anything had happened to you, anything at all, it would have been my fault. I couldn't have lived with that." Her voice cracked. She patted my knee and blinked back the tears that were trying to push themselves to the surface. "Being with you would mean giving up a lot for me, but you're worth it. I hope you know that. I would never pick my brood over you. Not when you really needed me."

I nodded, choking down my own tears. I didn't realize until now, until I heard her say that, how much it had hurt me to think she'd left me to figure this out alone.

"And we're going to free my sister, understand? Together."

"But how?" My voice was high and full of air, inflated with disbelief.

Summon narrowed her eyes on me. "Let me work on that. But trust me, okay? There is nothing they can do to hold your mother in there. Not if she wants out. Not if we want her out. I don't know what would've possessed her to confess, except her love for you. But I'll get to the bottom of it. I promise you that."

I looked up at her, grateful to finally hear the Summon I knew and loved. Everything would be okay.

She grinned. "Now are you going to explain the three men ready to kill one another and you, too, on your porch?"

I started to answer, but realized I didn't have one. Maybe Summon was right and my frequency was pulling together my own little web of caretakers.

"You stopped them," Jace said to her. "The same way Innocence—you can control them. Part of being a . . . a siren."

Summoned glanced up at him as if she was just noticing him again since the hallway, as if she just realized he was more than furniture. "Correction. I stopped them with my Ruger M77. Never hurts to keep a little firepower around when you're managing a brood." She spun on me. "You told your *genesis* about what we are? Are you sure that's wise?"

Her voice was a loud whisper from the corner of her mouth, as though Jace weren't right there and couldn't hear her as plainly as I could.

I shook my head. Brood, genesis—what the hell was she talking about? "What's a genesis?" I asked before she could throw out any other new vocabulary words I didn't understand.

"Christ," she muttered, looking at the floor. "You know nothing. Tempest was here and she didn't tell you about any of this?"

I shook my head. It seemed Tempest left a lot out, and most of what she did tell me wasn't true.

"She's been playing us both. Your mother was right not to trust her. Me and my bleeding heart."

I looked at Jace, his face a carefully sculpted blank. Did I want him hearing this?

Summon seemed to follow my train of thought. "Look, right now, I've got to deal with that man in the living room. Get him back to the hospital before he's missed and traced here. Why don't you see your gen—I mean, your boyfriend—out while I work on Phil. Then you can ride with me to the hospital. We'll talk on the way."

I nodded at Summon. Jace opened his mouth to protest but shut it quickly when my aunt turned her no-nonsense expression on him. He followed me out the door.

We walked slowly down the drive, each wondering where to even begin.

"So, as if PTSD weren't enough, now I'm supposed to believe that you're a siren?"

"It's just a word. One we got pegged with a long time ago. I'm not out of a fairytale, I'm flesh and blood. It's more scientific than the mythology would have you believe. We just—we emit waves, like a frequency, that other people can . . . pick up on." At his increasingly incredulous expression, I added, "I'll explain everything to you when I can, but right now, my mom—"

"That's another thing. Why didn't you tell me the truth about your mom?"

"How could I? You heard me in there. I barely know what's happening myself." I cut my gaze over to him, just in time to see his sigh.

"But you know more than you're telling. More than you're telling *me*, anyway."

"What's that supposed to mean?" I knew being defensive wouldn't help my case any, but I couldn't help it.

"I don't know," he said with a shrug. "Maybe you're talking to Kurt."

I rolled my eyes. "Talking to Kurt is about as intimate and personal as talking to a bag of rocks."

Jace laughed in spite of himself. "Well, at least I know we're on the same page there."

I was surprised he still wanted to be on the same *anything* with me. I looked at him, hoping he'd see the earnestness in my eyes. "I wanted to share everything with you, but I didn't even know where to start."

Jace reached out and brushed his fingertips across the top of my hand. "Well, let's start with what you *do* know. What you did in there with Phil—that was your *frequency?*" He tried the word out like he was tasting something for the first time, with curiosity in his eyes and tension in the muscles of his face.

"Yeah, more or less."

"And that's what exactly? Some kind of mind control? Hypnotrance stuff?"

I shrugged. "I guess. I don't really know. Tempest never explained very much. And you saw how cryptic Summon's message was."

He nodded, taciturn again.

"I think it's more than that," I said after a few seconds. "It's not a parlor trick. Not that stuff Criss Angel does on TV. There's more to it, but I don't know what exactly. It sounds scary, but it feels natural, good even."

He nodded again. "Have you . . ." he paused, feeling his way forward carefully. "Have you ever used it on me?"

"No!" God, no wonder he was so quiet. He probably thought everything between us was a lie. Could I promise it wasn't? "I mean, not intentionally. I think it works on its own though sometimes. Like a low-level hum or something. So, I don't know for sure if . . ."

"If that's what's between us?" He picked at a spot on his shirt, carefully avoiding my eyes.

I sighed. "Yeah. On your part."

"And on yours?"

I looked at him, his eyes round and blank, expectant maybe. Did it matter what I felt for him if everything he felt for me was fake?

"Of course not. It doesn't influence me." But then I remembered Kurt's kiss in the kitchen, and how good it felt to see myself through him. Still, that was nothing compared to what Jace made me feel, even with just a look.

I put a hand out tentatively and let my fingers rest on his. "How I feel about you, Jace? It's genuine. There's nothing artificial about what you do to me. And, for what it's worth, I've never felt that for anyone before. With or without the frequency."

He didn't speak.

"Say something," I begged after a moment, unable to contain myself. "Please."

Jace rubbed his palms over his face and crossed his arms, his brows pulled tight over his guarded eyes. I wasn't used to that. Jace's eyes were many things, but never guarded.

"I don't know what to say," he answered.

I'd just gutted myself for him—the least he could do was respond. "Start with what you know," I said.

"Let's see. I just found out that the girl I'm in love with is practically a fugitive, may have killed someone, and can mind-warp men into doing just about anything she wants. That she's been using people to get by like her mother taught her, and that she *likes* it. That she doesn't even believe she's human. Oh, and that whatever was growing between us may amount to nothing more than a steaming pile of siren song bullshit."

He sounded angry. Real angry. And hurt. And scared. And about a dozen other things that I couldn't pick out at the moment because I was reeling from his words as if he'd just punched me in the stomach. My mouth fell open, but there was nothing I could say to that. I closed it again with a click of my teeth.

Then, out of all the angry words, six of them floated up like a bubble of hope in a bottomless well of despair: *the girl I'm in love with . . .*

"You love me?" My voice was like a child's, disbelieving and frayed.

Jace's eyes were hard as turquoise nuggets, and his jaw muscles feathered when they clenched. "I thought I did," he said, looking away. "But how can I know anymore?"

That was just it. He couldn't.

And neither could I.

26

I came back in to find Aunt Summon rooting around in the freezer.

"He gone?" she asked.

"Yeah." I tried to hold it in, but my chin quivered anyway and the tears came.

"Oh honey," she cooed, patting the counter next to her with one hand. I hopped up obediently. She pressed a frozen bag of mixed veggies to my chin where Kurt had caught me. "Keep this here," she instructed.

I nodded, remembering the throb I'd felt earlier and letting the cool bag numb my face and heart.

"He'll be back," she told me then. "They always come back."

"I don't know. He was really angry."

"It's risky telling a genesis the truth—tempting, but risky. They don't always take it well. It's enough just asking them to share you with the brood."

Keeping the bag to my chin I said, "You mean, like your man-harem? Sam and all the others. That's a brood?"

She narrowed her gaze on me. "No wonder they were about to cream each other when I got here."

I laughed in spite of myself.

"Come on," Summon said, helping me down from the counter. "What do you say we deliver Mr. Strong in there back to the ER in San

Antonio? Maybe we can stop for margaritas after. I'd say you've earned a cold one after today—my treat."

We managed to dump Phil onto a gurney in the trauma center of a San Antonio hospital and sneak out again thanks to Summon's frequency and the male orderly who saw us in. On the way over, Summon worked on Phil, shifting his need to her, talking him through what he would do next, how he would let us stay in the house in Stonetop. We skipped the margaritas and headed home afterwards, too tired for much else. Summon tried Tempest's number on the drive back, but she didn't pick up.

"That girl . . ." she growled under her breath.

"Why didn't Mom trust her? Mom was so angry when she saw you were letting Tempest stay with you. But we never got a chance to talk about it."

"Bird, your mom's bad blood with your cousin and your Aunt Florid goes a long way back, all the way back to your daddy."

"Aleister?"

Summon nodded. "He was murdered. Brutally. And the way he died. There are similarities."

"Similarities? To?"

"Ray."

"I don't understand," I told her. "How?"

"It was another siren who did it, Songbird. Or made him do it to himself. Maybe more than one. Your mother was heartbroken. She'd lost the only possible love of her life, and she'd been betrayed by her own kind."

"But why? Why would a siren kill my father?"

"He was helping your mother. Or trying to, at least. Bird, your dad was brilliant, and charming, and very, *very* good looking. He was also your mother's null."

Another new vocab word I'd have to learn. "Come again?"

"A null—a nullifier or nullifying agent. It's just a term we use. It means someone who's immune to the frequency. A man who can't be a target." Summon tapped her fingers on the steering wheel, beating out the rhythm of a silent tune. "Anyway, supposedly every siren has at least one, but it's pretty uncommon for them to find each other. Your mom got lucky, I guess."

"Siren lotto?" I quipped.

She gave me a small smile. "Something like that."

"Would that be a problem? Enough of a problem to kill him?"

"No, but his research was. Because your mother had no power over him, your dad could get close to her in ways other men couldn't. He sympathized with your mother's 'condition.' And being the brilliant scientist he was, he was desperately curious. He wanted to know more about our family, about sirens. He wanted to get to the bottom of what was happening with the frequencies and how we were different from other women genetically."

"And that was a bad thing?"

Summon patted my leg. "Some people thought so."

"Some sirens, you mean."

"Yes. Your Aunt Florid chief among them. They weren't wrong to be afraid. I told Dall she was playing with fire. Your dad was a good man—he wanted to help. But in the wrong hands, his research could be very, very dangerous. Not just to our survival, but to the world at large."

"I don't get it. Why would it be so dangerous?"

She laughed dryly. "You see? That's the problem. I can't begin to explain your dad and your mom to you, our family history, until you have a firm understanding of your legacy. It won't make any sense."

"Start with the basics then, with sirens. What they, er, *we* are. Tempest never really elaborated. We're not half bird, and we're not half fish."

"No. We're all women, just . . ."

She seemed to be having trouble. So, I tried another angle. "Well, what are the frequencies exactly?"

"Can't say with a hundred percent certainty. It's not like there's been a lot of scientific research into the phenomenon. We kind of have to fly under the radar. That's where things got tricky with your father."

"But you have an idea," I said, hoping.

"A few. I mean, obviously it has to do with manipulating energy, and all energy is vibration. Creating the illusion that you are everything a man has ever wanted, even when each man is looking for something different from the next and there's only one you. But it's more than that. Your mom and I think that the frequencies work on several levels at once. That they adapt our pheromones to each individual. That they set off an explosive release of hormones and chemicals within the bodies of our prey, for lack of a better term. All the good feelings—dopamine, serotonin, oxytocin, to name a few. The frequencies also heighten our senses, probably through an adrenaline reaction of some kind, to feed us a host of details about our targets, helping us adjust energetically to each of them with the finesse of a silk glove. All the while, that connection allows our targets to tune into us, too. To know what we need sometimes even before we do. So they can provide it. And that connection grows stronger with increased contact—speaking, sight, touch. Touch is always the most powerful."

This was explaining so much. All the tiny details I picked up on the men around me, how someone like Kurt could think of someone like me as his perfect mate. Maybe even my PTSD. Yes, I'd suffered a trauma that haunted me, but this adrenaline spike could easily be exacerbating those symptoms, maybe even mimicking some of them. "Is that all?"

"We also know it interferes with brain wave patterns. Your dad recorded higher cycles of theta brain waves in men your mother was actively influencing. But the majority of this is conjecture, you understand. The most research done on it was conducted by your father, and he isn't exactly available to share anymore. And his research was stolen by his killers."

I suppressed a snarl and a shiver at the same time. So my dad was a null, immune to my mother's frequency. And he was the only person in history to research sirens. Was he researching me, too? Did he even know about me when he died?

"So, what's a genesis and why did you call Jace that?"

Summon rubbed absently at her forehead, her eyes transfixed on the highway. "It's the first, you know? When you form a brood. It's kind of like an alpha. We call them a genesis."

"I think—I think I've made some mistakes, and I need to figure out how to fix them. Without using the frequency anymore," I added.

Summon smirked. "It's not a switch, Songbird. You can't turn it off and on. There's not a plug inside you can pull for all that power to drain away. If I hadn't arrived when I did, you would have been a casualty of your own miscalculation."

I scowled but didn't respond.

Aunt Summon turned to me, an authoritative gleam in her eye. "You can focus it. With your eyes, with your hands, with your mind. You can direct it. But it's never gone, never dormant even. It's autonomous. Like your heart beating, or breathing, or digestion. It's always there, always acting and ensuring your survival. At least on some level."

If I didn't know better, I'd almost say Summon's tone was bitter. "But Mom's kind of a loose cannon," I said. "She didn't kill Ray, I did. She couldn't. She was too weak. And she doesn't hold a lot of control over her frequency. I think if she could have spared most of those men the side effects of loving her, she would have."

Summon shrugged. "Those were the finer points your dad was working on. He thought he could provide Dalliance with some level of control. Some way to turn it off and on. He thought his own ability to resist her, his genetic makeup as a null, was the key to an antidote, if you will, for both sirens and their targets. Being one of us isn't easy, but it's doubly hard for someone like your mother. No one can ever get too close. Anyway, he never got very far."

"Sounds lonely," I said.

"He was the first man, the only man, who could tolerate her indefinitely, who could really get next to her. The only one she could let in. She fell for him . . . *hard*. She loved him, not just for what he was—her null—but for who he was."

I let everything she was saying settle over my mind, but one thing kept prickling at my conciousness. "You said we can't turn the frequency on and off, but I can," I confessed. "I can control it. I can concentrate my frequency willingly if I try."

Summon studied me before speaking again. "Maybe. Some people can think a certain thought to slow or speed up their heart rate. Some can hold their breath for impossible amounts of time. It takes training. Discipline. But it's not the same thing as total conscious control.

"Your mom had a theory. Because you were Aleister's child, the only known offspring between a siren and her null, she thought perhaps you could choose to turn it off and live as a human would. I'm not sure I agree with her though. Can you honestly say you are able to completely shut it down for whole periods of time?"

I thought about Mr. Sikes and Kurt and the way they gravitated to me before I intended for anything to happen between us. Was Jace like that? "I don't know," I admitted with an ounce of regret. "Why do you keep referring to humans like you're not one, like I'm not?"

Summon glanced my way and turned back to the road. "Ever hear the term parthenogenesis?"

I shook my head.

"Did you know that at least seventy different vertebrate species can reproduce without male fertilization?"

I wasn't exactly ahead in my science credits. More head shaking.

"What about hybridization? Or interspecies breeding? Surely you've seen a mule?" Summon leaned forward in her seat.

"I knew a kid in Corpus who was raising one for FFA."

"Hybridization happens all the time, and has been for ages. It's one of the many wonders of evolution. Take a good, hard look at yourself," she said, flipping down my visor.

I stared at my reflection in the little mirror.

"You look more or less like any other girl in high school, right?"

I shrugged my assent.

"You're not. Hybrids are typically difficult to detect because of their physical resemblance to a parent species."

"What are you implying exactly?" I asked, getting more and more uncomfortable with where this was leading. I'd rather not think of myself as a special episode on *Wild Kingdom.*

"You see, the problem with parthenogenesis, or any asexual reproduction, is that the narrower the gene pool gets, the murkier the waters. And the problem with hybrids is that they're not always fertile. Two lefts don't always make a right, so to speak. We just found a way through Mama Nature's loopholes."

"You mean . . ." But I couldn't quite bring myself to say it.

So she said it for me. "We're a separate species."

27

"You see why I wanted to stick with the basics for now?" Summon said with a withered look as we trudged back into the lodge. I dropped onto the sofa, reeling with the biology lesson I'd received in the car.

"You mean scrambling men's brains like eggs in a pan? Those basics? How can you talk about this so casually?"

"It's not as bad as it sounds," Summon said, whirling to face me. "It's all designed by millennia of evolution to meet our biological requirements. It's survival. A symbiotic relationship that meets everyone's needs. We care for our mates generally."

"Generally?"

Summon sunk into the chair across from me and looked away. "Occasionally there are . . . anomalies."

"Anomalies." I swallowed. "Like mom. Like Florid. Like me."

"And maybe like Tempest."

"What do you mean?"

"Your mother always thought Florid and Tempest were the only ones strong enough to pull off your father's murder. Besides herself. She blamed them, feared them. But Tempest was so young then, just a kid. I could believe it about Florid, but not her, not a child. I supported your mother in her theory about Florid, but I told her to leave Tempest out of it. Being born to a psycho was a sentence, not a crime. She'd been punished enough already. But now I wish I'd listened to your mom. Tempest obviously hasn't been living as clean as she'd have me think."

"So we're really like them? Mom and me? We have the same *condition?*"

Summon blew out a long breath. "Your Great Aunt Florid is a chapter unto herself in the Byrd family saga. But your mother, Bird, she's not like Florid. Yes, she is an anomaly. Her frequency is unusually strong. Dangerously so. But she's not a sociopath. And neither are you."

"Aren't I?" I looked out the window, the dusky drape of night falling around us. "After what I did to Ray . . ."

Summon grabbed my hands in hers and shook my arms until I turned back to face her. "You did what you had to, Bird. Survival. It's no different than someone shooting an intruder in their home. Okay? It was self-defense. The only difference was *how*. And you're a damn good example of what I've been trying to tell your mother for years: having a frequency that powerful, being what you are, it's not all bad. And it doesn't make you bad. In that particular case, with Ray outside of Salinas, it saved two lives."

"By taking another," I whispered.

"So what? Are three deaths somehow better than one?" Summon's eyes searched mine, trying to make me see her logic.

"But it was her fault he was like that. Ours." Ray had been a normal man until we came into his life. Well, not exactly normal, but not psychotic.

"Honey, there wasn't much redeeming about Ray Caldera. Your mom had no business getting tangled up with such a worthless cause, and I told her so. But she was desperate, and after your father . . . well, she was always trying to find a way to redeem herself. She may have blamed Florid and Tempest for the murder, but she blamed herself, too. She couldn't help what she was, but she was always looking for a way to make some good out of her power. Leave men better than she found them. I'm not saying what happened to Ray was right. I'm just saying he was a weak character with a weak mind long before your momma bumped into him."

I pushed the intruding thoughts of Phil yesterday from my mind. "Is that why Mom couldn't live with you? Or me? Because of her, *our*, frequency?"

"More or less," Summon said. "It's been our way for generations. We stick together when we can. The one with the strongest frequency usually handles the brood. The other frequencies sort of submit to that one, supporting it instead of competing with it. But Dall's is so powerful, she can't stick with any man too long, or he ends up on the receiving end of a syringe of Risperdal. She couldn't maintain a brood like that. So we had to split up. She wanted me to have a chance at a normal life. Normal for us, anyway." Summon winked at me. "And then you came along. And anomaly or not, she needed to protect you. To keep your existence a secret from whoever killed Aleister. So you see, it never would have worked. But it wasn't because we didn't want it to."

My shoulders slumped and I tucked my knees up against my chest. My poor mother. What kind of existence was this? And like it or not, my heart cracked a little for Tempest, too. She'd told me how our family lived, the unfairness of it. "Tempest said her mother wasn't bad for wanting a different life."

"She wasn't. She was bad for the kind of life she wanted and how she chose to get it, no matter what Tempest says."

"She said she took something from Grandma Byrd. Something important." I was pushing her for details, trying to place where Tempest, my mom, Florid, and I all fit into this bizarre equation. Was I on the good side of our family tree, or the bad side?

"She did," Summon told me. "She took her genesis."

"You mean an affair?"

"Against his will," she added.

"She used her frequency to make him choose her over Harmonious?"

Summon's eyes clouded over the way my mother's sometimes did. "Exactly. Florid and my mother had been arguing over her frequency again. Even though she was supposed to use her power in a supporting role, Florid was always rebelling and using it to get her way. The other sisters wanted her gone, but our mother stood up for her. We had never tossed out one of our own, she told them. It wasn't the Byrd way. We took care of our family. Always."

"So what went wrong?"

"The way I heard it from my own Aunt Grace, your great-aunt, Harmonious was at the end of her rope. Florid had been sneaking out to meet a man in town—a married one. He bought her things, and she used him to get what she wanted. She enjoyed the sport of it all, even when he turned up with a shotgun at their property, threatening to shoot anyone who came between him and his love. He was deranged. He thought Florid would run away with him. There was a fight and he was shot, but one of the brood was arrested for it. They were small then, just trying to get by. And an innocent man was going to prison because Florid wanted to be the center of attention."

"What did Grandma Byrd do about it?"

Summon rubbed at her forehead. "The only thing she could. She threatened Florid, threatened to kick her out if she didn't stop making trouble."

"And that's when Florid turned on her?"

Summon nodded. "She seduced her genesis using the frequency, and then she made him kill himself before fleeing to a neighboring city. They found his body hanging the next morning in the barn. Our mother never recovered from the heartbreak."

Tempest had failed to mention those finer points. And here I'd been feeling sorry for her and her mom, buying into their sob story.

No wonder my mother thought Florid was responsible for my father's murder. "And Tempest? Where did she come into all this?"

"That was her father. Turns out Florid got pregnant from her little act of revenge. She tried to mooch money off a few distant relatives. When that didn't work because no one would take her in, she made her own way. At first, I think it was a lot like your mom and you. But eventually, she found she could get more from killing than just using her targets. She stole, she took money to kill, and she left a trail of unsolvable crimes in her wake, dragging Tempest along for the ride."

I was horrified. However bad I'd thought I had it all those years on the road with my own mom, I suddenly felt incredibly grateful. What we did, what we were, it was hard. It sucked in a lot of ways. But we wanted to be better, do better. We were good people underneath. My mom always tried to leave them *before* they were too far gone. She just miscalculated with Ray.

What kind of gene pool did I emerge from?

I pinched the bridge of my nose and squeezed my eyelids tight. Now that I knew so much more, there were huge chunks of it I wished I could forget. All my life, my real father was just a mystery, a giant question mark that barely registered on my conscious thoughts. Then he became someone I could name. A person. Like me. Only, I wasn't just a person. I was more. Different. And so was everyone I was related to. Because of what we were, what Florid was, my dad didn't even know I existed or was ever born at all. She stole him from me, just like she stole from Grandma Byrd and my mother.

Summon said my mother left as soon as she heard about his murder. She didn't want anyone to suspect she might be pregnant. She didn't want to risk the murderers coming after me next. If my mom's suspicions were to be believed, Florid's personal vendetta against our family, *her* family, found the perfect outlet in my dad's research. Killing my dad was just another way to take a stab at us. And once she started, who was to say she would stop? My mother ran to keep me safe. And thus our life on the road was born alongside me.

"Wine?" Summon's voice was in my ear too soon, and I heard the dull thud of her footsteps retreating to the kitchen for a little liquid comfort.

I gripped my knees, Florid's tale of killing sprees swirling in my stomach. I opened my eyes and blinked. Nope. Not a nightmare. "Pass," I told her.

Summon returned to her seat, wine in hand, and somewhere between us, less visible than the steam rising on the air, was my mother, Tempest, Florid, masquerading as ghosts.

"All this time, all this running, and it's been from our own family. Why do they hate her so much? Why would they want to kill us?"

Summon gave me a pitiful glance and sighed. "Florid never was a fan of competition, and your mother is the only other siren we know of who was strong enough to oppose her. Maybe she feared retaliation for killing Aleister. Who knows? Psychopaths don't need the same reasons we do to justify their actions. Your mom was afraid it would hurt you too much to know the truth. And that it would place you in greater danger. She really believed you had a shot at a normal existence."

"Do you think she would really confess to Ray's murder? Tempest made it sound like she was going to be convicted, but she wouldn't, right?"

"Oh, Songbird." She combed long, elegant fingers through her untamed hair. "I think your mom would do that and then some to protect you."

"How does that protect me? How does abandoning me keep me safe?"

"I know you're angry, Bird. And you have every right to be. But please try to understand, everything she's ever done has been for you. Even if it doesn't seem like it. Even if you don't understand how. Okay?"

I nodded, sniffling.

Summon pursed her lips and nodded back. "The only reason your mother would confess to Ray's death is because she was afraid they would come for you. They must have something she thinks would lead to you."

I thought about the last day I saw my mother. The panic in her voice, the fear in her wild, green eyes. It was Mrs. Kleberg calling her by our real last name that set her off. If I'd only registered under Phil's last name, *Strong*, would she still be here? It was all my fault, but I didn't have the heart to tell Summon that.

"Or else someone's threatening to give the police something that would lead to you," Summon said.

I looked into Summon's eyes, confirming who I knew she meant. "Tempest."

Summon took a long sip of wine. "Bingo."

"It makes sense, and I get why she kept me from the truth about our family, but I still don't understand why Mom wouldn't trust me with information about my own father."

"It's not that she doesn't trust you," my aunt told me. "You have to understand, your father wasn't a nobody. Telling you anything could have cause the whole sordid tale to eventually unravel before your eyes. Aleister single-handedly founded CAGE—the Central Authority on Genetic Experimentation. All that research, it costs money. He needed funding. People were worried about what he might be coerced into exchanging for financial backing, and I'm not talking pocket change here. Or what might happen if his research was stolen. He could deliver a weapon they'd never seen the likes of before."

"By 'people,' you mean sirens? You make him sound like an arms dealer."

Summon *hmmph*ed. "Yes, I mean sirens. Your dad was just a geneticist. Dalliance was the weapon. A woman who can control almost any man on the planet, except one—her null. They could make him her handler, use her love for him against her. They could use her to sway political officials, foreign dignitaries, business CEO's, opposing governments, anyone they wanted! And what about the rest of us? Think about it. With your mom on a leash, and with every major company or country on the globe still run primarily by men, someone could use her to get them just about anything. Hell, they could even have her kill people without ever leaving a fingerprint."

"Like Florid did."

Summon cringed. "Yes, precisely. And Florid was at the top of the list of sirens who didn't want our secret getting out to the world at large. She was fine with being deviant and evil on her own, but like I said at my place, she needed to be in control. She was not about to risk becoming someone's puppet. She pulled the strings, not the other way around. Plus, she didn't need her crimes coming back to haunt her. If the authorities knew what she was capable of, they could try to charge her, even put her in the electric chair for it. But only if Aleister succeeded in his theories and found a way to tap into his own immunity."

"And you think Tempest has picked up where Florid left off?"

Summon shrugged. "Florid's gone now. She finally died of natural causes. I hear it wasn't pretty toward the end. She was so far gone, so mental. I always felt sorry for Tempest. Because I loved you and Dall, I wanted to believe she was like you, cursed with too much power, and double cursed for having Florid as a mother. She had no one else. Our family had deserted them. I kept in touch when and how I could. And let her crash now and again. I never told your mom because I knew she'd flip. We disagreed about Tempest, though not about much else. But now I know she's been playing us. Turning up at my place acting normal, sending you texts through my phone and vice versa. Keeping us all under her thumb, her influence. That has Florid written all over it. Which means she was probably never the lost little girl I thought she was. And she doesn't just want you and Dall dead like your mother always feared. She wants Dall out of the way, but for what? And why stay connected to you? Why hang around? You were vulnerable all this time; she could have hurt you if she wanted to. She has something else planned. I just can't put my finger on it."

I mused over Summon's questions. We represented unlimited potential for power-hungry politicians, but what did we hold for Tempest?

To anyone else, my mom was the ultimate spy—she could probably access and deliver all kinds of top-secret intelligence. The prime negotiator—send a handful of men into a room with my mom and whoever had her on their side would see their terms met, no *ifs*, *ands*, or *buts*. The perfect weapon—one no one would ever see coming . . . or going. Which was even better.

She had to be the most valuable commodity a country could get their hands on.

Next to me.

I swallowed hard and tried to ignore the pinpricks of fear rising all over my body.

The only other person besides a null who would be immune to my influence and know how to use it would be another siren.

I suddenly had a very good idea what Tempest was saving me for.

28

We sat down to an uneasy breakfast the next morning. I needed to tell Summon what I thought Tempest was really up to, but I figured she deserved the chance to swallow a meal before I dumped that load on her along with everything else she'd learned yesterday. I was glad Summon was here. Glad to see her again and glad to have someone around who knew what the hell was going on and could tell me. Someone who wasn't secretly hatching her own diabolical plan for how she could use me. But I was also afraid of what her presence meant. Stonetop, Jace—these were uncertainties now. She would need me to help her free Mom. And then where would we go, what would we do? I knew, despite what I wanted to believe, that my dream of a normal life here with Jace was just that—a dream.

"He's cute," she said with mouthful of toast. "I'll give you that."

She meant Jace. I didn't respond. I still wasn't as certain as she was that he would be back for more after yesterday's showdown.

"I remember the first time I saw Sam. Gawd, he was gorgeous! I couldn't have been more than nineteen at the time. There he was, across the bar, tall, dark, and delicious. I took one look and I knew, I had to have him." Her eyes wore a dreamy cast.

I bristled at her words for some reason I didn't understand. I just knew I didn't like to think of Jace that way, as a *genesis,* as one of a number. Jace was all there was for me. I didn't want anyone else.

"Don't bother trying to hide it," she said, watching me as she sat her toast down and sipped her coffee. "I can smell your judgment from here."

I bit my lip and exhaled. I hadn't wanted to hurt her. I *was* judging her, her choices, her lifestyle. "Do you love him?" I asked.

"Sam? Probably as much as any woman loves a man. Maybe more. He was my first. He's my right hand. If the rest of them packed up and left tomorrow, I'd be okay as long as Sam was by my side."

"Then how can you . . . I mean, is it really the same? When the frequency is involved?"

Summon sighed. "I don't know, Bird. I've never been with a man where the frequency wasn't involved. All I know is that I defy anyone to tell me that what I feel for Sam is somehow less than what they call love."

She was so proud, leaning against the counter with her chin out and her hair falling around her face like lava. I hated to shatter that, but I had to know. "Maybe what you feel isn't, but what he feels is."

She shrugged. "Is it? Really? Is love anything more than a rush of hormones and a whiff of pheromones? It's just a biochemical reaction, Bird. Same as what I inspire in my brood. The difference is, I know that and most people don't. Don't let the way your mom raised you cheapen what we are. Dall did what she had to for your sake and hers, but that's not *all* we are."

Tears formed in my eyes, falling to make wet splotches on the tops of my bare toes. "But how do you justify so many? I mean, if you love Sam. If you really love him . . ."

Summon set her cup down and stared at me. "I love more than Sam. He's special, he always will be, but I hand selected every member of my brood, and they all hold a place in my heart. Who says love should be limited between two people?"

I wiped at my eyes and stared at her. None of this made sense to me. Jace filled my heart to bursting. I never wanted to think of anyone else there.

"Couples split up. They divorce. Someone's widowed. And then they find love again. It happens all the time. And it doesn't make the love they felt before any less real. We just bypass the chronological nature that humans have adopted. That's what works best for their survival, and this is what works best for ours."

I slapped my hands against my thighs. "Stop saying that! Is that all anything is to you and Mom? Survival?" Jace wasn't survival to me. If anything, I was risking myself to be with him.

Summon didn't get angry back. "What do you want me to say, Bird? Do you want me to tell you it's all some hormone-fueled fantasy land? That's not life. It gets real. It gets hard. And love is what pulls you through. It's the very physical shoulder you lean on. It's the person who sees you without makeup and still talks to you when you need to brush your teeth. Love, true love, is not some fairy tale. It's the people who see the worst you have to offer day after day and yet still stick around."

I glared at her. "How can you say that when you're keeping them there? Those men never see the worst of you. They see what we want them to see."

Summon rubbed her forehead and thought for a moment before responding. "Those guys out there, they matter to me. And I matter to them. And believe me, we've seen the worst of each other. The frequency is always there, and I can't help that, but I'm not powerful enough to totally override a man's free will. You understand? I'm not your mom, Bird. I couldn't make a man kill himself unless he already wanted to. I can't hold Sam by my side if some piece of him didn't want to be there. That's how it's supposed to work. So everyone gets taken care of. And it *is* survival, like it or not. I need that property. I need to tuck my frequency away from the world, and that takes a lot of land and a lot of help."

I nodded. "I get it." And I thought I did. I wasn't sure I agreed with her, but I could at least see where she was coming from. In some ways, Summon was right; love had a purpose. It played a role in keeping humans on the planet. And sirens. Maybe Jace felt different to me than Sam did to her. But it didn't make what she was doing or how she was living a crime. Morally and ethically questionable? Perhaps. But I didn't have the luxury of living in a black-and-white world anymore.

"So now what?" I asked. "Will you take me back there to them? Your brood?"

Summon eyed me for a moment. "You remember that night on the porch, when Sam was acting weird?"

All too well. "Sure."

"Well, that was your frequency overriding mine. It was like Dall all over again."

"Oh." I knew where this was going.

"I can't take you back there with me, Bird." Her voice was sorrowful.

"No, right. Of course not." We'd been over this. Some part of me wanted to live like Summon, in her big cedar house in the woods. But I was also relieved. I didn't want to leave Jace. Even if Summon's place was only a couple of hours away.

"But I won't risk leaving you by yourself either. Not anymore. You're not ready yet. I told Dall that's what would come of this, raising you without any understanding or training. And with Tempest lurking about, I think we should stick together. So I guess I have no choice but to stay here for a while, until we get the next step figured out." She leaned to put her elbows on her knees. "If you'll have me."

I grinned. "What about Phil? Do you think everything you told him yesterday will stick?"

Summon shrugged. "I think I can handle him. I'll pay him a visit in a day or two to reinforce things. I'll be weaning him from your mother's frequency to mine, but given the time and her absence, I can manage it. You'll have to stay away from him of course."

I threw my arms around her neck. "You mean we can stay here in Stonetop?"

Summon laughed, hugging me back. "We can try, Songbird. At least until we spring your momma. But once we have Dall back, we have to make her freedom a priority."

I knew that was coming. And I wanted my mother to be free and safe and back with us more than anything. I just hated that it would mean leaving Jace. "What about your brood? What about Sam and the others?"

Summon shrugged. "I might drive out to my place a couple times to tie up loose ends, make arrangements. But only if I can leave you with someone safe. Maybe that boyfriend of yours will come in handy."

I forced a nod. I wasn't sure I could call him that anymore.

"The guys and I have been together a long time," she continued. "I'm counting on that to hold them there, keep things running while I decide what the next step is. Worst-case scenario is they leave, scatter like ashes on the autumn breeze. I still have you. And we'll get Dall, too. If we can just get you through high school somewhere. Eventually, you should be able to set up shop on your own, maybe some place out of the country to be safe. With your genesis, of course. If you think he'll meet you."

Maybe. And maybe I could keep him somehow. If he got over yesterday, that is. We could keep in touch by phone. It was only another year and a half, then we could go to college together. He could apply to be a foreign exchange student. We could make this work.

Summon prattled on. "I'll stick with you and your mom for a while, at least until you've learned the ropes. Then I'll start over somewhere fresh. The guys can join me. If they've bailed by then, I'll form a new brood. Sound like a deal?"

Summon put a hand out toward me and I clasped it eagerly. "It's a deal!"

She laughed again. "One look at you and Mr. Sappy Eyes out there and I knew it'd be easier to peel paint from a brick wall than to try and drag you away from him. I know what it's like. Sam and I were young once."

Sam and Aunt Sum both still looked like Calvin Klein underwear models, so I wasn't sure what youth she was referring to, but I didn't care. There was a way to keep Jace, as long as he still wanted me. With Summon here, I could go back to school. Summon would handle Phil, and I could drop the frequency to keep Jace happy until we rescued my mother and had to leave. Everything was going to work out.

"So how are we going to free Mom?" I asked her.

Summon's eyes looked pained. "We have to tread lightly here. She doesn't want the police changing their focus to you. We need a good plan in place, and when we strike, we have to do it fast."

"So that's it?" I asked. "We just go up there to the precinct and spring her?"

Summon shook her head. "It won't be that easy, and it's going to take a little time because you need to learn how to use your power so you can help me, and I need to square some things away at home and solidify our getaway. And I need to find out where they're holding her. She may not even be in Stonetop anymore, not if they have a confession."

In other words, I would need to engage in target practice, so to speak.

"It shouldn't take that long, Bird. You leave the planning to me, and you work on gaining control of that frequency of yours."

I nodded but didn't respond right away. "What about Tempest?"

Summon glanced at the Ruger she left leaning near the back door when we came in, and I was suddenly glad to never have crossed her. "She'll get what's coming to her, one way or another."

29

It was only a couple of days before the trouble started. Summon was on her phone constantly. If she wasn't talking to Sam or one of the guys, she was talking to Phil. If she wasn't talking to Phil, she was talking to his attorney. She'd even started to put in a call to the station, then second guessed herself, deciding it might be better for everyone if Reyes and the feds went on thinking Tempest was my only relative, if they didn't know Summon's face when *Operation Spring Dalliance* went into effect.

Phil spent half their conversations asking about me, which caused my aunt to shift her wary green eyes onto me, the color of poison ivy. I kept my mouth shut. Sam spent half their conversations asking when she'd be home. Then the phone would get passed from guy to guy while my aunt worked tirelessly to appease every member of her brood from a distance. The attorney had a bajillion questions about my mom, about me, about her. The only reason she entertained them was because he was filing half a dozen petitions at once, clogging up the process with paperwork while we figured out what the hell to do. *Stall tactic,* Summon had told me, and a smart one. Apparently, as long as the feds couldn't proceed with their case, they couldn't transfer my mother out of state, which was sure to be one of their first moves without those petitions to hold them at bay. She may have been arrested here in Stonetop, but

Ray died in California, and that's where they would try her. No matter where they took her, Summon promised me they couldn't keep her from us, but everything would be a hell of a lot easier and faster if she were still here. We were already by the border, for crying out loud. One good drive and we could be safely into Mexico, scoping out land for a coffee crop or an avocado farm before the FBI knew what hit them.

In between phone calls, she sat at my laptop at the dining table, looking up maps and checking accounts, shuffling money around. That's where she was now, the screen glowing with a list of properties from Durango to Oaxaca. Meanwhile, Sam was on the line, plotting the asking price of her place with her, telling her about the conversation he'd had with the real estate agent that day.

I heard Summon give a weary sigh. "I know, Sam." Her back was to me, rounded before the laptop, her hair tied up in a frazzled knot on top of her head. "Just be patient. I'm working on it."

I loitered in the kitchen doorway behind her, eavesdropping. It had only been a few days since her heroics on the front porch, and for the first time in her life, Summon was showing a bit of her age. The juggling was wearing my aunt out. She'd let me stay home "sick" so I could help her get her bearings, but my absences were adding up and I needed to get back. From the look of her, I hadn't eased much of the burden anyway.

"Okay. Okay," she said, half-listening as she agreed with something he said. "You, too." She made a quick peck at the phone and hung up. When she turned, she saw me standing there. "Hey, Bird."

"Everything okay?" It was a stupid question. Of course everything wasn't okay. My mom was in jail. Summon was giving up a brood and a home she'd spent years building. And our entire future was about as clear as a defunct Magic 8 Ball.

"Perfect," she said tightly.

I frowned. "Sam?"

Summon moved to the kitchen and poured a glass of milk, brushing past me. "Sam's fine. Don't worry about Sam."

"So he'll do it? He'll handle selling the property and meet us in Mexico?"

"He'll do it," she said. "The rest are cooperating, but it's a lot to ask. They don't know why, what's going on. There are a lot of questions I just can't answer yet. Some of the guys are getting restless. It's to be expected." She took a few swallows of milk and sat the cup down, losing interest.

"But not Sam? I mean, he's going to stick with you, right?" Somewhere in the last few days I'd convinced myself that if I could just help Summon hang onto Sam, I wouldn't feel so guilty about how Mom and I were wrecking her life.

She gave me a shallow smile. "Right." Even she didn't sound convinced.

I blew out a long breath. "Maybe you should go down there. Just for a day."

Summon eyed me, her irises going all suspect green, the color of toxic plants, like they did when she thought I was up to something. "Bird, it's only been a few days."

I grabbed her milk and poured it out, rinsed the glass. "I know. But I'm fine, really. And they need to be reassured. Especially if . . . if they're coming undone so soon."

Summon opened her mouth to protest, but I wouldn't let her.

"Just hear me out. Go for a day. Get everyone back on track. Settle things down. Once they *see* you, they'll feel differently. I'll be fine. I'll go to school and Jace or Kurt can come over after. In the meantime, I think—" and here's where I needed to finesse a bit. "I think you should let me handle Phil."

Summon appraised me quietly. "Innocence, we can't afford mistakes right now."

"I know," I told her. "It's just, I've been watching you. And I think the reason the guys are giving you a hard time is because you're spread too thin. You're working over all of them, *and* Phil, *and* his attorney. All remotely. It's too much. It's making your frequency weaker. I need the practice, you said so yourself. And the truth is, I'd already hooked Phil before you showed up. I needed to know he'd let me stay here. So I know I can handle him."

Summon drew a breath, sat quietly. "That's why he keeps asking about you."

I nodded. "Let me take him off your hands. And you go and take care of your brood for a day. Come back the next, no biggie." I left out the fact that I couldn't practice my frequency on anyone at school because I couldn't let Jace know I was using it. And that I was hoping for a night alone with him. All this planning was making my near departure much more real and substantial than it had been before. I wanted a little time with Jace before I couldn't see him again for months, maybe years. Time to memorize the details of his face, his laugh, every freckle on his skin. Time to be sure he wouldn't forget me.

Summon glanced around, then stood and stretched. She picked up her phone, punched in a few things, then walked over to me, holding it out. The screen glowed with Phil's name. "Here," she said, giving me a tired but genuine smile. "I'm going to pack an overnight bag."

Phil had been easy; Jace was harder.

He tried avoiding me in the halls and didn't show up for our usual lunch date. There were no texts or calls. But I could feel him in the building, and I could feel his resistance to me, too. He was still brooding, and I couldn't blame him. But I also couldn't leave it alone. I used our tether to bump into him after fifth period. He tried to brush past me, and when that didn't work, he spun on me. "Back off, Innocence."

"Jace . . . I—"

"I can't right now, okay?" His eyes were pleading. "I just . . . I need some time."

And that was that. All I could do was wait for him to come around.

In all fairness, I did drive past the café after school in an attempt to honor Summon's wish that I not be home alone. And I considered stopping and going inside. But the thought of all those eyes on me, of having my frequency go off and tag some pimple-faced waiter or greasy cook I'd have to fight off later, of possibly running into one of a dozen people I didn't want contact with ever again, was exhausting. Just considering it gave me cause for a nap, and within a matter of minutes I found myself unlocking the gate, driving up the cloudy path, and lumbering into Phil's lodge by myself.

I fell onto the sofa and kicked off my shoes, picking up my phone, trying to decide if there were any words that would possibly convince Jace to give me another chance.

I heard the door open. Some clicks, a *whoosh,* a tiny squeak when the hinge betrayed my intruder. I'd forgotten to close the gate behind me. My first wildly hopeful thought was that Jace must have let himself in. He was coming back to me like Summon said. I turned as someone came into the room.

At first, all I picked up on was the red hair, glowing like a cascade of hot embers down her shoulders where it turned to ice. Then the tight, ripped jeans. The oversized, dyed jacket with all its patches. The wolf-under-a-full-moon silhouette on her t-shirt. The half a dozen necklaces of varying lengths. The raven in flight on her hand where she was propping herself against the molding. The heavy eyeliner, white skin, doe-brown eyes.

Tempest stood in the entryway to the living room, staring at me, smacking her gum. "Miss me?"

"Uh . . ." I froze, then stood too rapidly, my head going fuzzy and my vision swimming. My movements were jerky, too fast or too slow, not planned, not fluid.

Tempest grinned. "Relax. I know about Summon."

Like it was a secret or a betrayal. Like I was in the wrong somehow and not her.

"You do?" I fell back to the sofa on my butt, deflated, unsure. Of course she did. How else would she know to come the first time Summon left?

She shrugged. "'Course. You think I'm stupid?"

No. Not anymore. I was beginning to think Tempest was much smarter than anyone gave her credit for, and this whole lost-puppy, rebel-without-a-cause act was part of her keeping people off guard, off the scent of her diabolical, brilliant mind. The hairs on my arms rose. I opened my mouth, closed it, opened it again. "You've been going back and forth this whole time. Using our phones, playing us both."

She moved into the room, flopped into a chair across from me, too casual to be believed. Not an inch of her unnerved. "You make it sound so seedy."

"It is!"

She laughed. "Boy, did your momma name you right. Could you be more naïve? This ain't nothing, kid."

"How long?" I asked now.

Tempest sat up straight, leaned forward onto her elbows, her ridiculous hair swinging forward. I had to say, despite the Black Sabbath look she was going for, she had the Byrd beauty underneath, like a light you just couldn't cover no matter how many coats of eyeliner you used to try to conceal it. It bled through, alive and threatening, a terrible, fierce beauty that spelled disaster. "You wouldn't believe me if I told you."

"Try me. Did you follow us here? Did you always have this in mind?"

"Summon was always my only means for finding you. I kept in touch, cried on her proverbial shoulder, dropped in to 'crash.' I knew one of these days you or your momma would turn up. Or call while I was there. Or something that would give you away. I've been tracking you, Innocence. Following your scent like a cadaver dog. I must say, it got real thick in Salinas. Before that, you were just a legend that wouldn't quite materialize. But after, you were practically calling to me."

"You're crazy," I spat. "Delusional."

She leaned back again, amused. "Am I?"

"Why? What do you want with me?"

Tempest *ahhh*ed, like my question was refreshing. "Always with the wrong questions. What don't I want with you? I mean, at first you were just another assignment. *The* assignment, really. The assignment of my lifetime. It was her dying wish. 'Never give up,' she told me. 'Burn them out—the eldest line.' I promised her like a good little girl would. And then I was all alone in the world. For the first time. Really, *really* alone."

I glared at her. "You're breaking my heart," I sneered.

Tempest smirked. "I think things changed then, though I hadn't realized it yet. I was more obsessed than ever, hunting you and your momma. Trailing you. I thought it was because I owed it to her, because I wanted to finish this and be free of it finally, of her. Snap it like a cord that tied me to this shithole life and somehow live happily ever after."

She crossed her legs and uncrossed them. This part, at least, wasn't an act.

"But I think I just wanted to feel connected to someone else in this world, someone *like* me. Do you know what it's like to feel completely and totally on your own? Like there is not another person on the whole planet who could relate to you?"

In a way, I could. Because I'd felt so much that way growing up. But unlike Tempest, I'd always had my mom. She stood between me and the isolation that threatened to consume me. Without her, without Summon, what would life feel like? Could I even bear it? I nodded at Tempest without elaborating.

"Anyway, once I caught wind of Salinas, that's when I knew I wasn't alone anymore. You—you were like me. Your mother, she was strong like mine, on her own. But you, you're the one who knows what it's like to be raised by someone like that. To come into your own power, to be greater, stronger, and so terrified of what's rising up within you but so drawn to it at the same time. You could understand me. You could be me."

That was where I begged to differ. I shook my head until my eyeballs rattled. "You're wrong. I'm nothing like you."

"Hey, whatever helps you sleep at night," she said with open hands. "But deep down you know better. You and I, we're the same."

"When did you find us? How?"

"Easy. After Ray, I knew your mom would head inland, skip state. And I knew where Summon was already. Dalliance would need to regroup. You forget, I've been through this routine a million times before with my own mom. Once she dropped a target, left a mark, we'd go far, try to hunker down a bit, put space between us and the hit. Wait for the next contact, the next assignment."

"Assignment?" Why did she keep saying that?

"It's just a word, Innocence. Not anything special like Summon with all her siren terms—brood and genesis and null. My mom, she never bought into all that crap. It was just mumbo jumbo to keep little sisters in line. The men my mother . . . *helped,* they were our assignments. She was paid to take care of her targets. And she did it well."

"You mean *killed,* don't you? Or do you honestly think you were helping those guys?"

Tempest glowered at me. "We never killed anyone. Never touched anyone in violence. If they wanted to die, that was their problem. We merely sped it along."

"With your frequency. By driving them to it, overriding their own will."

Tempest shrugged again, loose. "Semantics. At least we made it quick. Not like your mother, leaving a trail of crazed and drooling lovesick freaks behind her. You know how long it takes those guys to recover? They're never the same. No one else will ever be good enough.

It's depraved, what she did. The rest of their lives are a string of psych prescriptions and empty hookups. They're shells."

I covered my ears. I didn't want to hear this. It wasn't like that. And even if it was, we didn't mean it. "Shut up!"

Tempest sat quietly until I calmed down and lowered my hands. She lit a cigarette even though she knew we didn't allow smoking inside. "You," she said in a focused tone. "You're different, Innocence. You're not like your mom. You know better. You're stronger. Ray was your work."

I couldn't deny that, but I wouldn't say it.

"I knew it the second I heard. I was used to your mom's mark after years of trailing you. This was something new, or rather some*one* different. You were coming into your own. Ray was your first mark."

"Maybe," I whispered, tears filling up my eyes. I remembered how it felt to use my frequency that day, like unfolding a long limb, some part of myself that I let out to see the sun. It felt good.

Tempest smiled softly. "Now we're getting somewhere. Anyway, I scouted area records, caught wind of a new student registration at the school, one *Innocence Byrd*. And bingo! There you were. On the map. Traceable. I hopped down to Summon's with my latest sob story and waited. And then you and Dalliance walked in, practically on cue. It was too perfect."

Damn that registration.

"And then all hell broke loose that night, and that's when I knew. I wasn't hunting you to kill you—not anymore. I was hunting you to train you. With your real name finally on record somewhere, it was no leap to call in an anonymous tip to the FBI about Salinas, compel a witness, drag your mom into the light to answer for her crimes, separate you."

Tempest was a shadow that fell over our family the day my dad died and followed us wherever we went.

"I'm used to the FBI; I know how to finesse them. In a business like mine, you rub elbows with feds all the time. Sometimes they're hiring you; sometimes they're looking for you. It's all the same. And once I threatened to use my frequency to convince the feds *you* were the killer, she confessed quick enough. Anything to save her precious fledgling." Tempest's eyebrows lifted and fell, like this was a ridiculous show of weakness on my mother's part. "And now here we are."

"And where is that exactly?" I baited her, waiting to see what it was she really wanted.

"My proposition." She grinned, lacing her fingers and stretching them out so the knuckles popped, the way piano players do right before they dive into some super complex concerto. She was a prodigy in a way, but not the good kind.

"Which is?"

"You stay with me, train with me, work with me. And I'll make sure your mom doesn't get lethal injection. Forget about Summon and Mexico and a brood of your own. Together, we would be unstoppable, kid. We could hold the friggin' world in our hands, you get that? Anything we wanted. No assignment would be beyond us. We could cover this great, green earth in our marks. Ask for anything we wanted."

She made it sound tempting. Unlimited power. Ludicrous wealth. Ultimate freedom. But she was forgetting something. "What about anyone?"

Her face contorted. "Huh?"

"What if I don't want things? What if I want a person?" Like Jace, like my mom, like Summon. What if power and wealth fell short of love and happiness?

"What are you talking about?"

"I'm talking about my dad."

The room went dark the way it does when the sun ducks behind a bank of clouds. Tempest screwed her lips up, realizing what I was asking. "He's dead, kid. Leave it."

I swallowed and trained my eyes on her. She looked hard and lean and wild, but she wasn't any stronger or better than me. She wouldn't want me if she didn't think I was more powerful than her. I used that to give me confidence. "He was your first, wasn't he?"

She leaned back in the chair, her face drifting behind a shadow. "I said, 'leave it.'"

"Did your mother help, or just put you up to it? Did she make you a proposition like you're making me right now?" I leaned forward, pressing in for the kill.

"Don't, Innocence. Don't pick at that scab. You won't like what's underneath."

"I already know what I'll find, Tempest. You aren't fooling anyone. At least, you aren't fooling me. Not anymore. I just want to hear you say it." My voice was thick with rage, grittier than I'd ever heard it.

Her cigarette burned in the shadows, the smoke curling like a white ribbon in the air. "I killed him. Happy now? Yes, Aleister was my first. And it was unbelievable. My mother coached me. She . . . got him there right at the brink, and then I pushed him over. And it felt so good. I kept pushing, again and again and again. I'll admit, I got a little overzealous. Careless, even. But I was so young. It's to be expected."

Now, she scooted to the edge of her seat so her eyes could bore into mine as she continued. "Do you know how much power it takes to make a man stab himself twenty-seven times?" She exhaled a ring of smoke, blew it at me.

I wouldn't let her get to me like this. She was trying, but she didn't know who she was dealing with. I glared back. "Actually, I do. I know exactly how much power it would take to make a man stab himself twenty-seven, twenty-eight, or even twenty-nine times. The difference is, I don't use it just because I can. You're wrong about me, Tempest. I. Am. Nothing. Like. You."

She shrugged one shoulder. "Suit yourself. But if you don't take me up on this, you'll be sorry. If you aren't with me, you're against me. And if I can't convince you, then I have no choice but to bring you down like Mother wanted. I don't tolerate competition."

I stood, my legs wobblier than I would have liked. "Don't worry, cousin. You don't have any. I'm way out of your league."

She stubbed her cigarette out on the arm of her chair and got to her feet, a wicked smile stretching across her face. "There's something you're going to learn about me, kid. I love nothing more than a challenge." She moved toward the door and opened it, grinning into the sunlight. Then she glanced back at me. "Don't you want to say goodbye?"

I glared at her. "What are you talking about?"

"Come see."

Cautiously, I stepped to the doorway, careful to keep some distance between us. "What?"

She pointed toward her damaged sports car in the drive, then waved cutely at it, like a mother to a waiting child.

That's when I saw his face beaming from the passenger seat, eyes locked on Tempest like she was an oasis in the desert. It was Kurt.

I swallowed. "Tempest, don't. You wouldn't."

"Relax, Songbird," she said, mocking my Aunt Summon's voice. "I don't go around stomping kittens just for fun." She took a step out onto the porch, then turned back to me. "Or do I? Until we meet again."

"I'm not sure what your plan is, but take it from me, I don't give free passes. If you harm him, if you fuck with my family again, Tempest Byrd, and I will push you out of the nest for good."

"Don't worry, kid. I'm done with family. I've got yummier plans in mind." The last thing I saw was that raven tattoo on her hand as she pulled the door closed behind her.

30

A normal person would have called the police. But if I'd learned anything through all this, about myself, about my family, it was that we were anything but normal. I had to tread delicately, let Tempest think she was in control. I couldn't risk Kurt being hurt in any way because if she was willing to go after Kurt, Jace would be next.

I would cross any line to keep Jace safe. Just as I would, and had, my mother. But some lines can't be crossed again. Once on the other side, I might be too much monster, too little Innocence, for him to want.

Better not to find out. I walked into school, and for the first time since my frequency started plaguing me, I deliberately turned the volume up. Male bodies in the building moved about my consciousness like tiny marks on an inner radar. I couldn't find Kurt, his rocky arrogance laced with fumbling sweetness.

I concentrated on Jace, my mind conjuring a montage of favorite images. Jace doodling the Xavier Institute in the corner of his notebook, Jace picking up his mom's prescriptions so she wouldn't have to face the pharmacist, Jace treating his car like it had actual feelings. Then Jace in Tempest's arms, his lips on hers, Jace hanging from the end of a rope in a barn, Jace's eyes flat and gray and dead as slate.

"Hey, you're Innocence, right?"

I startled. A dark-haired kid, pink slip in hand, interrupted me in the hall. I hadn't yet made it to class. If I couldn't find Jace, I wasn't going to stay. My hyped-up frequency zeroed in on him, and he blushed a crimson so deep it was nearly purple. I should have cared. I should have felt bad. But it felt like nothing more than a nuisance.

I softened, and he held the slip out like it would bite and was careful to avoid my gaze as I took it from his fingers.

"This is from Mrs. Kleberg, the counselor?" I gave the kid an interrogative look, wagging the pink slip.

"Yep," he answered. "Something about your absences. You didn't turn in a note this morning."

"Where's Jace? You know, the guy who usually delivers these, blond hair, sloppy t-shirts?"

The kid winced at my demanding tone, then shrugged. "Must be absent. They pulled me from the registrar's office."

He kept walking but I froze. I reached out, dumping frequency into the air, reaching to the farthest corners of the school, trying to feel something of Jace, some semblance of his presence in my psyche. But I came up blank. *Absent.*

"Hey, you okay?" The kid asked, doubling back to me. His nonchalance had been replaced by focused concern. He reached for me and I bolted toward Wanda's office.

I flung open the door, suppressing the urge to shout.

"In here, Innocence!" she called from her open office, oblivious to my panic. Wanda was behind her desk in a red blouse, her hair held in a loose bun at her neck with a pencil. "There you are! We've been missing you around here," she said amiably.

I gulped air. "Where is Jace?"

She frowned. "Innocence, Jace is absent today. I thought you knew. I didn't call you here to discuss Jace, however. We need to talk."

"Is he sick?" I ignored her. "Did someone call? His mother?"

Wanda stared at me, wide eyed.

I slammed a fist on her desk, sending her dish of jelly beans to the floor in a clatter. "I asked you a question! Was it a woman's voice or his?"

Her mouth worked soundlessly for a moment. "I told you I would not tolerate another outburst after Kurt. I clearly misjudged your desire to get better. You can head straight to the office. I was sending you there anyway, but I wanted to warn you first. My mistake. We're done here." She looked rattled.

"Office? Why? Why would you need to warn me?"

Wanda smoothed her hair and stooped to pick up her candy dish. "You can see for yourself. Go out the door next to this one, it'll take you straight to the front offices." She rose and pointed, her finger trembling.

Something in her tone, like day-old coffee, made me anxious. Her fingers rested lightly on the surface of her desk, too lightly. Her face was pale but her neck was flushed, growing redder around the collar of her blouse. They were all tells, but I wasn't sure of what. I hitched my backpack higher on my shoulders.

I let my hand linger on the door knob a second too long, but she just returned to gathering the jelly beans off the floor. There was something more going on here. For the first time since I met her, Wanda Kleberg was doing the hiding instead of me. I needed to figure out what was happening, then I need to find Jace before it was too late.

I ducked out her door and exited the way she told me. Sure enough, I found myself in the hall that connected all the admin offices and meeting rooms, leading to the front desk where Miss Clair would be waiting with her pink lipstick.

Ahead, the flood of fluorescent lighting waiting at the opening end of the hall told me the front office was close. That and Miss Clair's high Texas drawl floating down the hallway. I could make out the tick of each of her acrylic nails on the Formica she was no doubt leaning on.

"I'm sure Wanda is ready to see you, if you'll just give me a minute to phone her," Miss Clair was saying. "You'll still need a visitor's pass to access the halls though. And for that I need to see some ID, even though I believe you all are who you say you are."

"No problem," a masculine voice replied.

I approached the corner slowly, intending to peek around it into the office before entering. A strange scent reached me where I was still encased in shadows. Lemongrass and crushed peppery leaves, like antique roses. It was a man's scent, backed by a strong foundation of tobacco and vanilla. I pressed myself against the wall, my heart speeding up in my chest, my frequency feeding me information about this mystery man before my eyes could.

The sound of the sticker machine running off the visitor's pass filled the silence. Then Miss Clair said in a satisfied tone, "Here you are, Mr. Monroe. Can I just say, that is a very interesting badge you have there."

My breath hitched. *Mr. Monroe? Badge?*

"Thank you," the man replied sounding bored. "But I don't go by *Mr.* Monroe. It's Special Agent, please."

"Oooh, a real special agent, huh? Like in the FBI? We don't get many of those around here," Miss Clair went on. "Sometimes the police bring the drug dogs in just to sniff out lockers. You know, kids these days. Always on that pot. The boys especially. Such a shame!"

I could see her pink lips droning on in my mind; I didn't need to look. With any luck, she'd bore Special Agent Monroe to death before he ever stepped out of the office. And yet, I had to know for sure. Was he really out there? Why?

I eased myself parallel to the edge of the doorway and angled my head so that the room beyond filled my vision. My eyes, my nose, a fair bit of my profile would have been visible but for the shadow of the wall and Miss Clair's gift for distraction.

"Yes, well. I'm not exactly here for that," the special agent told her, letting authority and a hint of impatience fill his words. "I'll need to examine only one particular locker belonging to one particular student."

He reached for the sticker pass in Miss Clair's hand, but she suddenly jerked back with a jolt.

"Really? Do tell!" she begged, her inner gossip getting the better of her with a giddy laugh. "I mean, I'll need a name in order to tell you what class the student in question is currently attending."

She shifted to her other foot, leaning the hand without the sticker on the counter, and I was able to see the tall, blond man in his black designer suit before her. It was him all right. The very same man with the placid face who stood in my driveway the day they took my mom. And behind him, behind the glass double doors that set the front office apart from the foyer, stood a small crowd of men in matching dark suits, waiting.

His hair was clipped short at the neck, parted and combed perfectly over his face. Deep crow's feet laced his dark gray eyes shaded by strong brows. An impending five o'clock shadow added to the definition of his jaw. His lips were thin and straight, brooking no argument, favoring a frown over a smile, which he was flashing Clair now in order to try and scare the visitor's pass from her grip.

"Not much escapes you, does it?" he said with a sigh, an undercurrent of distaste riding behind his words. "Her name is Innocence Byrd."

Miss Clair was oblivious to his irritation with her. "I thought there was something off about that one from day one," she replied.

Her back was to me, so I couldn't see the spastic batting of her lashes that was no doubt deflecting Agent Monroe from noticing me. All I could make out was the rather large wag of her denim-covered rump as she flirted shamelessly with the federal agent sent to arrest me as she pulled my schedule up on her computer. Monroe did have a certain James-Bond-on-a-bad-day finesse that worked.

"Well, Mr. Monroe, it appears she's normally in algebra class right now but was called to the counselor's office. Let me just ring Wanda. I'm sure she's expecting you then."

"Thank you," he replied graciously, though her behavior hardly merited it. The last thing I saw was Miss Clair finally handing over the visitor's pass.

I swallowed hard and ducked back into the hallway. That was no *Mister* Monroe. That was the Agent who had come for my mom. And now he was coming for me.

I tugged my phone from my purse and texted a furious message to Aunt Summon, praying she would get it right away. *Feds are here at my school. Come home asap!*

31

I hit the door out to Wanda's office so hard it flew back on its hinges, smashing into the wall and probably leaving a doorknob sized divot in the drywall. The dark-haired kid shrieked and flew off the love seat. But I was bolting through before Wanda could stick her head out and get a word in edgewise.

I turned down one hall and then another. I had to find a way out of the school that wouldn't take me down any of the main halls. The boy from the registrar's office was on my heels within a couple of minutes. "Innocence!" he shouted, flagging me down.

I tried to outrun him but he caught up, tugging at my arm. "This way," he insisted, pulling me down a hall I'd never used before.

It took me a moment to realize what was happening. When I'd unleashed my frequency earlier, the kid had been nearby, caught in its beam. Now, in my rush and fear, it was feeding him information, pumping into him what I needed before I could so that he could help me stay one step ahead of the feds.

We sped down the hall toward a set of double doors, which he crashed through without slowing. The gym was full of freshman in oversized red-and-white uniforms who dropped their dodgeballs long enough to watch our flight across the polished floor to an opposite set of doors. The coach's whistle blew at our backs, but we hit the next set of doors with even more force than the first and spilled out onto a sidewalk that skated the atrium between the buildings of the gym complex.

"This way," the kid gasped as we turned right, then left, finally coming to another heavy door with an inset window. He stopped short just before turning the handle. "This is the wood and metal shop. There's another door on the adjacent wall. That'll take you into the mechanic's and Ag wing. Go through there, out the door at the end of the hall, and into the garage. It opens onto the back of the student lot. Find your car and go. Understand? Just don't let any administration see you. Without a pass, they'll try and hold you here."

I nodded brusquely. "Thank you." Before he could say anything else, I pushed through the shop door and left him behind.

I was three steps into the shop room when Kurt appeared around a shelf of power tools, right in my path.

"Going somewhere?" he asked, his expression a mixture of adoration and fury.

I stiffened—both in relief that Tempest hadn't hurt him and in panic because if he was here, Tempest had to be nearby.

"Kurt, let me pass. I'm leaving." I pushed against his chest with one arm, but he didn't budge. I never realized he took shop. It wasn't exactly on our homework list.

"We need to talk." His jaw was set and he widened his stance.

I looked back over my shoulder, but the kid was gone. He was no match for Kurt anyway. I was on my own here and the clock was ticking, every second bringing the feds a step closer. I didn't have a choice.

I turned my eyes up to Kurt and curled my lips around a sultry smile. "Of course." The words sounded eerily seductive, and I had to force down the revulsion it built in me. "But I need something from you first, Kurt."

I put a hand to his cheek. His will was like a wall before me, but my frequency was already worming its way into his weak points, finding every vulnerable crevice and taking his resistance apart brick by brick. He was already mine; he couldn't refuse.

"Anything," he muttered, uncrossing his arms.

"There's a man in the office. He's tall with blond hair. He's on his way to see Mrs. Kleberg, the counselor. He wants to hurt me. I need you to stop him. Don't let him leave the campus."

I took my hand away from Kurt's face but kept my gaze firmly fixed on his. "There's other men with him. Hold them off. Do you understand?"

"Absolutely. I'll pound the motherfuckers. They won't know what hit them."

In spite of myself, I smiled. Thank God I hadn't managed to fully convert Kurt to a nice guy just yet. I doubted he could really *pound* a swarm of FBI agents, but at least he'd slow them down.

"This time, the *how* is up to you," I told him.

He grinned menacingly and started past me, but I grabbed his arm. I might not see Kurt again after this. He wasn't Jace, but he'd meant something to me just the same. "And Kurt, thank you. For everything."

"Sure," he said with a shrug. "Whatever you need."

Unfortunately, what I needed was a pass. I was all the way down the hall of the Ag wing, the door to the garage in sight, when Ms. Jaimes, the Ag teacher, stopped me.

"Going somewhere, young lady?" she asked with a grin that said *try me*.

I went for friendly and naïve. "Oh, I was just getting something out of my car. A textbook. I totally forgot it this morning, but you know Mr. Sikes, he's so demanding."

"I do know Mr. Sikes," she said, coming between me and the door in two big strides. "And I know he would never send a student out to their car without a pass."

I blinked. "Right! Well, I had one, but I, uh, dropped it in the hall on the way here. I bet if you look, you'll find it."

"Nice try," she said, pressing her already nonexistent lips into an even thinner line. "Do you know how many students try to sneak off campus through the garage per day?"

Why, oh why, couldn't they have hired a man to teach Ag? Ms. No-Nonsense Jaimes was completely impervious to my siren skills.

"Come on," she said. "We're going to visit the office."

That, I simply could not do. Agent Monroe was in the office. "But you'll leave the door unattended. I'll go back to class."

"Nope." She clamped her fingers down on one of my elbows and began to tug. "Back this way. Together."

We wrestled all the way down the hall and through the door back into shop class, where my savior Kurt was nowhere to be found. I was halfway through my explanation of why she didn't need to escort me beyond this point when the door across the room opened and a disheveled Agent Monroe entered with Wanda at his side.

"Oh, Ms. Jaimes! You located her. How wonderful." Wanda's cheeks were pink with effort and the flush of being next to the agent's good looks. Monroe grinned at me like a barracuda, and the Ag tyrant finally dropped my arm.

I turned, frantic, and sped back the other way. I had one small window, and I needed every inch of it. Half a dozen feet pounded after me, punctuating my called name, but I didn't spare a second to look back. I charged headlong through the door to the parking lot, sunlight flooding my vision. Agent Monroe's black, unmarked sedan waited in the first visitor's parking spot, shiny as an exoskeleton in the morning light. The windows were nearly as dark as the paint. Officer Reyes's patrol car seemed downright friendly by comparison. Monroe's tobacco and lemongrass scent walled around me, and I realized my frequency was working overtime again.

Alone, I might have a chance to overpower him, but as a group it could prove too much for me to manipulate at once. The memory of those men in matching Monroe suits in the school foyer was fresh on my mind. They would also be making their way to this end of the school inside a heartbeat. I had to keep running, but maybe, just maybe, I could still use my power to slow him before the rest caught up. I dodged left, coming up behind the rear of the vehicle, throwing my frequency and my voice behind me as I shouted at my pursuers, "Stop! You don't want to do this."

I never missed a step, even as my voice rang out around the cars, but someone behind me did. I heard the collision as Monroe came up short, and they all tumbled forward in a series of cracks and slaps on pavement. Mrs. Kleberg's gasped and said, "Mr. Meier!" followed by another grunt. He'd bought me a few extra minutes at least. I sprinted across the parking lot just as a familiar Mercedes skidded around a line of cars, glinting like a lighthouse in a storm.

"Get in," Aunt Summon shouted from behind the steering wheel, and I obeyed. As we sped away, I looked back just in time to see Monroe regaining his balance and his senses, his eyes trained on our license plate. It was only a matter of time before they found us again.

"That was close," Summon said as we pulled onto the street. "Now what?"

"Tempest has Jace," I told her.

We sped toward Jace's house. I twisted in my seat, scanning the roads for Tempest's car. I knew she'd been at the school, but maybe she'd left, confident Monroe and the other agents would stop me. Or worse, she realized they *weren't* going to stop me, and she ran to secure her last trump card.

Summon and I never got as far as Jace's house. Three miles due east, our little Mercedes was surrounded by a swarm of unmarked black cars. Summon gunned the engine, but two vehicles pulled in front, calling her bluff.

"Son of a bitch," she swore as she pressed the brake, bringing our getaway to a skidding halt. The other vehicles stopped alongside, so close we could barely open our doors.

Summon stood next to the driver's side, hands up in surrender, but I could taste her frequency flooding the air around us. Several agents caved, moving to her defense, but the others talked them down.

Monroe only needed that brief moment of distraction before he was right next to us, his will like an iron wall breaking up Summon's frequency.

I realized all too quickly that Summon wasn't going to be able to get us out of this. And Jace didn't have time for it. If I was going to get to him before Tempest did something she couldn't take back, I had to save us this time. Not Summon. Not my mom. Me. It was time to be the siren I really was underneath.

Monroe spun me on the hood of the car, ready to slap on cuffs thanks to my flight routine earlier. He barked orders at the other agents to take those Summon had manipulated into custody and to get her into a sedan. It was obvious he was in charge. If I could get him to cave, I could get the others. I knew it. I let my arms go limp in his grasp. "Hear me out. Okay? You've got this all backwards. I'm not the one you're looking for."

Monroe ignored me. "No talking. I ask the questions, you answer. That's how it goes."

Several agents crowded around Summon, urging her into the back of one of their cars. I had to secure Monroe before they separated us; her frequency could support mine if we remained together.

I threw myself back, slamming into him. My skull cracked against his chin, sending us both stumbling several steps.

"Goddammit!" he cursed, but he managed to stay upright.

The back of my head felt wet, and I couldn't tell yet if I'd cut my head on his tooth or split his chin. What mattered was that I'd broken his grip and I spun, planting both of my hands on his face as I opened myself, letting the force of who I was unravel around us, drawing on the years of fear and terror, every labored breath, every counted number, every tremor, every nightmare. I threw the weight of my experience behind my eyes, my words, my will. He *had* to hear me. "Please! I need you to listen to me. You're confused. You're being manipulated. I know the truth and I'll tell you, but not here. We have to go somewhere else. We have to go to my mom."

Monroe couldn't avoid my stare as he tried to reestablish his dominance. His gray eyes were cold as polished steel but for a flicker behind them. Once I saw it, I knew what it was—uncertainty. And that was all I needed.

"Please," I repeated. "You know I'm right. I need you to believe me, or it'll be too late."

Before he could peel my palms from his face, I let the image of Ray putting that gun into his own mouth flood every wrinkle of my brain, and I pushed it at Monroe, through every pore in my skin.

Monroe blinked dully and shook his head as if he were trying to fend off a nagging fly. But his defenses were crumbling, splintering to dust around us; I could taste his doubts in my mouth. Gone were the rose and tobacco notes from earlier, replaced with the first smell of fear, lacing the air with the bitterness of acid.

The others grew restless as he shifted under my fingers. The frequency was pumping out of me with such force that they were caught in its web as collateral damage. He turned his head sharply from my touch and spun me around so fast I thought I'd lost, and then I felt his fingers at my wrists unlocking the cuffs he'd only just gotten on me. He jerked open the door to let Summon out and called to his men to follow him.

"Get in," he shouted as he ducked into the driver's seat.

He didn't have to tell me twice. I was pulling the door closed as the tires screamed beneath us. The other agents scrambled for their own vehicles. Monroe wove through the lot with the deftness of a Grand Prix winner. Within seconds we were leaving Stonetop in a trail of dust.

I rubbed at my wrists and glanced back at Aunt Summon, who gave me a tiny nod. She was a pro at this. She would entrain her frequency to mine, making us both stronger than we were alone. "Where are you taking us?"

Monroe glanced at me. "Your mother. You said you wanted to see your mother, right?"

I nodded. But leaving Stonetop hadn't been part of the plan. Jace needed me. I couldn't afford to go very far. "Where is she? Why are we leaving Stonetop?"

Monroe grunted. "Not far. We're holding her outside town in a classified location for the bust. She's been detained in Austin for weeks." He glanced at Summon in the rearview. "Your attorney made sure of that. Couldn't get her outside the state. But we were hoping we could use her to persuade you to be honest, to give yourself away," he told me. "We've been planning this from a nearby local. She's there. Under guard, of course."

Monroe's gun lay menacingly across his lap, and I was suddenly very aware that this could end badly for me if I couldn't keep him connected, keep him focused on me, on *my* needs. "You saw it, didn't you? The memory of Ray shooting himself. My memory."

His eyes darted from mine out the window. "I saw . . . something. It—I don't know, it felt foreign. Like it wasn't mine. But like I was there. I've never experienced anything like that before." He glanced at me. "You some kind of witch or psychic or something?"

"Yeah." I exhaled. "Something like that." I didn't know the frequency could do that, but then again, there was a lot I still didn't know about myself and what I was capable of. I could feel Summon's eyes on me, but she was quiet, lending all her strength to me.

Even now, Monroe's will fought mine. This was not any ordinary man. This was a man of intense presence, a man who bled authority. He had his own power. Nothing preternatural, but still a force to reckon with. And he had been trained to dominate, to manipulate, to overpower, and to recognize when he was being trifled with. This was not the same as getting Mr. Sikes to give me a pass on my algebra homework.

And to think Tempest was maneuvering more than one of them. She was scarier than I thought.

"I been working this case a long time," he said now. "On the surface, it's suicide, cut and dry. I-I believe what you showed me. Back there. I believe your memory. But there's more to it than that. And I saw her in your vision."

I swallowed and fixed my attention on him. "Her?"

"Your mother," he said. "I saw her lying on the bed in the background. She was tied, or had been."

A shiver ran through me, and the old familiar habit pressed in on my consciousness. *One . . . two . . . three . . .*

"Yes," I told him. "So was I."

He looked at me hard, and that's when I realized he wanted to believe me—*us*. Not just because my mother was beautiful, but because there was something else there under the surface, something more than the frequency, that spoke for itself, the presence of truth. I didn't have to convince him we were innocent; I had to convince him to trust what he already knew inside and to help us escape. There was no allowing the system to take its course, especially when Tempest was toying with it. I had to get Monroe to risk everything to let my mom out and let us go. Now. Today.

"There are things that happened in that room that I can never explain," I said to him, angling my body toward his as I spoke. "Things you would never understand."

"You'd be surprised what I've seen."

"Don't make me relive a nightmare I've lived too many times already."

Monroe nodded. My frequency had cracked his stony façade. His words carried a filterless quality, thoughts flowing freely between us. "I hear you. There's shit I seen I can't erase. I close my eyes at night, and there it is, bright as day. Can't sleep. Can't eat. Can't pretend this world is a safe place because we know it's not."

We. That one word gave me hope. "No, it's not. And putting my mother and me behind bars is not going to make it any safer."

Monroe eyed me, shaking his head as the car slowed. "I know that, but I got a job to do, people I report to."

I glanced at Summon; her eyes were focused on Monroe. I poured my will into my words. "All I need is a head start and a vehicle. We can manage the rest. You can make up a lie about how we got away. For now, you report to me. Today, your job is setting us free."

He was quiet but complacent. He gave a brisk nod, and I felt his need to follow a chain of command transfer itself to us, to *me.* I was in charge now. Not Monroe. Not the FBI. And I had one mission: freeing my mother so I could save Jace.

32

Monroe marched me into the barn, his hand protectively on the small of my back. Behind us, a cloud of feds escorted Summon only a few feet away. My shoes made light clacking noises against the brick floor, and the smell of fresh hay was sweet in the air. But there were no animals to be seen, and no foul stalls to sweep. This barn was high class, with fluorescent track lighting, storage, offices, a full vet facility, and an elevator. Monroe had filled us in on the way over. A flustered agent jumped up from his post near the door when Monroe told him to hand over the key to the room where they had my mother.

"I've got her waiting in holding room B," he stammered, handing out the keys.

I didn't have to use my power on him. He was under Monroe's command, taking orders. But I did anyway. Because I could.

I gave him a dazzling smile. "Thank you."

He quickly moved from handing the keys to Monroe to handing them to me.

"Stay out of our way," Monroe told him. "You call me if anyone else shows."

Monroe led me back to a narrow, white door. I slipped the key in the knob and turned, swinging it inward. The room was sparse, with a table and two chairs, a small stack of magazines, and a pallet made out of horse blankets. My mother was sitting stoically at the table, her hair pulled neatly over one shoulder as she flipped through an issue of *Horse & Rider*.

"I told you to bring breakfast when you came back," she said without looking up. "You can't try me if you starve me to death first."

I was so overjoyed to hear her voice I almost choked.

Then she looked up. Her eyes glossed over and the magazine fell from her hands. She stood, shaking with emotion, as I rushed into her arms.

"Oh baby, my dove. What are you doing here? What's going on?"

Monroe signaled and Summon stepped into the room behind him, wrapping her arms around both Mom and me in a classic bear hug.

We broke apart for me to fill Mom in as Monroe ordered one of the agents to bring a change of clothes.

Dalliance looked from me to Agent Monroe to Aunt Summon. I could see the disbelief trapped behind her gaze, but she, like my aunt, was no novice. She quickly pulled her energy in, focusing what strength she had behind mine. Between the three of us, Tempest and the FBI didn't stand a chance.

Another agent passed Monroe a pair of jeans and a flannel, which he handed to my mother. "You can't march out of here in that orange garb," he said. "Change first."

Monroe handed me a set of keys. "These go to the black jeep outside the barn. It's your best bet because there won't be any tracking devices installed, but you better ditch it for another vehicle as quickly as you can."

"Right," I told him, knowing that would be no problem. We could swing by the lodge and grab another car, after I knew Jace was safe.

Monroe looked at his watch. "I'll step outside for her to change. You've got about three minutes."

When the door closed, my mother pulled me to her again. "This was so dangerous, Innocence. You shouldn't have come for me. Your safety is my only priority."

"Just get dressed," I told her. "I have it under control."

"You were right, Dall," Summon said as my mom buttoned up the flannel. "She's something else. I've seen her do things today that would make Grandma Byrd turn over in her grave. She's special."

"Tempest—" my mother started to say.

"We know," I told her. "She's behind everything. Just hurry. I think she's got Jace." I leveled my gaze on her. "He's my boyfriend, FYI."

She let that roll off of her. It was no time to argue whether I'd earned the right to date. "What do we do when we walk out of here?" My mother asked then, zipping her jeans. "Once we pull out and get very far, your hold on them will break. Then what? They all come barreling back after us and this time get to take three for the price of one?"

I hadn't thought about that. I just thought about leaving, getting Mom out. She was right. I needed to think of some way to keep them off of us.

"Earlier, in the car, Monroe said you showed him something, a memory of you and Ray." Summon lowered her voice as she spoke.

"Yeah, so?"

She looked from me to my mom. "Dall, you always thought you could do good with the frequency. But your control issues made it impossible. Innocence isn't like you. She's strong, but she manages it. If she can show a man her memory, could she take one of his?"

My mom brushed my cheek. "You can do that? Show him a memory?"

I nodded. "It's amazing what you figure out when your life depends on it."

"It's worth a shot," she said. "Get Monroe in here and we'll do our best to support you while you give it your all. But first, you've got to get him to let you in."

I nodded and opened the door. "Monroe, we need you."

Like a loyal Labrador, he stepped inside.

"Close the door," I told him.

When it clicked shut, I moved close to him, looking up into his face. "What if I could erase them for you?"

"What are you talking about?"

"Like the memory I pushed into your mind before." Like me, Monroe was suffering with PTSD. Maybe I could lighten his trauma load. Give him a few years of peace. "What if instead of giving you my memories, I could take some of yours?"

He looked wary and confused and that made him dangerous. Our connection was fragile. I couldn't risk breaking it by pushing him too far, and yet that was exactly what I was doing.

"Just the bad ones," I added as an afterthought.

"I don't want you rooting around in my head. Nobody wants that."

He was right, of course. But I had to convince him. "Monroe, you can't stop me." I didn't say it aggressively, but with an air of resignation because it was true, and I was counting on him to recognize it.

He looked at me, at my mom, at Aunt Summon, and back at me. "Go on."

"You helped us. Now let me help you. I'll take your memory of our escape so they can't punish you. You'll pass a lie detector. And I'll take the other memories, too. The ones that keep you awake at night."

He was quiet a moment, thinking.

"I know what it's like," I told him. "To live in fear. I can give you your life back, Monroe." And as I said it, I knew it in my bones. That was my father's gift to me, the benefit of being the child of a siren and her null. I could do a lot more than will men to give me cars or money or fall in love with me. I could actually *help* them, like my mother had always wanted.

He glanced at me. "You certain?"

I nodded. "Yes."

"I'm all yours."

I placed both hands on Monroe's face as I had done in the parking lot when I wanted him to see my memory of Ray shooting himself. His mind parted like butter under a warm knife, laying him open to me like a biology dissection. My frequency, this thing I'd carried for so long, this extra limb, reached in with a surgeon's nimble delicacy and picked through a host of thoughts and memories, identifying the ones that made their way into his nightmares—a drowned child, a woman so brutally raped she had to be medicated the rest of her life—and simply plucked them out like bad seeds, willing his mind to let go, to release, including his recollections of today, from the parking lot onward.

Behind me, my aunt and my mother stood with a hand on each of my shoulders, feeding their strength into my own, driving me forward.

"You're never going to reach for these memories again," I began. "You're going to be free of all the trauma from your past. You're going to go home, kiss your wife like the first time you met her, and build the life for the two of you that you've always wanted. I need you to be happy from now on, Dennis Monroe, and I need you to forget everything about this day, about my mom, Summon, and me, about the pain you've witnessed. You're going to sleep through every night, breathe deep, and enjoy every second of the rest of your life. Can you do that for me?"

The agent nodded candidly against the heat of my hands, his eyes locked on mine. And for reasons I couldn't explain, I felt oddly maternal toward him, protective. I was setting this man on a new path, and I would be damned if I let anyone get in the way of that. I brushed a hand across his forehead and gave him a hug. "Thank you," I whispered before he could come to his own senses, knowing he'd never remember it, but it mattered just the same.

I turned to my mother and aunt. "Come on. Jace needs me."

We sped toward the back of the barn, tumbling into the warm afternoon. The jeep was waiting for us. And in between—Tempest.

Her ripped jeans were replaced by pressed slacks, her hair dyed a dark auburn and pulled into a French twist. She'd have looked positively domestic if not for the exposed raven tattoo on her hand and the fact that her eyes were a touch too wide, borderline manic, her lips dry and tight at the corners. A flicker of surprise rippled through her expression at the sight of us together, my mom blinking in the bright daylight. Then Tempest's face rearranged itself into sour acceptance. Her car was pulled haphazardly next to the jeep, a swerved track of dirt behind the tires, but Jace was nowhere to be seen.

"I wondered," she said, "if you'd be able to undo my frequency after they took you in, when I was too far away."

I swallowed, stalling for time, unsure what move to make.

"But now I'm here," she finished with a hint of a smile.

The implications were obvious. She could interfere with my hold. She could bring the whole lot down on us before we got far enough away. Her frequency against mine. I could already feel it picking at the seams of my power.

Inside, Monroe was a clean slate, and the other agents would hold off while he made no move to stop us . . . for a while.

I had one shot to fix this.

I looked at my mom and Summon. "Run," I whispered, squeezing the jeep keys against Mom's palm. And then I let out the loudest, most blood-curdling scream of my life.

Tempest froze, her eyes bulging as Mom and Aunt Summon rushed toward the waiting vehicle.

Before she could blink, a dozen agents spilled out into the sunlight like ants from a hill. Still tuned into my now-desperate need for protection, they barreled toward Tempest without another command.

Panicked, she ran, diving into her sports car before the first one could grasp her. Her engine kicked up a cloud of dust over us.

In the confusion, my mom circled around, pulling the jeep up before me. I climbed in and she sped off, hoping the agents would feel my fear receding, that they wouldn't follow. I had to find Jace before Tempest reached him again, or the agents reached us.

Barreling down a country road in the stolen jeep, my aunt and mother's frequencies layering mine, I closed my eyes and concentrated on reaching out for Jace. Whatever Tempest was up to, our tether remained, and I traced it until I was certain of him. Even at this distance, it was like I could hear the thumps of his heart in my own chest. He was at Phil's—the lodge. And we wouldn't find him alone. Tempest was between us, heading his way, her frequency creating interference in my own like feedback from an electric guitar.

As we neared the property, we rolled down the drive, unsure what we were pulling into. Jace was alive, and that was all that mattered. I'd figure the rest out.

Jace stood stock-still in front of the porch, a pistol in one hand. His face didn't even flicker with recognition as I moved toward him.

Behind him, Tempest stood on the top step, her rigid stance trembling at the edges.

"What have you done to him?" I spat.

Tempest sidled down the steps, resting an elbow on one of his shoulders. "Let's just say I made a few improvements on the original."

"No," I screamed stepping forward, but Jace's arm shot up, the pistol aimed squarely at my chest.

"Nah-uh," Tempest warned. "That thing is loaded. One more step and your boy toy will make you the heartless bitch you are." Then she leaned over and licked his cheek with a long, slow stroke of her tongue. "Mmmm . . . yummy."

I shuddered with rage I couldn't release.

"You can't take us all," Summon said coldly. "Hurt Innocence and Dall and I will be all over you. You're finished, Tempest. Let it go."

"Don't think I haven't thought of that," Tempest said calmly. She snapped her fingers and Jace lifted the barrel of the gun to his temple.

"No, please!" I shouted.

My mother moved between us before I could dash forward again. "Leave us alone, Tempest. It doesn't have to be like this."

"Yes, it does!" Tempest shouted. "I promised her."

"Promises can be broken," Dalliance said, pulling herself into the statue of solidarity I knew her to be.

Tempest shook her head violently, and her hair fell, revealing long bloodred tips to complement her dark roots. "No. Not anymore. It ends today."

I drew myself up next to my mother, Summon at my back, and sized up the vision before me. My frequency surged at Jace, trying to punch holes in whatever hold she had on him, but she had him well barricaded. She had either completely deprived him of his memories of me or pushed them so far down that even the sight of me wouldn't trigger them.

If I couldn't break through to Jace, I would have to focus on her. Her power was spiked, but desperate at its edges. Her madness was showing. The red-rimmed eyes. The trembling revolver in her hands. The look of sheer desperation. And having been here before, with Ray, I knew there was only one way out of this. My frequency could feel her vulnerabilities even when it could find none in Jace. And like with Monroe, I owed it to myself, to my mother, to Jace, to try.

"Tempest, don't do this. You'll regret it," I said, carefully pulling my voice into a soothing cadence. "We're the only ones who understand you." I took a step closer around my mom.

Instinctively, my mother's hand reached out to pull me back, but I shook her off. I needed to get closer, even if it meant staring down the barrel of a gun.

"Without us, it'll be like before. Remember? You'll be completely alone." Another step. Then another.

She planted her feet, shifted, planted again. "No." Her head shook. "You're lying. You don't know me. You're nothing like me. You said so yourself."

Jace's hand began to shake, the gun barrel quivering at his temple.

I held still and opened the doors that held my power in, letting my will course into the air around us, tasting her weak points. "That's because I was afraid. But you were right all along." I kept taking small, easy steps in her direction.

"No!" she shouted. "Stop lying!"

"The whole world, remember? That's what you said. We could have the whole world to ourselves. You, me, and Dalliance. Like we're meant to. The little sisters rising up to claim their power. We're the strongest sirens of all." I was so close now, but Jace's hands were still trembling and his trigger finger shifted restlessly like a prowling cat. I didn't want to spook either one of them. I couldn't lose Jace, not like this.

"See the car?" I continued. "You can come with us. We'll start over. Together."

Her eyes were watering now, dropping big, loose tears onto her pallid cheeks. But a stubborn vengeance held her fast, and Jace kept the gun pointed at his head. "No. There is no *us*. There's only room for me. You have to die. You and your mother. It's what she wanted. The end of Harmonious's line."

I took a breath and reached deeper than I ever had. Maybe she was a woman. And maybe she was a siren. But she had weaknesses and vulnerabilities just like anyone else. The anticipation of it built in my frequency, like a trained dog. We were on her scent—we just had to follow it.

"What do you want, Tempest? Florid's gone now. But you're still here. This is *your* life. It's time for you to think about the things you want."

She chewed a lip, mascara running to her chin in black drips.

"Do you want to be alone again?" I was so close now I could reach out and touch the gun if I didn't think she'd shoot my fingers off.

Behind me, my mother and aunt were catching on, their own

frequencies following mine, strengthening it. "Your mother was wrong to keep you away from us. It's time you be with your family."

A little shudder coursed over her, and Tempest sniffed. "I-I want . . ."

"Go on," I encouraged her, waiting to hear alarms or car engines at any moment. We needed to hurry this thing along if we were going to escape at all. "Tell us."

"I want . . ."

She didn't know what she wanted because her mind was so crippled from the years of brainwashing under her mother's care—but I was on her. She was stumped, uncertain, confused by her own inability to answer, and her secrets began to flow through my frequency. What she wanted, in the end, was me. To have me, to be me, to kill me. There was really no difference when she was this far gone. But it didn't matter. I'd found my *in*. And I would finish this.

"I need you to give me the gun, Tempest," I said, letting my frequency course over us both, sensing how it confounded her. It was a feeling she'd never experienced before, one she'd never expected. But she gave over to it easily enough, tired of the weight of her own psychosis.

"Give me the gun. Before it's too late. We have to go. Now." I made a *gimme* motion with my fingers, pushing the full weight of my will into my words.

At last, she crumpled against it. Jace's hand slipped to his side, the gun hanging there as she cried beside him.

I reached out and slid it from his grip, hoping my touch would awaken something. He blinked, but no more. Disappointed, I held the gun out behind me. My mother quickly retrieved it.

I turned to Tempest and gripped her face with both hands before she could shrink from me. "Look at me, Tempest." Jace would have to wait.

She was a puddle in my grasp, her eyes darting everywhere but to mine.

"Look at me," I commanded with a shake, and she finally landed them on me.

"What are you doing?" she asked through her tears. "What are you going to do to me?"

"I'm going to take it all away," I told her quietly. "Now hold still."

She obeyed . . . at first. But when she felt my frequency reaching deeper, plucking out every last memory she had not only of her mother, of her murders, of me and my mom and Summon, but of who and what she was herself, everything that made her a siren, every time she had ever used her own frequency, she clutched her hands over mine, trying to tear them off. The raven tattoo was the only thing I let her keep.

I could still hear her screaming when we drove away.

33

Jace stared at me with blank eyes.

"Can you hear me?" I asked him again. "What's my name?"

He lifted a hand to my face, which I took as a good sign. We were in the back of Tempest's dented sports car on our way to Jace's house. I had precious minutes with him before we'd be gone to a motel in Gillespie County, and he had yet to recognize me. Summon had agreed to drive. My mother rode shotgun next to her.

I'd spent the last ten minutes pouring my memories of us into him using the frequency. I didn't believe Tempest knew how to erase them, but she'd overlaid her will so thickly in order to override his feelings for me that they'd been forced deep into the unreachable parts of his mind. By showing him our time together through my own memories, I had hoped it would trigger his subconscious to release them. I still wasn't sure it worked.

"Jace," I said again. "Come on. You know me. What's my name?"

I was beginning to panic.

"I . . ."

I clutched his hand in mine. "Yes?"

His voice was weak, like someone waking from a coma.

"I love you, Innocence."

I let out a sob and wrapped my arms around him. "Oh thank god!"

After a few minutes of holding each other, Jace looked up and asked where we were headed.

"We're taking you home," my mother said, all business.

"And Innocence?" he asked her.

I couldn't bring myself to tell him. My mother was silent.

Jace looked at me. "You're leaving."

"I don't have a choice. If I stay, you'll lose me forever."

He swallowed. "Let me go with you."

"Jace—" I started.

"No, I'm not asking you." He leaned between the front seats. "Let me come. Innocence is everything to me. If you take her away, what's left? I can help you."

My mother sighed. "No, you can't. You'll be in the way. Your family will look for you. You'll bring more feds down on us. If you love her, you'll let her go." She looked at him in earnest.

Jace leaned back. "So that's it?"

"No." I laid a hand on my mother's arm. "Give us tonight. At the motel. He can go home tomorrow. We'll call a cab. And then we're gone."

My mother glanced at Summon, who shrugged and said, "Can't hurt." She winked at me in the rearview mirror.

"What about his parents? Or money for the cab? That's a long ride."

I said quietly, "That's what the frequency is for." I knew that now, and I owned my truth.

My mom pursed her lips and nodded once. "Tonight. That's it. Then we're gone and he stays behind."

I looked at Jace. "Tonight," I told him.

"Tonight," he agreed.

When we pulled into the parking lot of the motel, Sam stood leaning against the weathered paint job of Summon's truck, one boot up on the bumper, his arms crossed over his flannelled chest. "Going somewhere without me?" he asked her as we got out of the car.

Summon walked toward him, the surprise on her face quickly dipping into concern. "Sam, don't do this. We talked about it. I need you here. The guys need you here. The farm won't hold without—"

"Screw the farm," he insisted, grabbing her wrist.

My mother stepped forward. "Let go of her."

"Go inside," Summon said to my mother. "Go get a room, Dall. I'll handle this."

"Like hell I will," my mother replied, holding her ground.

I carefully tucked my frequency deep where it wouldn't interfere, gave Jace a reassuring pat on the shoulder, and moved to my mom's side. "Mom, she's right. Your frequency will only make it worse."

"I won't leave my sister!"

"Sam won't hurt her," I whispered, turning to her. "If he tries, I'll take care of it."

Mom inhaled and then moved reluctantly toward the leasing office.

Summon shot me a thank-you glance before turning back to Sam. "Please, baby. There's no other way. You know that."

Sam drew close, his lips only a breath from her own. He dropped her wrist and wrapped a leanly muscled arm around her waist. "There is nothing on that farm for me but you. Don't you know that?"

Summon's eyes glazed over, and she looked down at the pavement. "Sam, please. I can't do this. Not now."

"Tell me you can do it at all," he said. "Tell me you can walk away from this, from us. Tell me you can leave me. If you can say that and mean it, then you're already gone. And I'll leave you alone."

"I don't have a choice," she whispered as the tears began to roll.

"Summon Byrd," he said so gently he might have been talking to a child. "There is always a choice."

My aunt dropped her head against his chest and wept.

Every judgment I ever held about her, about her ability to love, about her relationship with Sam and the others, simply fell away. It was clear that trying to leave Sam was tearing my aunt apart.

Sam stroked her hair, holding her against him, and his tenderness toward her was unmistakable. Frequency or not, this man loved my aunt fiercely. Nothing could change that. "I've never been to Mexico," he said with a quiet smile.

Summon looked up and started laughing through her tears.

"You could make my dreams come true, Summon."

She punched him playfully in the chest and wiped at her eyes.

"Take me with you," he said now, echoing Jace in the car.

That's when I knew. Jace *was* my genesis. Summon had been right all along. And I had no fear of that, no resistance. I had only pride and love. I had chosen well. And because I was unique among sirens and humans, it was likely he was all I would ever need. But even if he wasn't, it wouldn't change how I felt. It wouldn't change us.

"Sam," my aunt said, her playfulness gone.

"Bring him," I said, unable to hold back. "We can work it out."

"How?" she asked, turning to me.

I shook my head. "I don't know, but we will. We're family. That's what we do. We make sacrifices for each other."

Summon didn't look convinced, but she was softening.

"And I'm special, remember? You said so yourself."

"Yes, you are, Songbird," she said. "But there are limits even for you."

I looked from Jace to Sam to Summon, and I knew we could make it work. "There are no limits where love is concerned. You won't make it without him, so bring him."

She stared at me a long time before finally turning to Sam. "You're gonna look hot in a sombrero."

Jace and I both laughed at that. "I'll go tell Mom we need a third room."

Our room was small but clean. More importantly, it was private.

"Jace." My voice was small, unsure. "You should know, we'll probably toss our phones, get burners. I won't be able to contact you until we're knee-deep in chili peppers and corn tortillas somewhere outside of Tijuana. And even then, we'll have to be careful."

He stood at the window, his face a mask of resignation. "What are you saying? Innocence, are you breaking up with me?"

I took a breath. "Of course not. I'm just saying we might be more distant for a while than either of us would like. I want you to be prepared. And, well, since this is our last night alone together. I-I want it to be memorable."

I walked over to him and took his hand in mine, squeezing his fingers. I knew Jace was crazy about me, but this was asking a lot. He'd always been the one to pull back, and now I was asking him to rush headlong into the storm while we watched the time we had together eke away with every touch.

Jace put a hand to my face, brushing my hair back. "It will be. Every minute with you is etched on my mind. She couldn't take that from me."

"I know. But I'm talking about something else."

He leaned in, his breath warm against my lips. "What are you asking me exactly?"

I let my gaze travel over the curve of his lips, the tangle of blue in his eyes. "Tonight, when it's time to go to bed, don't sleep on the floor. Stay with me."

"Inn, you know what'll happen if I do that." His voice was soft, pliable.

"I know," I told him, refusing to look away. "And I want it to."

Jace sucked in a breath. "Are you sure about this? You know I don't need that to stay faithful to you when you're gone. Are you afraid you'll lose me somehow if—"

"No," I stopped him. "That's not it. I've never felt like this about anyone. And I may never again. Maybe Aunt Summon is right. Maybe I am still a siren when it comes to you. But even if that's true, nothing will ever feel this real to me. And I want the whole experience. I want to know I didn't short myself. When I'm out there on the road, I want to take every piece of you with me."

Jace's hand tensed against my cheek. "You're scaring me, Innocence. You're acting like we'll never see each other again. Promise me this is it for us."

"It's not," I told him, and I meant it. "I have a plan."

Jace listened while I explained the ideas I had about him joining me in Mexico after graduation, maybe going to school there or volunteering with a nonprofit. "Or anywhere," I finished, worried he wouldn't like the idea. "I meant what I said to Summon out there. There are no limits where love is concerned, and I love you, Jace Barnes. We can travel the world, or you can apply to a university in whatever country you like and I'll come to you. I can finish school on my own and then get a place with—" I stopped just short of what I'd been about to say: *with you*. I barely caught myself in time. That was taking Jace's assent for granted, like Summon did. Like he was a genesis. Jace had a mind of his own, and I wanted him to decide for himself if he wanted to live together when high school was over. Even if it meant facing rejection. I held my breath while I waited for him to respond.

"What was that?" he asked, his eyes a piercing turquoise.

"I'll have to get my own place eventually," I said casually. "Can't live off Mom and Summon forever, can I?"

"No. Before that. You were about to say something else, but you stopped." Jace scrutinized me.

"I was thinking, I mean, only if you're into it, but we could, maybe, move in together after school. But you probably have a college picked out here already. It's fine. I can totally get my own place. You know, we'll Skype or whatever. No biggie."

Jace leaned down, his face inches from mine. "Is that a proposal, Innocence? Are you asking me to move in with you?"

Oh god, oh god, oh god . . . "It was just an idea."

He bent down and kissed me long enough to make today, Tempest, Mexico, all of it feel a million miles away.

"Of course I want to get a place with you," Jace said, pulling away. "But you're right, college is important to me. It should be to you, too. So maybe we try and go somewhere together, like you said, or at least in the same country. I hear great things about Trinity College in Ireland. And Dublin's a cool city. It has a music scene to rival Austin, several campuses, plenty of places to live, our choice of fine pubs, and a legal drinking age of eighteen," he said. "We can get an apartment there."

He leaned over and kissed my neck, which sent shudders so strong down my spine that I nearly buckled.

"Right. Sounds perfect. Dublin." Apparently, Jace's kiss rendered me incapable of more than a couple syllables at a time. Maybe *he* was the siren.

"So Dublin. It's a deal?" His voice was husky as he drew the curtains together across the window of our room.

"Yes," I agreed. "On one condition."

He looked at me, waiting.

"Promise me you won't hold back tonight. I don't want anything to remain undone between us." If Jace was my boyfriend or my genesis, it really didn't matter. I loved him. Only him. And tonight would never come again.

He looked hesitant, so I kissed him again, slow and savory, letting all my hunger bleed into my lips. If it was my frequency, my willpower, or my desire that tipped him over the edge, I'll never know. But I didn't care. I felt his hand slip from my face to my waist, felt his lips hovering over mine, felt his own passion spilling over. And then my shirt was on the floor, his skin warm and damp against mine, and there simply wasn't enough of him to fill me up.

He never said the words, but he kept the promise I asked of him. He stayed with me the whole night, and he held nothing back. When morning finally came, we were still folded against one another, our bodies inseparable, breathing in time.

Epilogue

Mexico, as it turned out, was as hot as Texas. Worse, because you couldn't get a bite of anything to eat that wasn't riddled with jalapeños or hot sauce. But the coast was beautiful, a stretch of white sand beaches lapped by waves the color of Jace's eyes. And the tourists made easy pickings for Mom. There was a never-ending buffet of spring-breakers, honeymooners, and day-trippers. Men who came for the tequila, cigars, and women. It was like shooting fish in a barrel. She did, at the very least, steer clear of the newlyweds at my insistence. I'd rather we weren't responsible for breaking up marriages before they could even start.

We kept a steady pace. Always putting distance between us and the last place. And we worked as a team. She reeled them in, and then I erased their memories of her, weaning them from the addiction before it could ever get out of hand.

The locals kept a wary eye on us. I heard the word *bruja* tossed around a time or two, but mostly they just stayed out of our way. And whatever they thought we were, they were always happy to take our money.

Summon and Sam stuck with us through most of Chihuahua and Durango, keeping contact remotely with their realtor while they waited for the Hill Country place to sell. Somewhere in Zacatecas they got the good news, and shortly after that they found some land near San Miguel they decided to buy, to lay down new roots. Most of her brood dispersed except for Alvaro, oddly enough, and a couple of others who joined them there.

As for Tempest, there was no doubt the rest of the agents caught up with her drooling on the drive outside Phil's lodge. But she wouldn't have meant much to them without her frequency to keep them in line. I didn't strip it from her, not exactly. She was more like a computer who still had her motherboard. I just erased her hard drive. Or something like that. I was never very good with computers.

With any luck, she'd stay that way.

Jace told me he'd come to see us over the winter break. He bought a ticket and everything. Mom and I planned to spend the holidays in Mazatlán at a beautiful resort. While he was there, Jace and I would go over his application to Trinity College. He never dropped the Dublin thing after I brought up the idea of him joining me someday. At least red hair would be common in Ireland, and there'd be less of a language barrier since English was there primary language. Which was great considering my Gaelic was likely to be even worse than my Spanish.

I could never leave my mother behind. I told Jace that, and he understood. On her own, she couldn't make it without causing damage and risking her own safety. But with me, she had some kind of chance at normalcy, which is ironic, considering I always wanted her to provide that for me. Instead, I was the one who had the ability to give it to her—and myself. I was grateful, though. Grateful to be who I was, *what* I was, and to know all of myself finally. There would never be any denying the siren in me. My life would always be filled with open roads and damage control, but it would also be full of the people I loved and who loved me. I would always be a Byrd. But unlike Tempest, I was more than that, and I knew it. For the first time in a long time, the road ahead didn't scare me, and the road behind didn't haunt me. I was living in the moment, in the space of each heartbeat, one breath at a time.

Acknowledgments

I would like to acknowledge a handful of extraordinary people who were essential in making *Songbyrd* a reality.

First and foremost, my agent Thao Le. Thao, you have been a tremendous support and a wonderful partner in this journey to publication. Thank you for loving and championing my work. Innocence, Jace, and the Byrd women are better because of your input.

Second, my editor, McKelle George. It has been a tremendous experience to share this vision with you. You are a consummate cheerleader and a brilliant coach. Thank you for sharing your gifts with me and my story.

Third, my dear friend and author, S. E. Babin. I can't imagine having traveled this road without your steady stream of kind words and delicious baked goods. The journey has been much improved with you as a travel companion.

And finally, my husband and children. You have all sustained your fair share of plot debates, proofreads, and neurotic, at times incoherent, rambling as a result of my madness for writing. Thanks for loving me through it.

ANNA SILVER is an author and artist living in the greater Houston area with her family, pets, and overactive imagination. Her art has been featured in the Houston gallery Las Manos Magicas. She studied English Writing & Rhetoric at St. Edward's University. She's freelanced for private clients and small publications like the Hill Country Current. Her *Otherborn* series has been featured on two of Amazon's bestsellers lists.